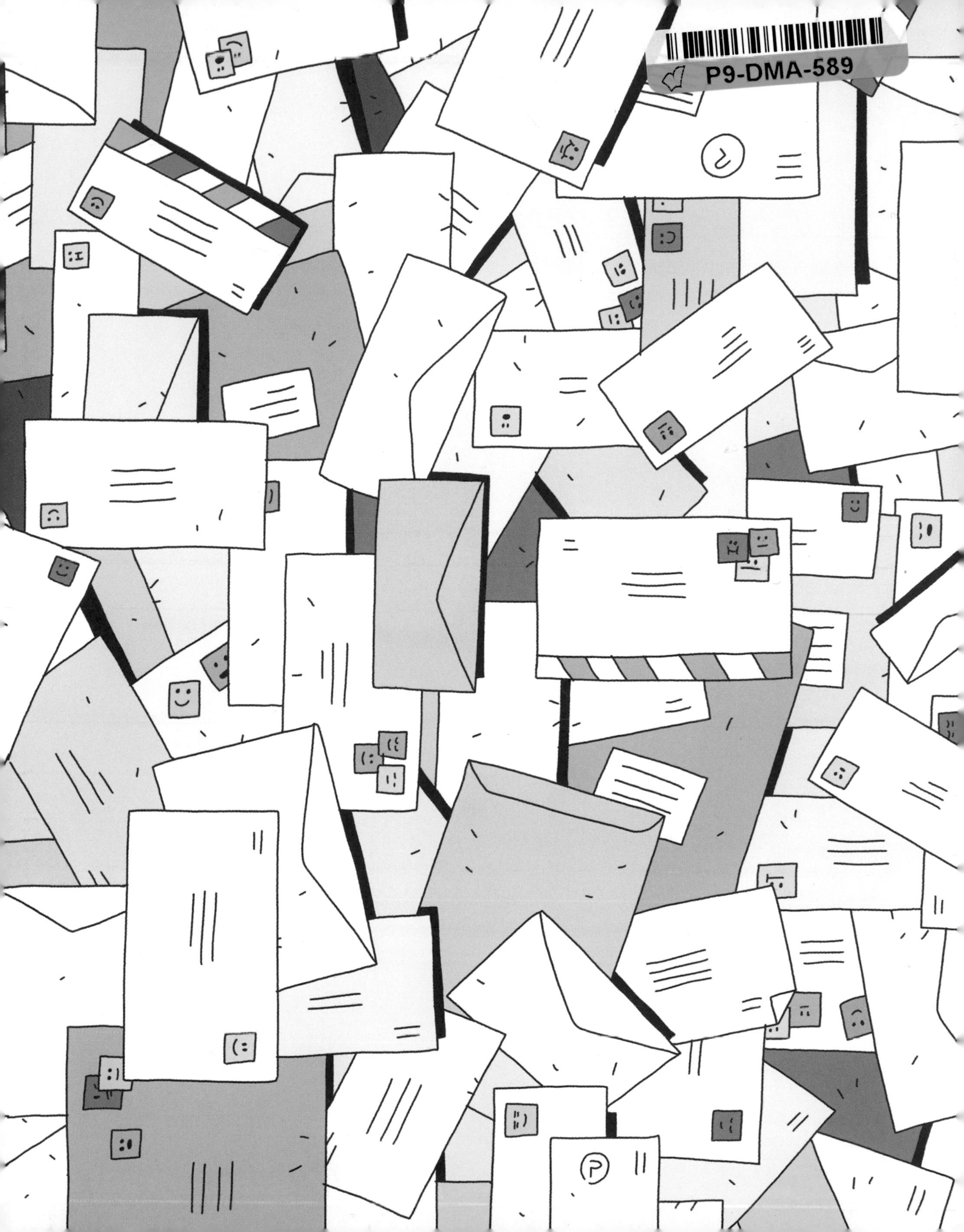

THE POSTMAN
FROM SPACE
THE BIKER BANDITS

THE POSTMAN
FROM SPACE
THE BIKER BANDITS

by Guillaume Perreault

Translated by Françoise Bui

HOLIDAY HOUSE · NEW YORK

[redacted]

Bob, our postman from the Planetary Post,
has definitely gained a lot of confidence
since we last met him.

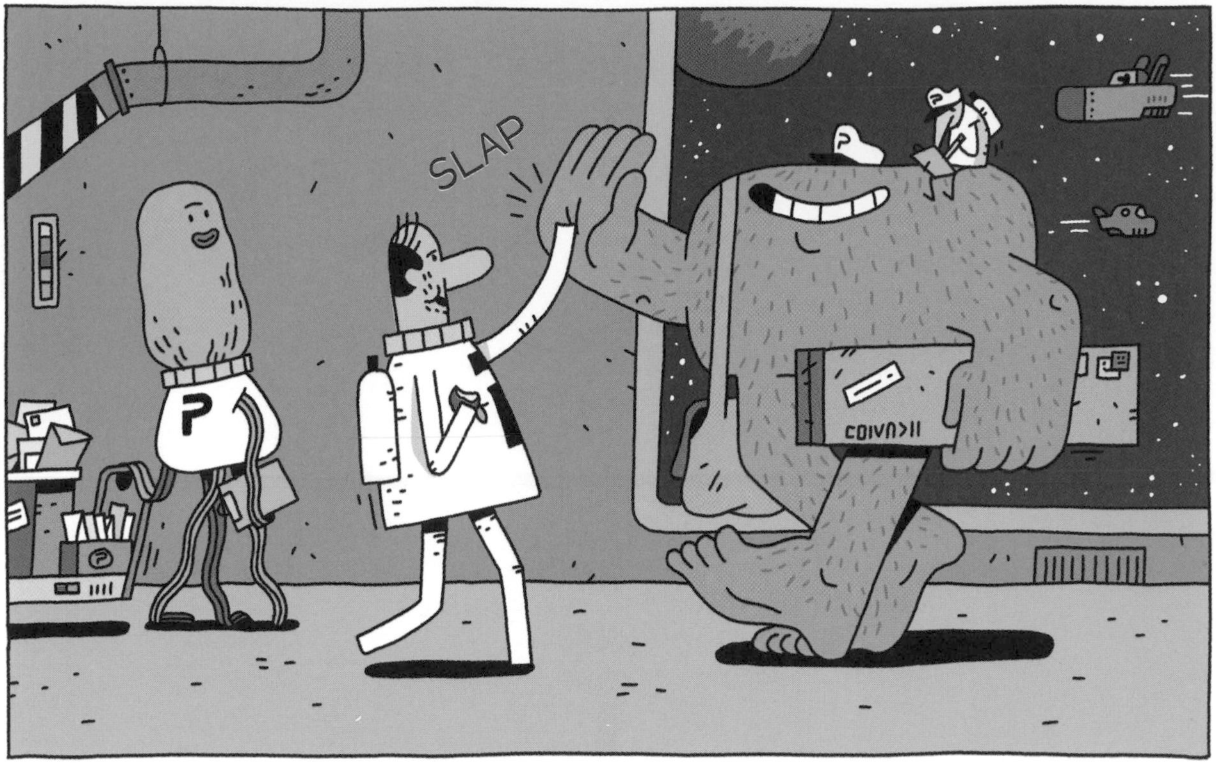
SLAP

He starts his day with a puffed-out chest . . . and a slightly swollen head!

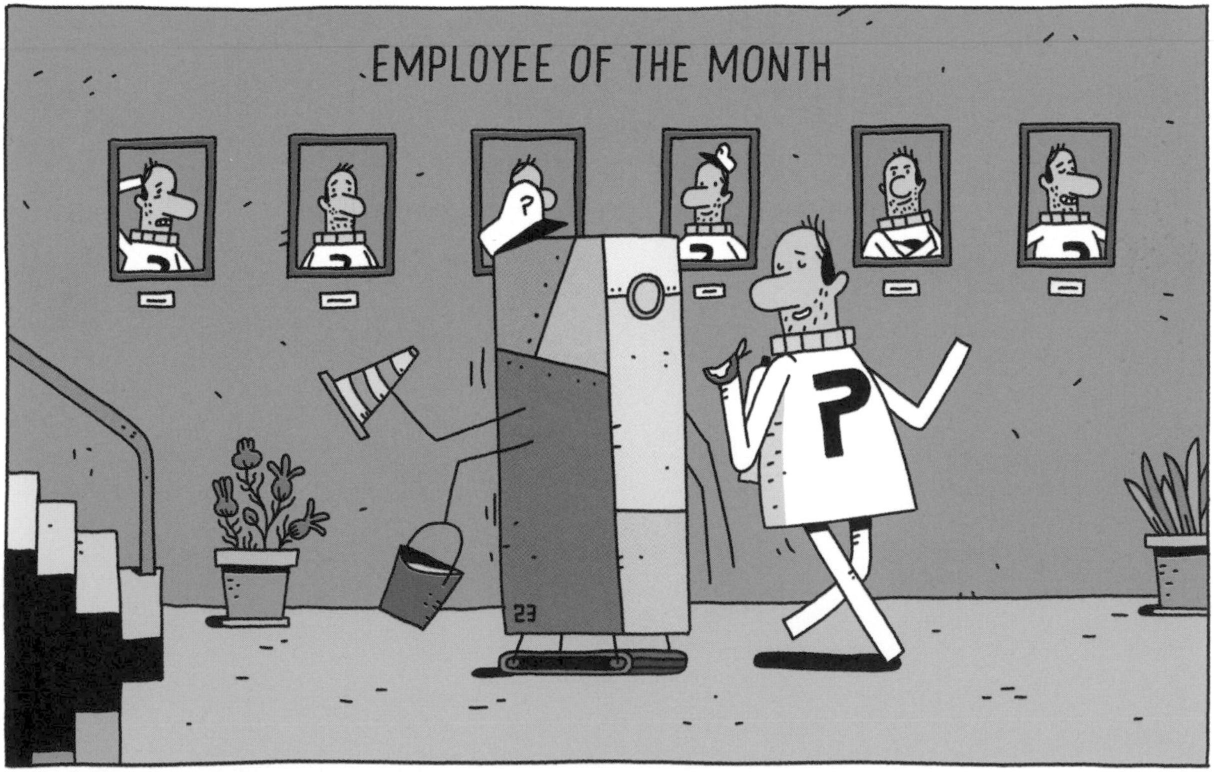
EMPLOYEE OF THE MONTH
23

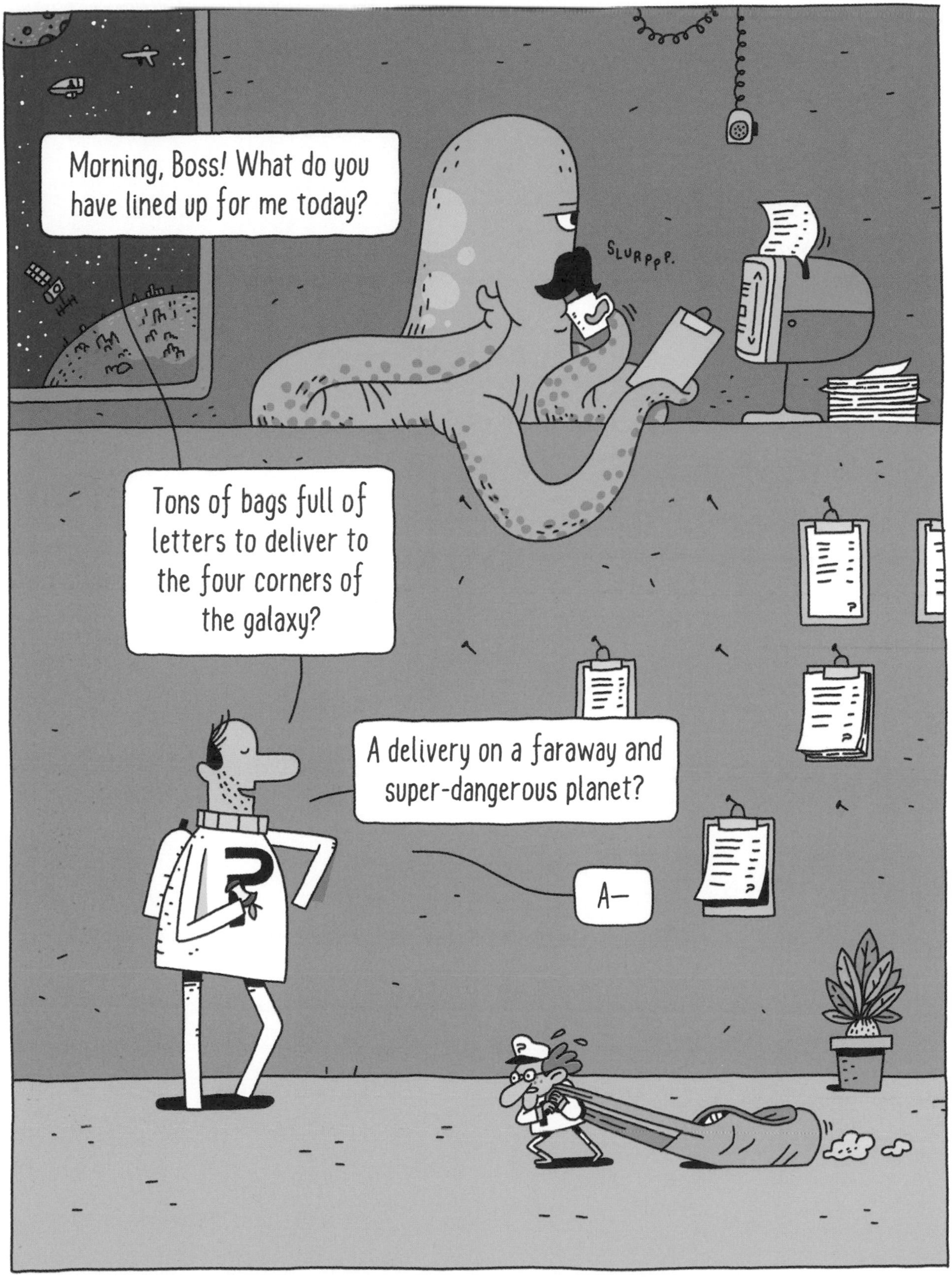
Morning, Boss! What do you have lined up for me today?
SLURPPP.
Tons of bags full of letters to deliver to the four corners of the galaxy?
A delivery on a faraway and super-dangerous planet?
A—

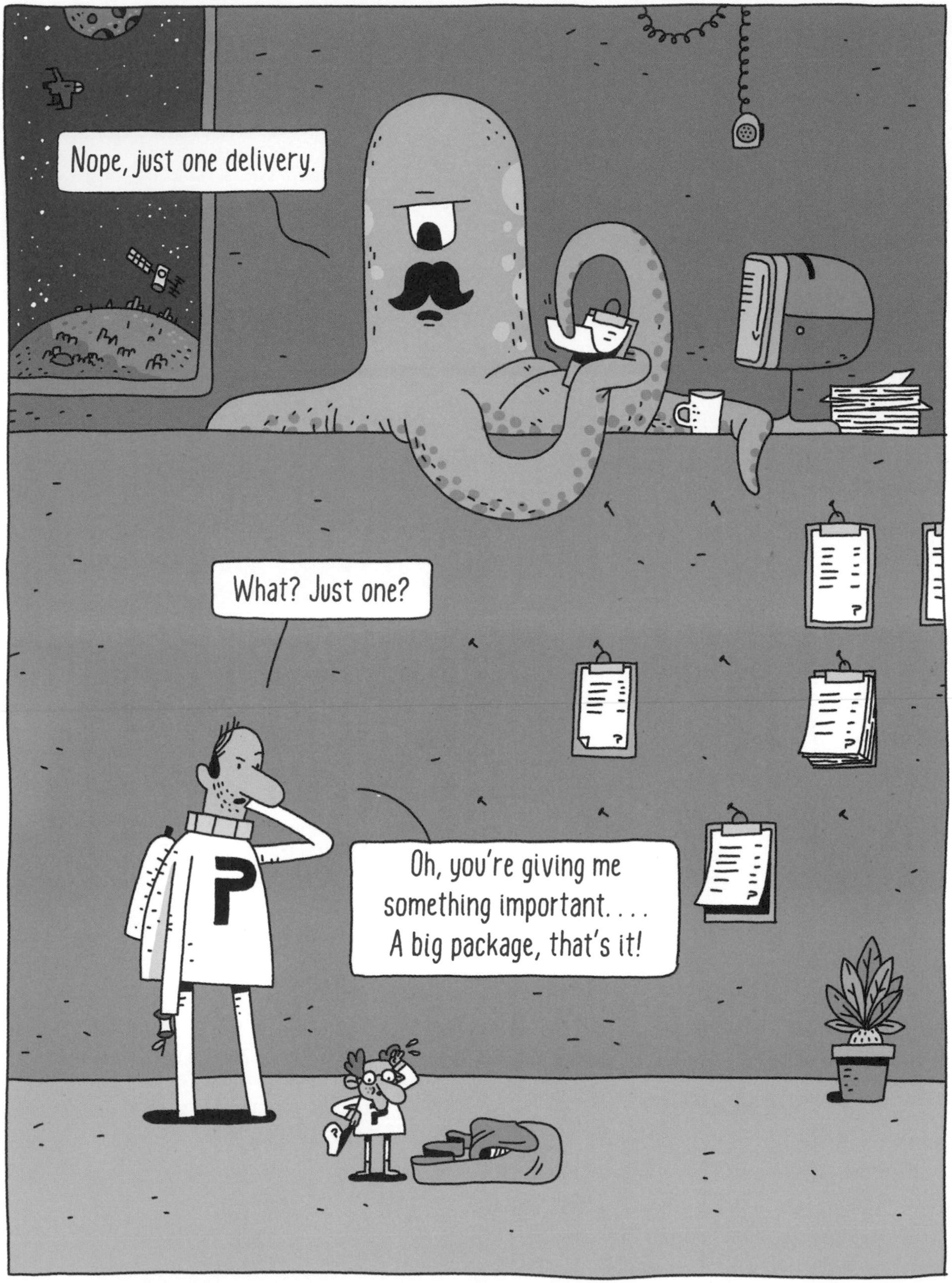
Nope, just one delivery.
What? Just one?
Oh, you're giving me something important. . . . A big package, that's it!

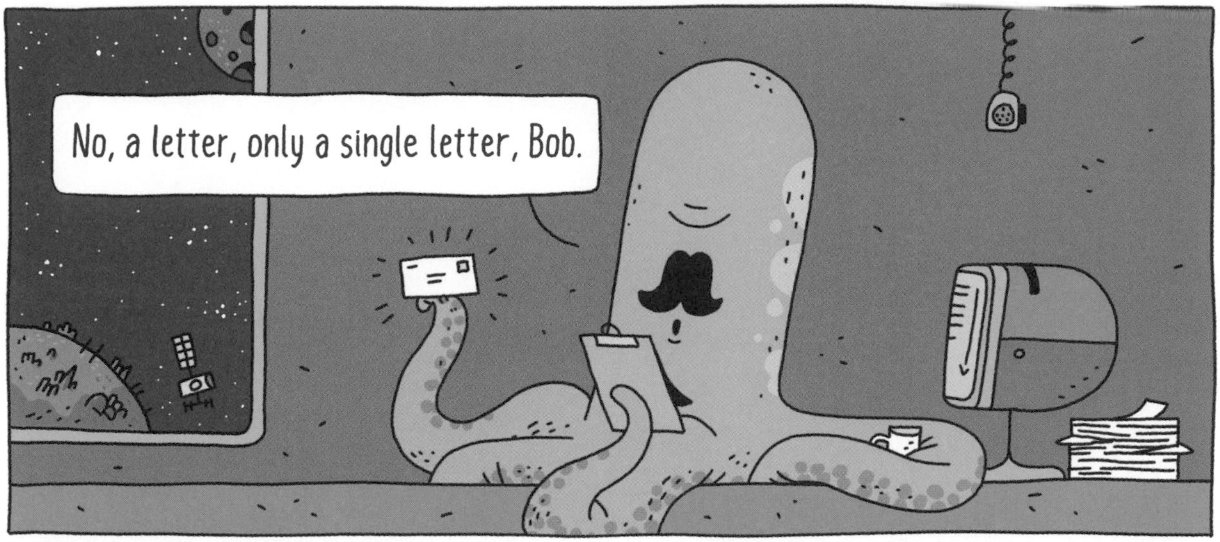
No, a letter, only a single letter, Bob.

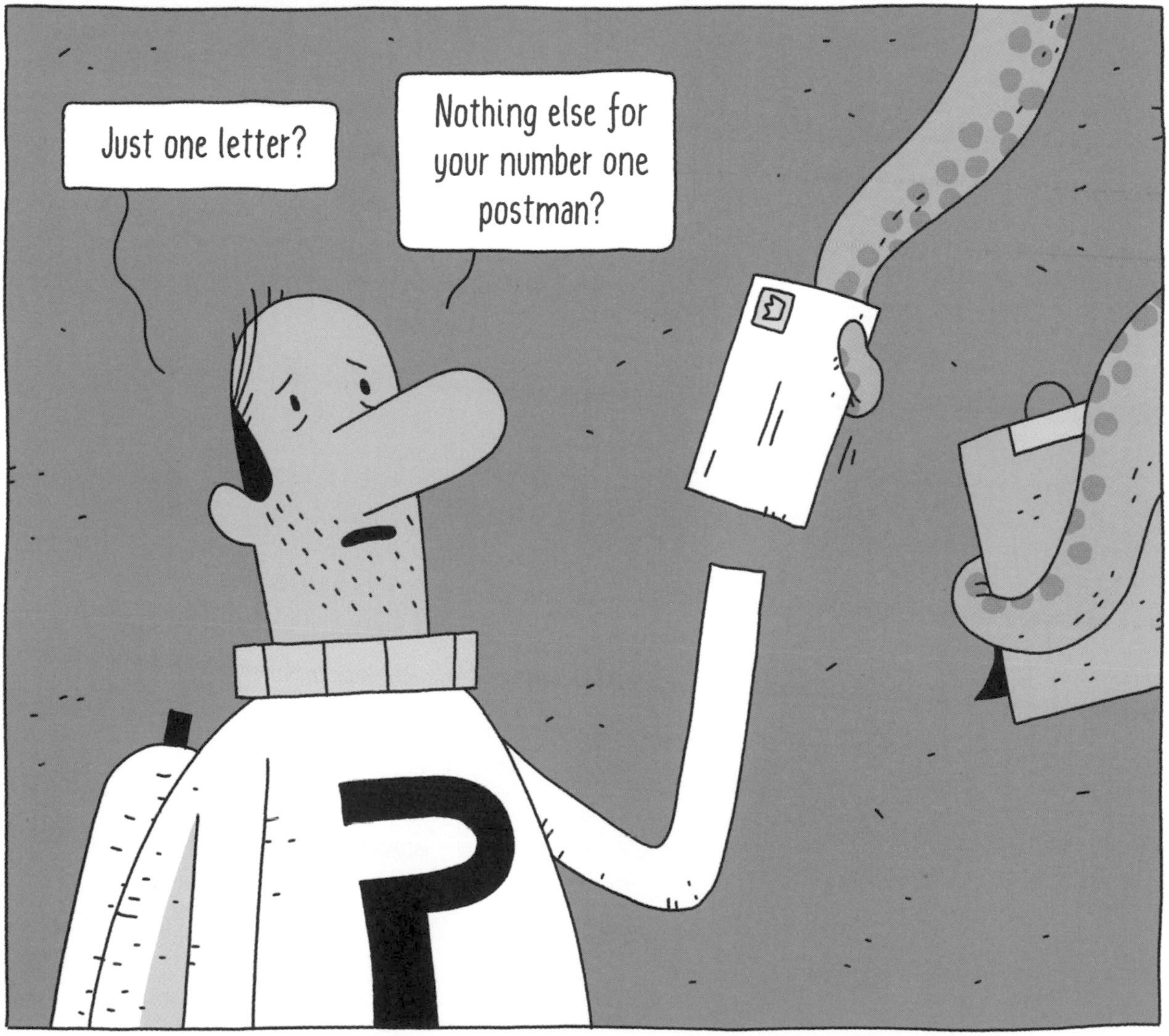
Just one letter?
Nothing else for your number one postman?

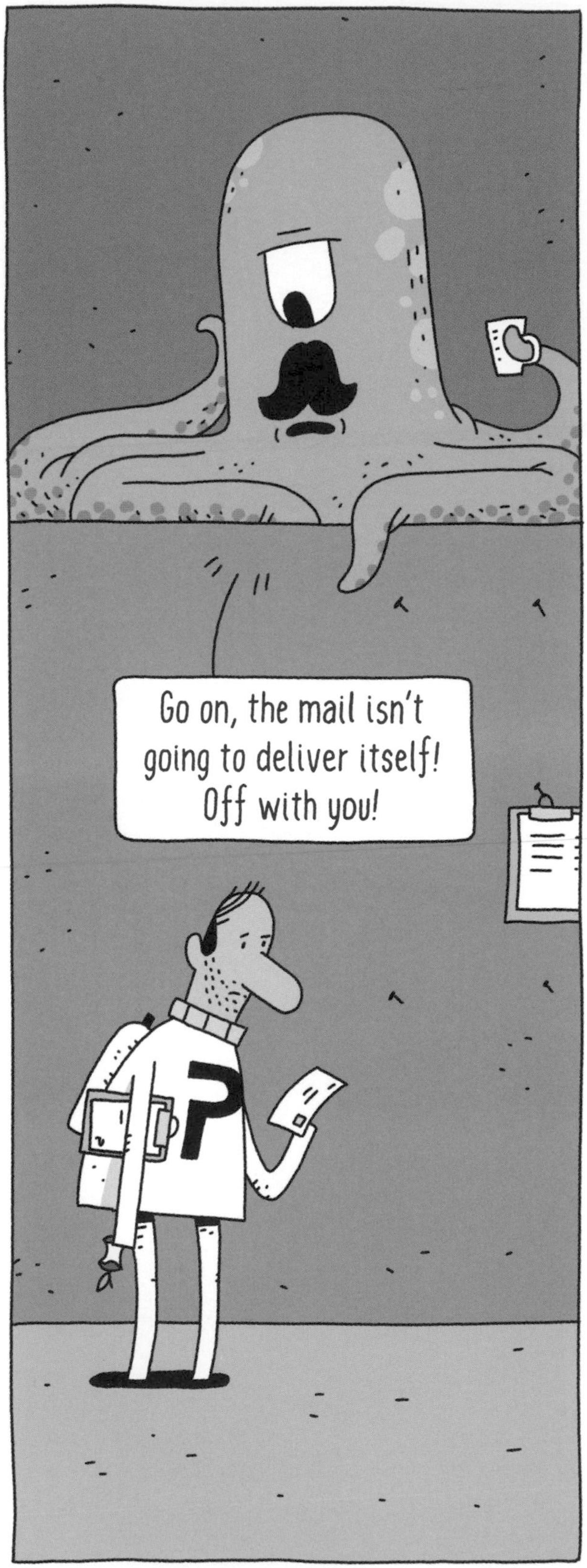
Go on, the mail isn't going to deliver itself! Off with you!

Now that he was used to more significant tasks, our friend seemed somewhat annoyed with the slim letter.
But oh well, mail delivery is sacred, so time to get cracking!

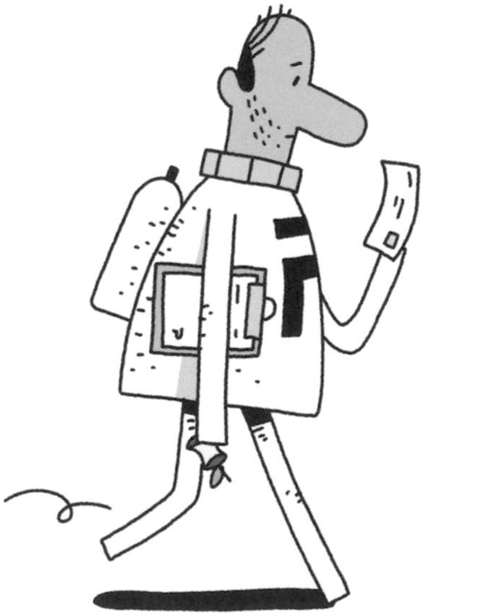

BOB!

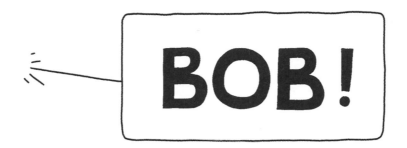

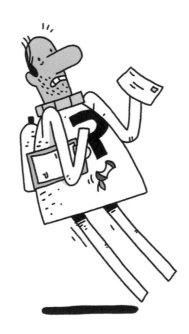

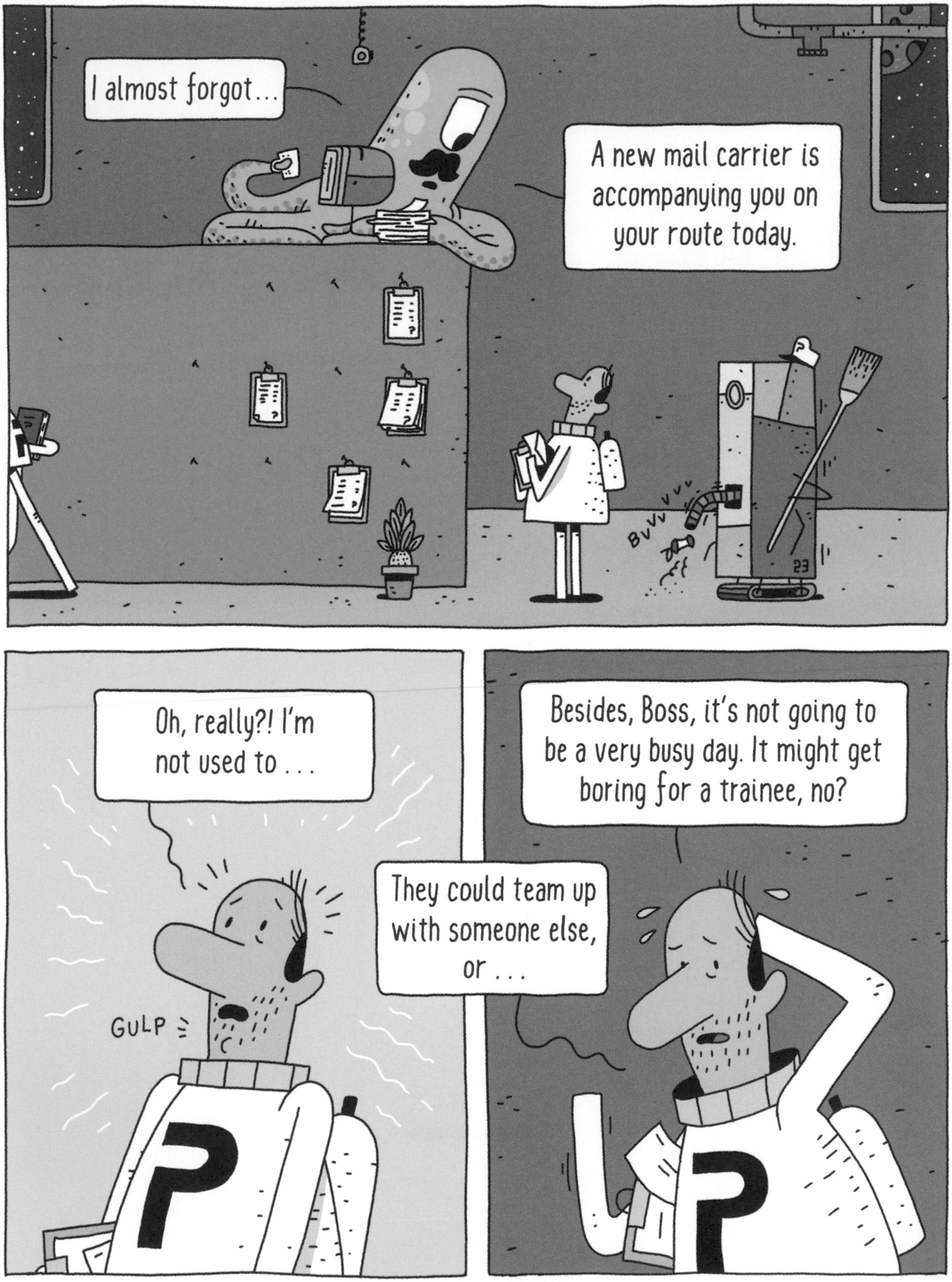
I almost forgot...
A new mail carrier is accompanying you on your route today.
BVVVVV
Oh, really?! I'm not used to . . .
GULP
Besides, Boss, it's not going to be a very busy day. It might get boring for a trainee, no?
They could team up with someone else, or . . .

Ah, there she is.

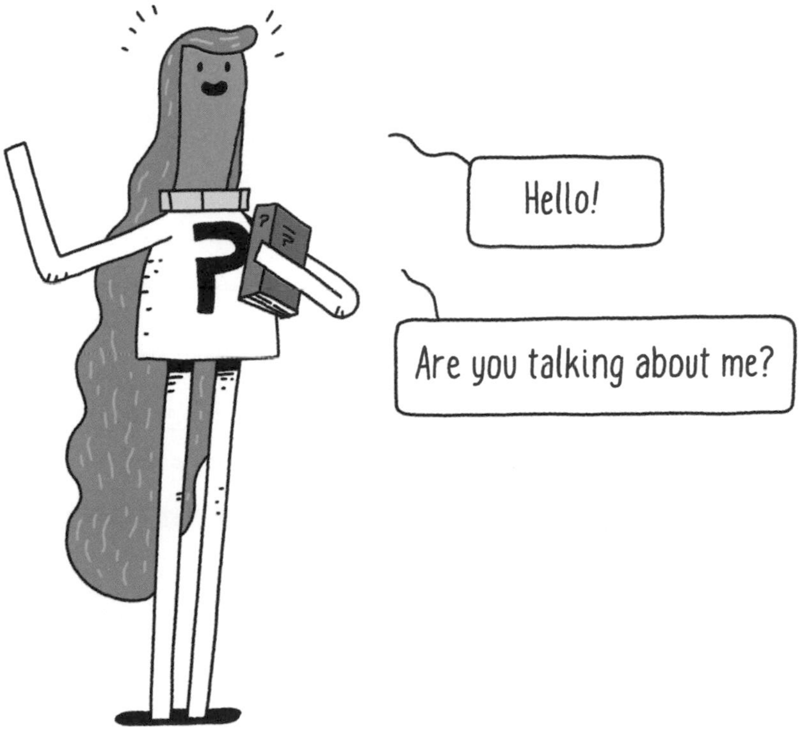
Hello!
Are you talking about me?

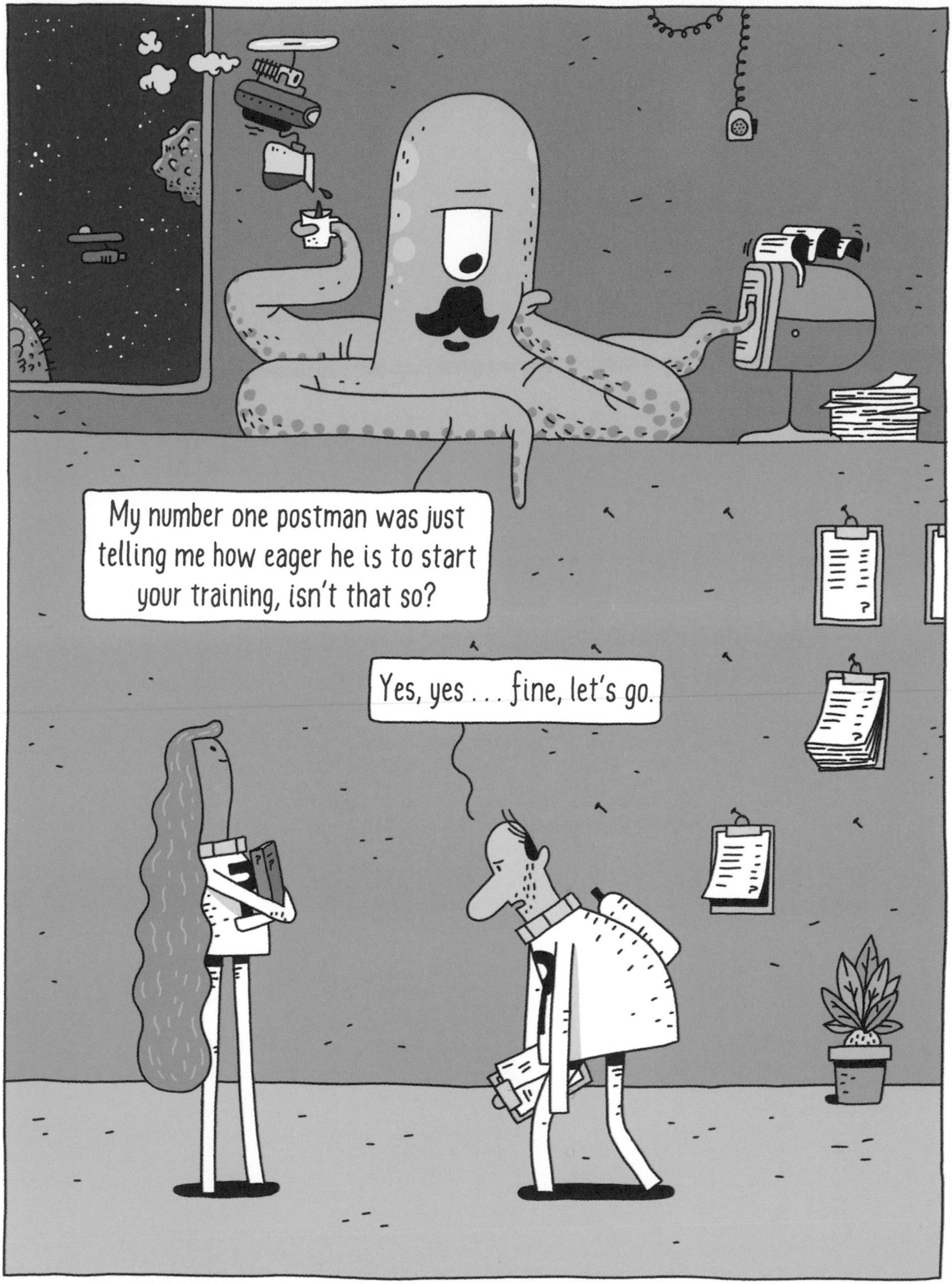
My number one postman was just telling me how eager he is to start your training, isn't that so?
Yes, yes . . . fine, let's go.

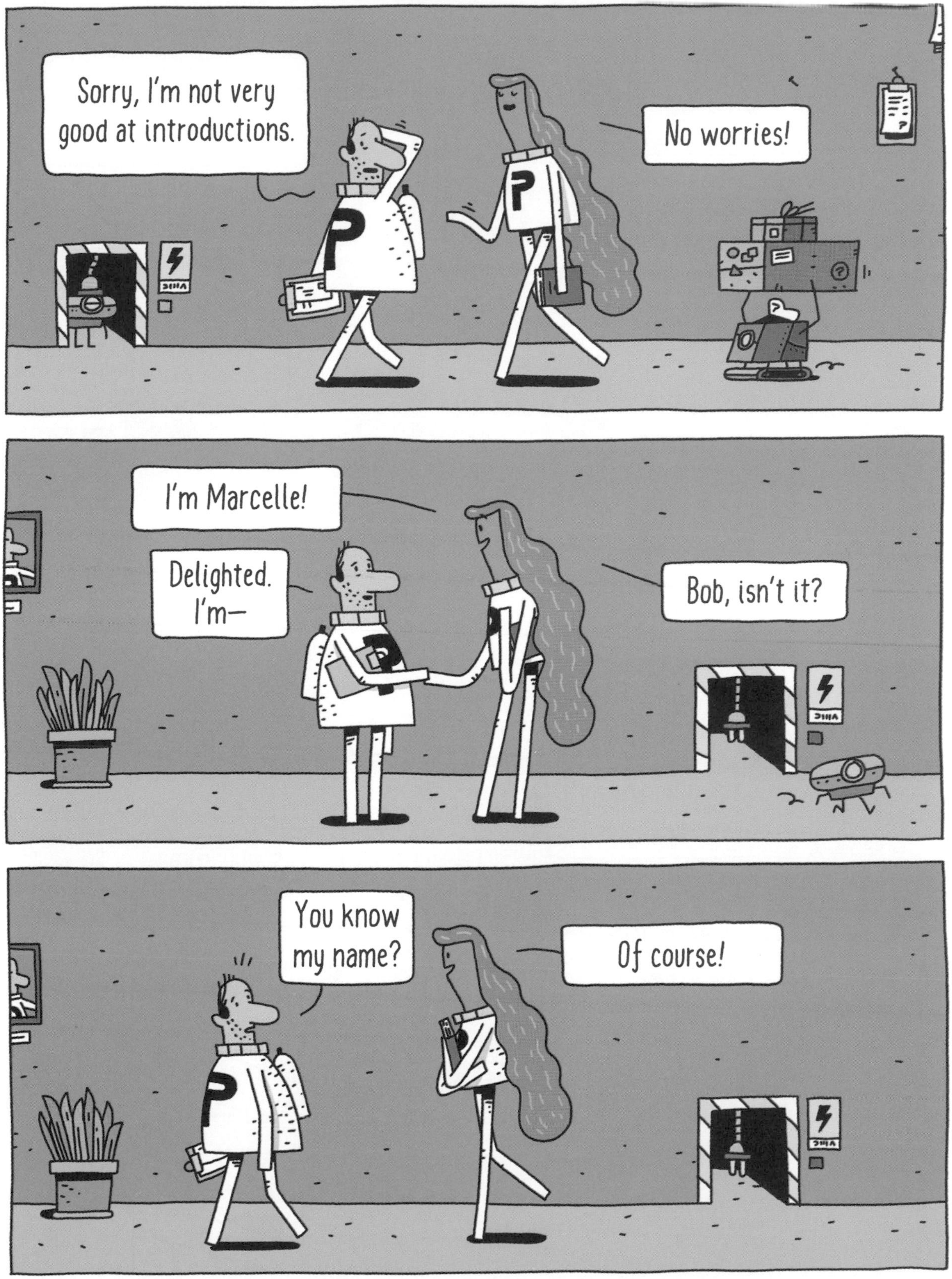
Sorry, I'm not very good at introductions.
No worries!
I'm Marcelle!
Delighted. I'm—
Bob, isn't it?
You know my name?
Of course!

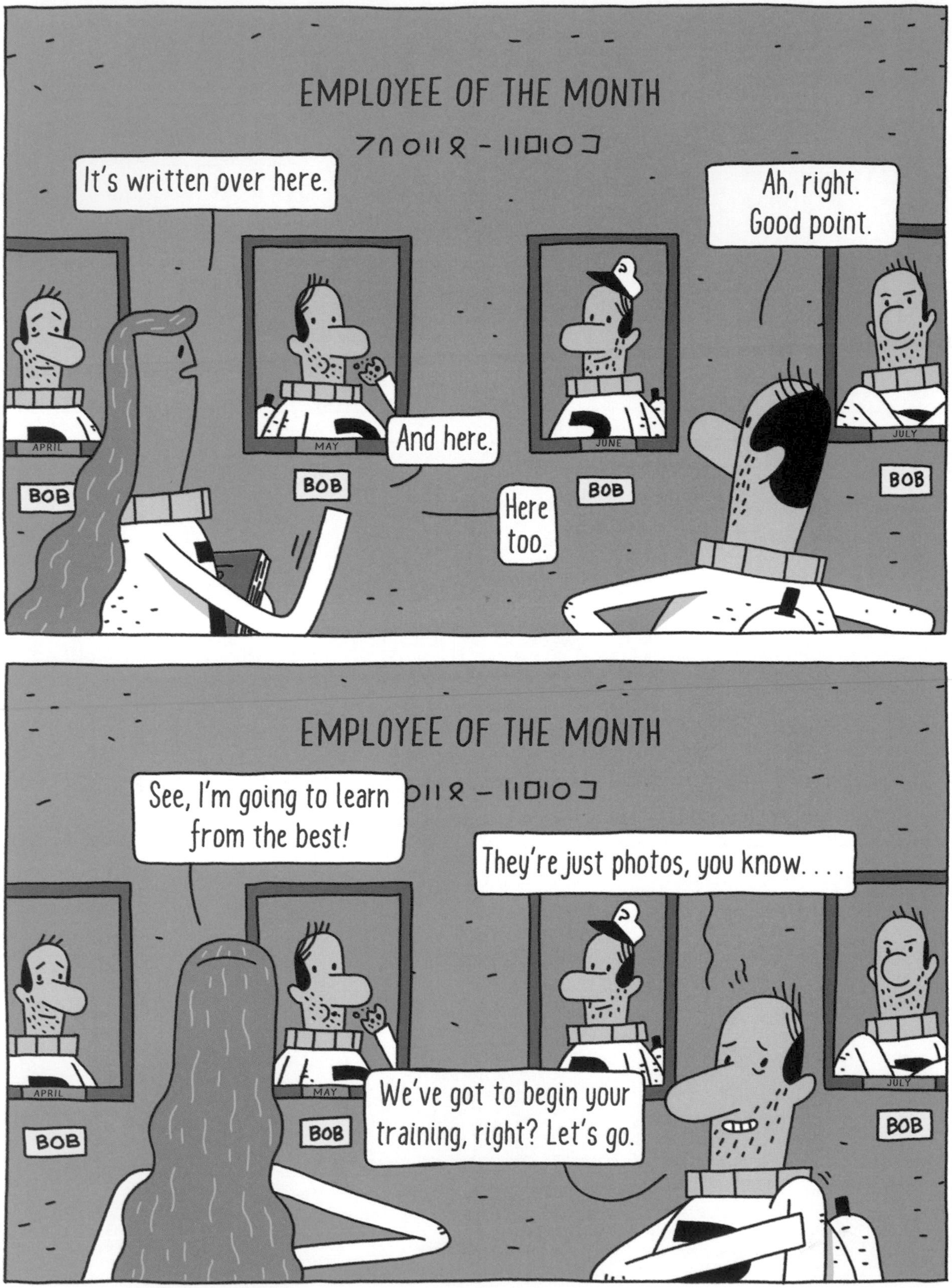
EMPLOYEE OF THE MONTH
It's written over here.
APRIL
BOB
MAY
BOB
And here.
Here too.
JUNE
BOB
Ah, right. Good point.
JULY
BOB
EMPLOYEE OF THE MONTH
See, I'm going to learn from the best!
They're just photos, you know. . . .
APRIL
BOB
MAY
BOB
We've got to begin your training, right? Let's go.
JULY
BOB

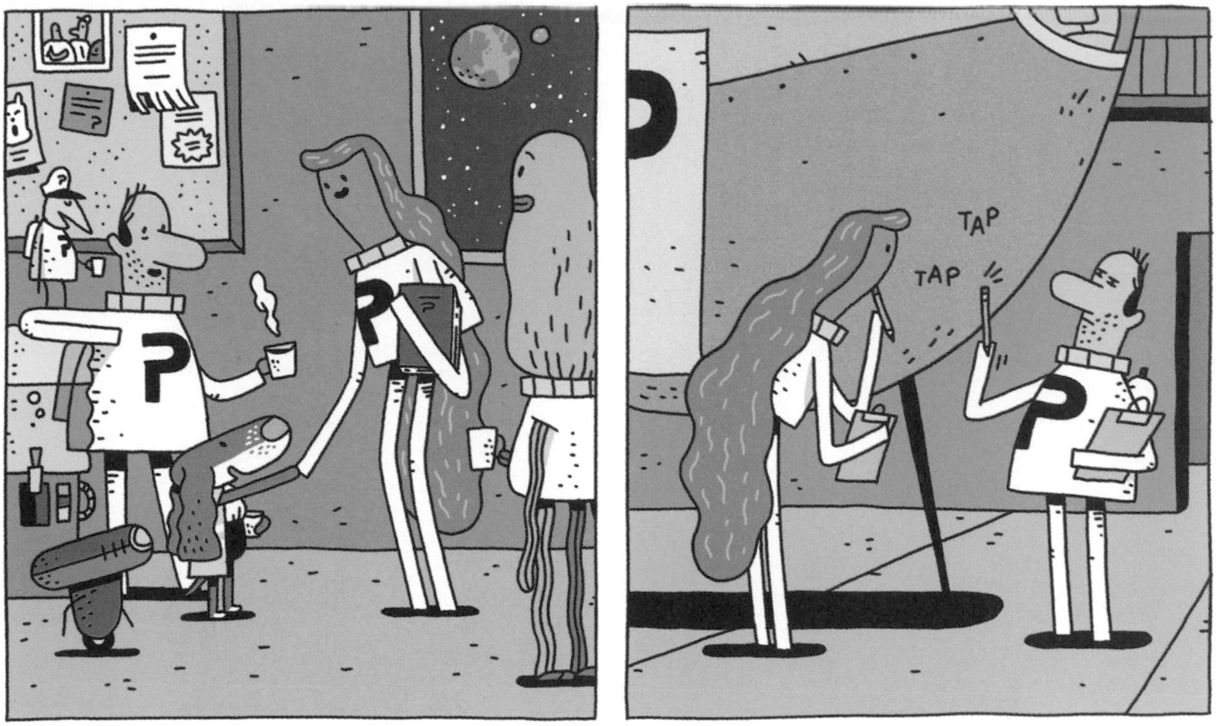
TAP
TAP

After greeting friends, inspecting the spacecraft, and filling up the gas tank, our duo is ready!

Speaking of duos, Bob is uneasy at the idea of having a partner for the first time. . . .
But, after all, what could possibly go wrong?

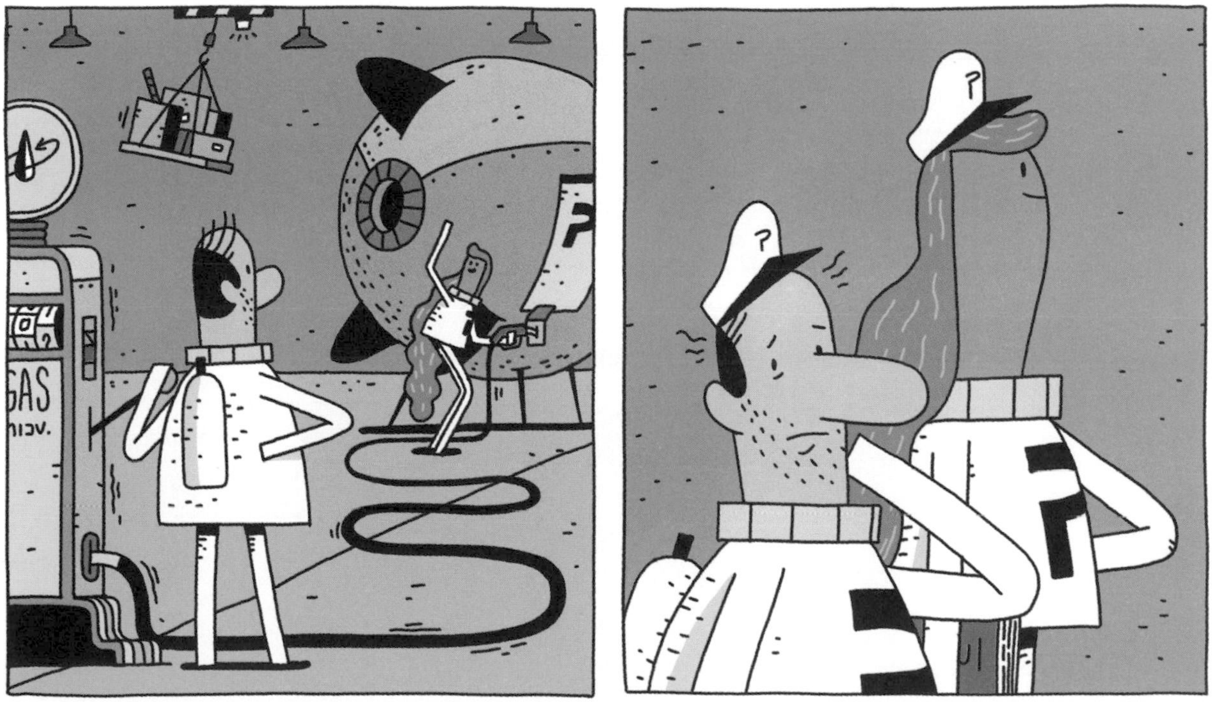
GAS

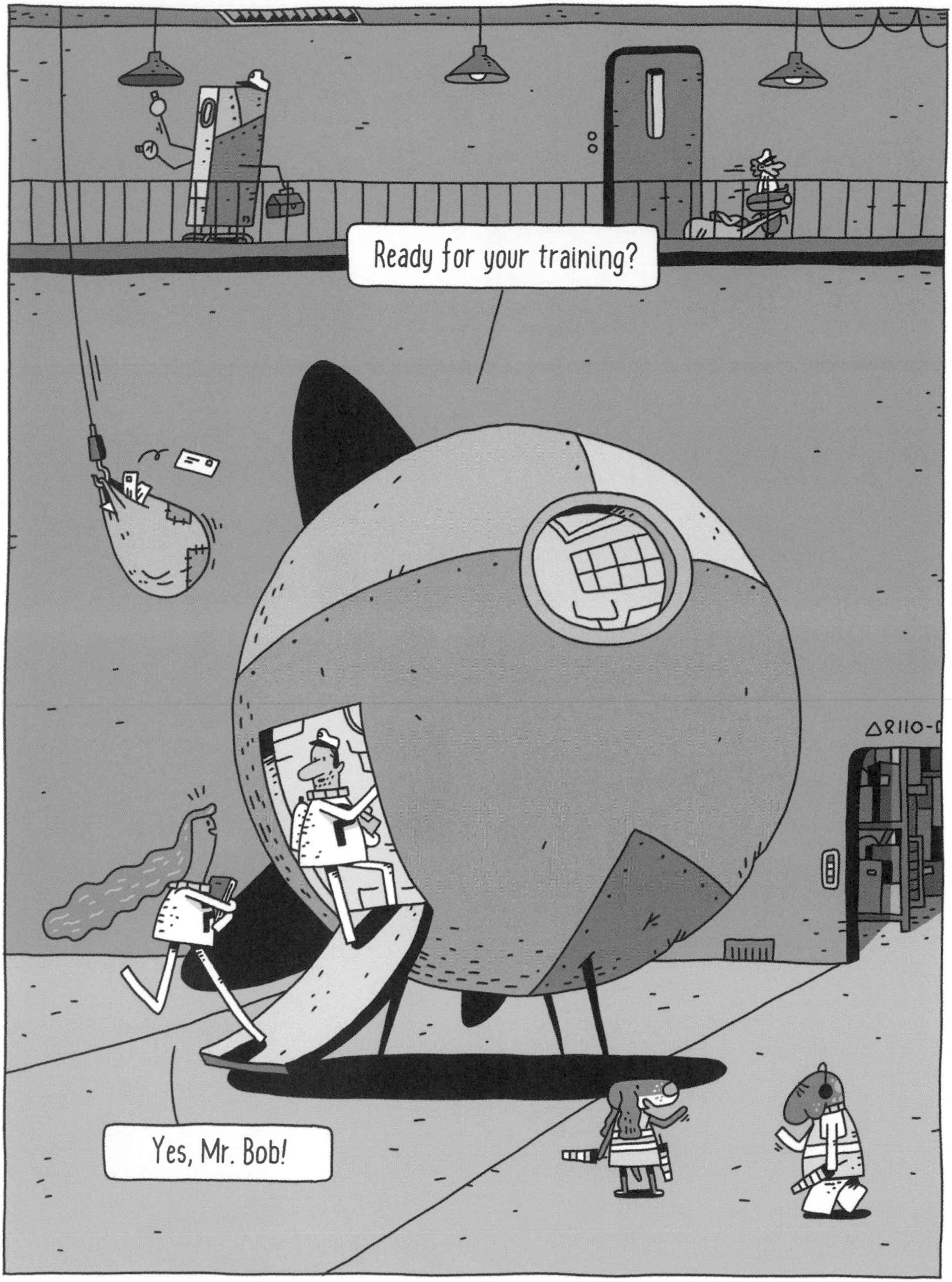
Ready for your training?
Yes, Mr. Bob!
Δ8110-

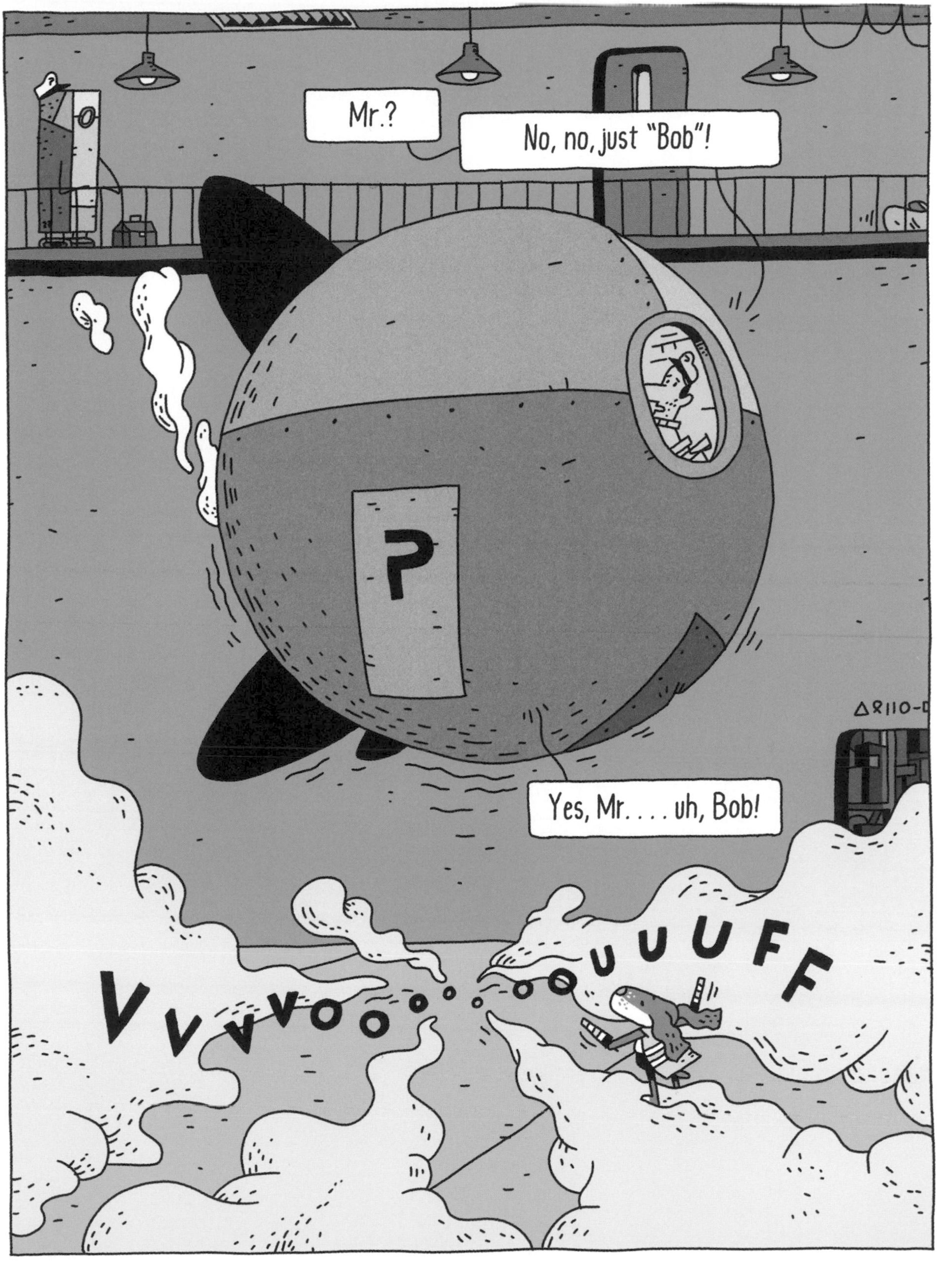
Mr.?
No, no, just "Bob"!
Yes, Mr. . . . uh, Bob!
VVVVOOOooo.ooUUUFF

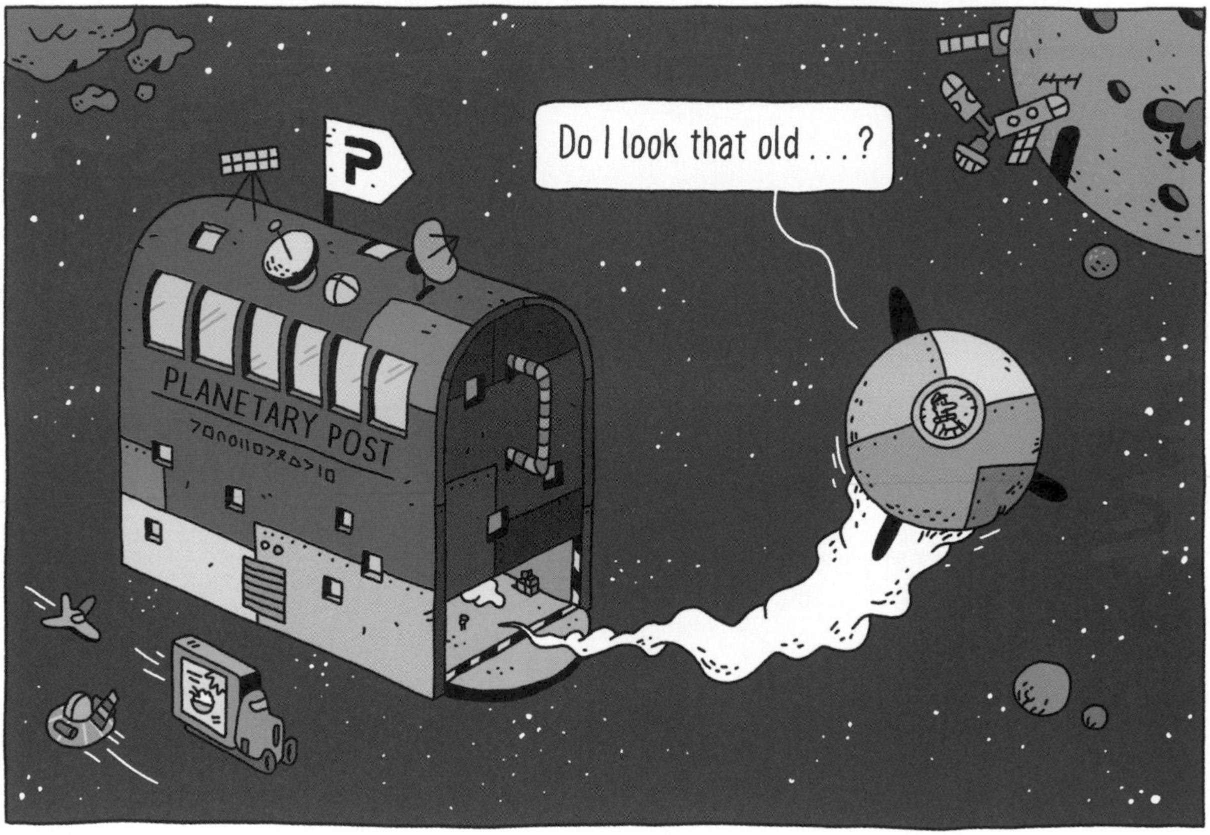
PLANETARY POST
Do I look that old . . . ?

STOP #1

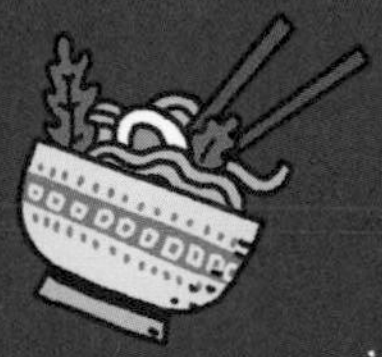

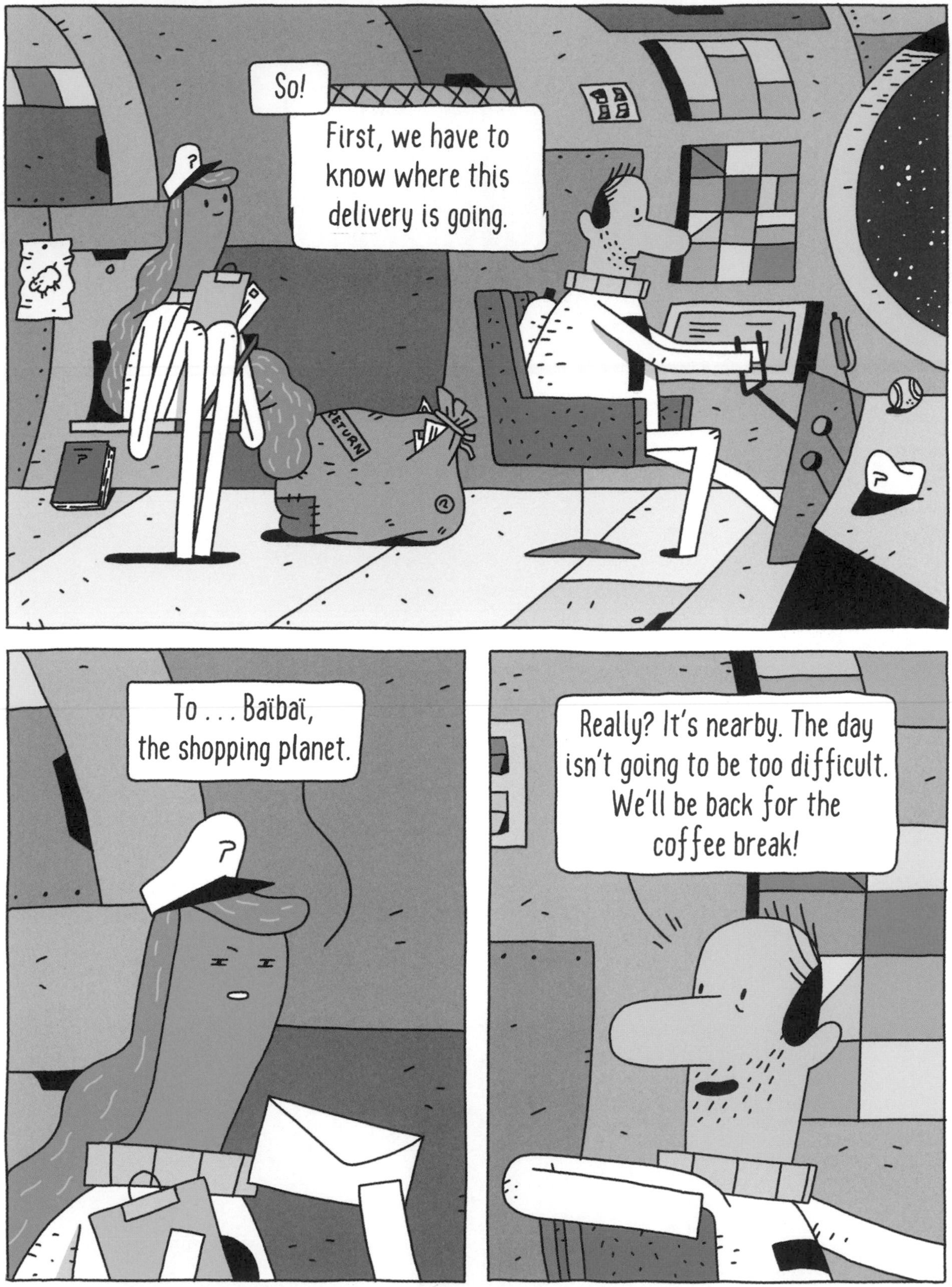
So!
First, we have to know where this delivery is going.
RETURN
To . . . Baïbaï, the shopping planet.
Really? It's nearby. The day isn't going to be too difficult. We'll be back for the coffee break!

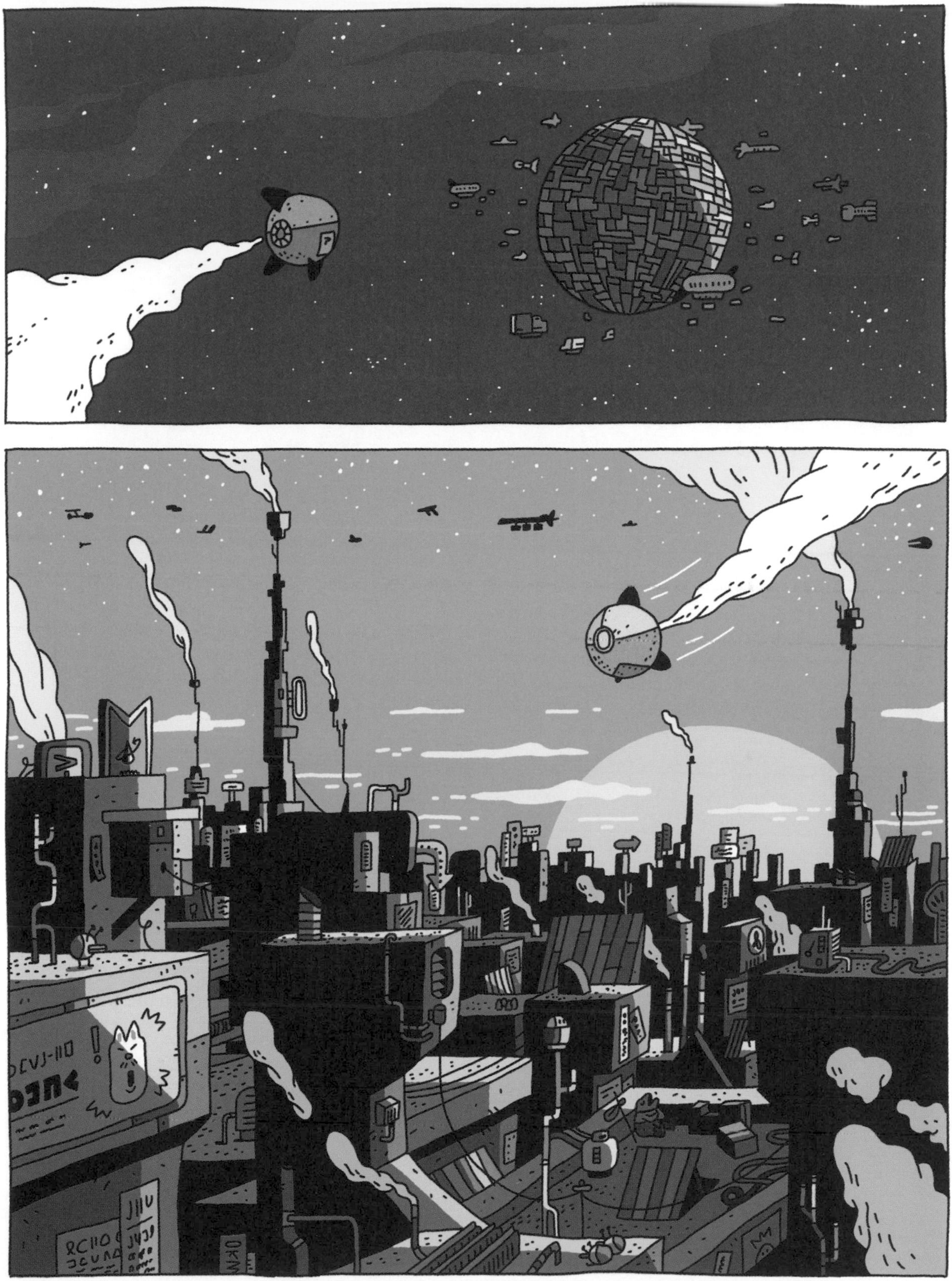

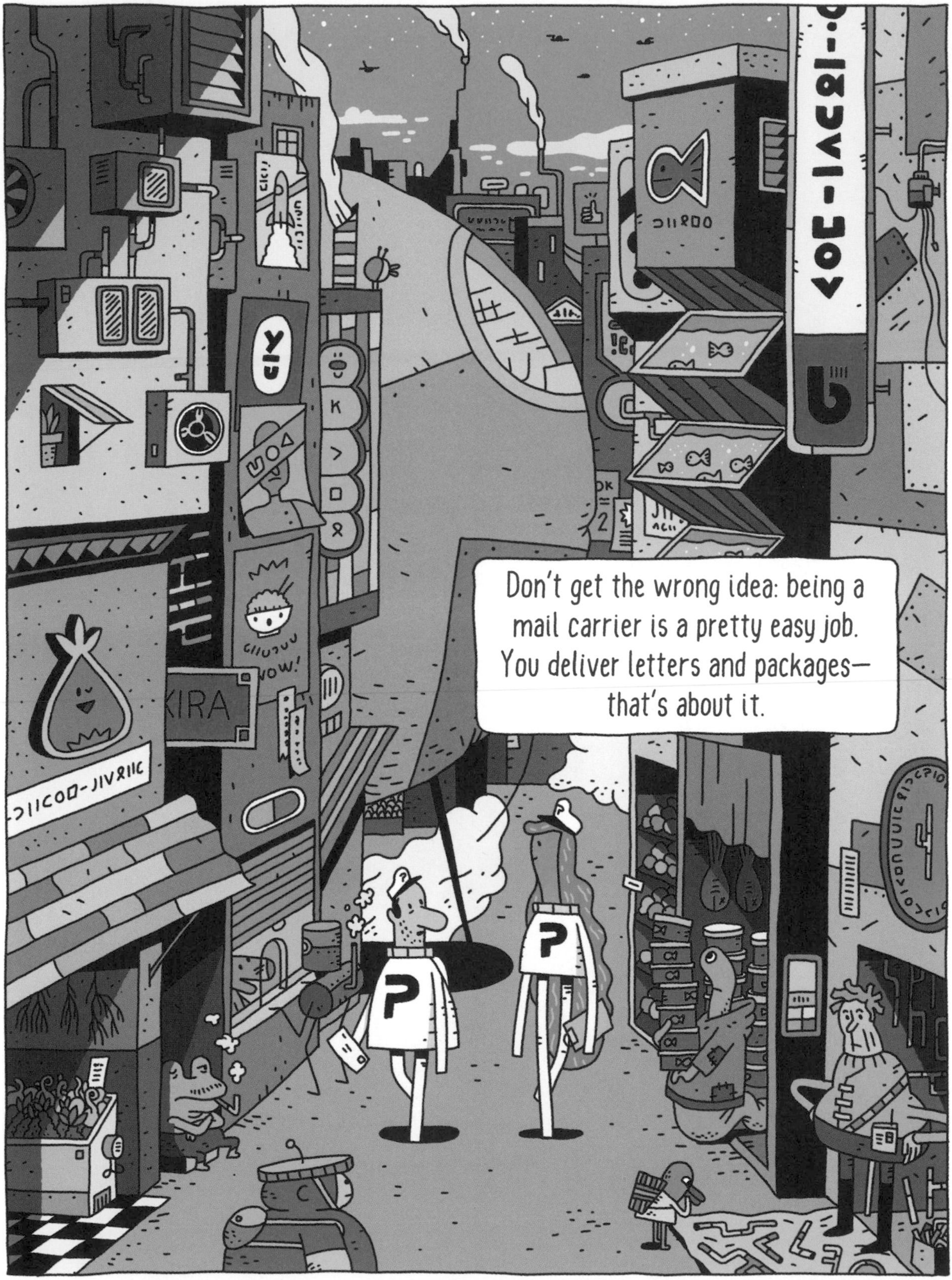
Don't get the wrong idea: being a mail carrier is a pretty easy job. You deliver letters and packages—that's about it.
KIRA
NOW!

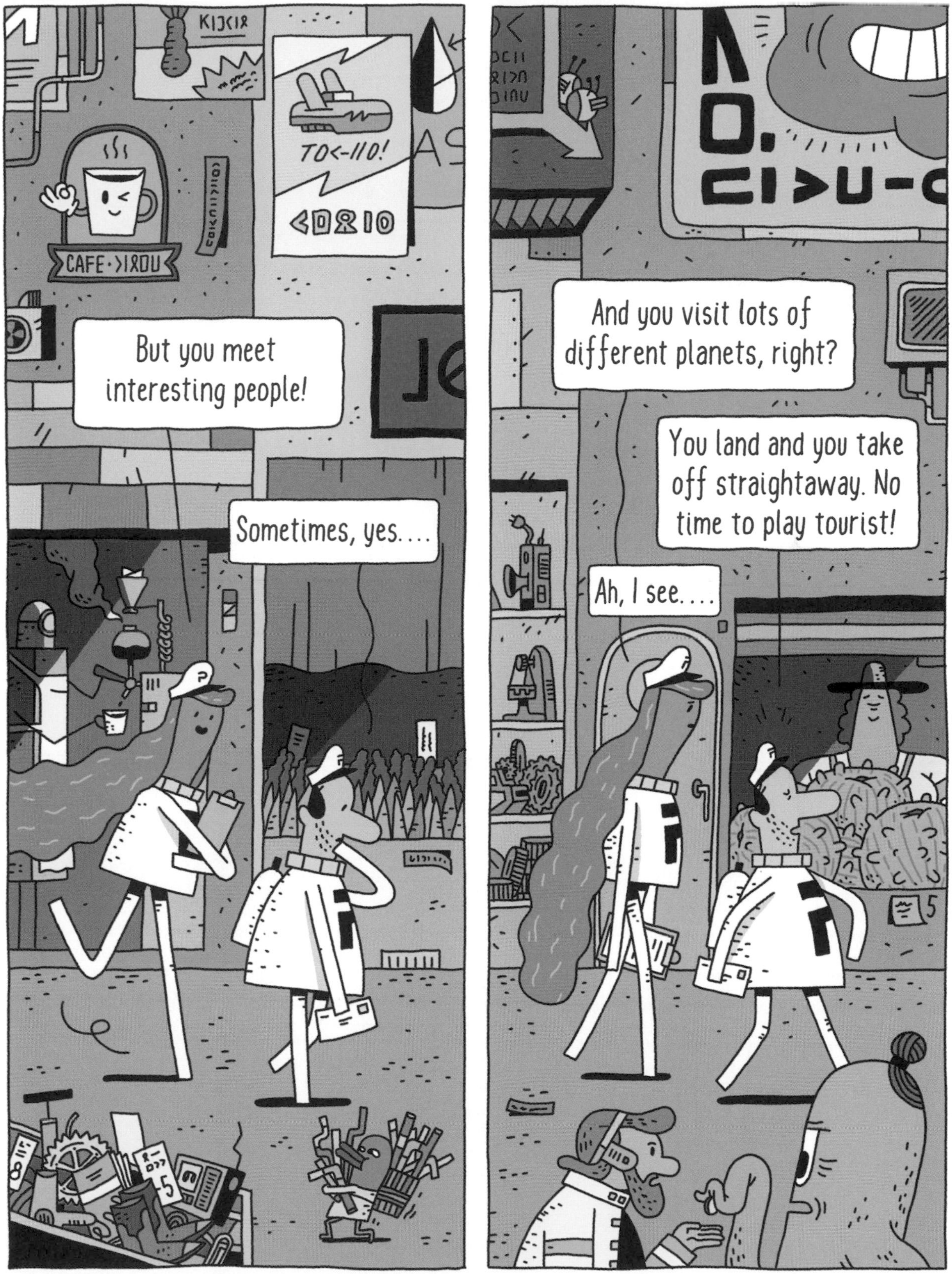
But you meet interesting people!
Sometimes, yes. . . .
And you visit lots of different planets, right?
You land and you take off straightaway. No time to play tourist!
Ah, I see. . . .

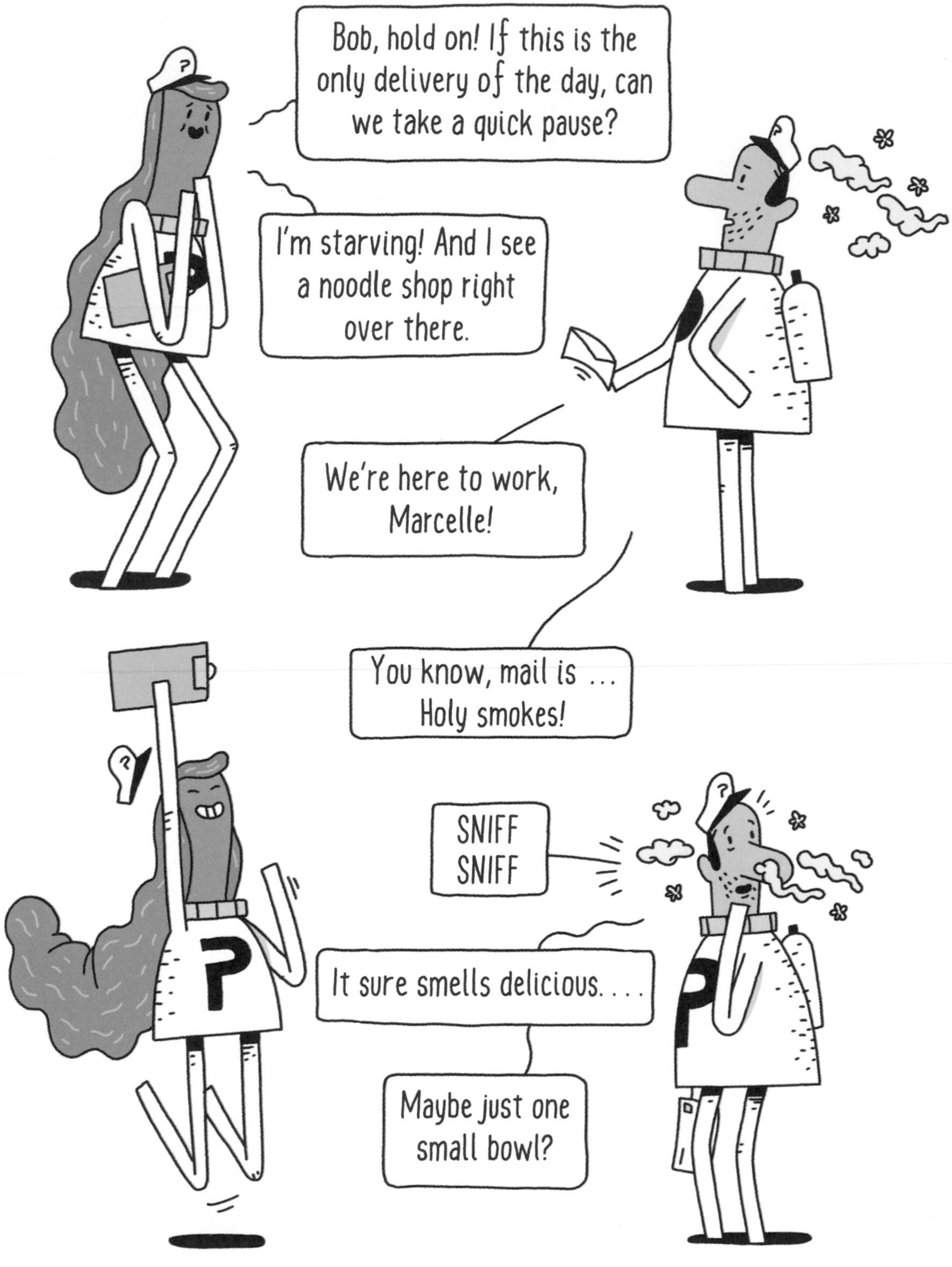

Bob, hold on! If this is the only delivery of the day, can we take a quick pause?
I'm starving! And I see a noodle shop right over there.
We're here to work, Marcelle!
You know, mail is ... Holy smokes!
SNIFF SNIFF
It sure smells delicious. . . .
Maybe just one small bowl?

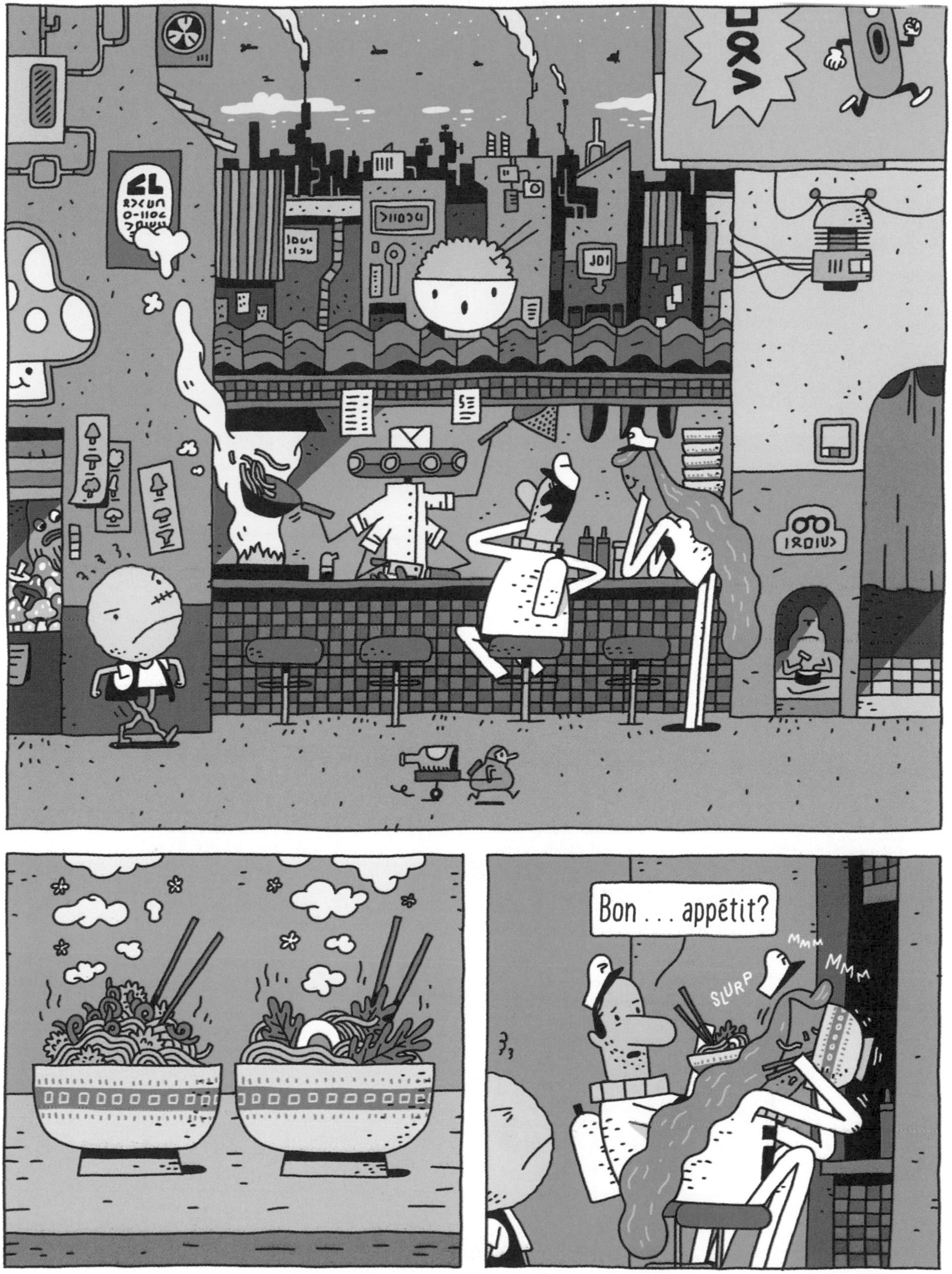
Bon . . . appétit?
SLURP
MMM
MMM

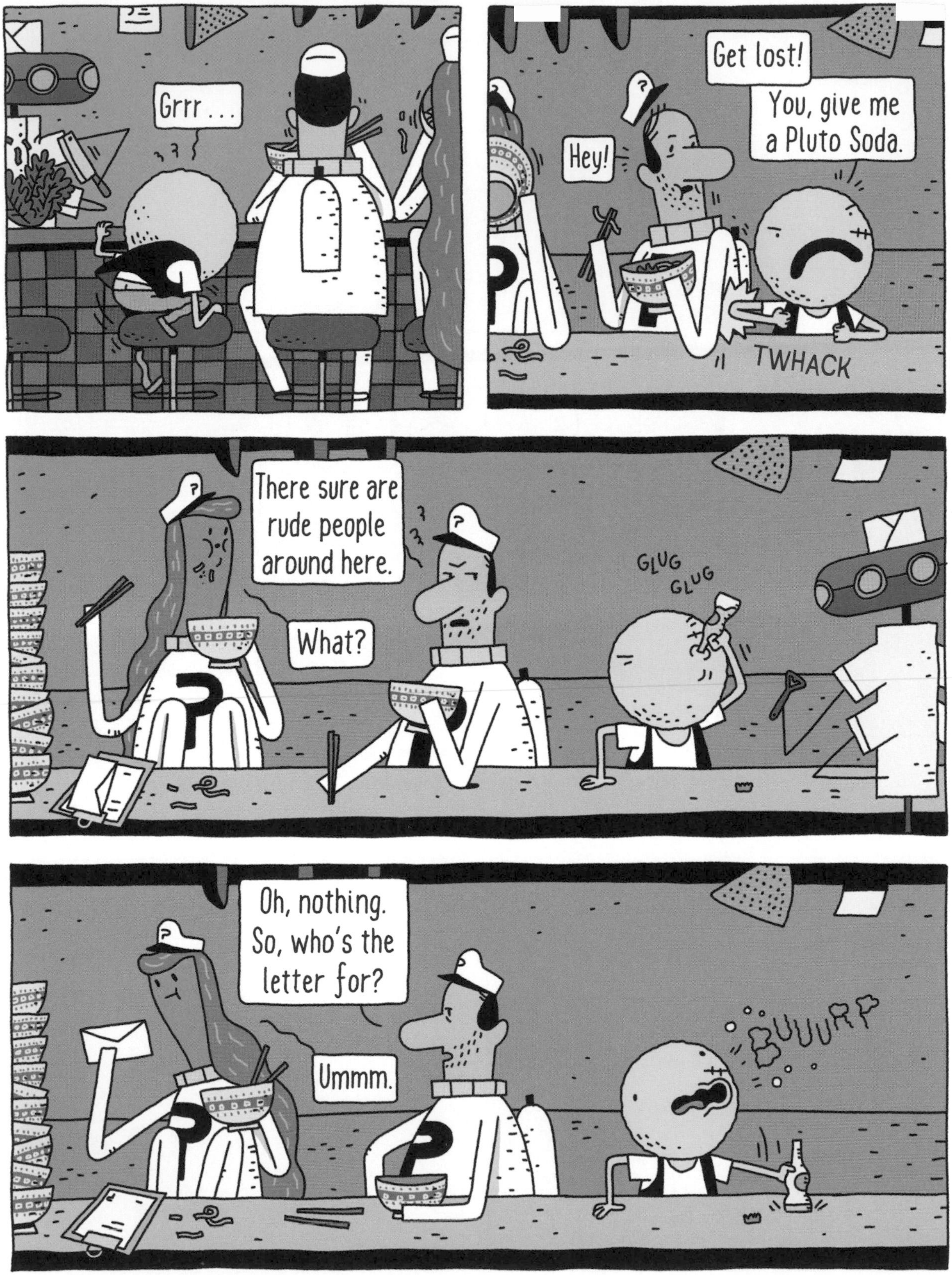
Grrr...
Hey!
Get lost!
You, give me a Pluto Soda.
TWHACK
There sure are rude people around here.
What?
GLUG GLUG
Oh, nothing. So, who's the letter for?
Ummm.
BUUURP

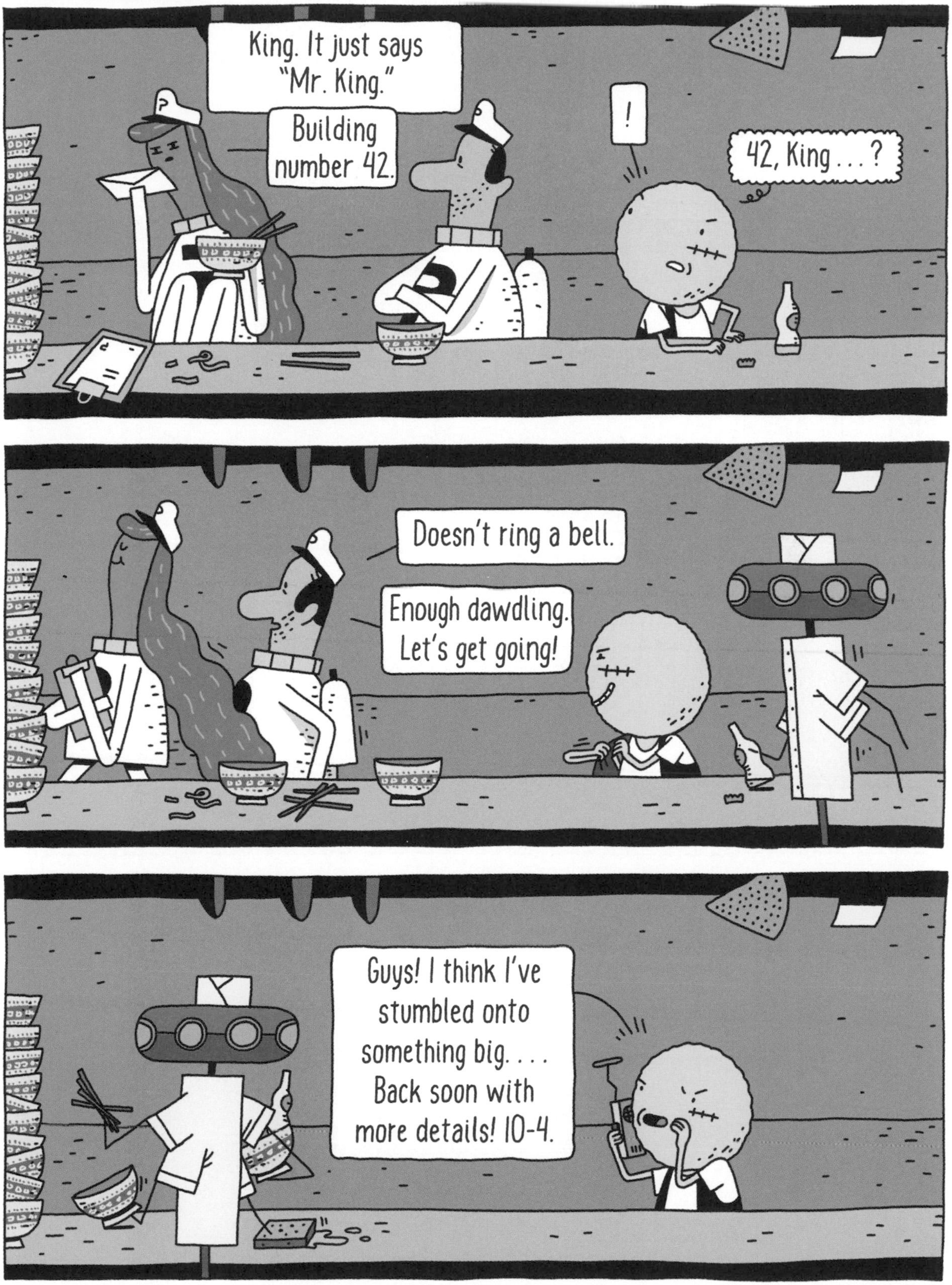
King. It just says "Mr. King."
Building number 42.
!
42, King . . . ?
Doesn't ring a bell.
Enough dawdling. Let's get going!
Guys! I think I've stumbled onto something big. . . . Back soon with more details! 10-4.

With full stomachs, Marcelle and Bob go searching for building #42.
It may not be so bad working as a team after all!

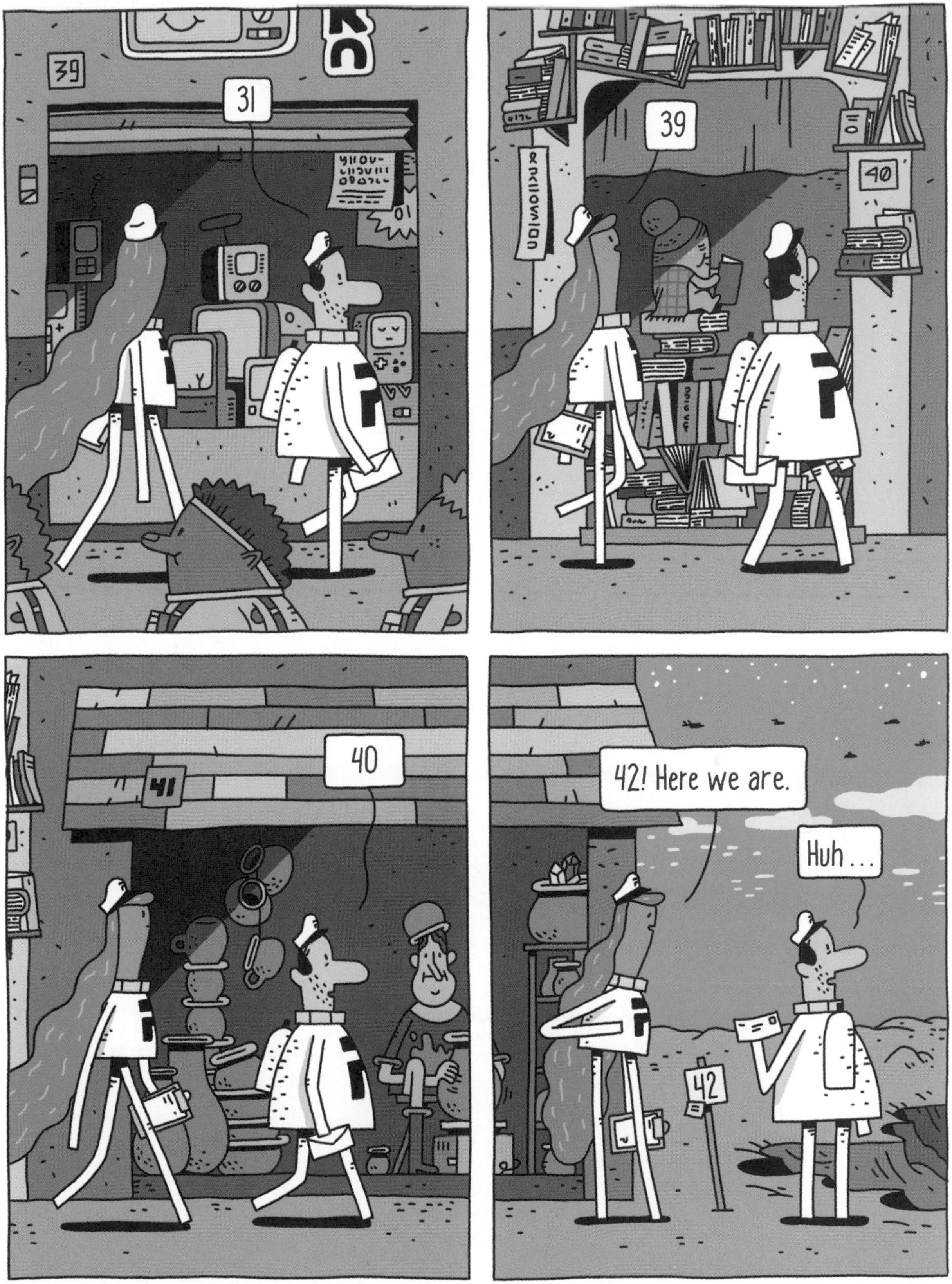
31
39
40
42! Here we are.
Huh . . .

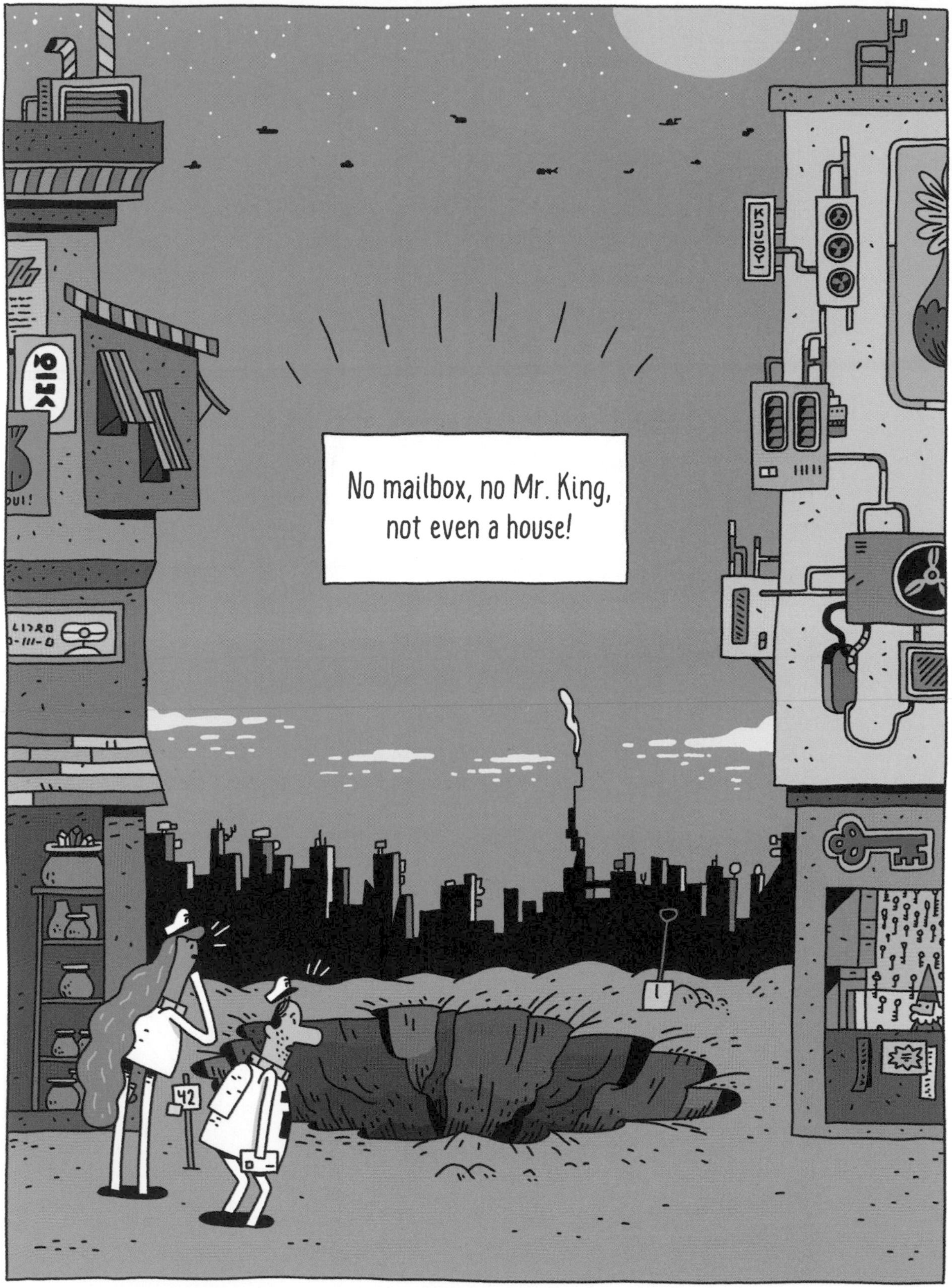
No mailbox, no Mr. King, not even a house!
42

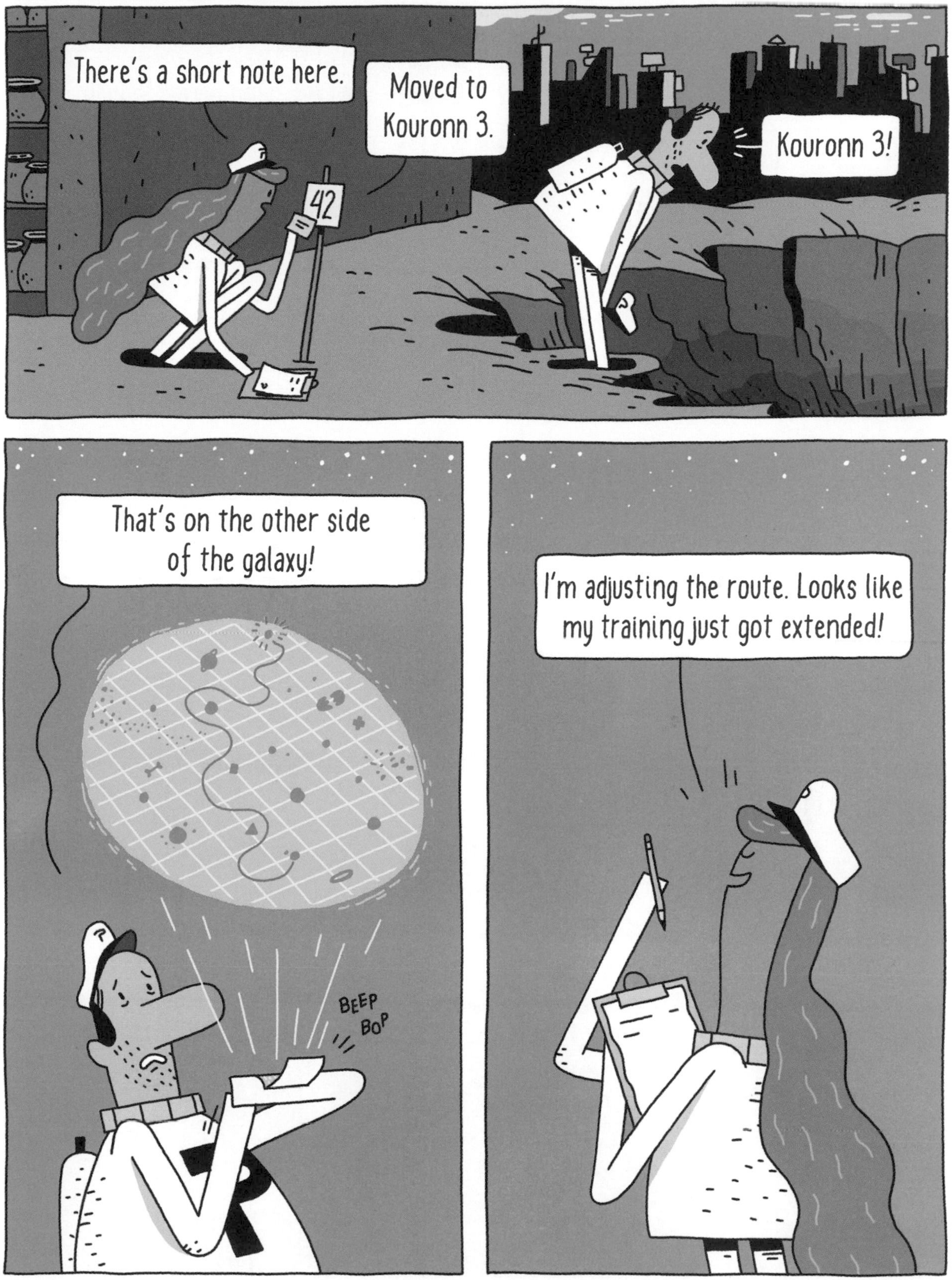
There's a short note here.
Moved to Kouronn 3.
Kouronn 3!
That's on the other side of the galaxy!
BEEP BOP
I'm adjusting the route. Looks like my training just got extended!

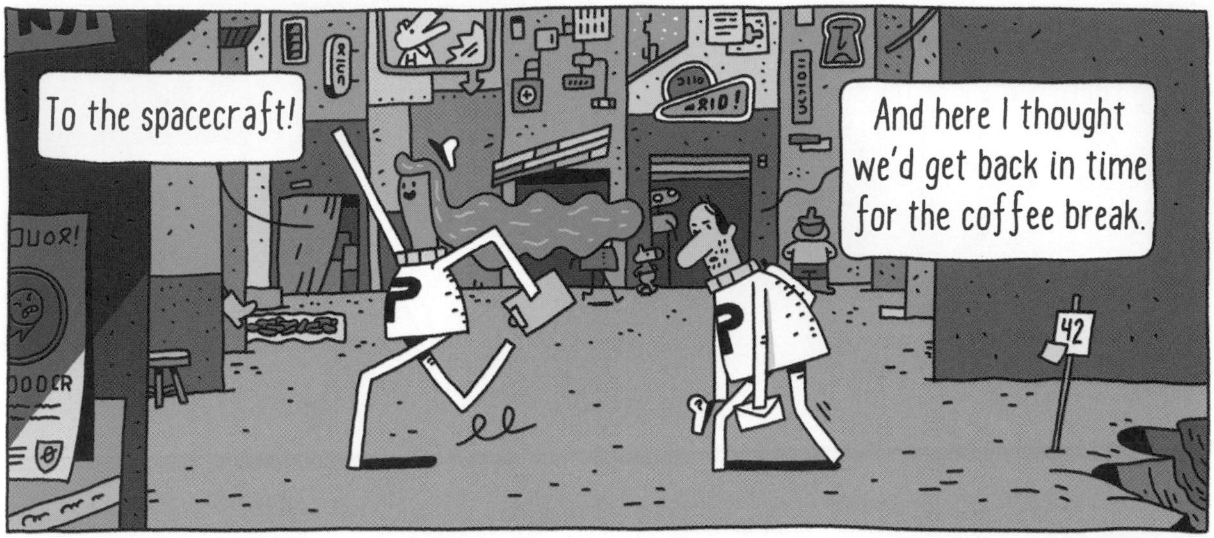
To the spacecraft!
And here I thought we'd get back in time for the coffee break.
42

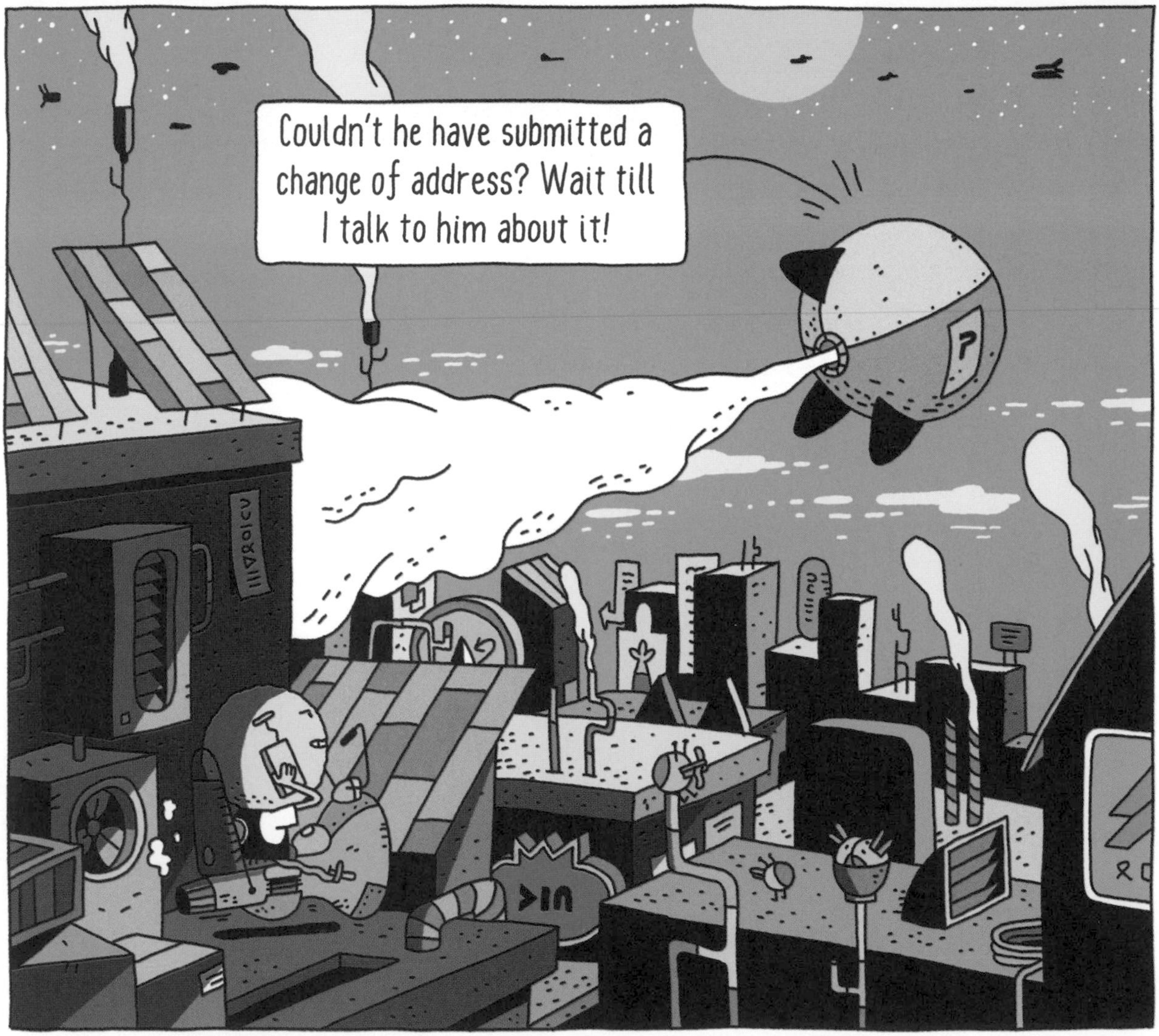
Couldn't he have submitted a change of address? Wait till I talk to him about it!

STOP #2

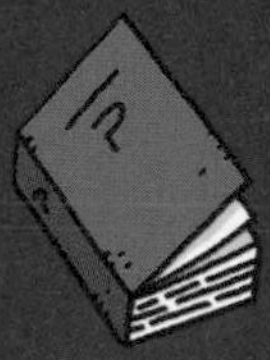

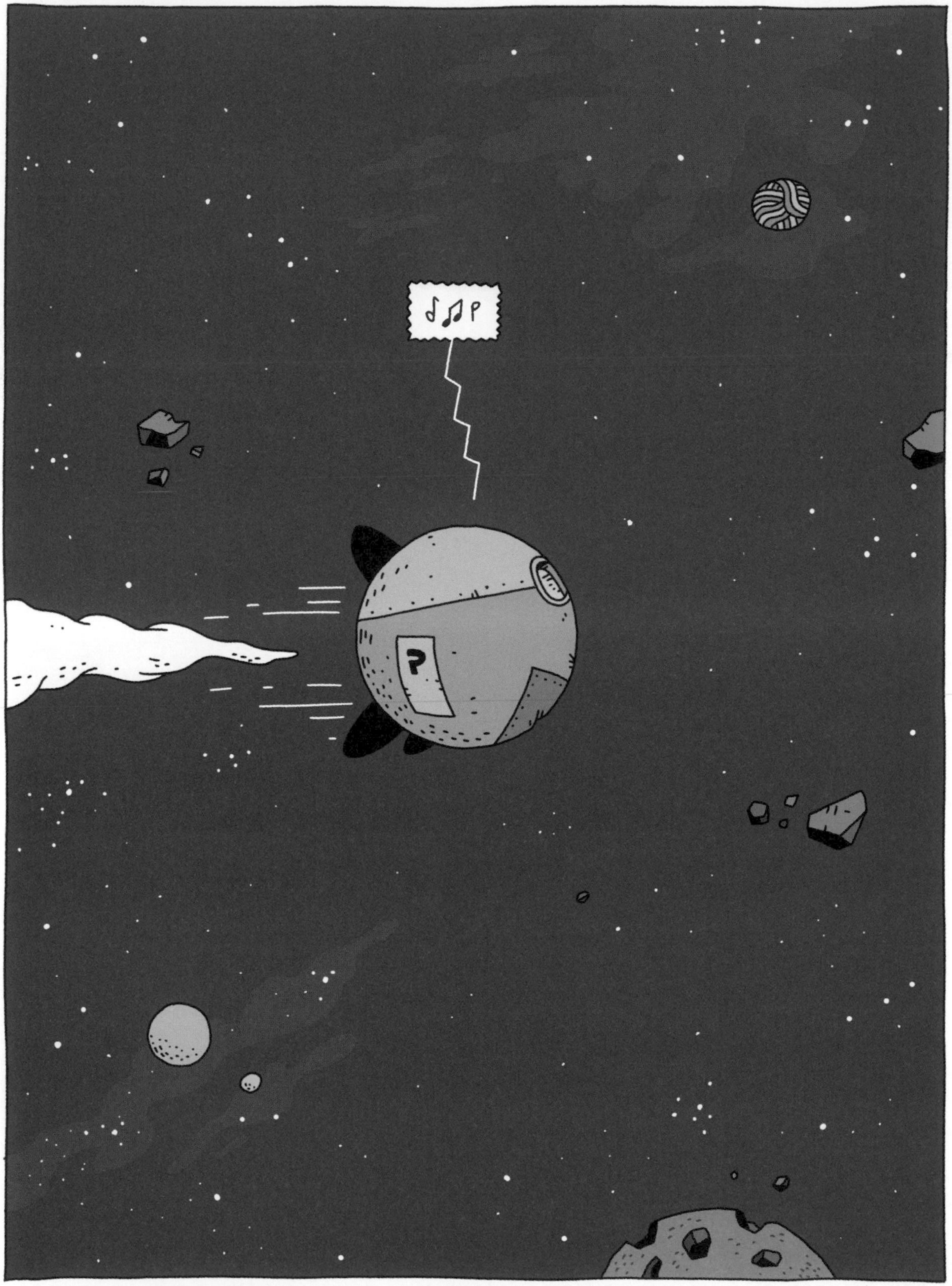

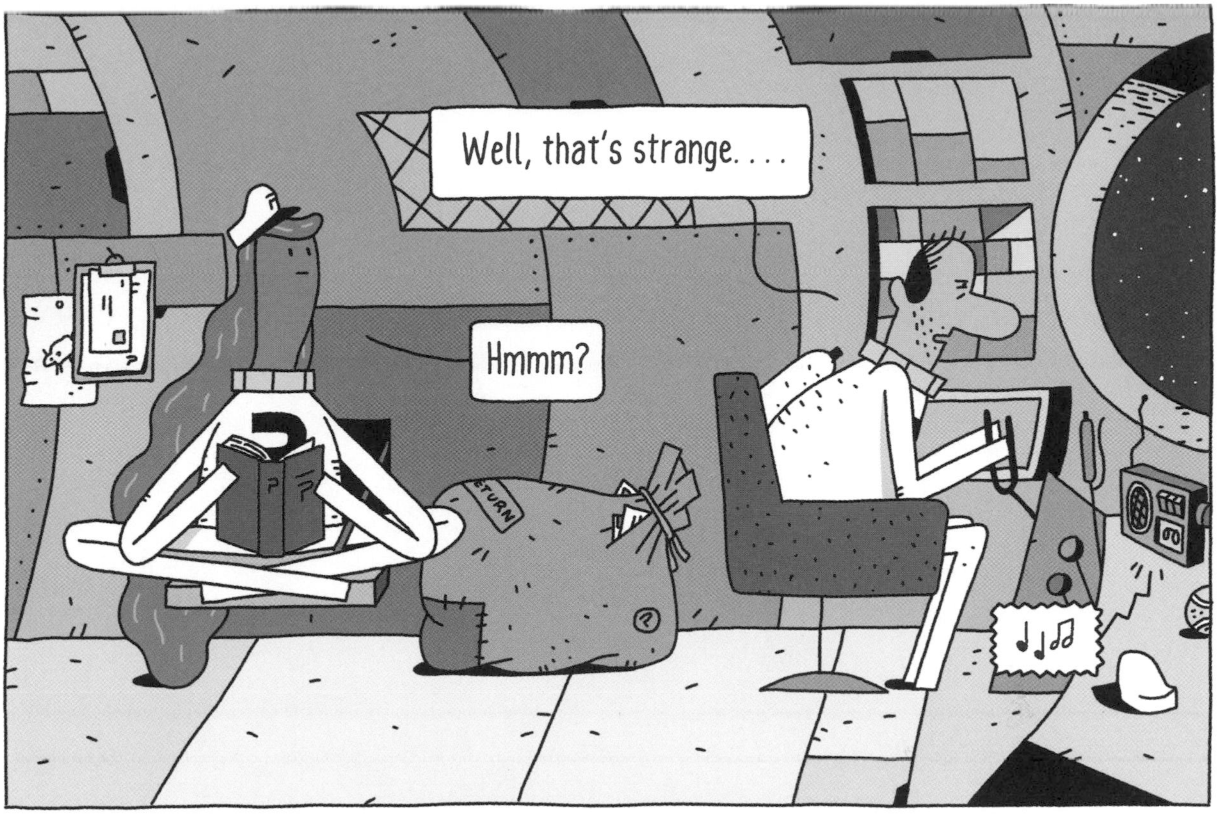
Well, that's strange. . . .
Hmmm?
RETURN

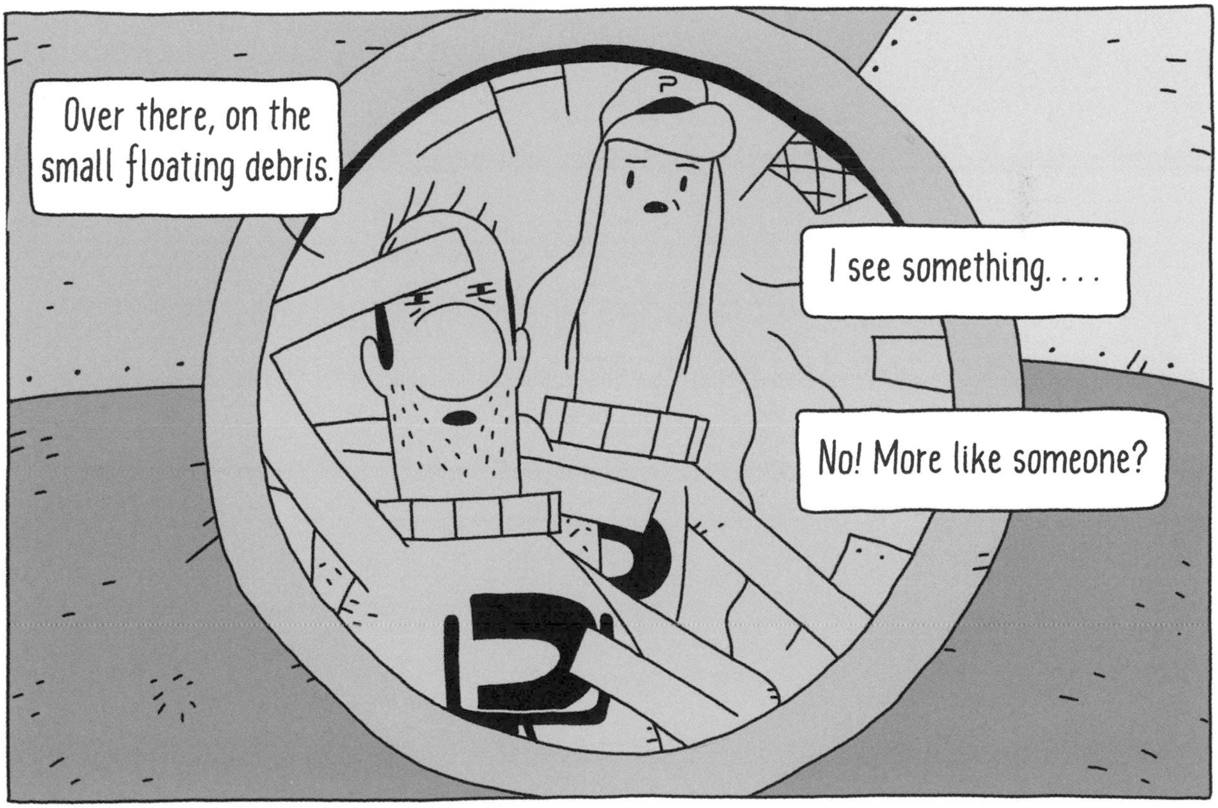
Over there, on the small floating debris.
I see something. . . .
No! More like someone?

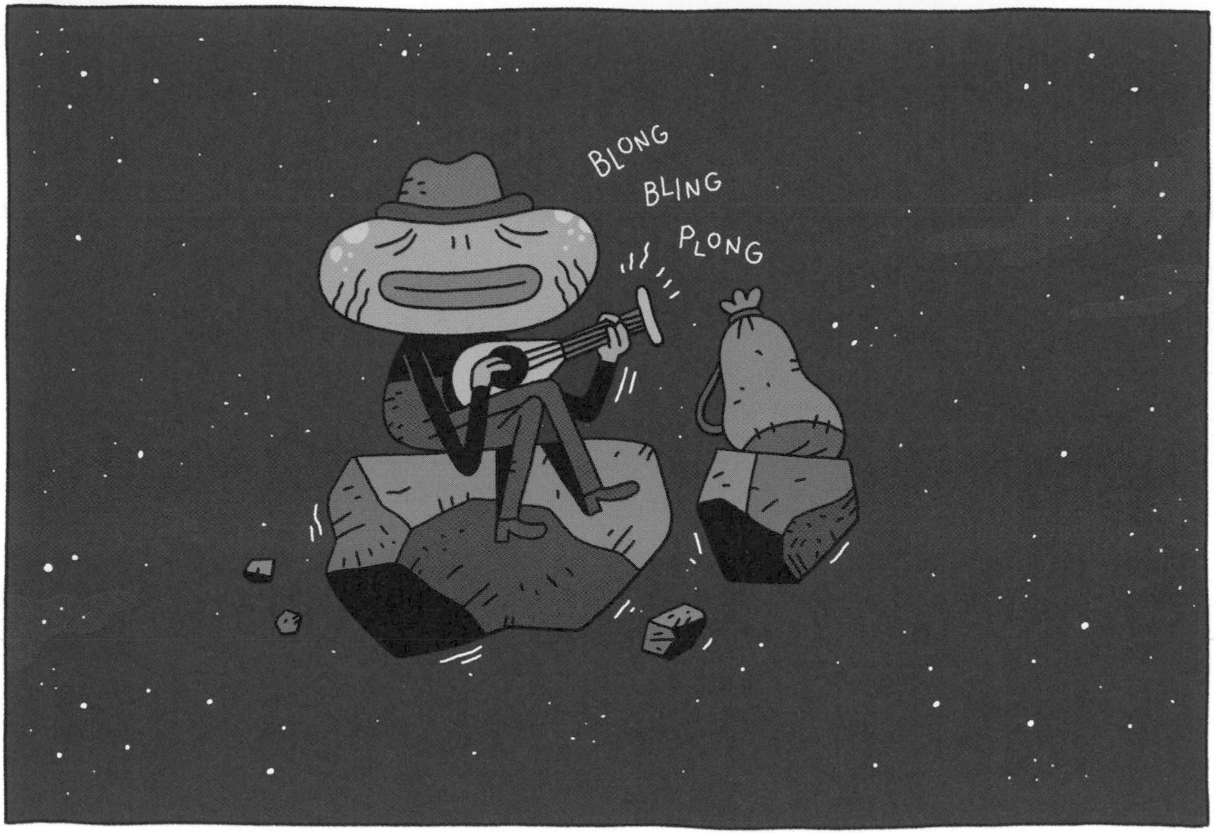
BLONG
BLING
PLONG

Holy smokes! Marcelle is totally right. An odd-looking individual appears directly in front of them, smack in the middle of space.

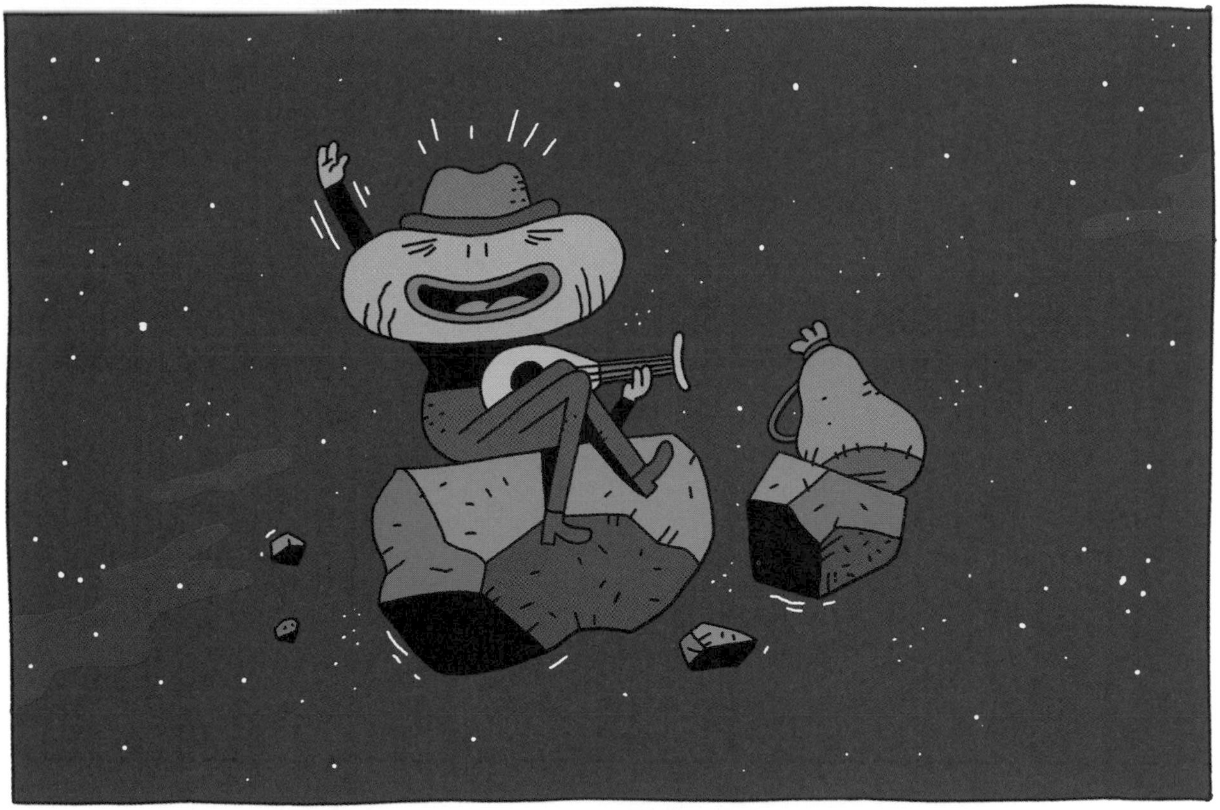

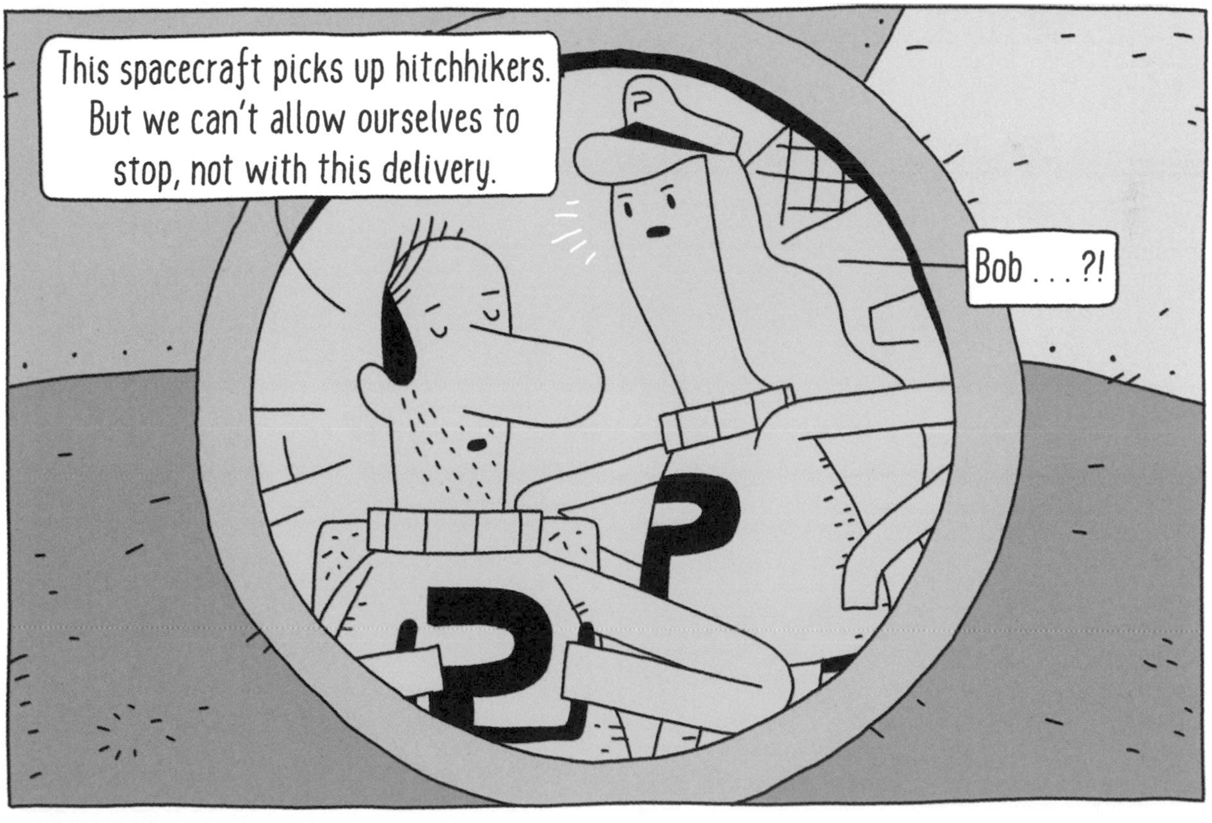
This spacecraft picks up hitchhikers. But we can't allow ourselves to stop, not with this delivery.
Bob . . . ?!

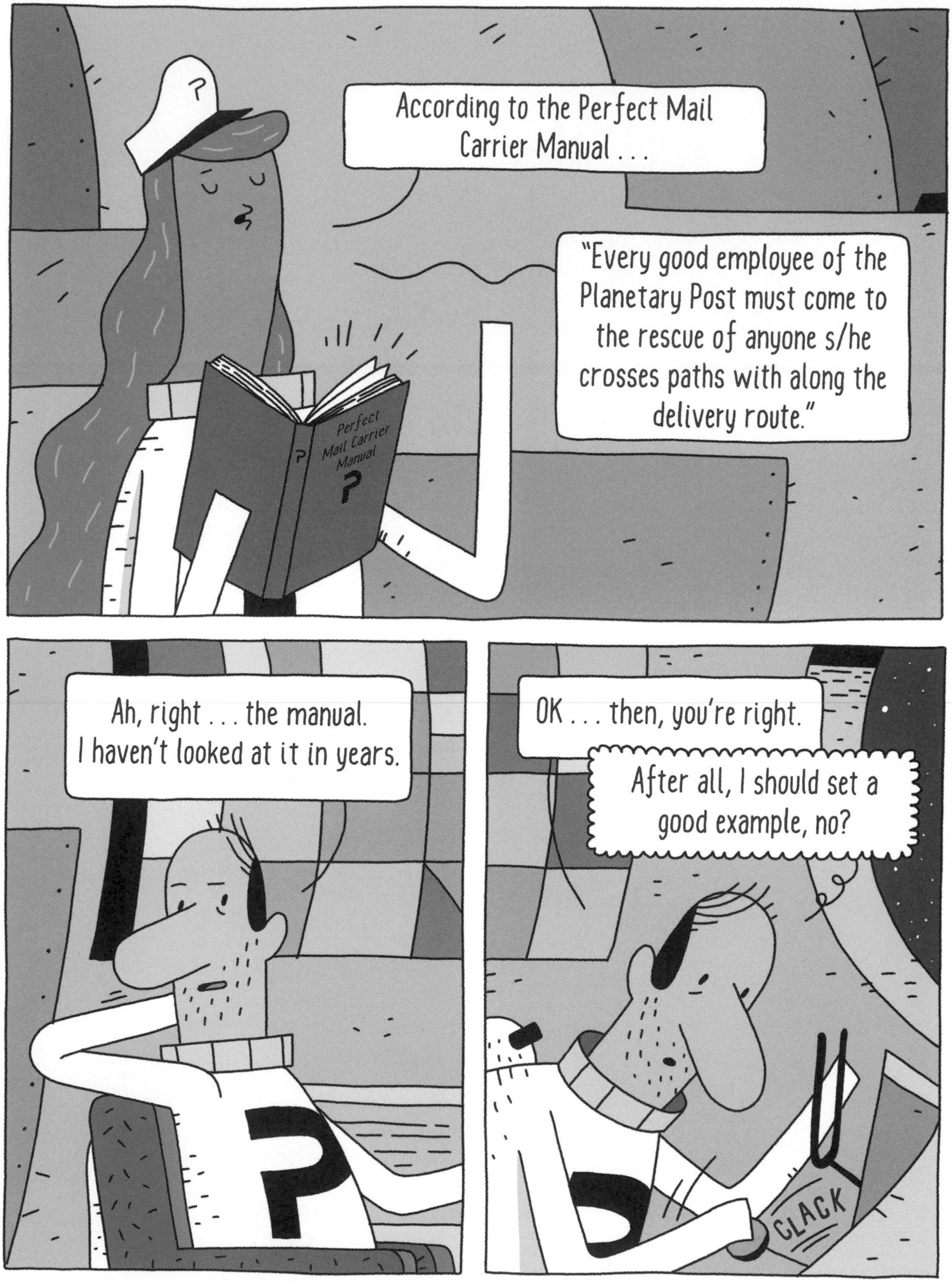
According to the Perfect Mail Carrier Manual . . .
"Every good employee of the Planetary Post must come to the rescue of anyone s/he crosses paths with along the delivery route."
Perfect Mail Carrier Manual
Ah, right . . . the manual. I haven't looked at it in years.
OK . . . then, you're right.
After all, I should set a good example, no?
CLACK

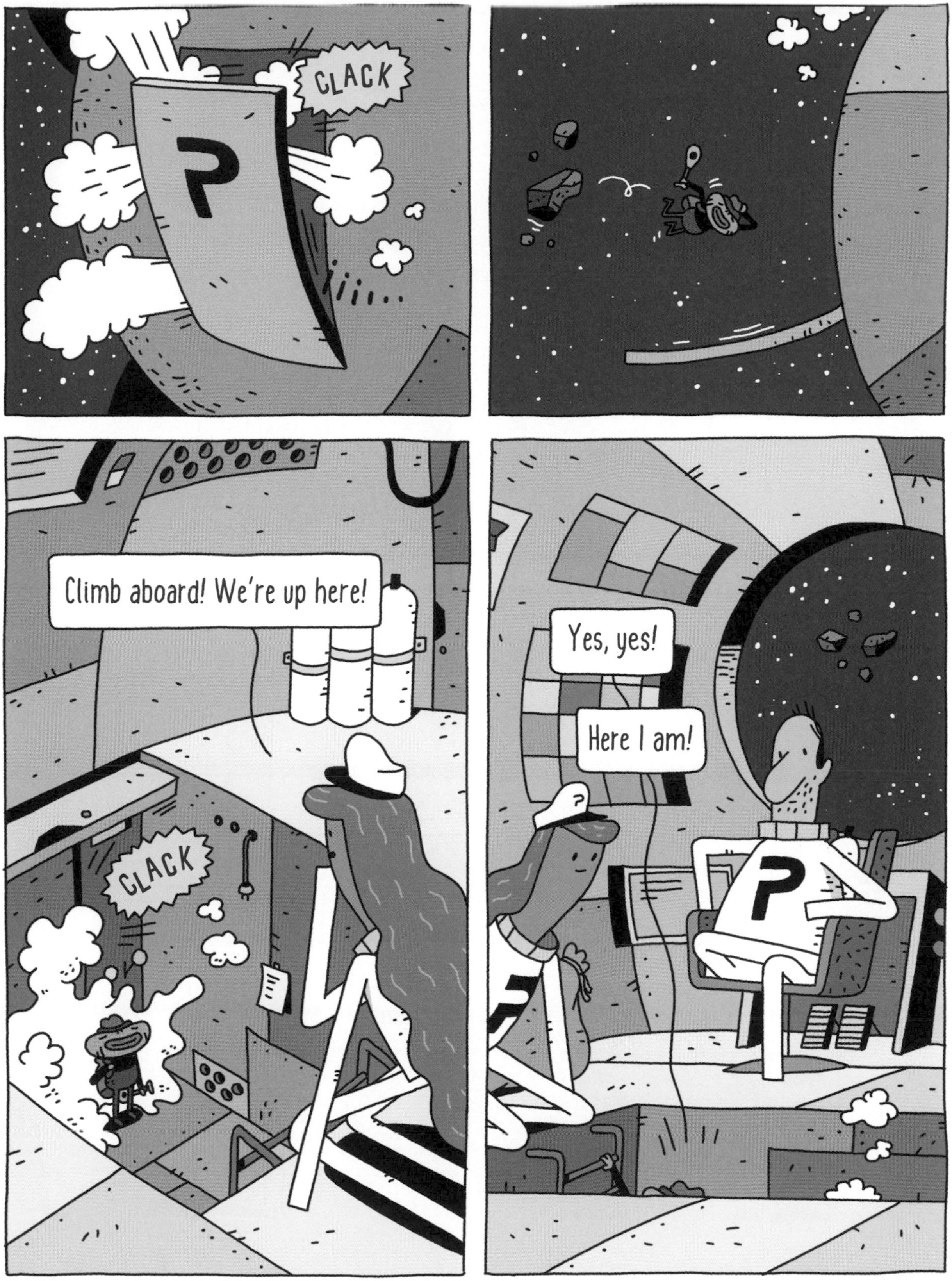
CLACK
Climb aboard! We're up here!
CLACK
Yes, yes!
Here I am!

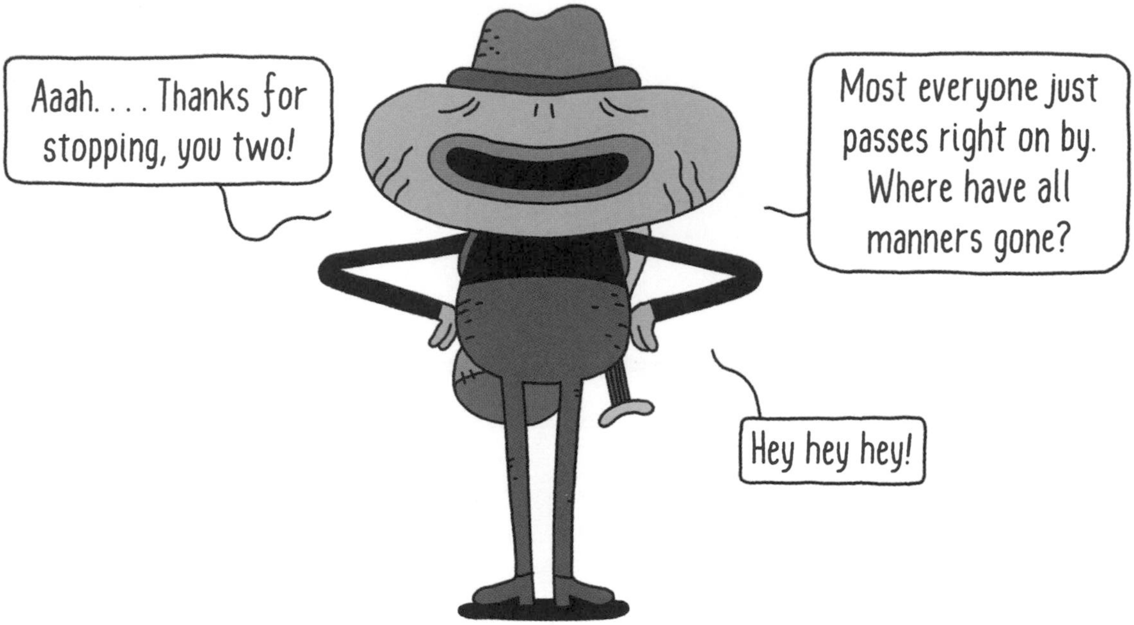
Aaah. . . . Thanks for stopping, you two!
Most everyone just passes right on by. Where have all manners gone?
Hey hey hey!

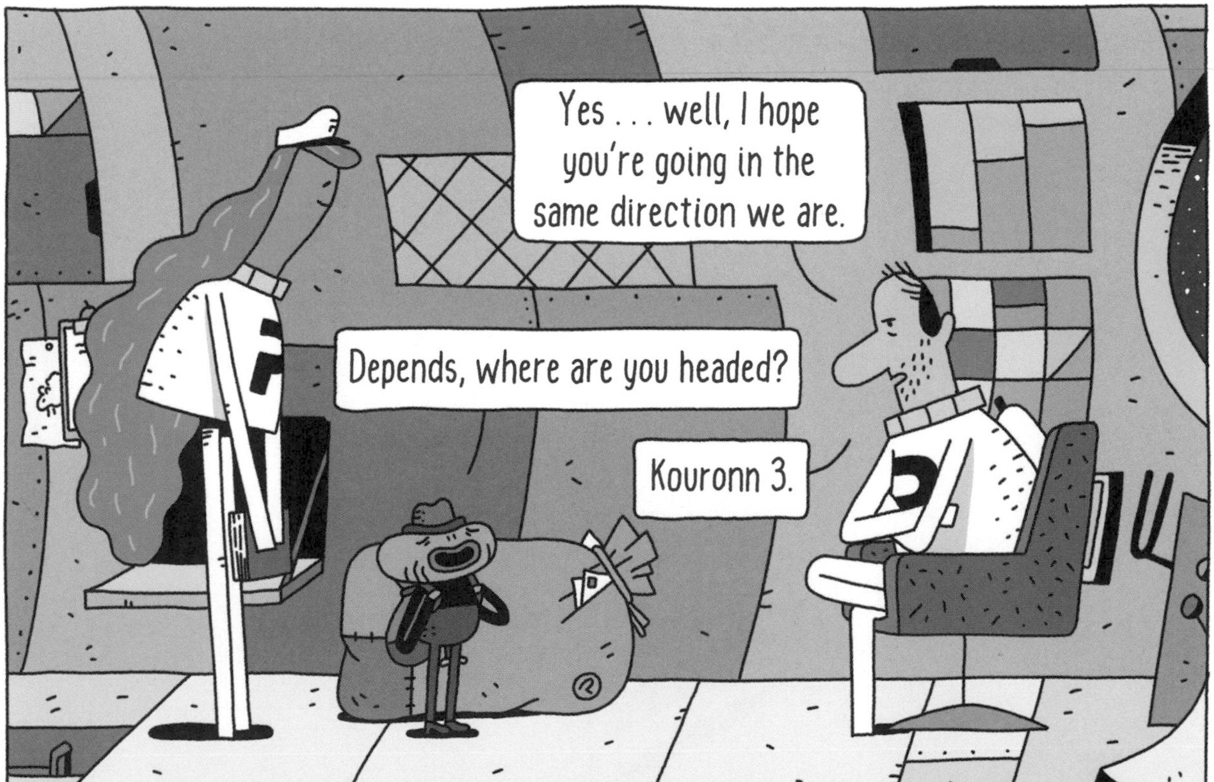
Yes . . . well, I hope you're going in the same direction we are.
Depends, where are you headed?
Kouronn 3.

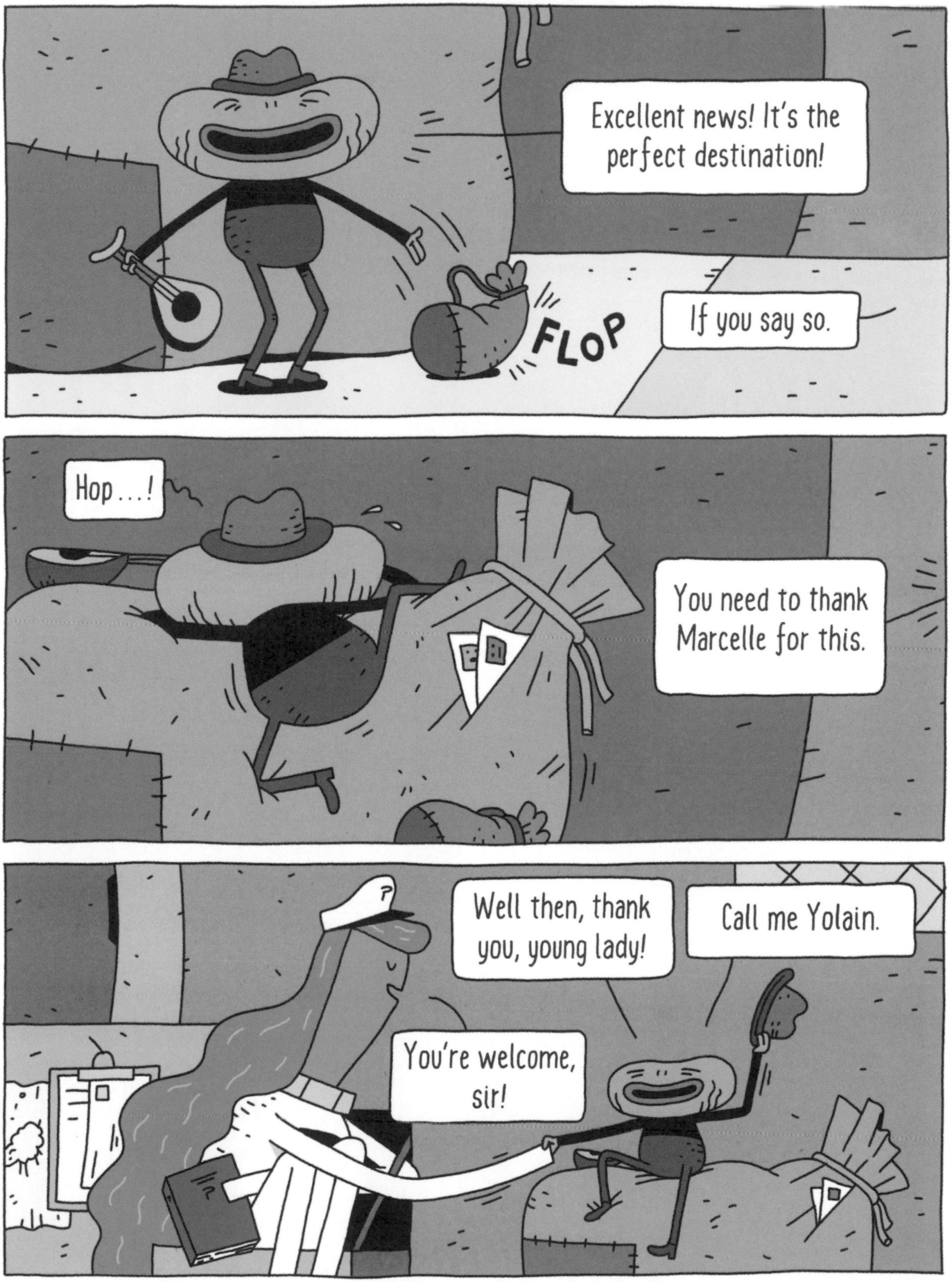
Excellent news! It's the perfect destination!
FLOP
If you say so.
Hop...!
You need to thank Marcelle for this.
Well then, thank you, young lady!
Call me Yolain.
You're welcome, sir!

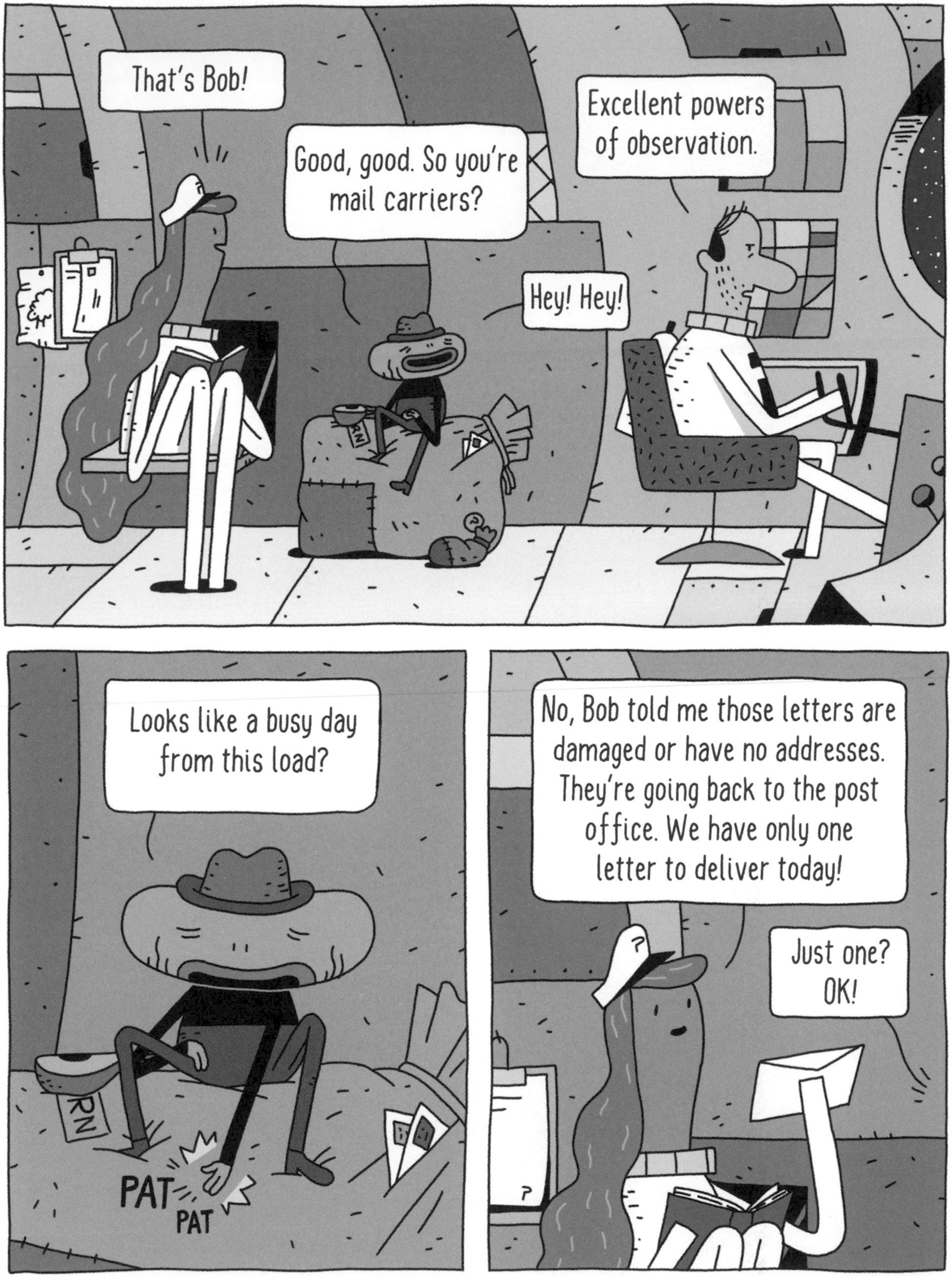
That's Bob!
Good, good. So you're mail carriers?
Excellent powers of observation.
Hey! Hey!
Looks like a busy day from this load?
PAT PAT
No, Bob told me those letters are damaged or have no addresses. They're going back to the post office. We have only one letter to deliver today!
Just one? OK!

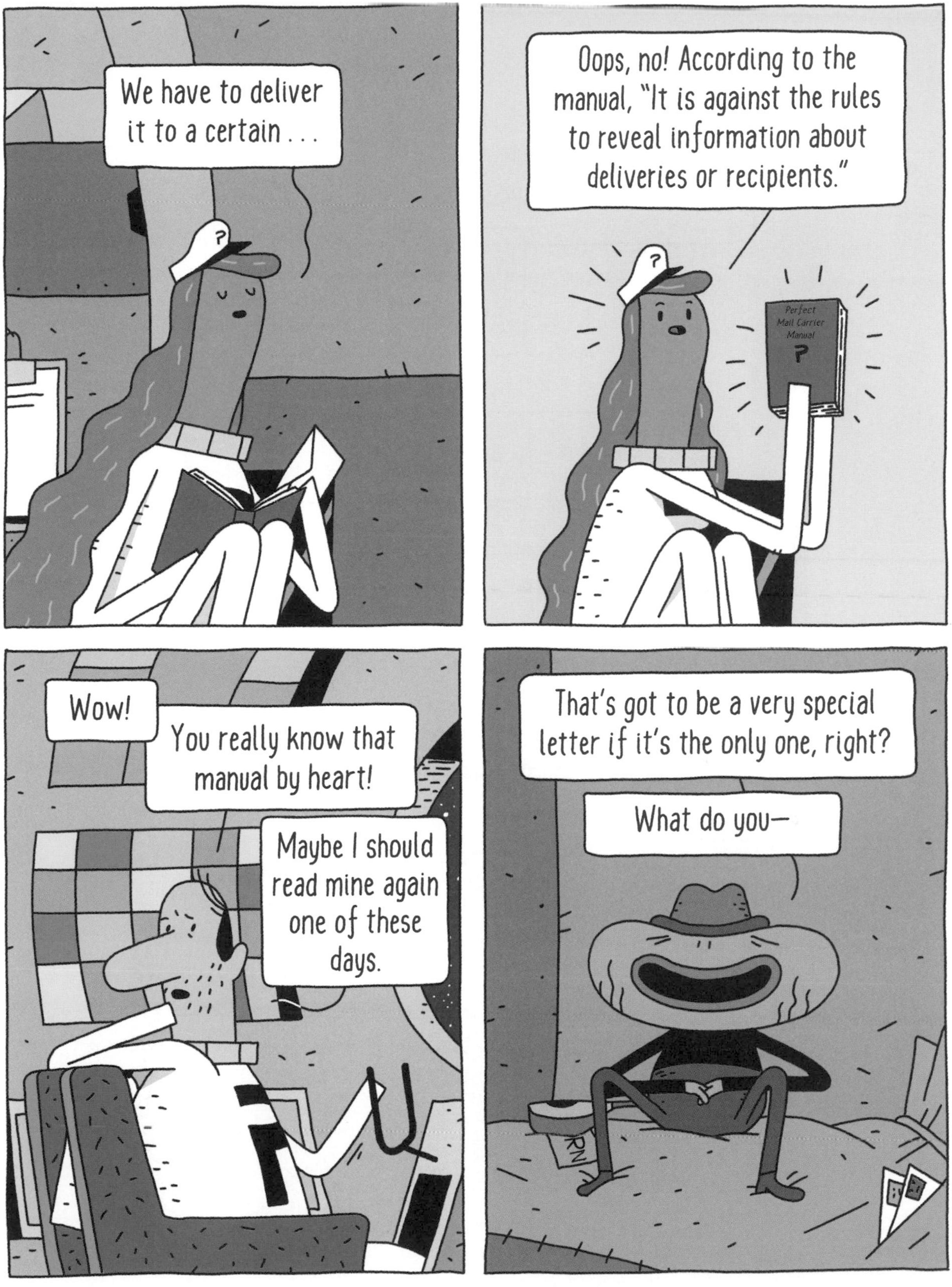
We have to deliver it to a certain . . .
Oops, no! According to the manual, "It is against the rules to reveal information about deliveries or recipients."
Perfect Mail Carrier Manual
Wow!
You really know that manual by heart!
Maybe I should read mine again one of these days.
That's got to be a very special letter if it's the only one, right?
What do you—

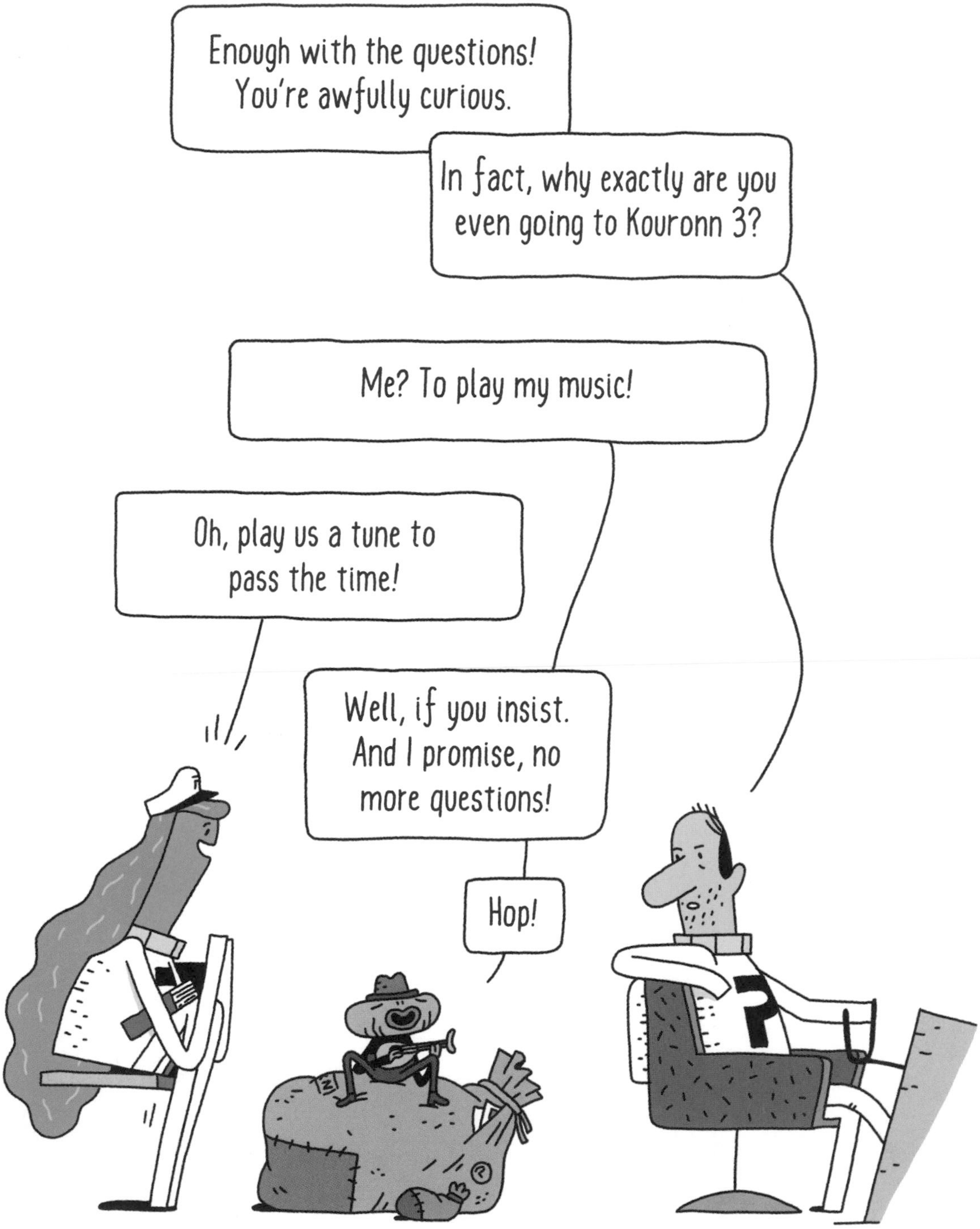
Enough with the questions! You're awfully curious.
In fact, why exactly are you even going to Kouronn 3?
Me? To play my music!
Oh, play us a tune to pass the time!
Well, if you insist. And I promise, no more questions!
Hop!

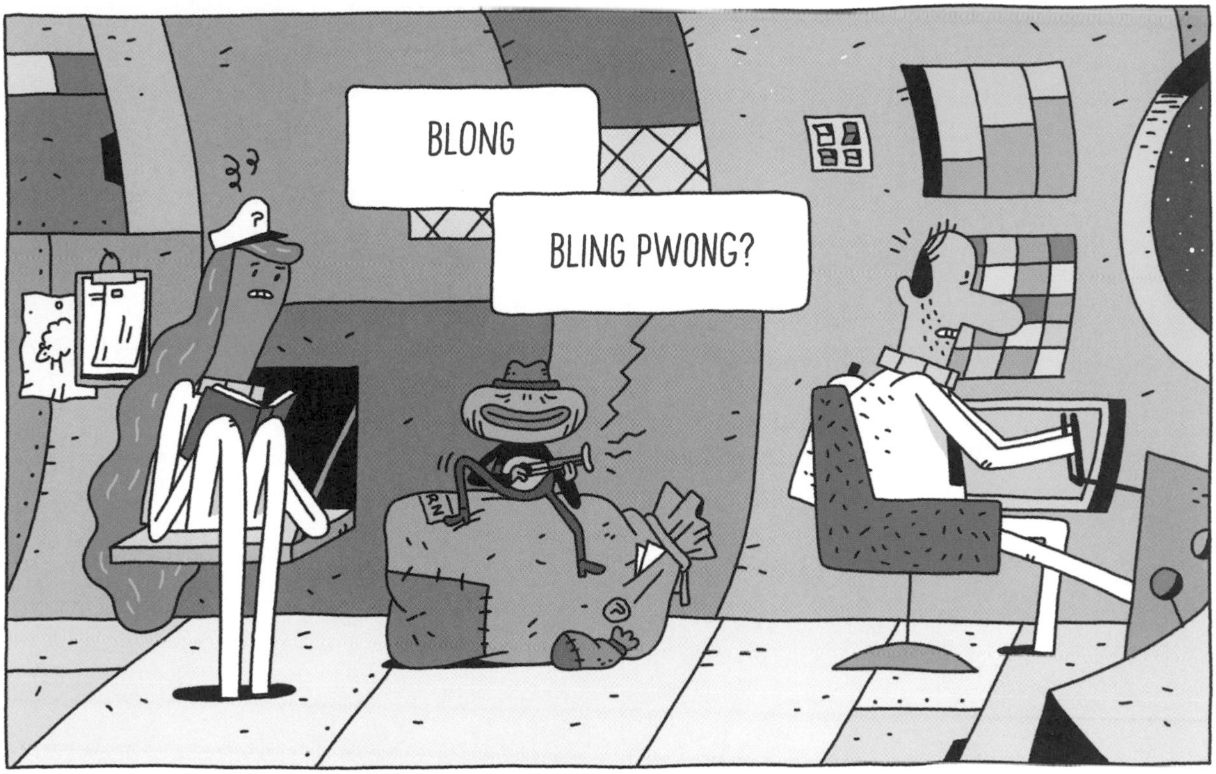
BLONG
BLING PWONG?

To Bob's delight, the journey continues with a melody . . . more or less harmonious.

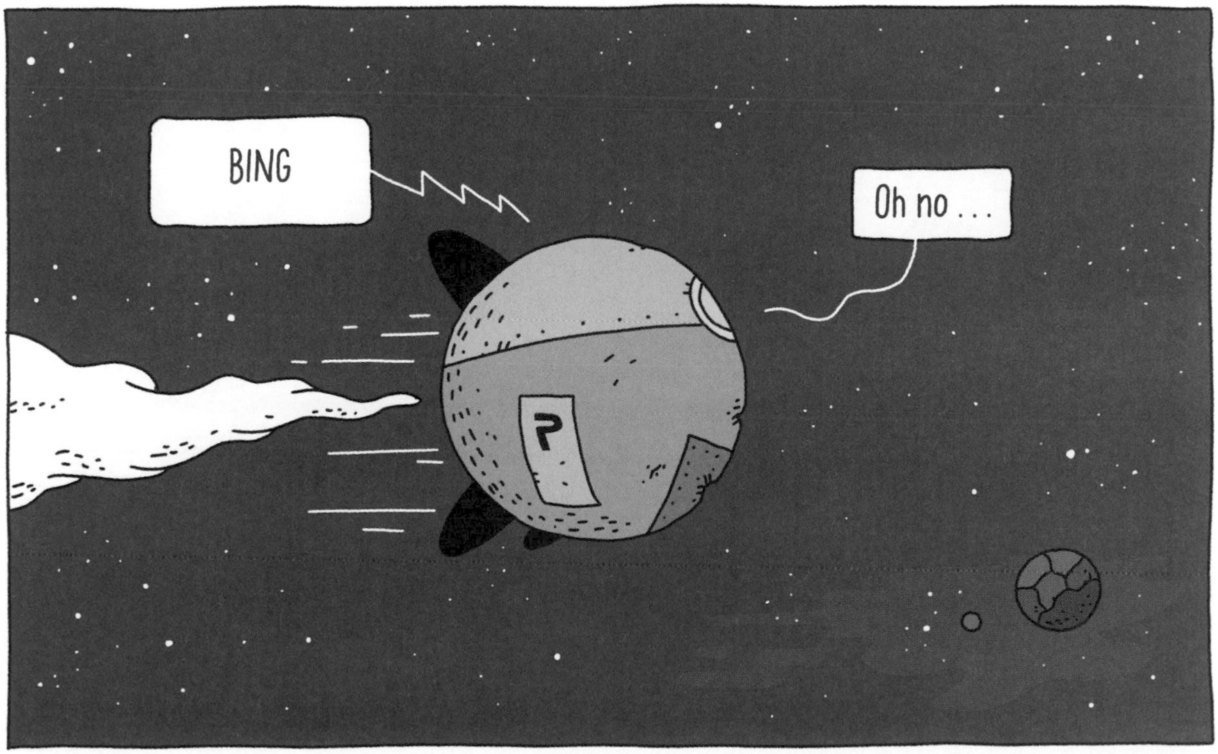
BING
Oh no . . .

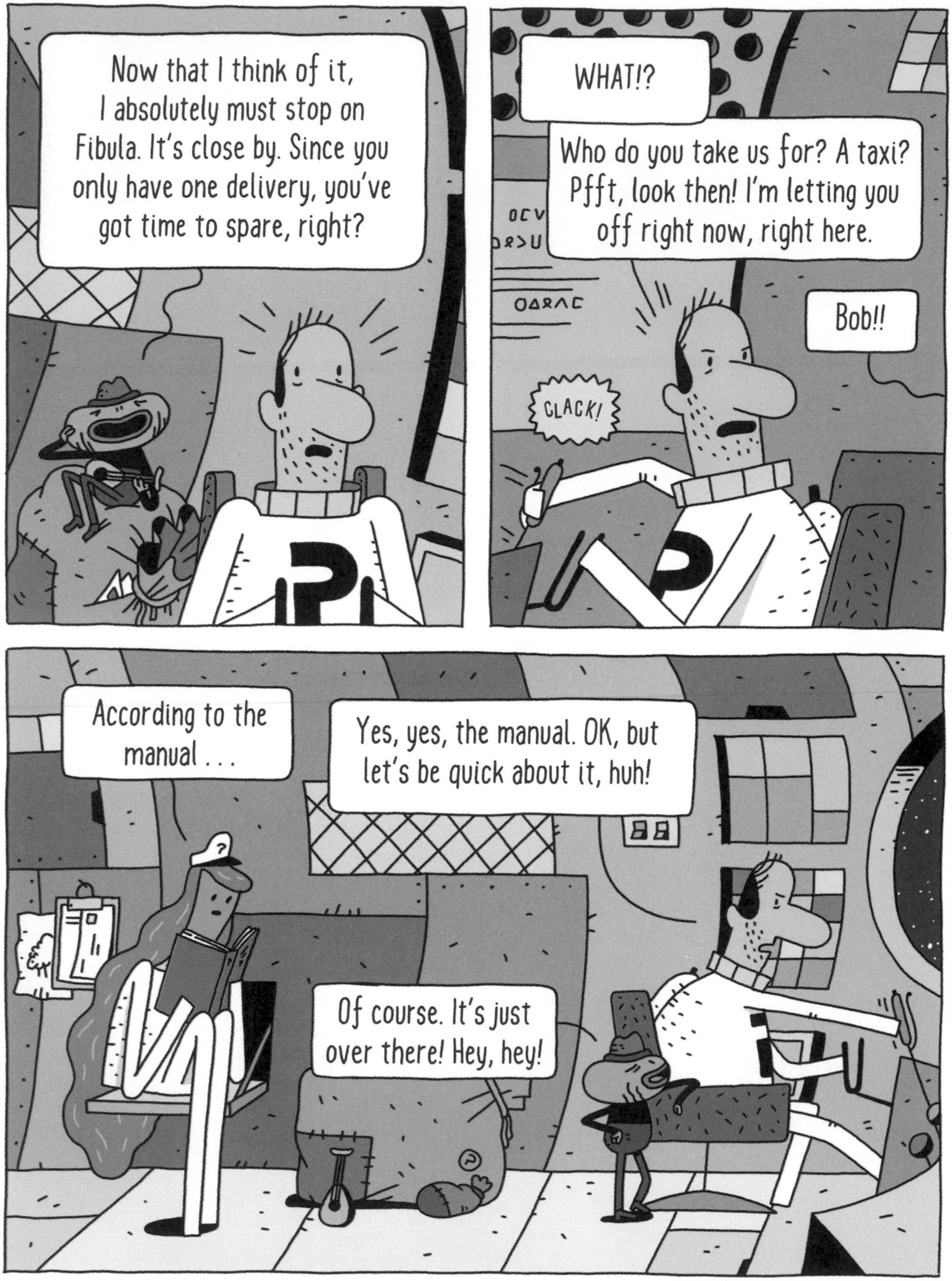
Now that I think of it, I absolutely must stop on Fibula. It's close by. Since you only have one delivery, you've got time to spare, right?
WHAT!?
Who do you take us for? A taxi? Pfft, look then! I'm letting you off right now, right here.
Bob!!
CLACK!
According to the manual . . .
Yes, yes, the manual. OK, but let's be quick about it, huh!
Of course. It's just over there! Hey, hey!

STOP #3

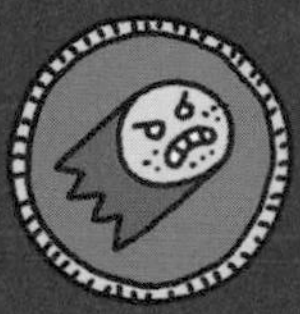

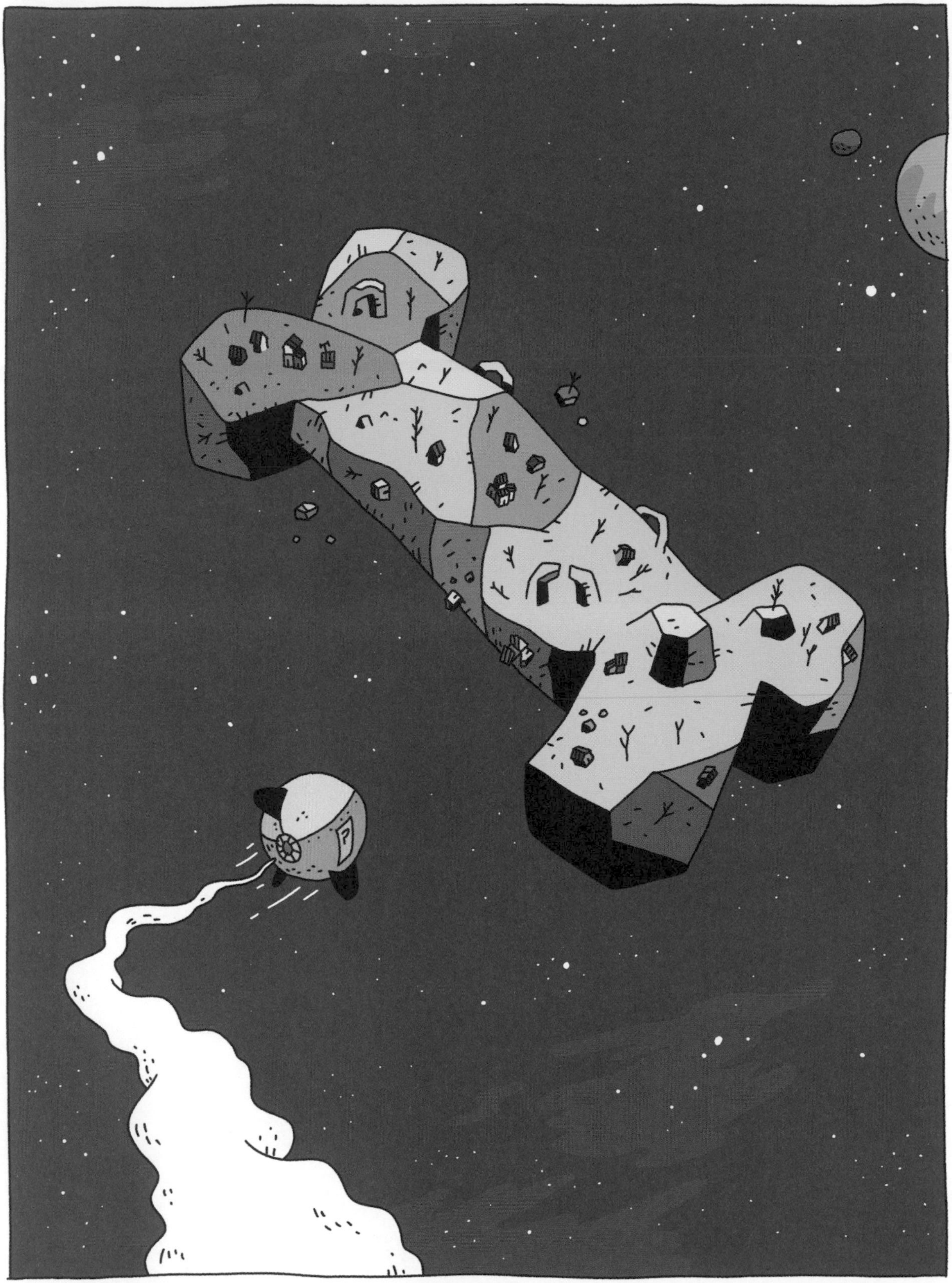

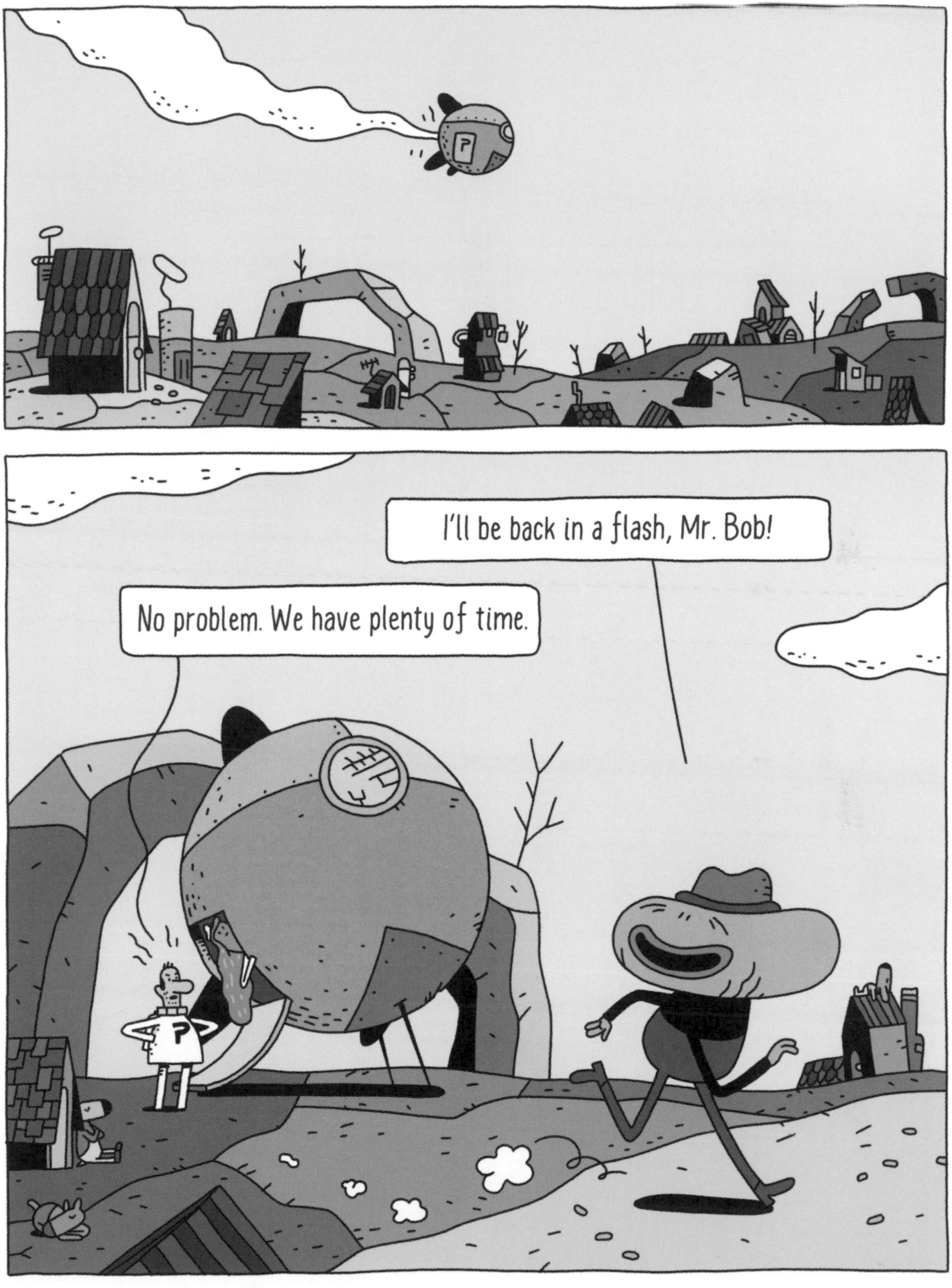
I'll be back in a flash, Mr. Bob!
No problem. We have plenty of time.

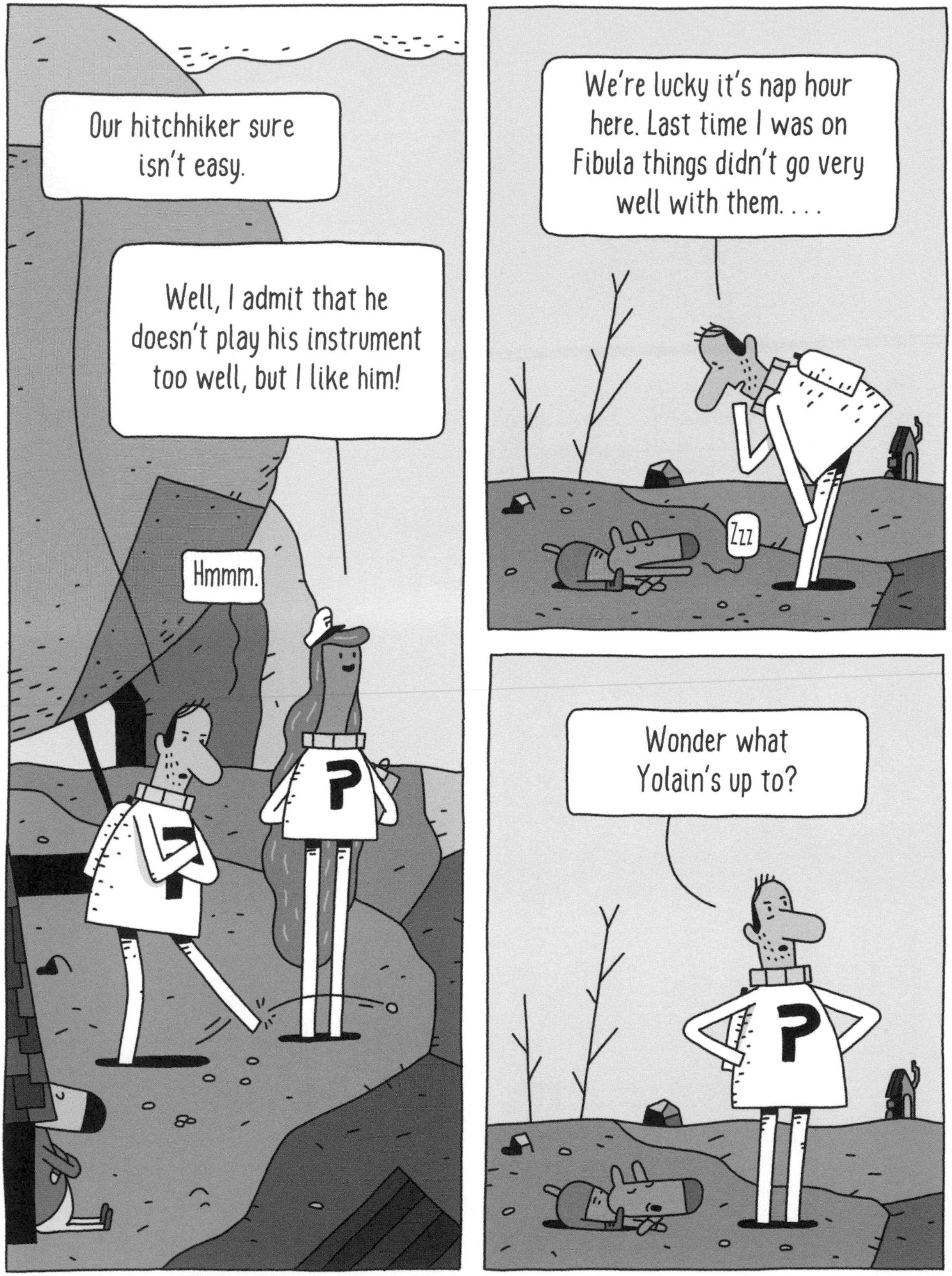
Our hitchhiker sure isn't easy.
Well, I admit that he doesn't play his instrument too well, but I like him!
Hmmm.
We're lucky it's nap hour here. Last time I was on Fibula things didn't go very well with them. . . .
Zzz
Wonder what Yolain's up to?

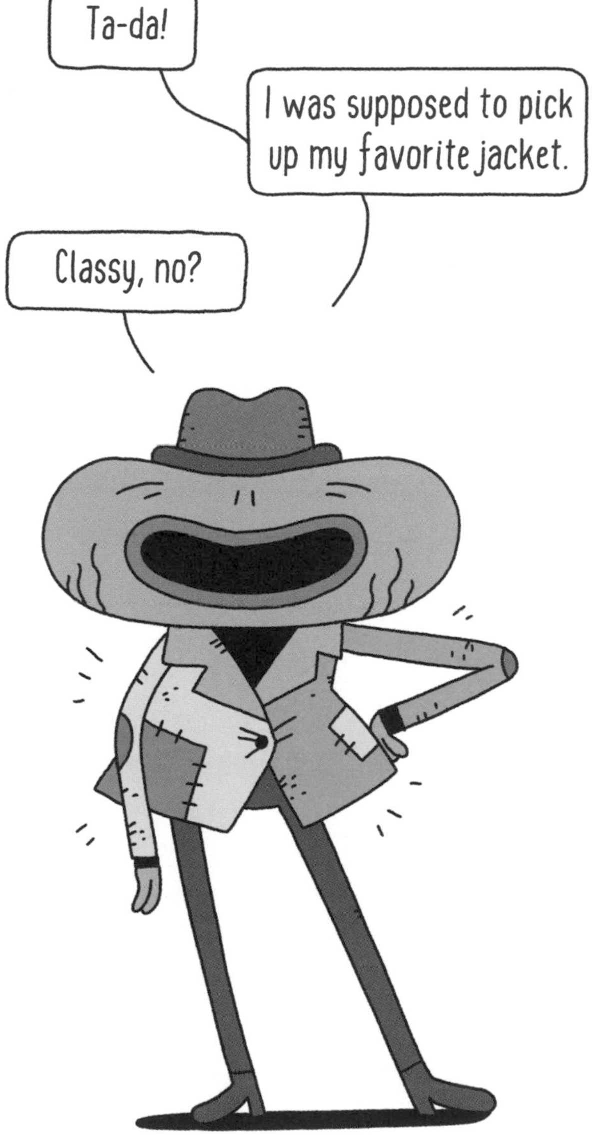
Ta-da!
I was supposed to pick up my favorite jacket.
Classy, no?

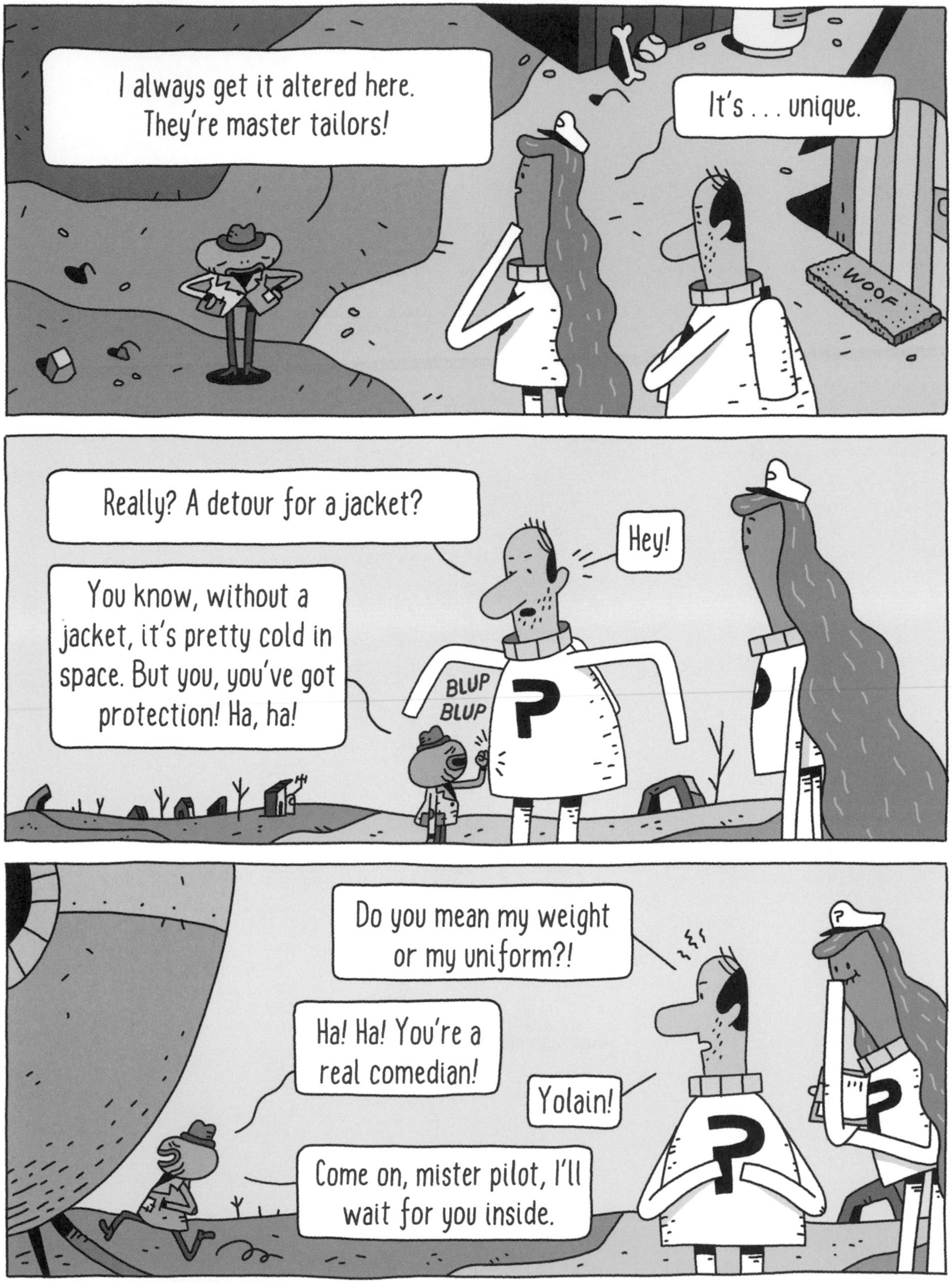

I always get it altered here. They're master tailors!
It's . . . unique.
WOOF
Really? A detour for a jacket?
Hey!
You know, without a jacket, it's pretty cold in space. But you, you've got protection! Ha, ha!
BLUP BLUP
Do you mean my weight or my uniform?!
Ha! Ha! You're a real comedian!
Yolain!
Come on, mister pilot, I'll wait for you inside.

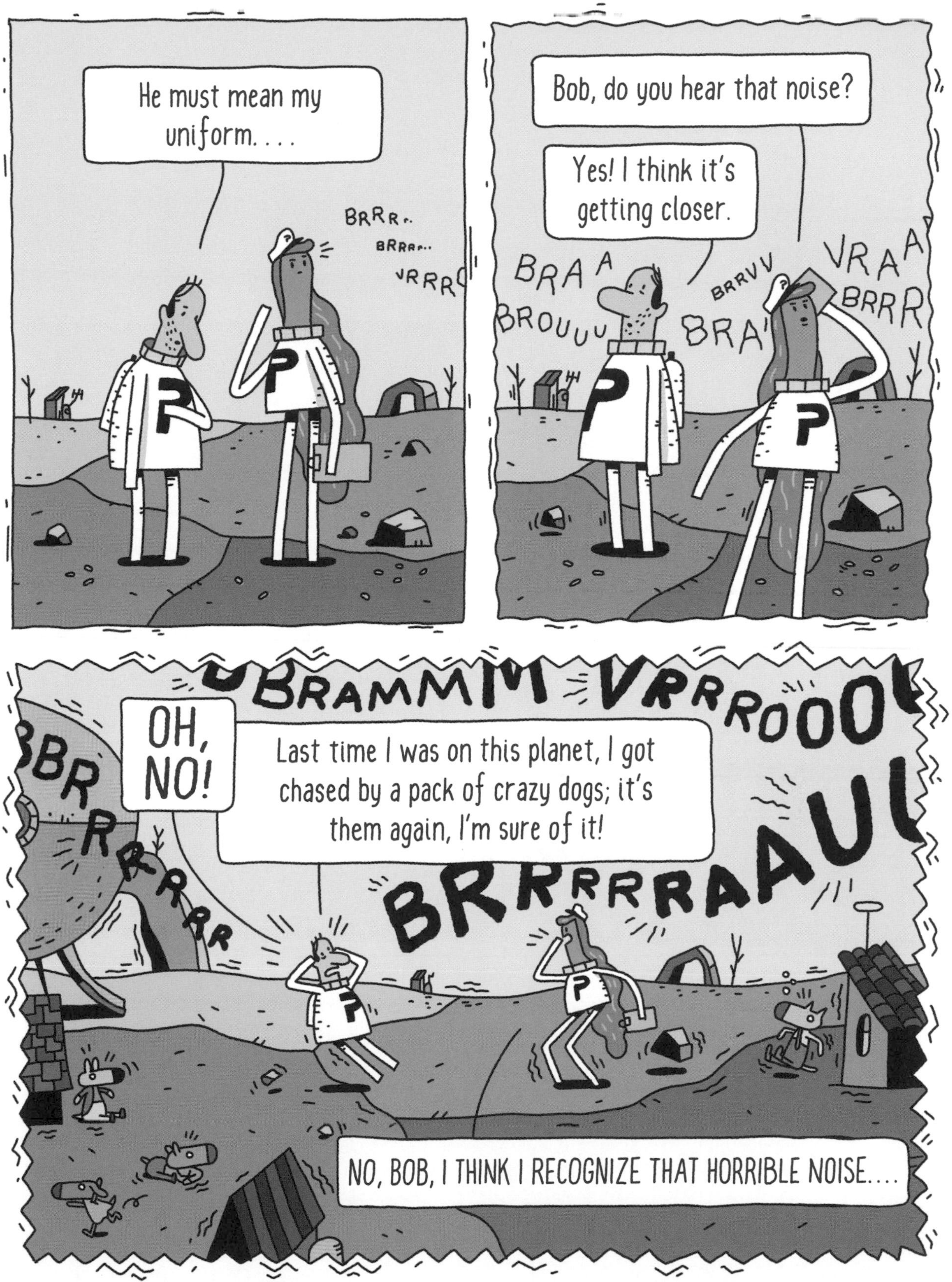
He must mean my uniform. . . .
BRRR..
BRRR...
VRRRO
Bob, do you hear that noise?
Yes! I think it's getting closer.
BRAA
BROUUU
BRRVV
BRA'
VRAA
BRRR
BRAMMM
VRRROOOO
BBRRRRRRR
OH, NO!
Last time I was on this planet, I got chased by a pack of crazy dogs; it's them again, I'm sure of it!
BRRRRRRAAU
NO, BOB, I THINK I RECOGNIZE THAT HORRIBLE NOISE. . . .

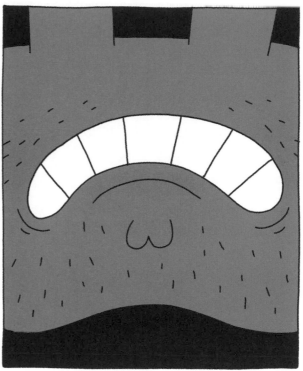

Battered spacial motorbikes, lots of dumb faces, bags brimming with loot, and vests with patches. The training manual is clear on the subject: these are . . .

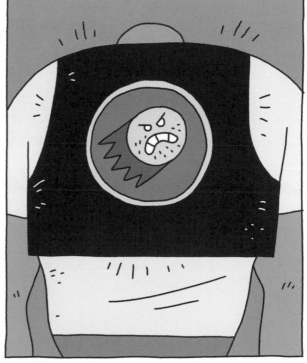

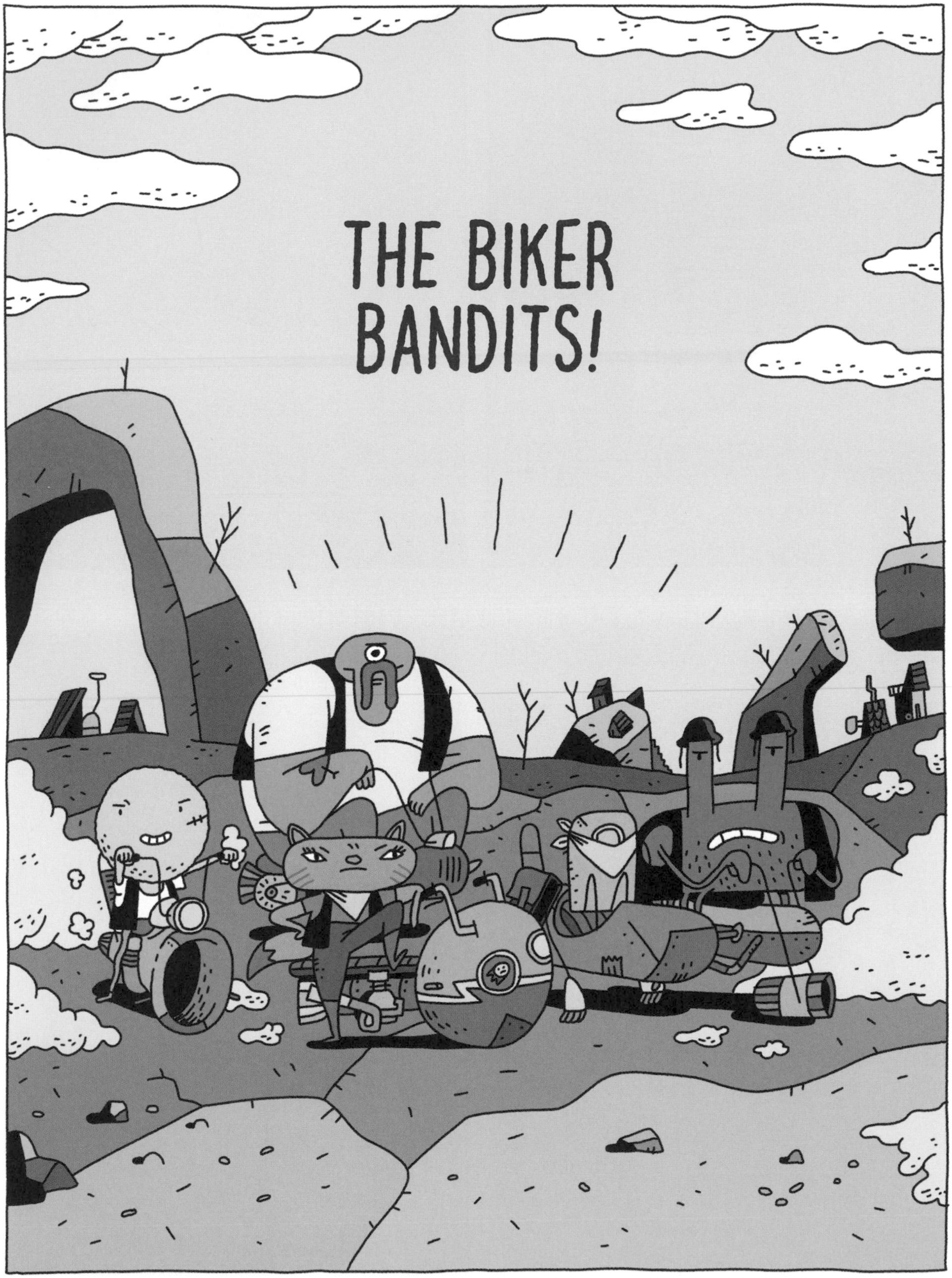
THE BIKER
BANDITS!

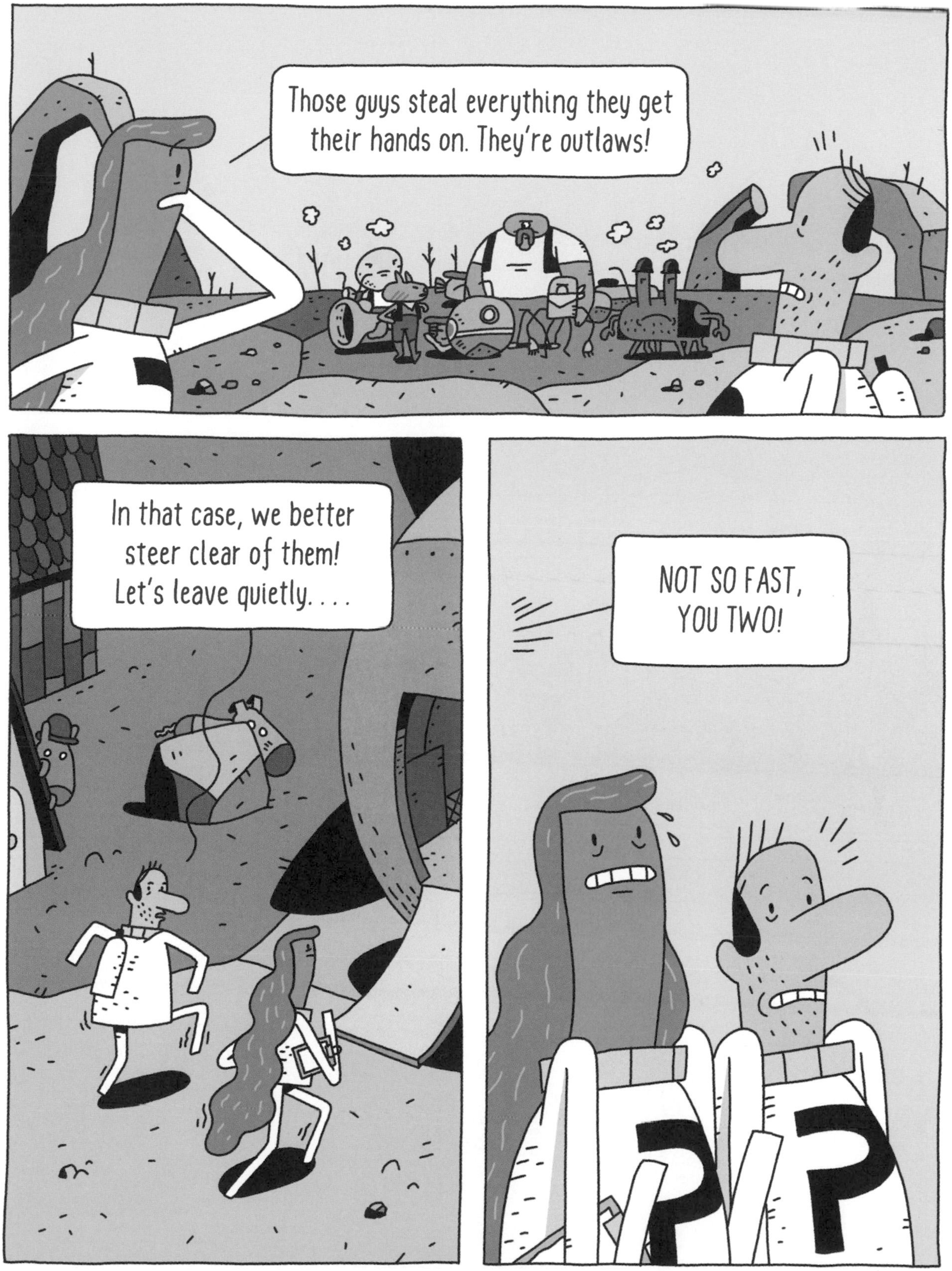
Those guys steal everything they get their hands on. They're outlaws!
In that case, we better steer clear of them! Let's leave quietly. . . .
NOT SO FAST, YOU TWO!

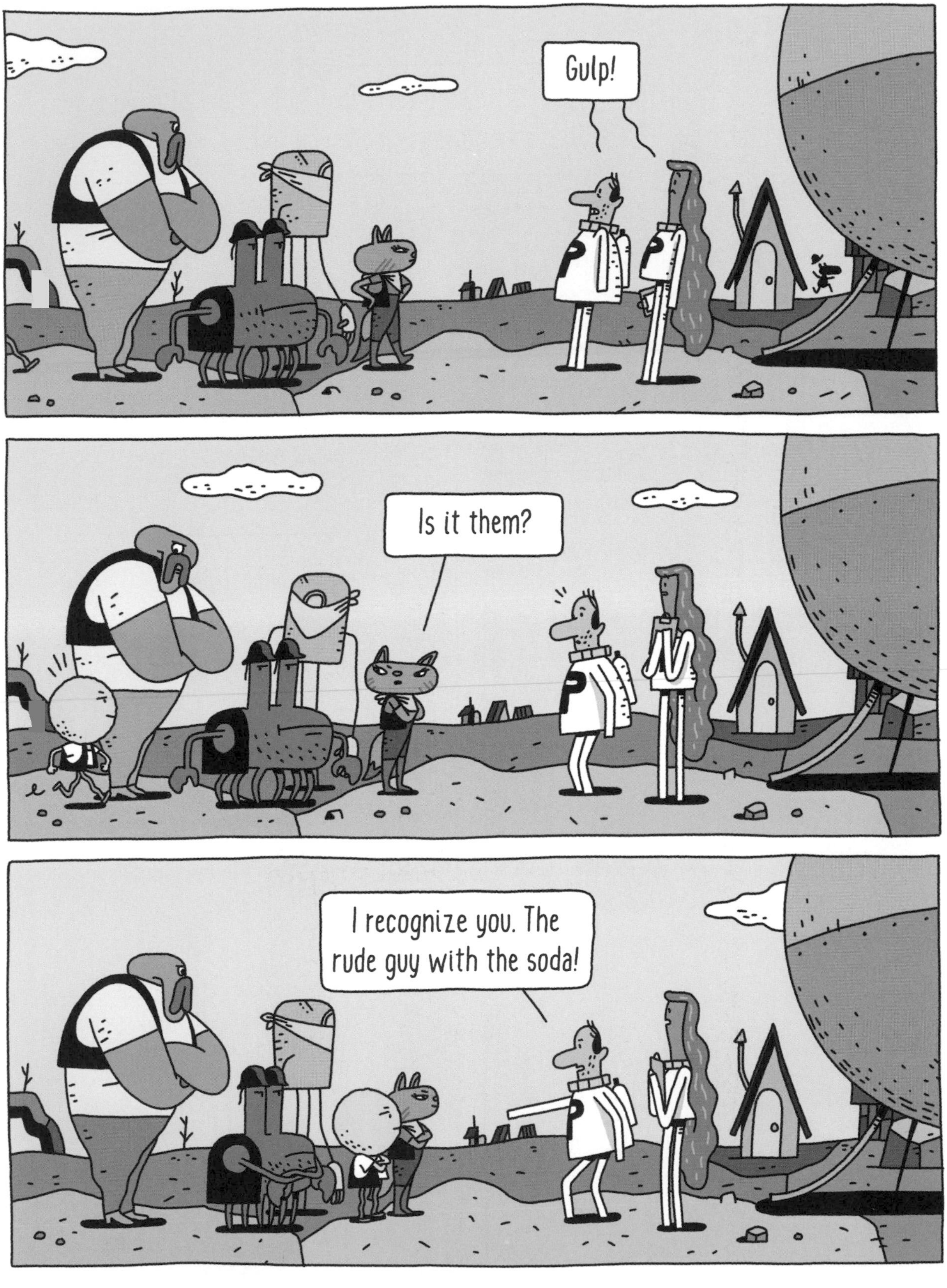
Gulp!
Is it them?
I recognize you. The rude guy with the soda!

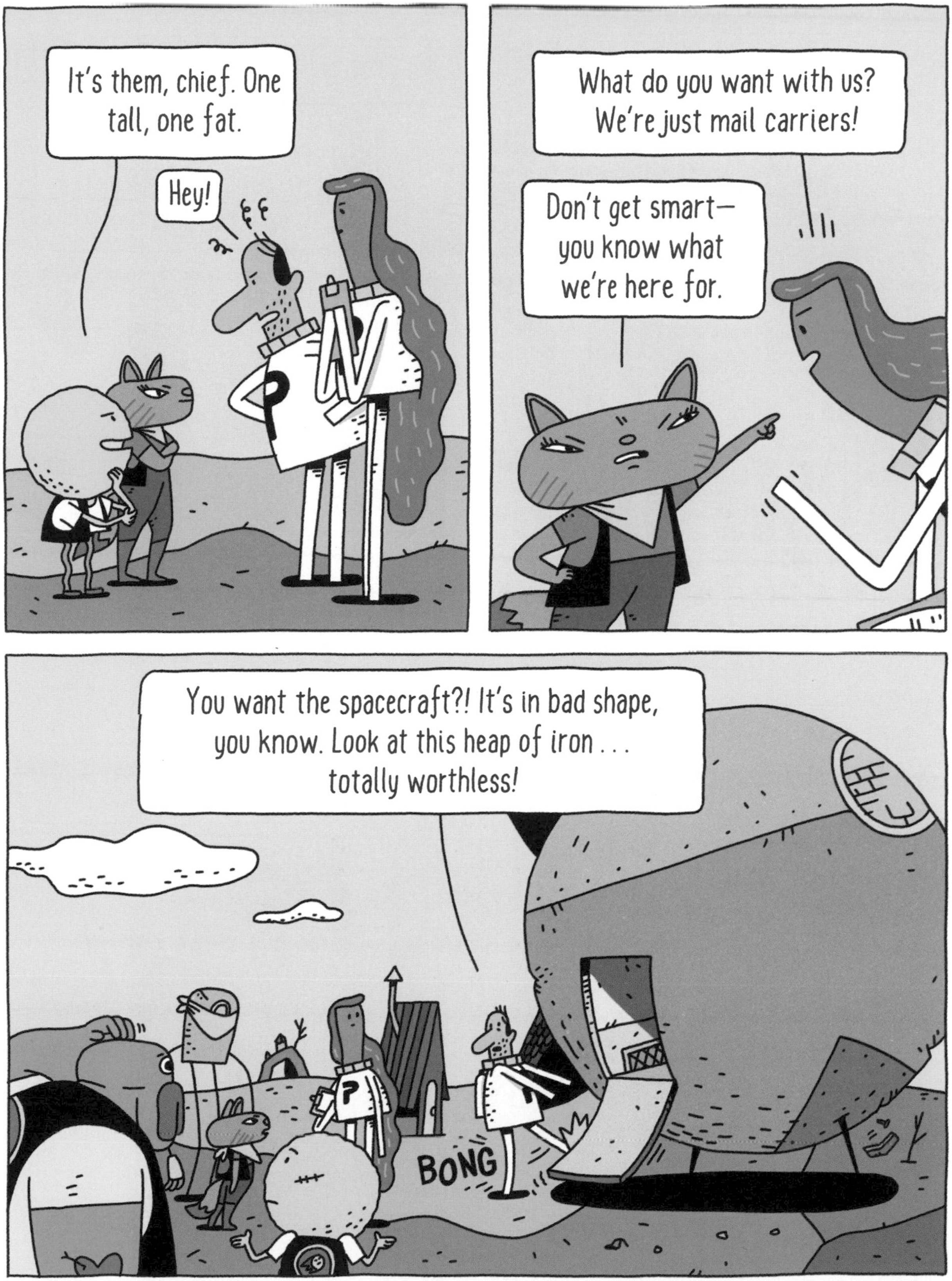
It's them, chief. One tall, one fat.
Hey!
What do you want with us? We're just mail carriers!
Don't get smart— you know what we're here for.
You want the spacecraft?! It's in bad shape, you know. Look at this heap of iron . . . totally worthless!
BONG

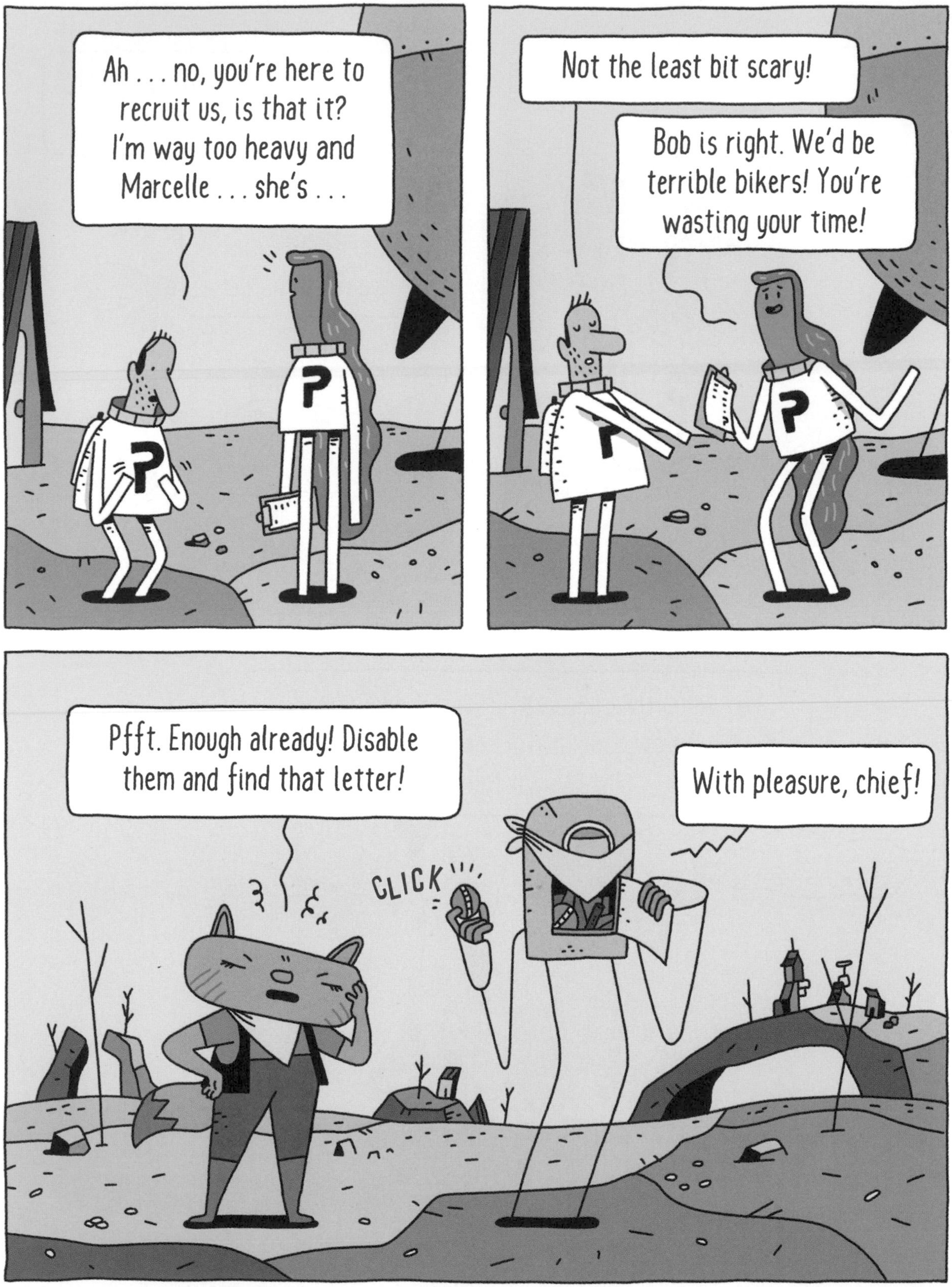
Ah . . . no, you're here to recruit us, is that it? I'm way too heavy and Marcelle . . . she's . . .
Not the least bit scary!
Bob is right. We'd be terrible bikers! You're wasting your time!
Pfft. Enough already! Disable them and find that letter!
CLICK
With pleasure, chief!

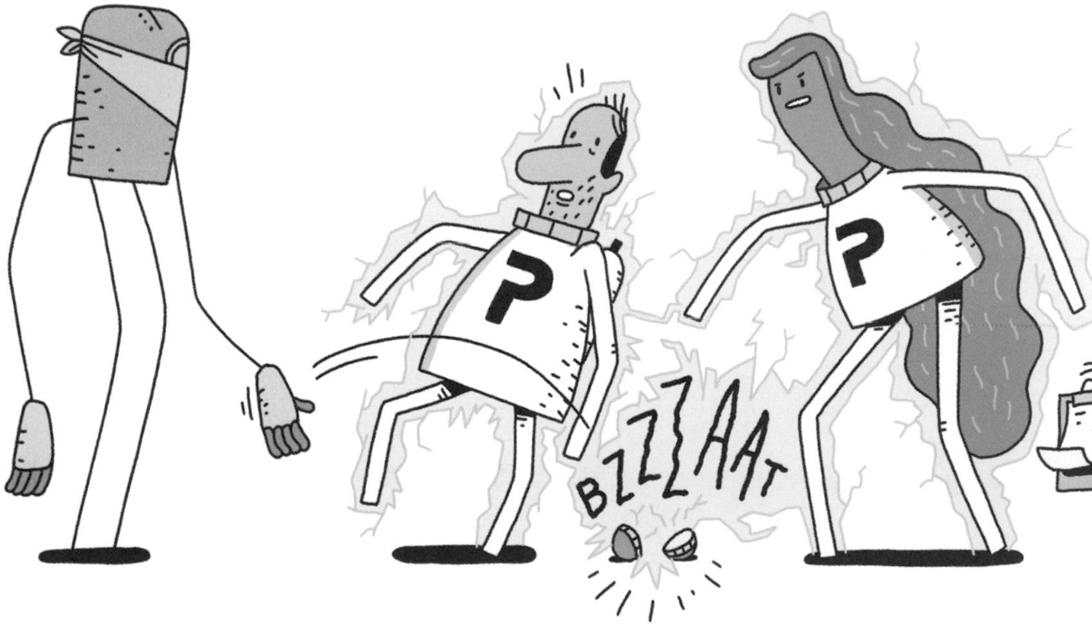
BZZZAAT

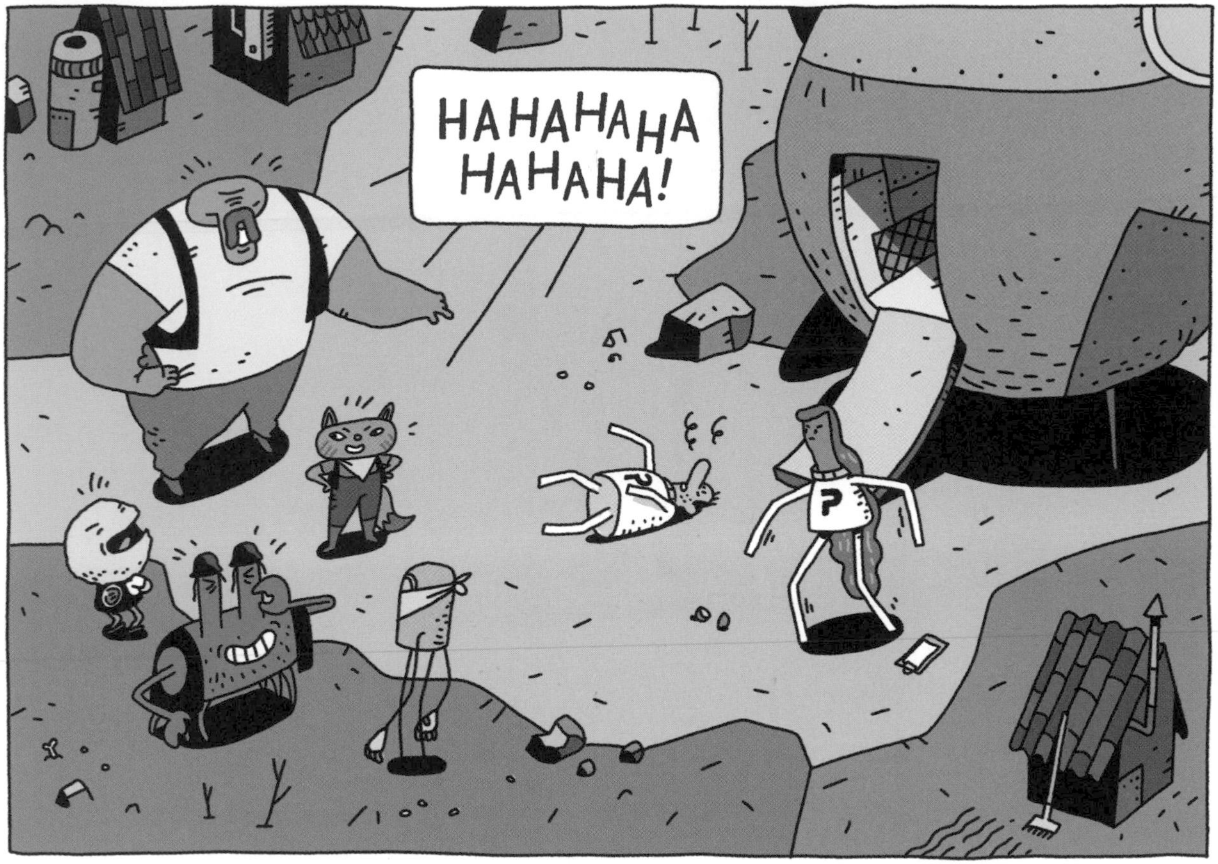
HAHAHAHA
HAHAHA!

The biker bandits are so busy roaring with laughter at Bob, who lies as motionless as a turtle on its shell, they don't notice that Marcelle isn't the least bit paralyzed.

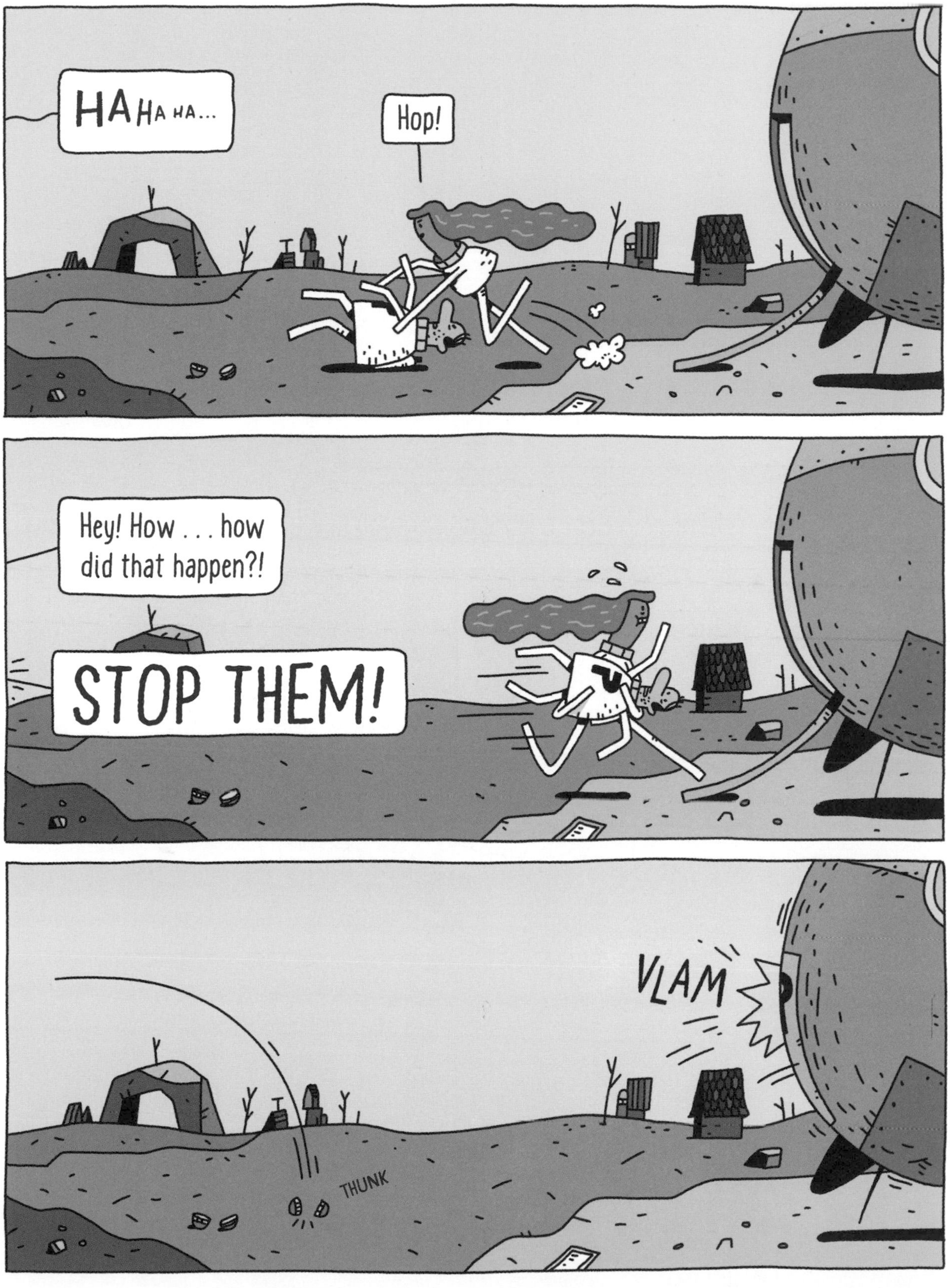
HA HA HA...
Hop!
Hey! How . . . how did that happen?!
STOP THEM!
VLAM
THUNK

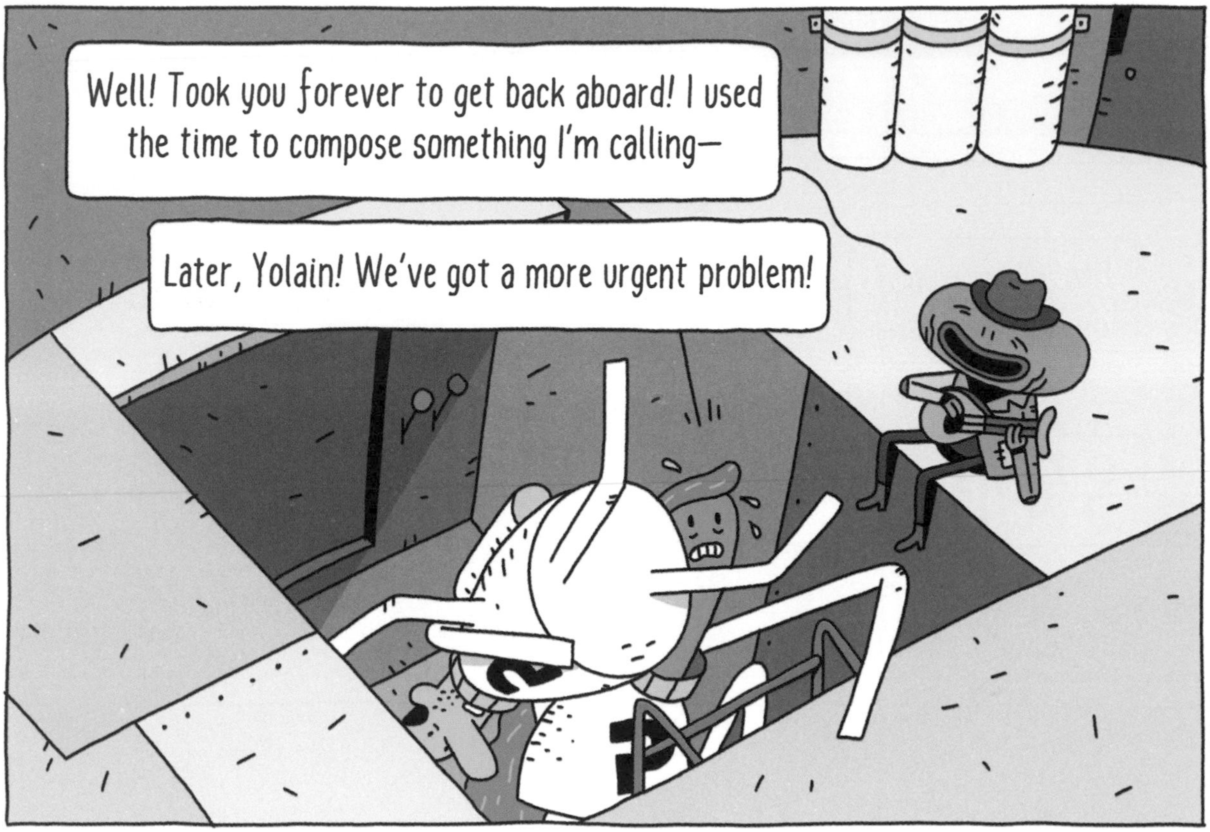
Well! Took you forever to get back aboard! I used the time to compose something I'm calling—
Later, Yolain! We've got a more urgent problem!

STOP #4

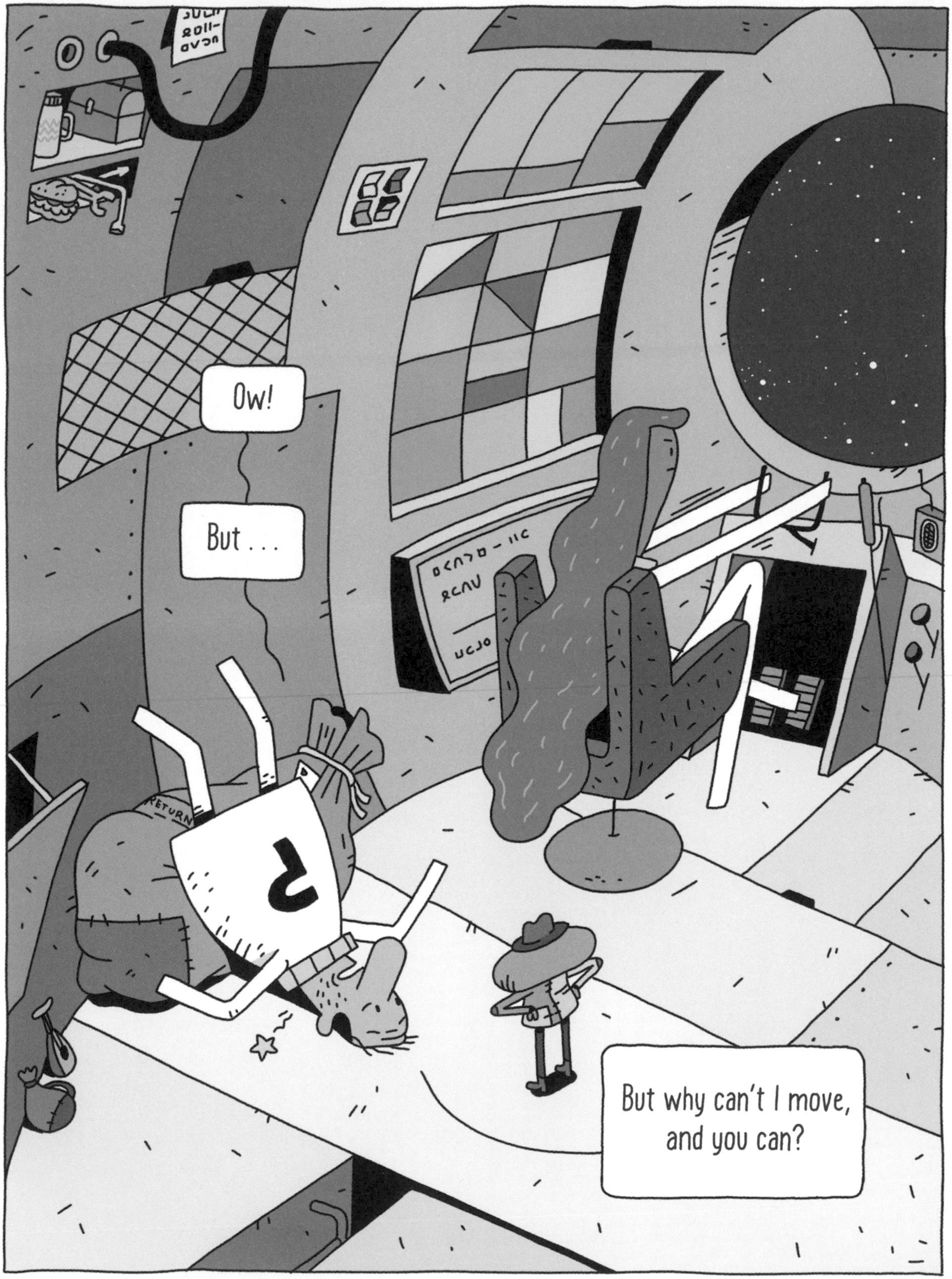
Ow!
But . . .
But why can't I move,
and you can?

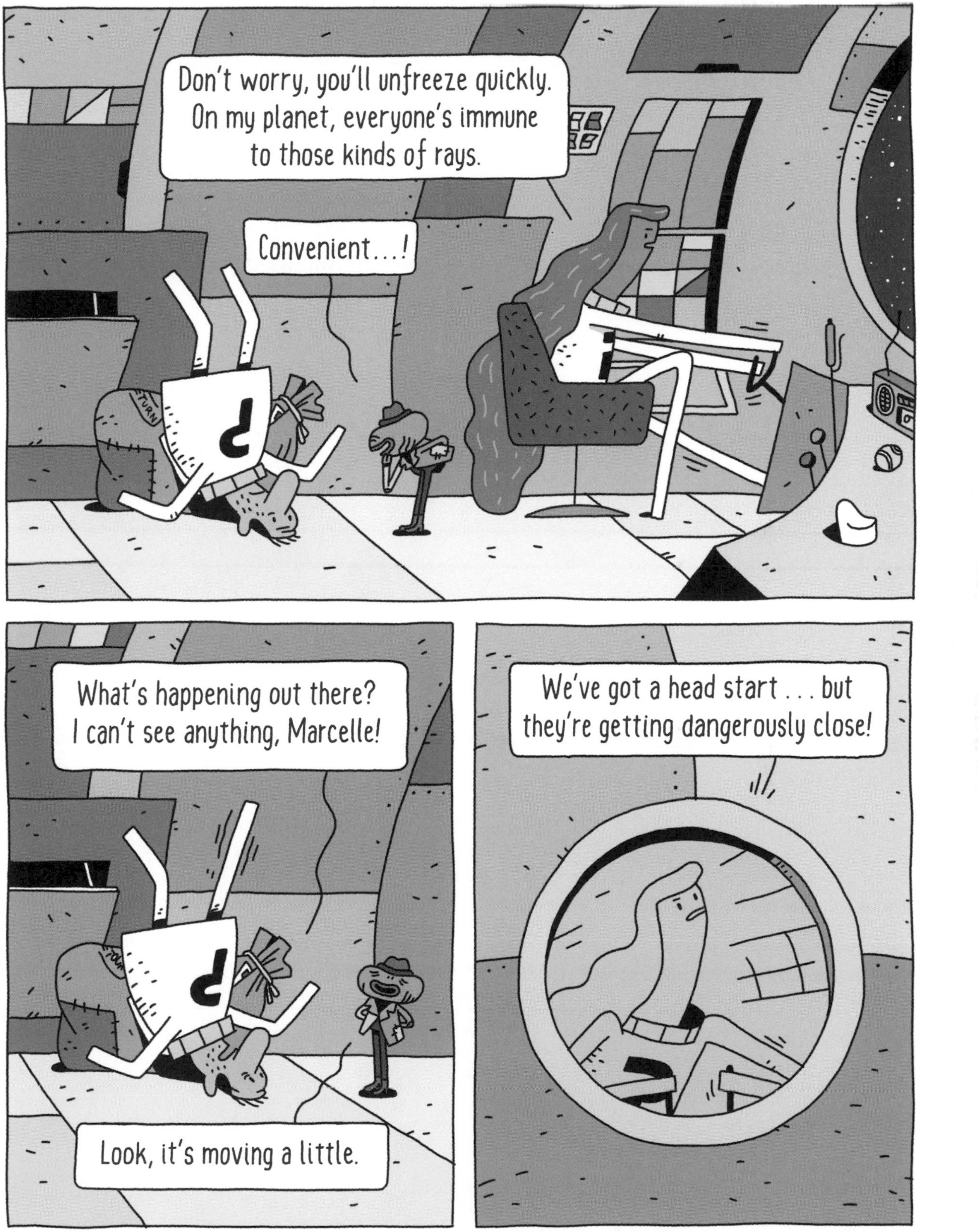
Don't worry, you'll unfreeze quickly. On my planet, everyone's immune to those kinds of rays.
Convenient...!
TURN
What's happening out there? I can't see anything, Marcelle!
Look, it's moving a little.
We've got a head start . . . but they're getting dangerously close!

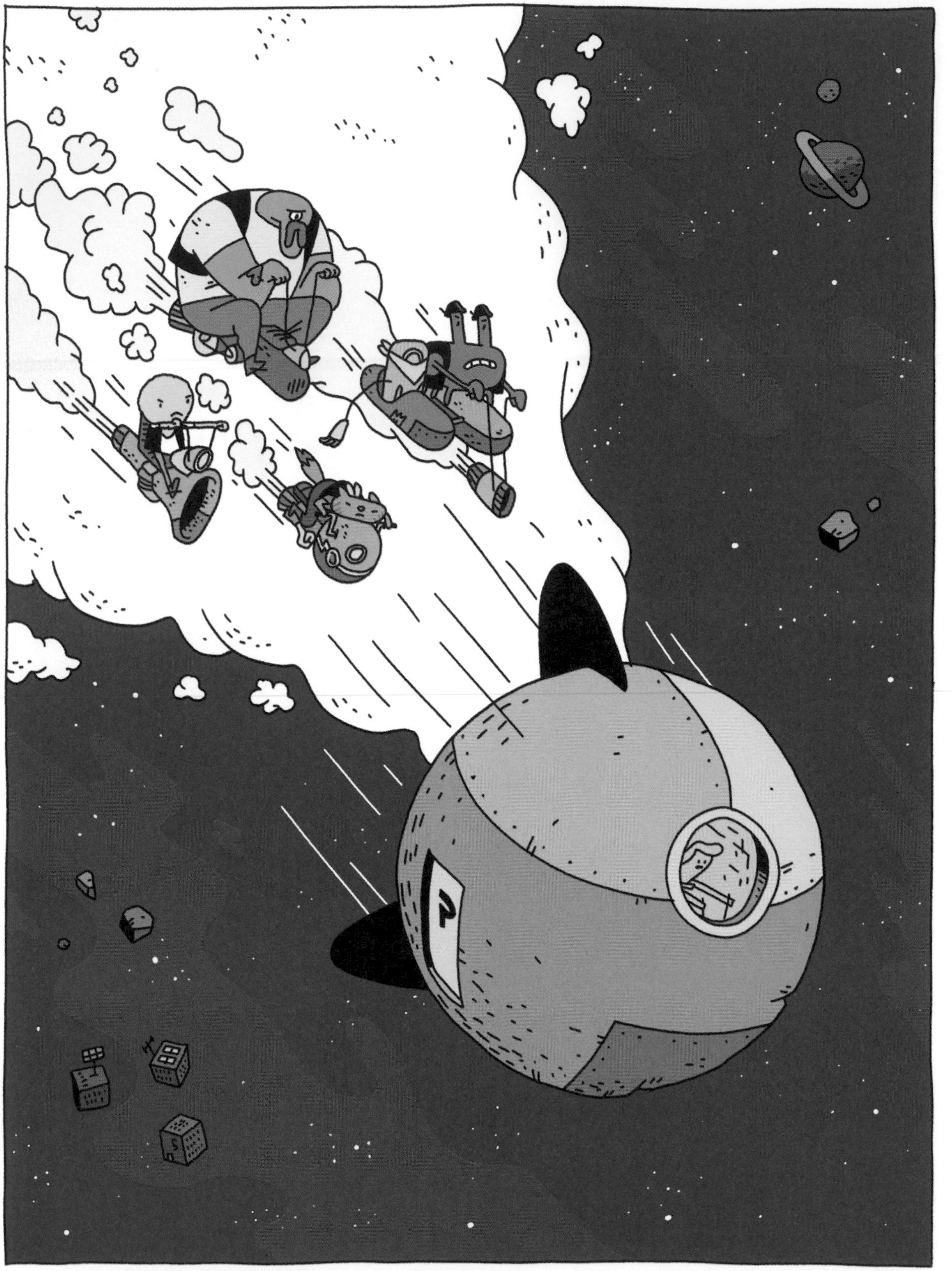

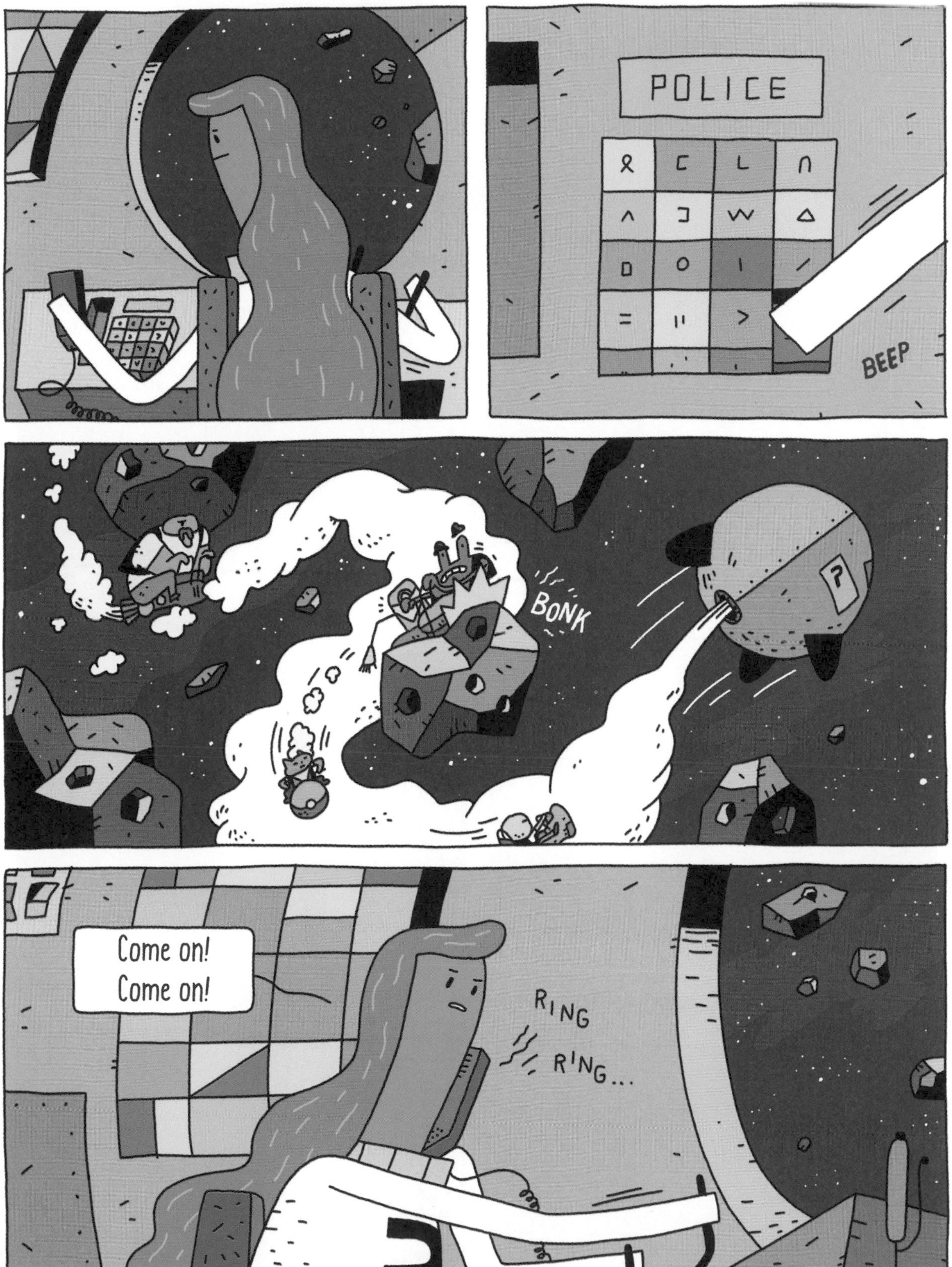
POLICE
BEEP
BONK
Come on! Come on!
RING
RING...

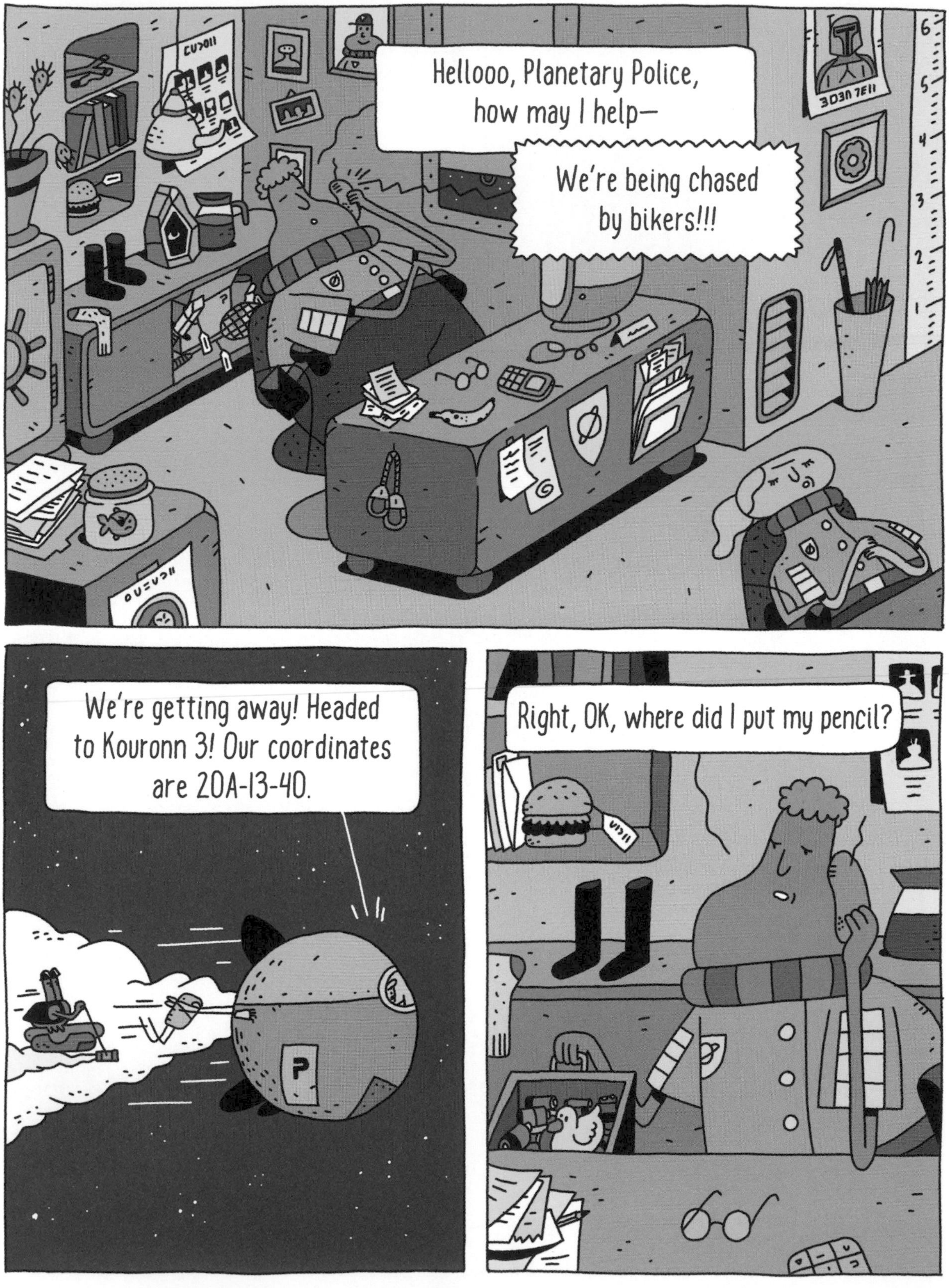
Hellooo, Planetary Police, how may I help—
We're being chased by bikers!!!
We're getting away! Headed to Kouronn 3! Our coordinates are 20A-13-40.
Right, OK, where did I put my pencil?

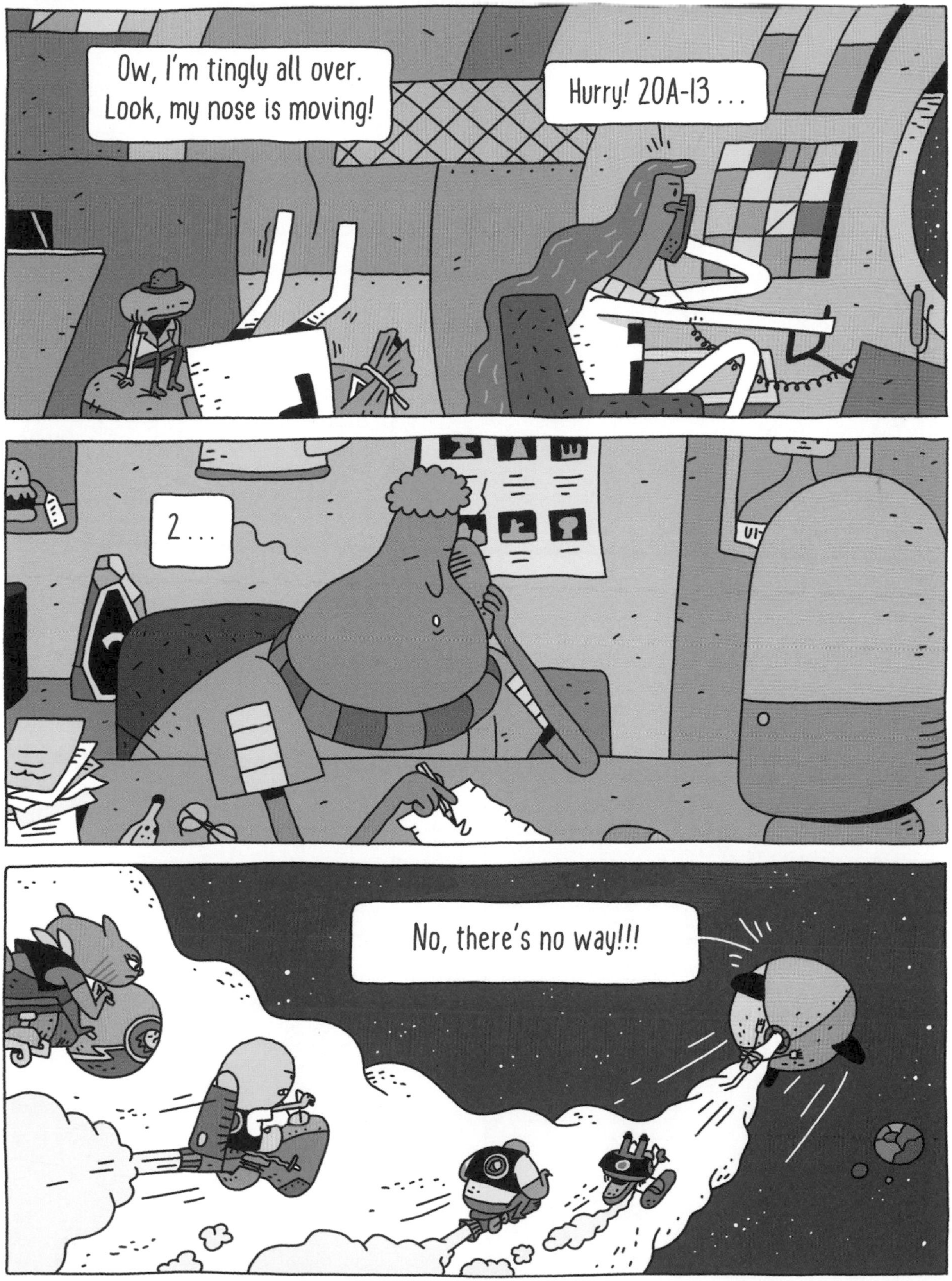
Ow, I'm tingly all over. Look, my nose is moving!
Hurry! 20A-13 . . .
2 . . .
No, there's no way!!!

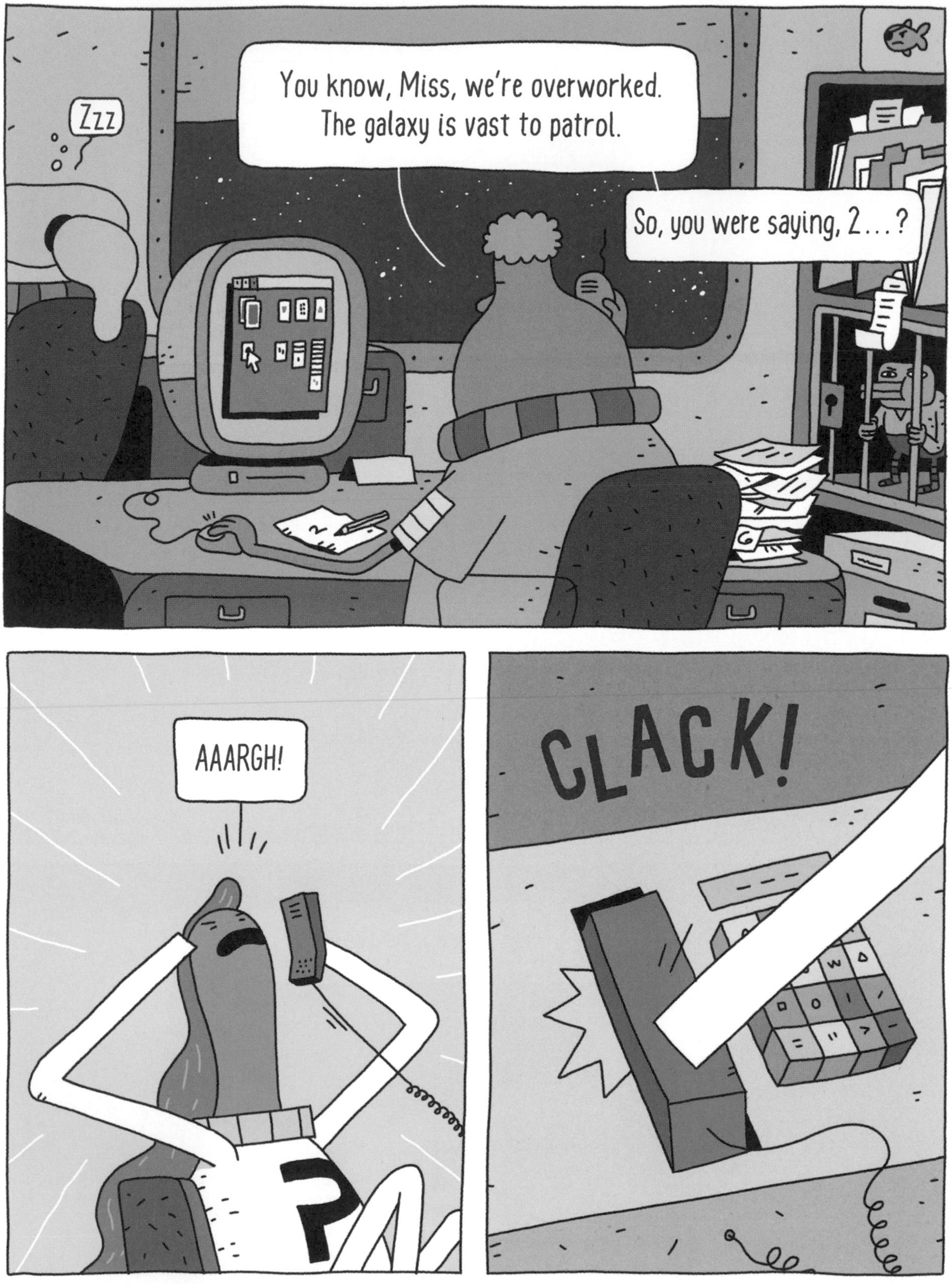
Zzz
You know, Miss, we're overworked. The galaxy is vast to patrol.
So, you were saying, 2...?
AAARGH!
CLACK!

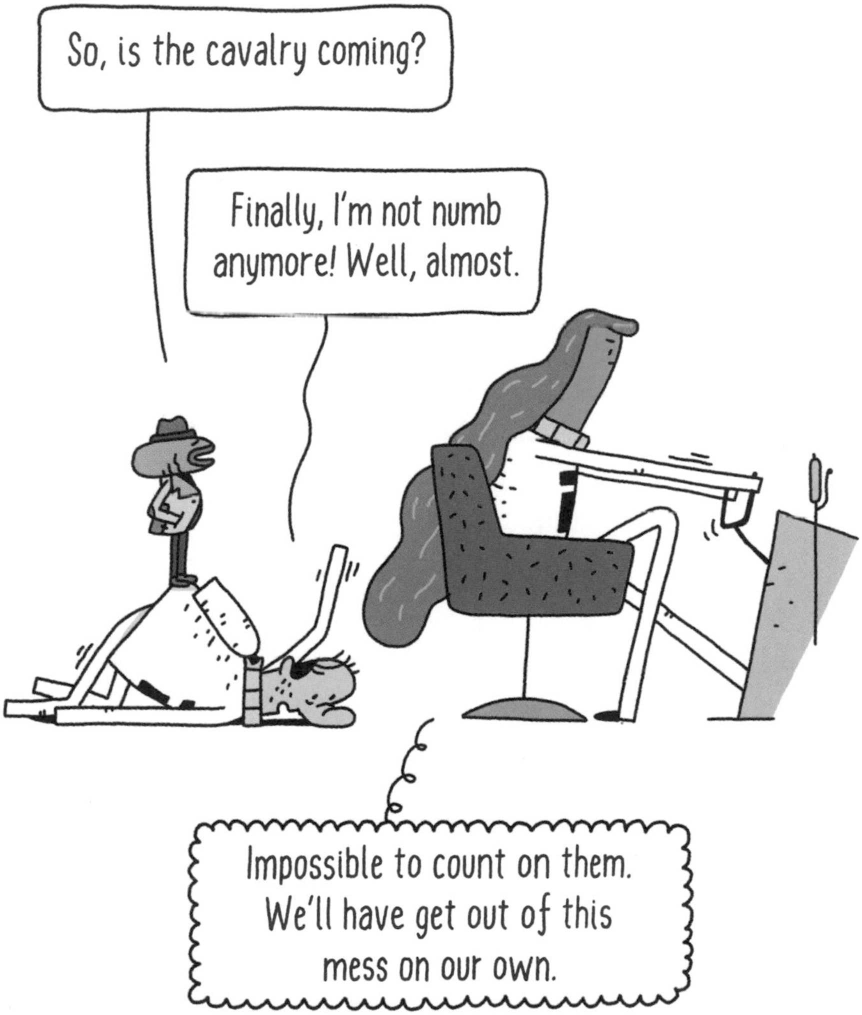
So, is the cavalry coming?
Finally, I'm not numb anymore! Well, almost.
Impossible to count on them. We'll have get out of this mess on our own.

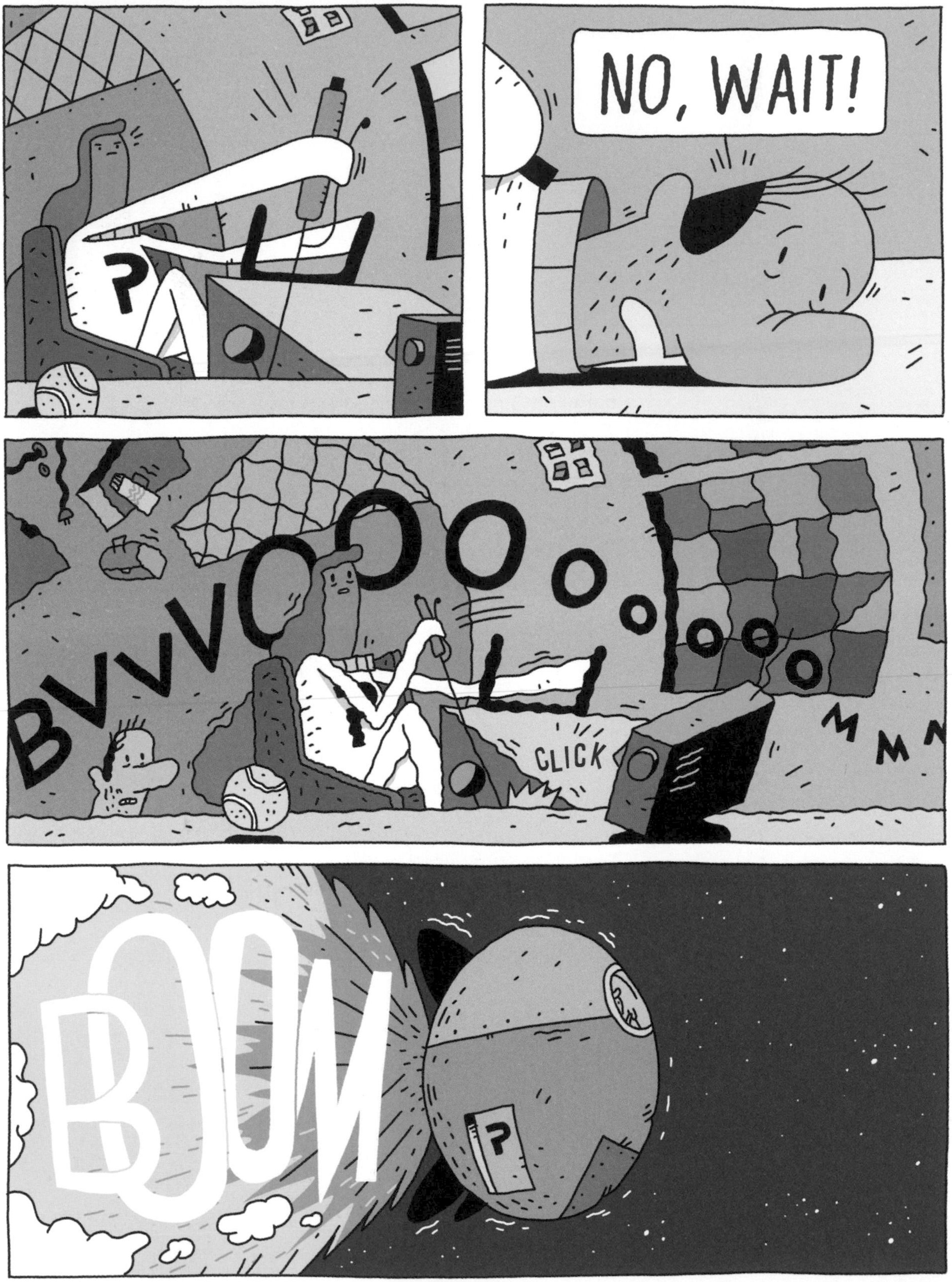
NO, WAIT!
BVVVOOOOoooooo
CLICK
MMM
BOOM

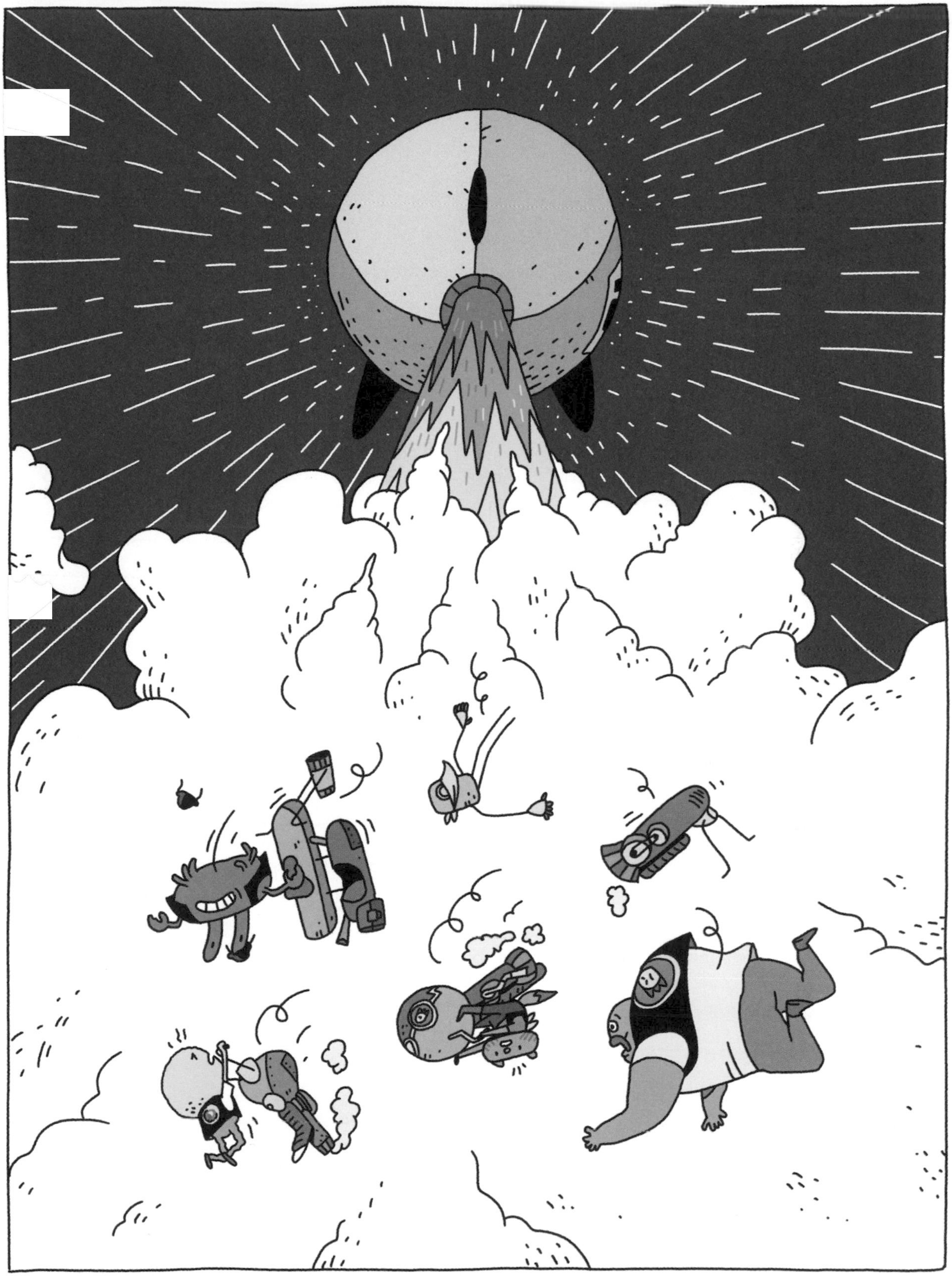

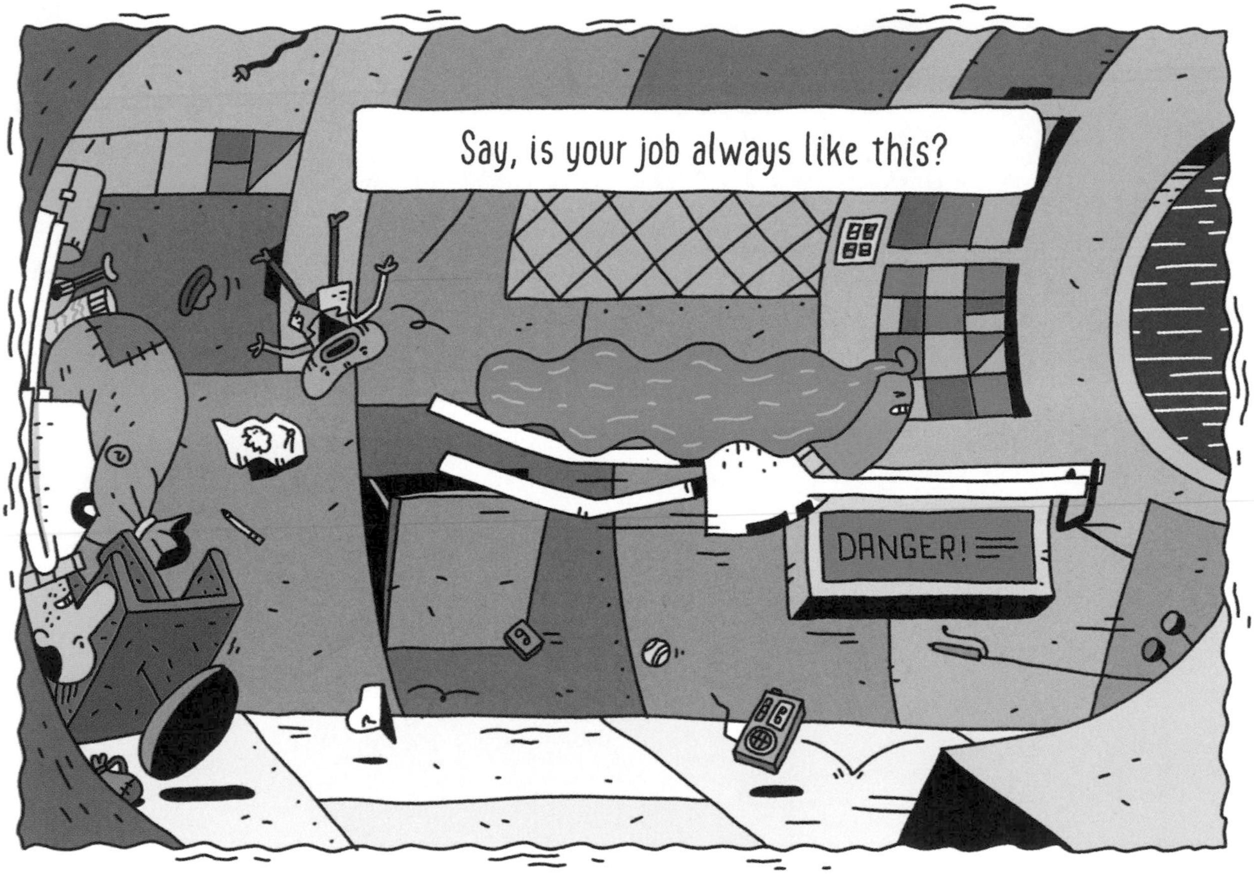
Say, is your job always like this?
DANGER!

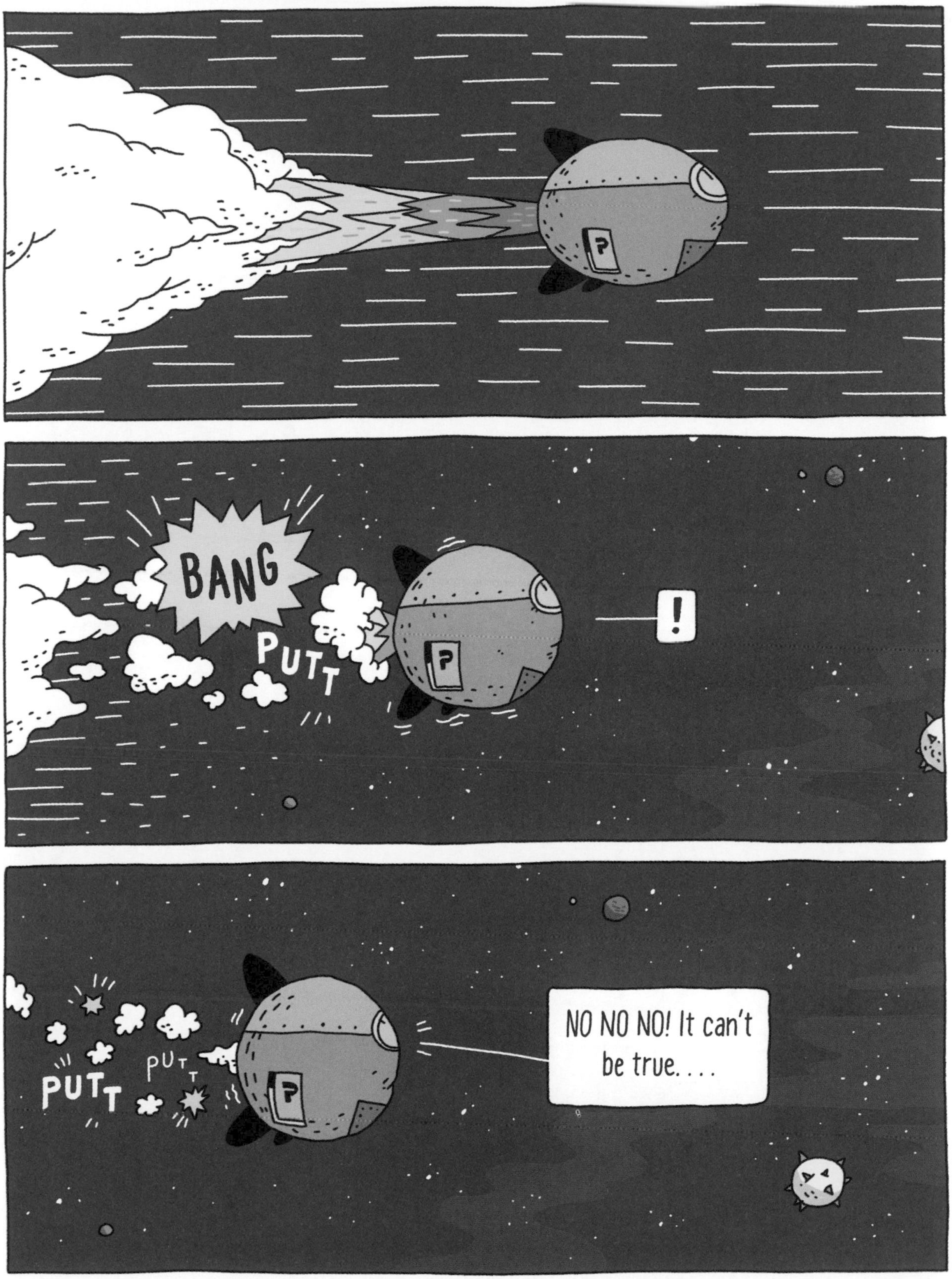
BANG
PUTT
!
PUTT
PUTT
NO NO NO! It can't be true. . . .

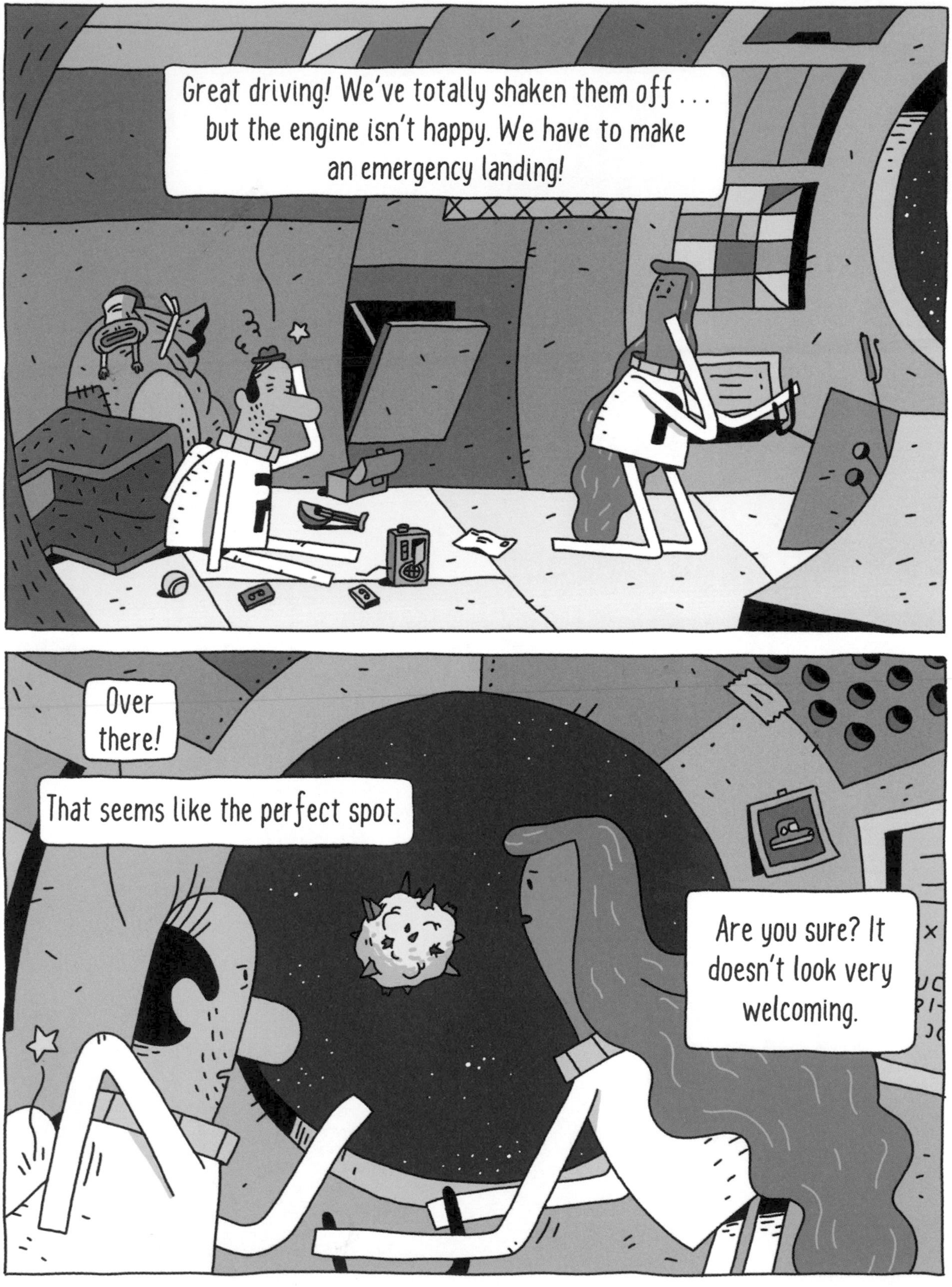
Great driving! We've totally shaken them off . . . but the engine isn't happy. We have to make an emergency landing!
Over there!
That seems like the perfect spot.
Are you sure? It doesn't look very welcoming.

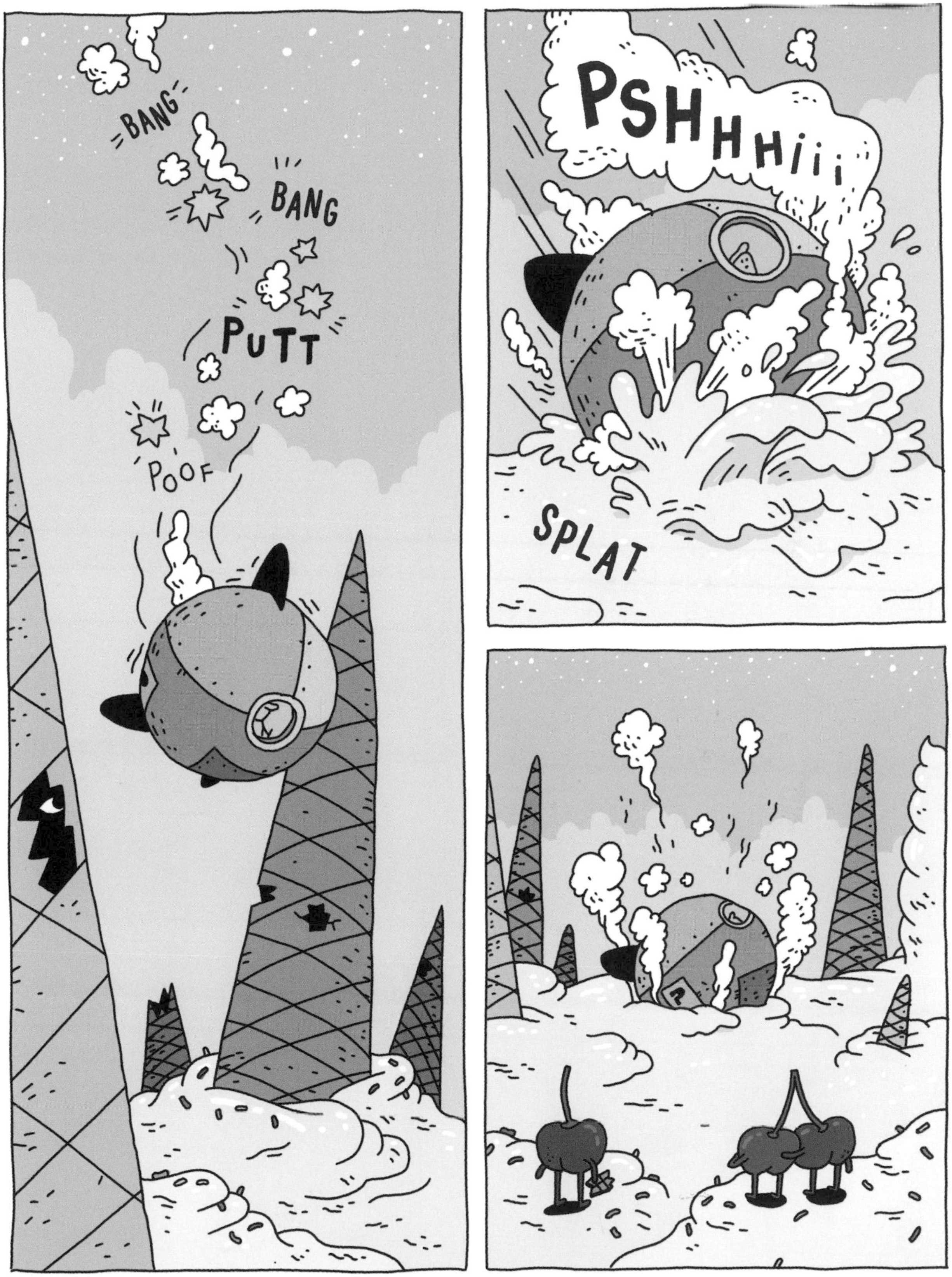
BANG
BANG
PUTT
POOF
PSHHHiii
SPLAT

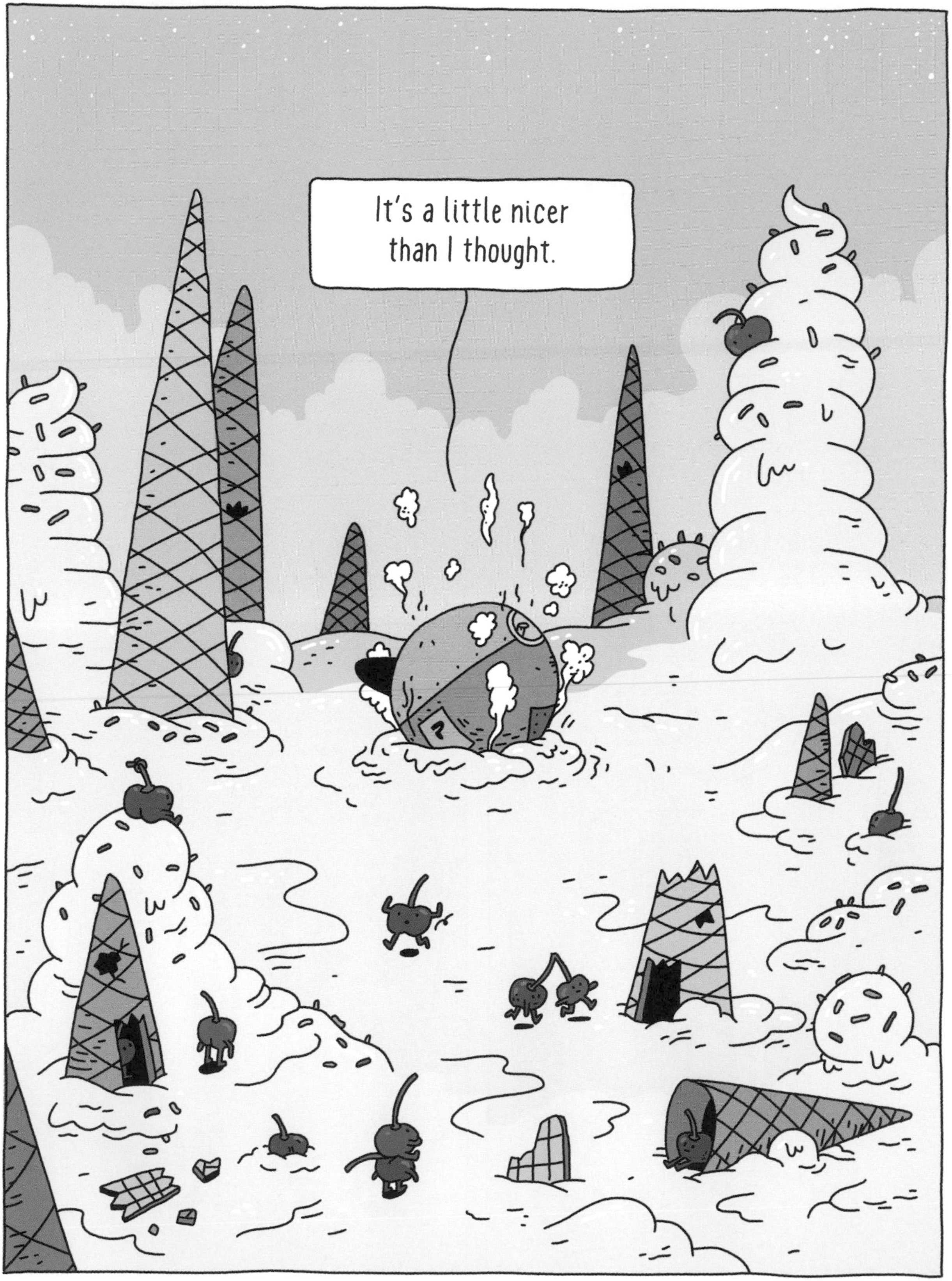
It's a little nicer than I thought.

STOP
#5

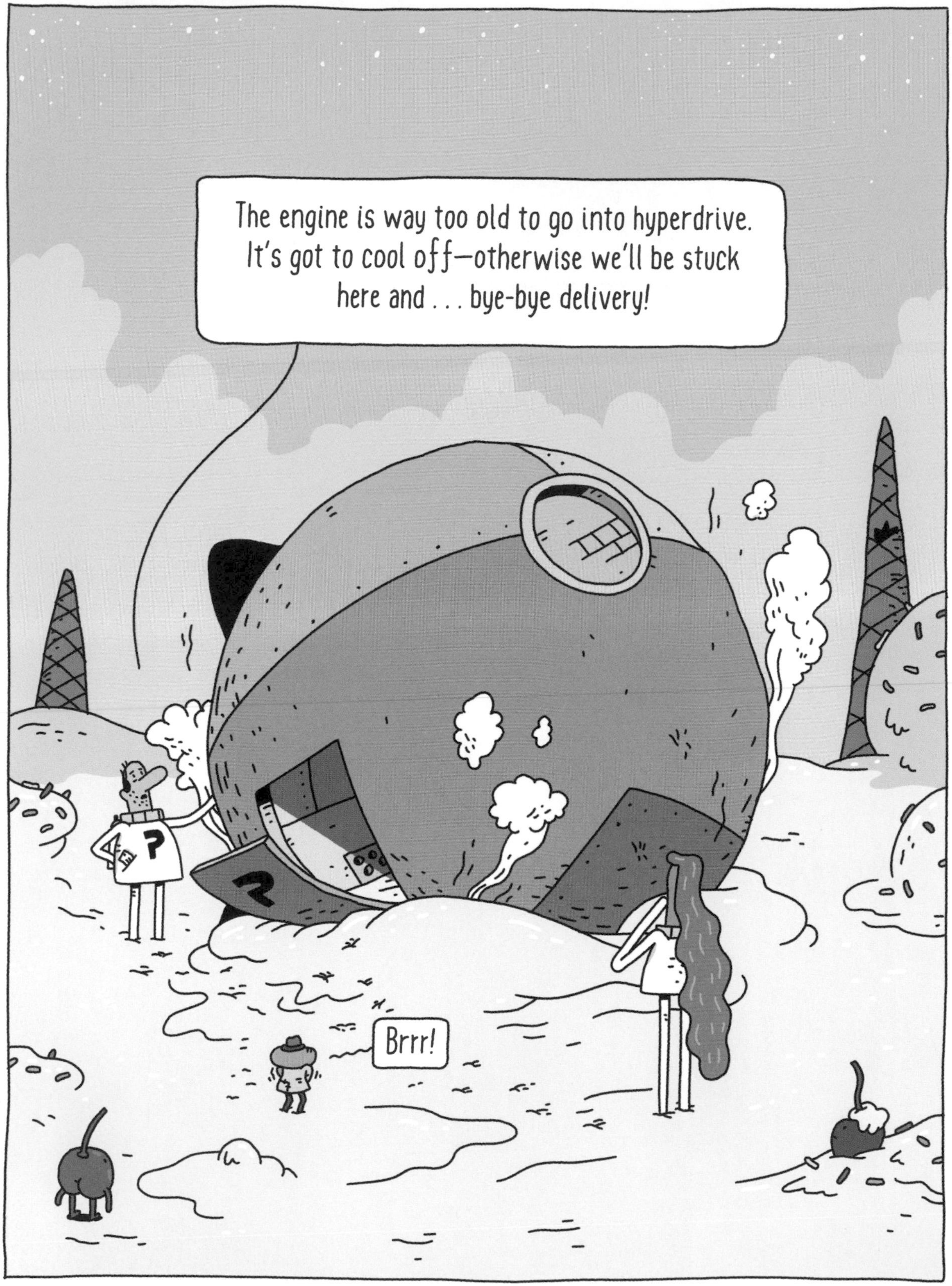
The engine is way too old to go into hyperdrive. It's got to cool off—otherwise we'll be stuck here and . . . bye-bye delivery!
Brrr!

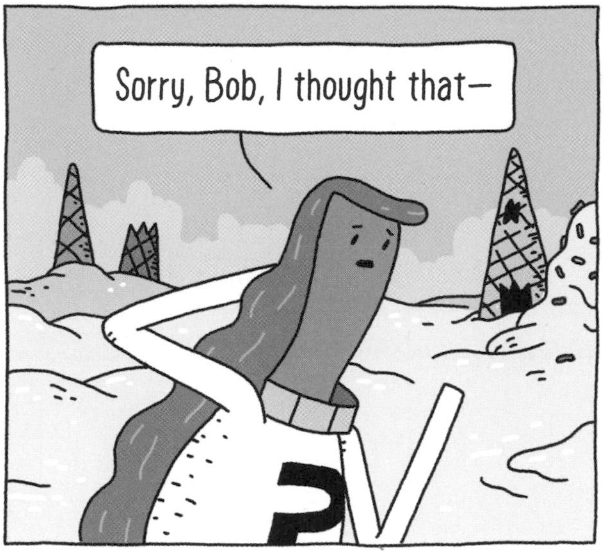
Sorry, Bob, I thought that—

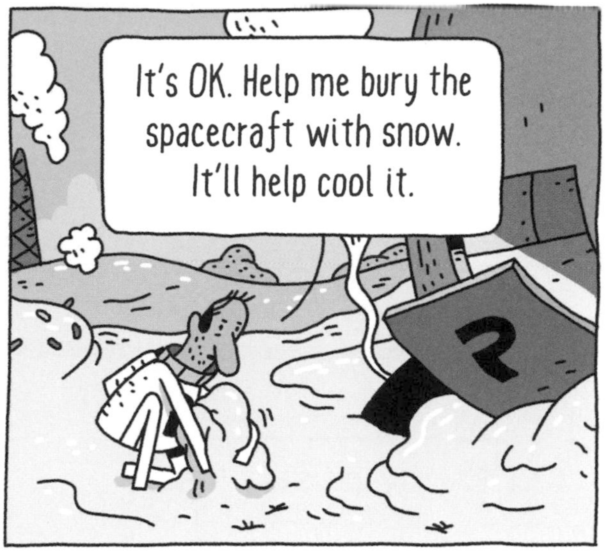
It's OK. Help me bury the spacecraft with snow. It'll help cool it.

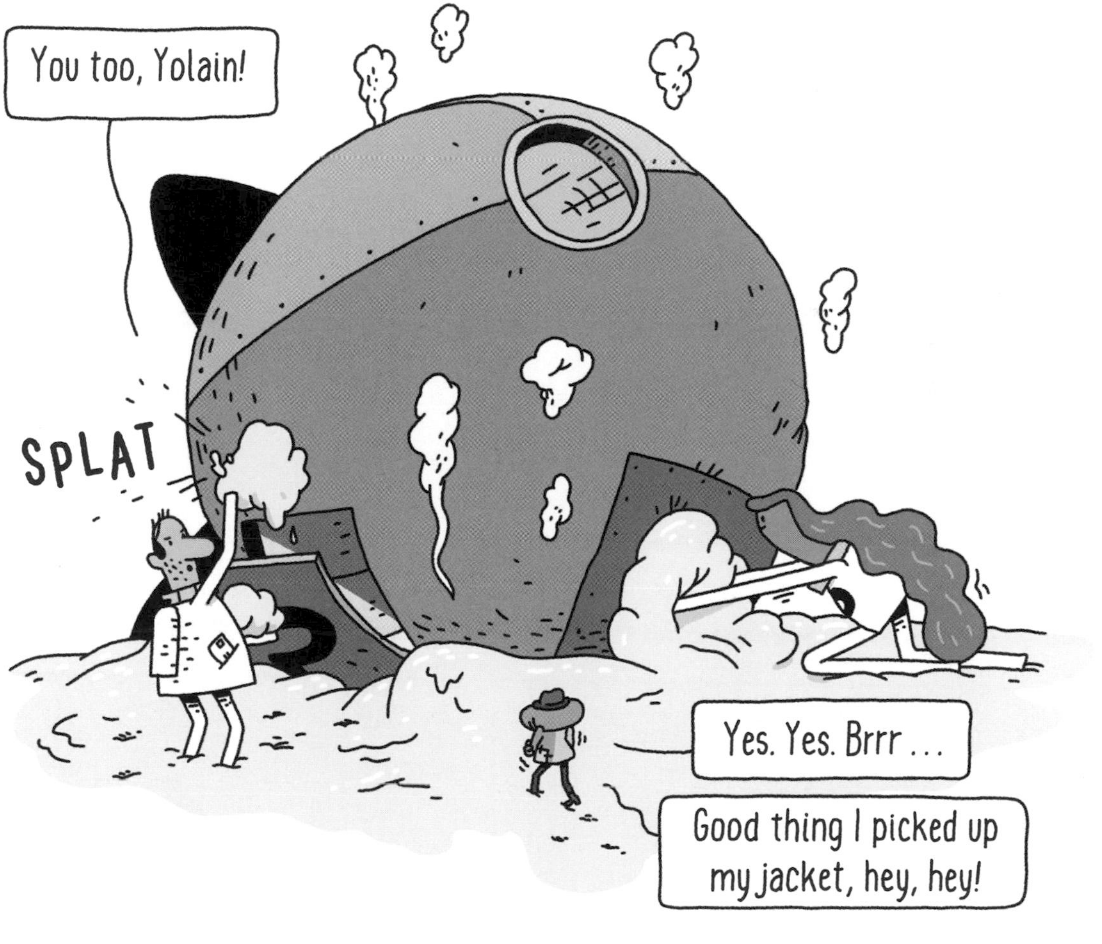
You too, Yolain!
SPLAT
Yes. Yes. Brrr . . .
Good thing I picked up my jacket, hey, hey!

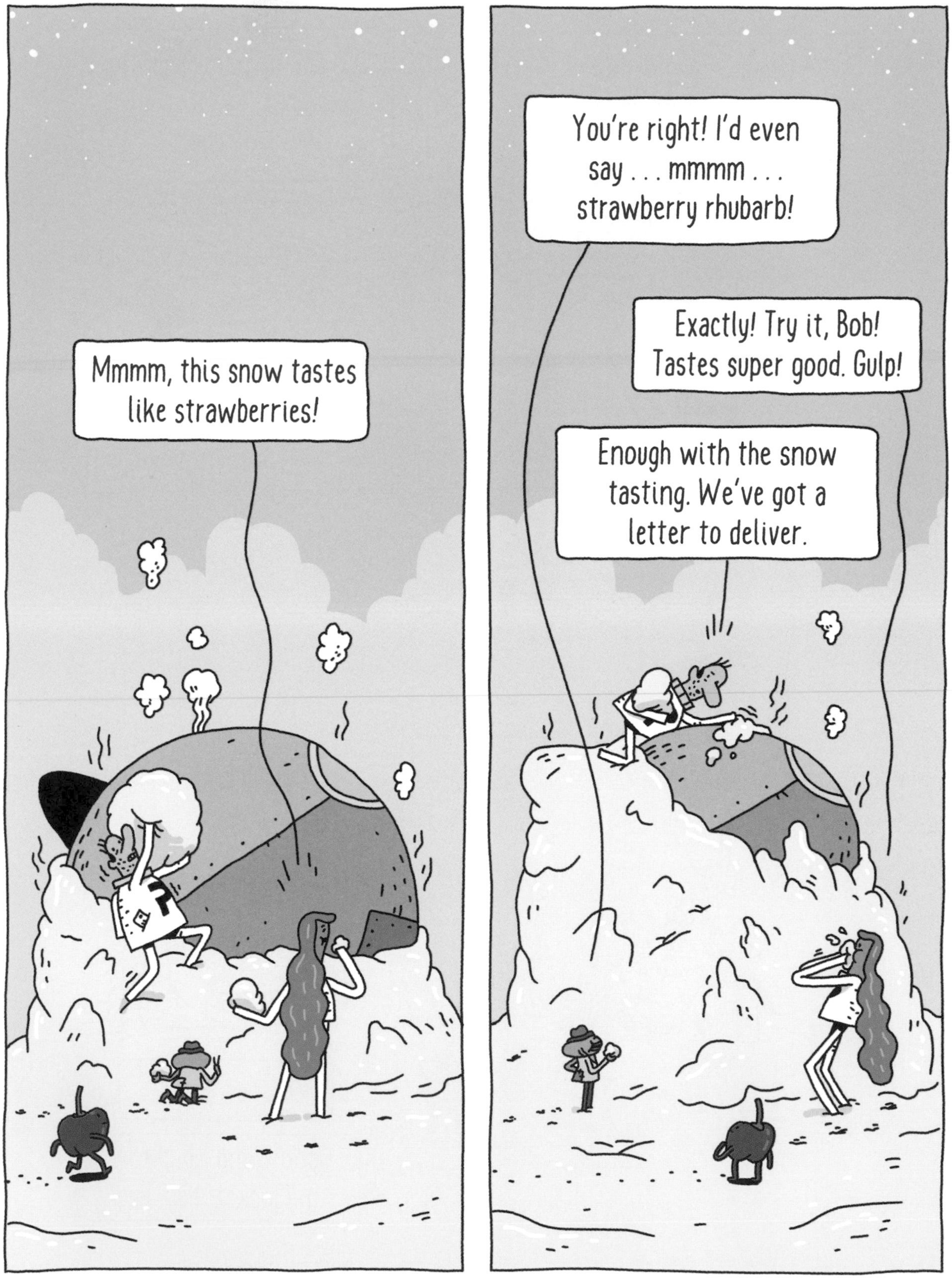
Mmmm, this snow tastes like strawberries!
You're right! I'd even say . . . mmmm . . . strawberry rhubarb!
Exactly! Try it, Bob! Tastes super good. Gulp!
Enough with the snow tasting. We've got a letter to deliver.

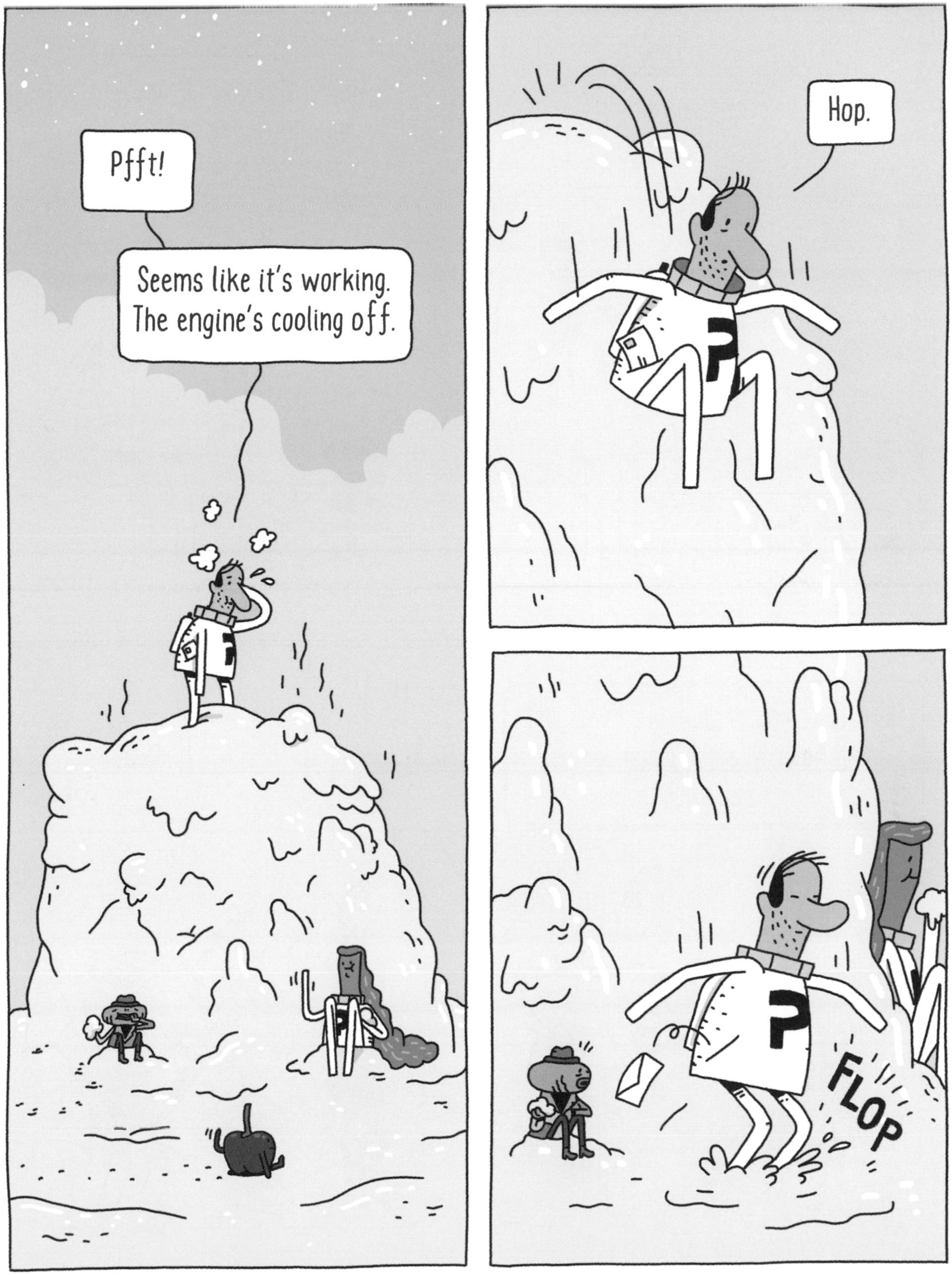
Pfft!
Seems like it's working. The engine's cooling off.
Hop.
FLOP

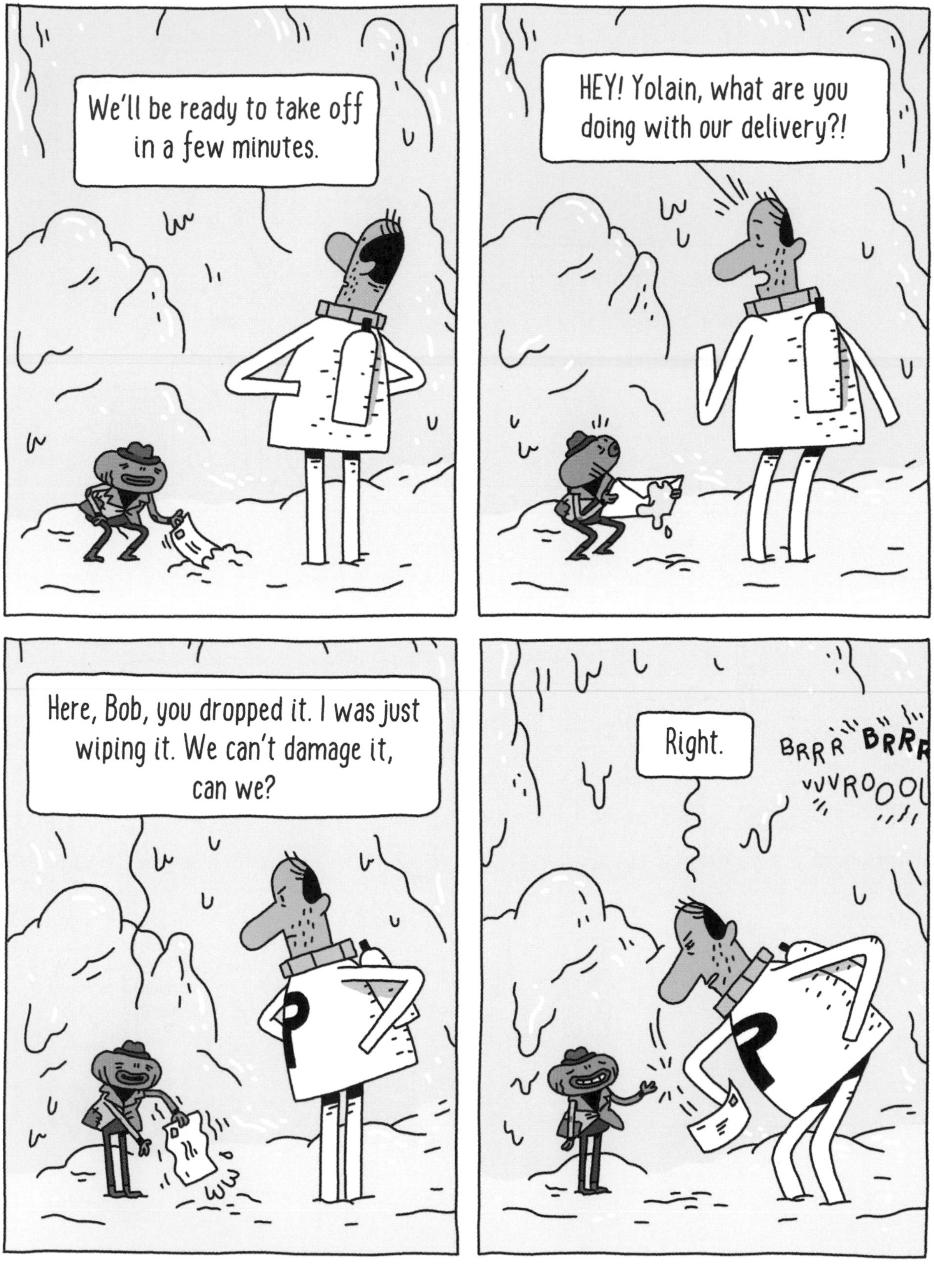
We'll be ready to take off in a few minutes.
HEY! Yolain, what are you doing with our delivery?!
Here, Bob, you dropped it. I was just wiping it. We can't damage it, can we?
Right.
BRRR BRRR
VVVROOOU

Do you hear that?
BRAAAOOOOMM
VVRROOO
VROOM
VROOM
This can't be happening!
BRRRRAAAMMMM
VRRRO
They've tracked us down!

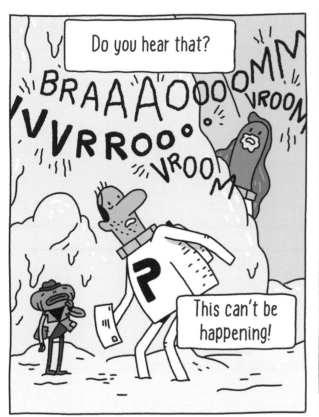

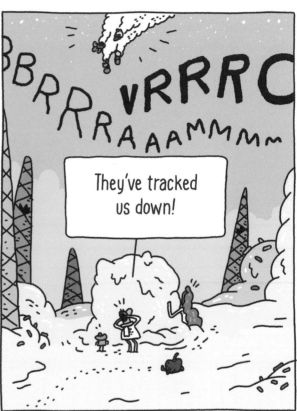

But it's impossible for our friends to flee.
The engine is too hot!

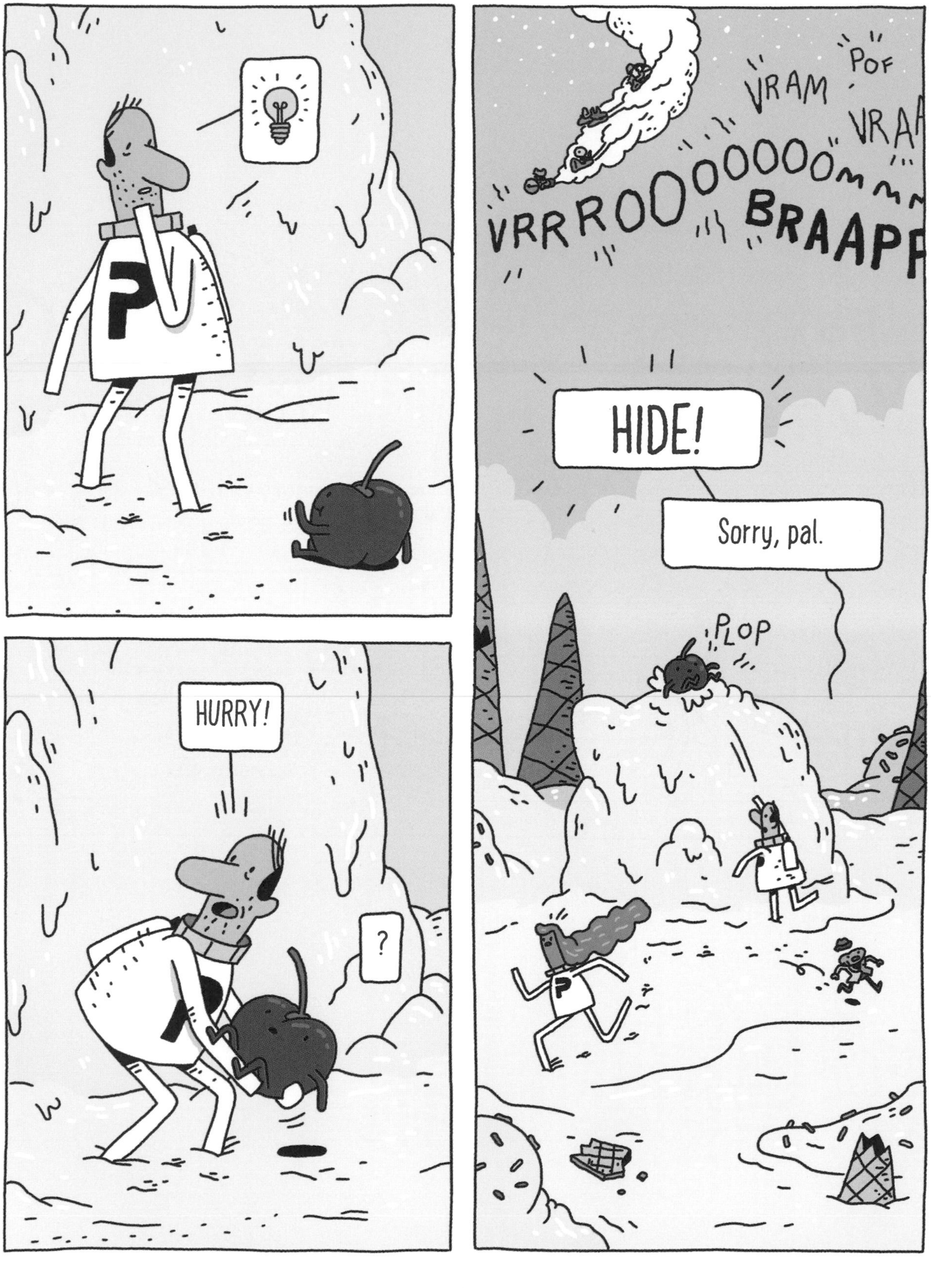
HURRY!
?
VRAM
POF
VRA
VRRROOOOOOOOmmm
BRAAPP
HIDE!
Sorry, pal.
PLOP

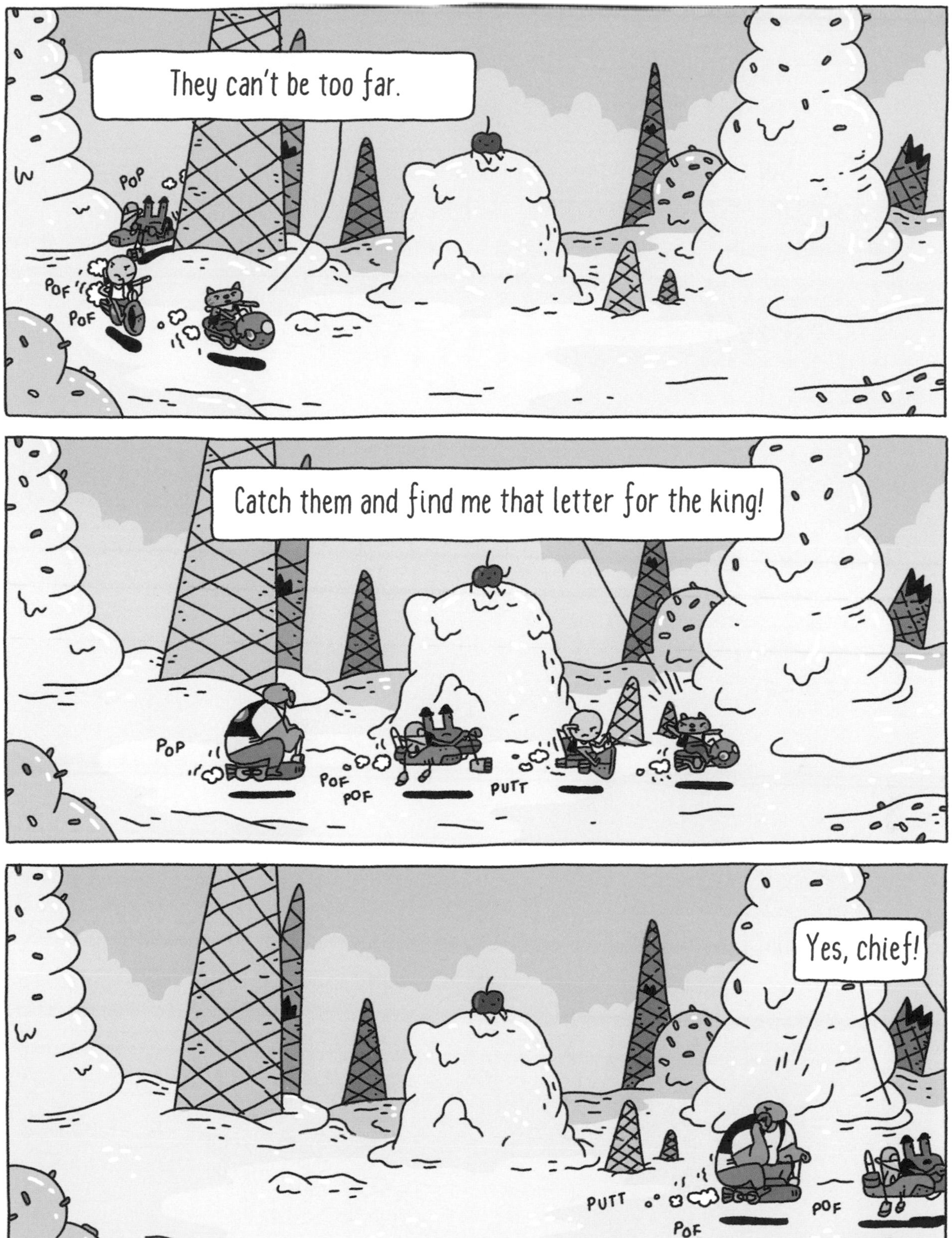
They can't be too far.
POP
POF
POF
Catch them and find me that letter for the king!
POP
POF
POF
PUTT
Yes, chief!
PUTT
POF
POF

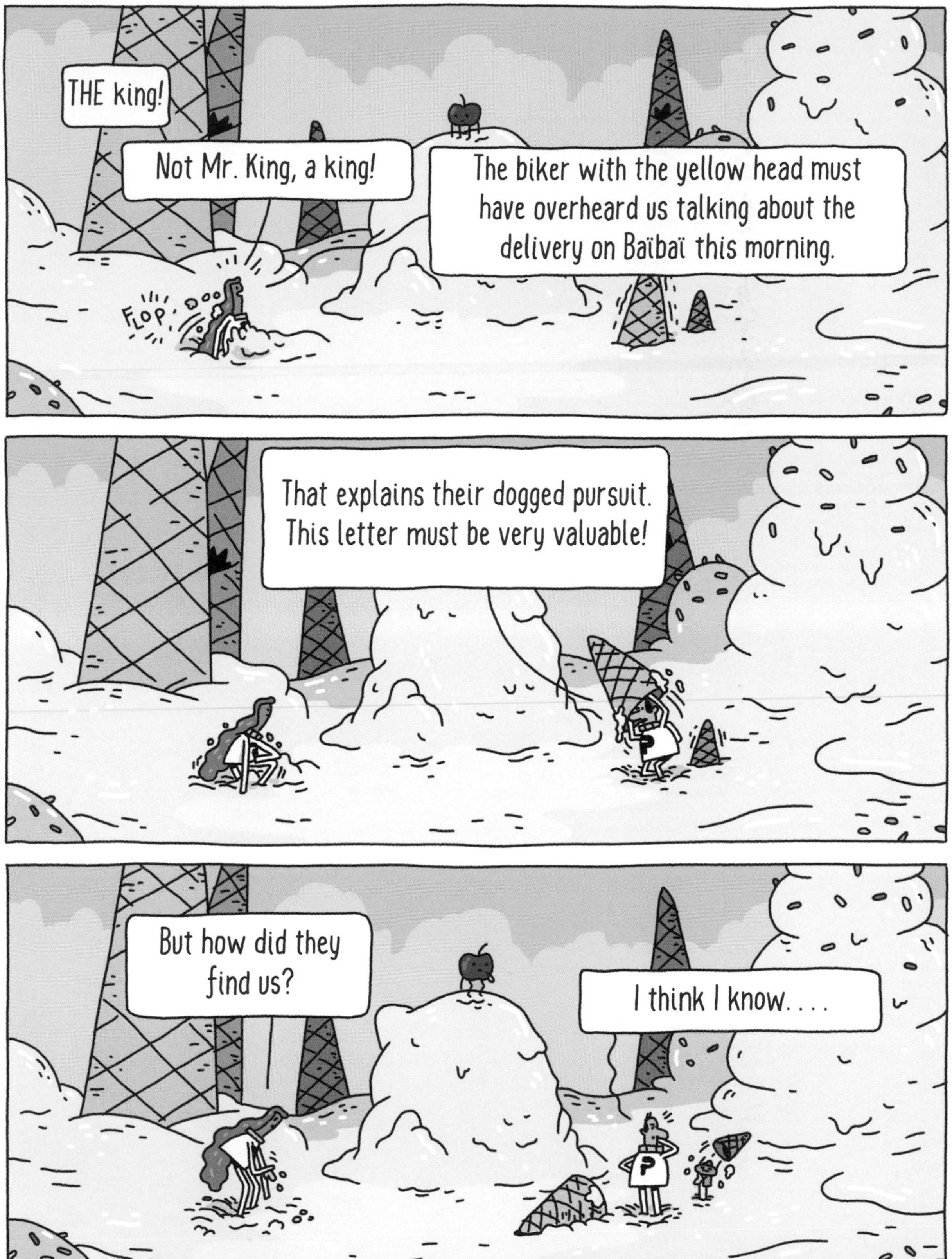
THE king!
Not Mr. King, a king!
The biker with the yellow head must have overheard us talking about the delivery on Baïbaï this morning.
FLOP
That explains their dogged pursuit. This letter must be very valuable!
But how did they find us?
I think I know. . . .

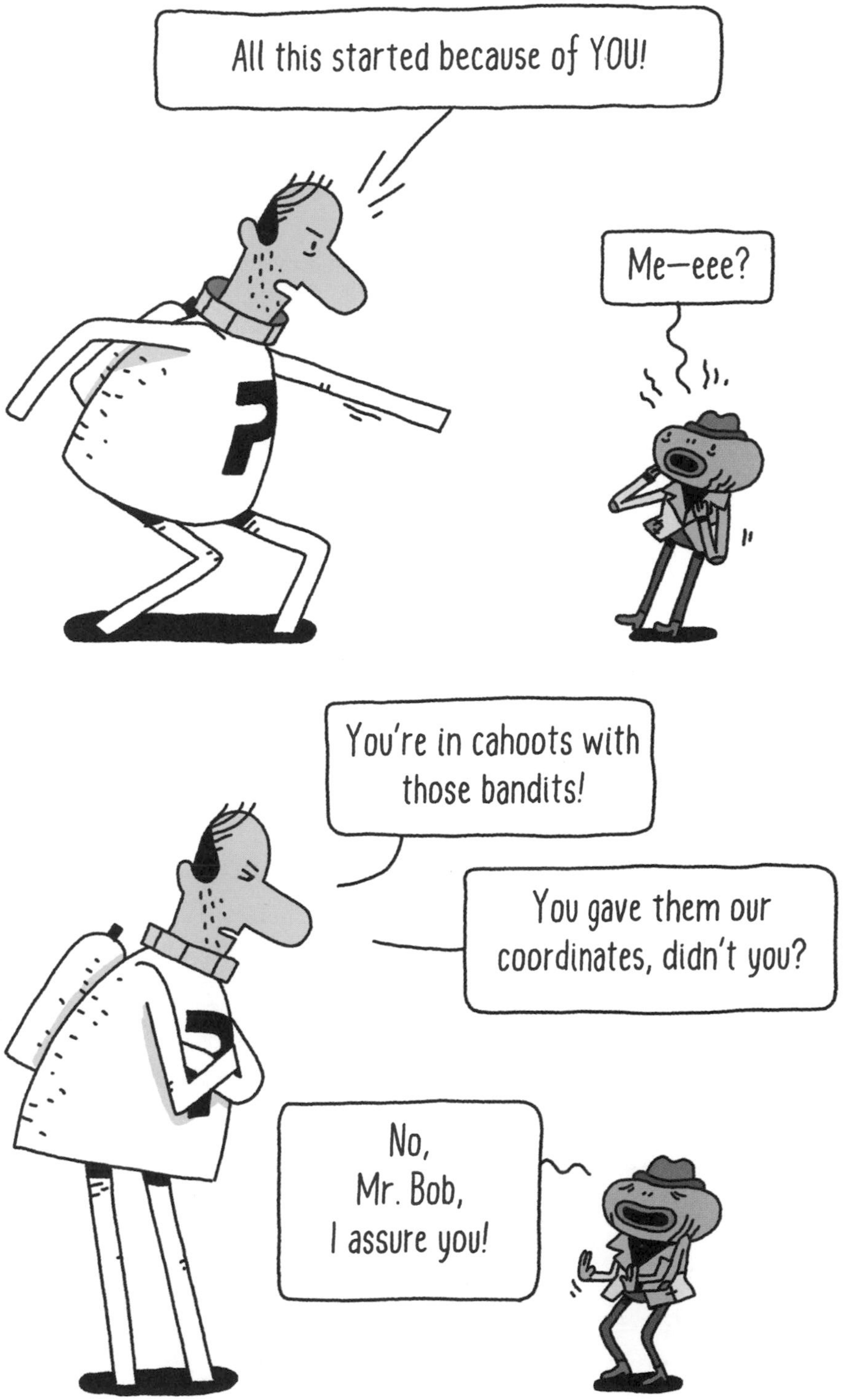
All this started because of YOU!
Me—eee?
You're in cahoots with those bandits!
You gave them our coordinates, didn't you?
No, Mr. Bob, I assure you!

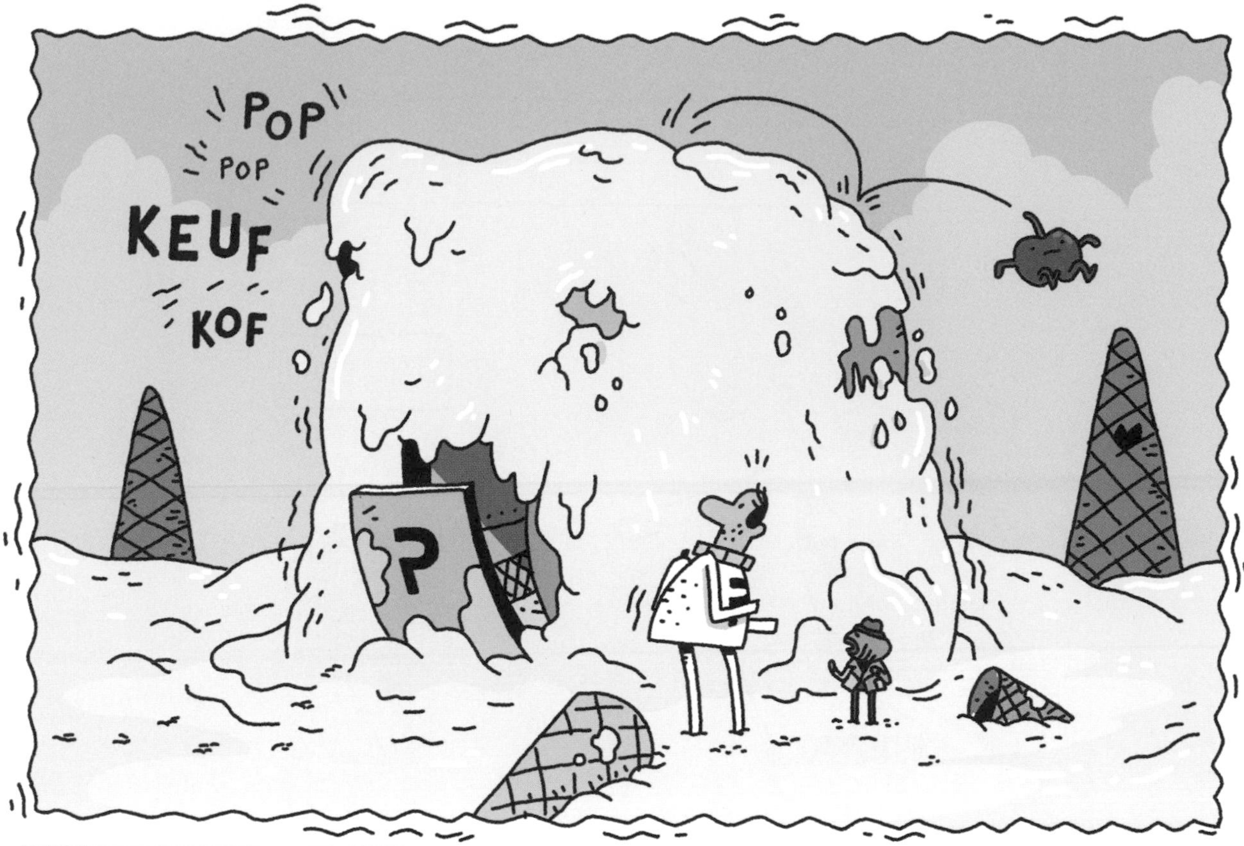
POP
POP
KEUF
KOF

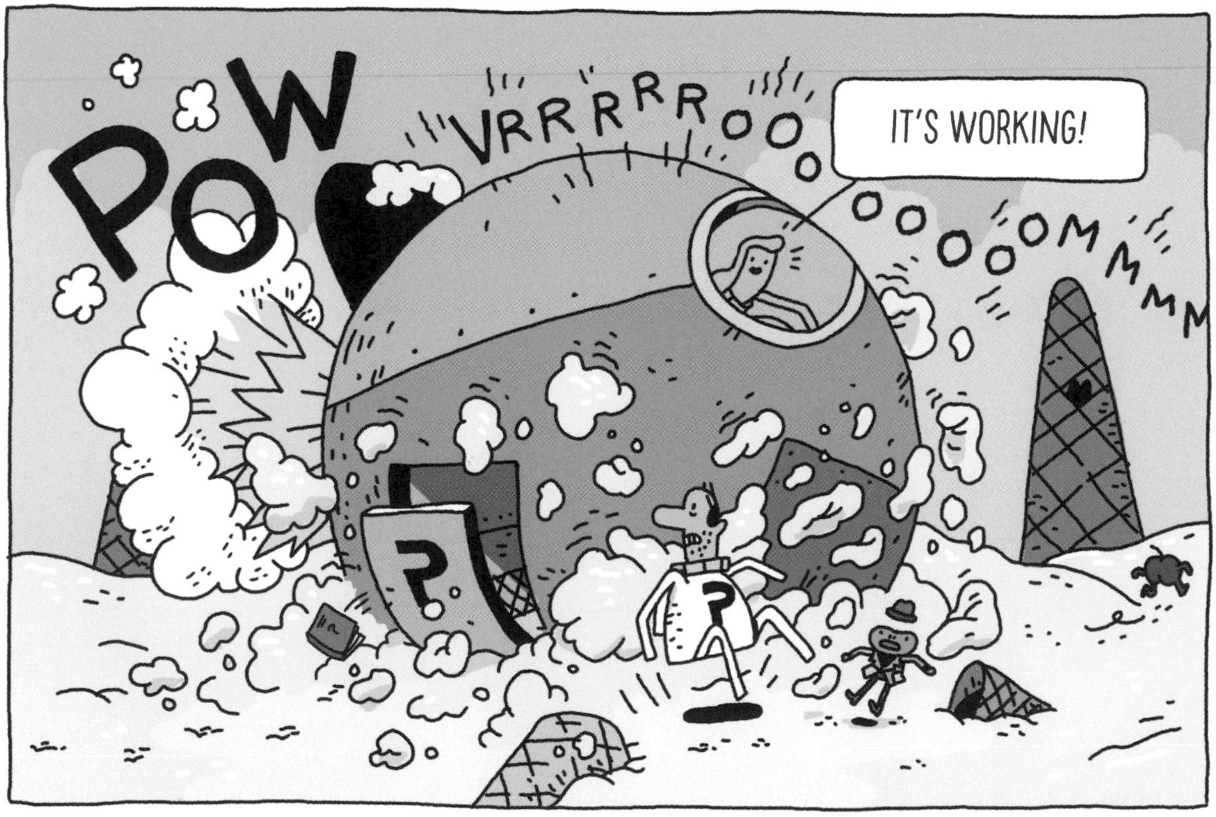
POW
VRRRRRROOOOOOOOOMMMMM
IT'S WORKING!

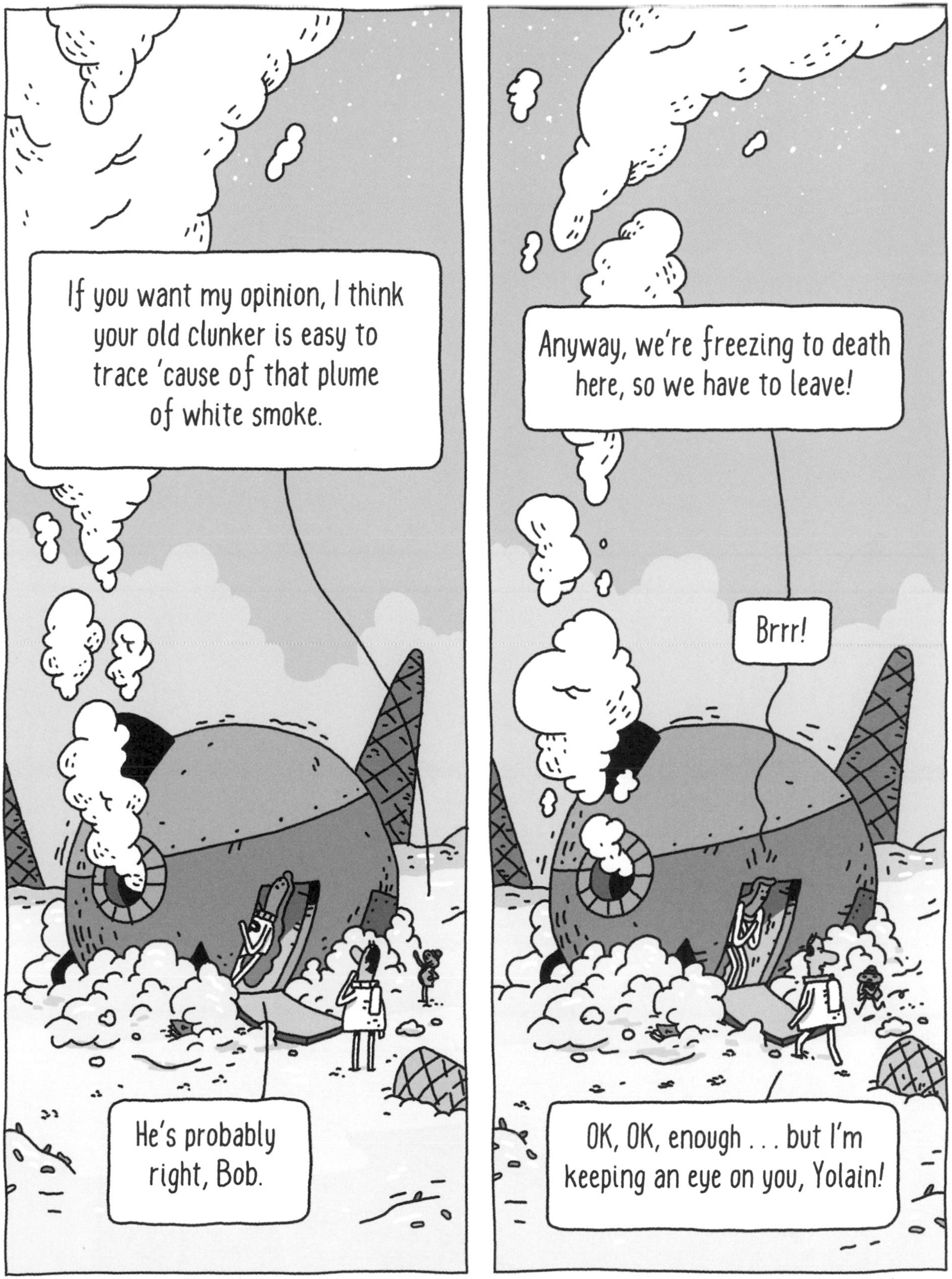
If you want my opinion, I think your old clunker is easy to trace 'cause of that plume of white smoke.
He's probably right, Bob.
Anyway, we're freezing to death here, so we have to leave!
Brrr!
OK, OK, enough . . . but I'm keeping an eye on you, Yolain!

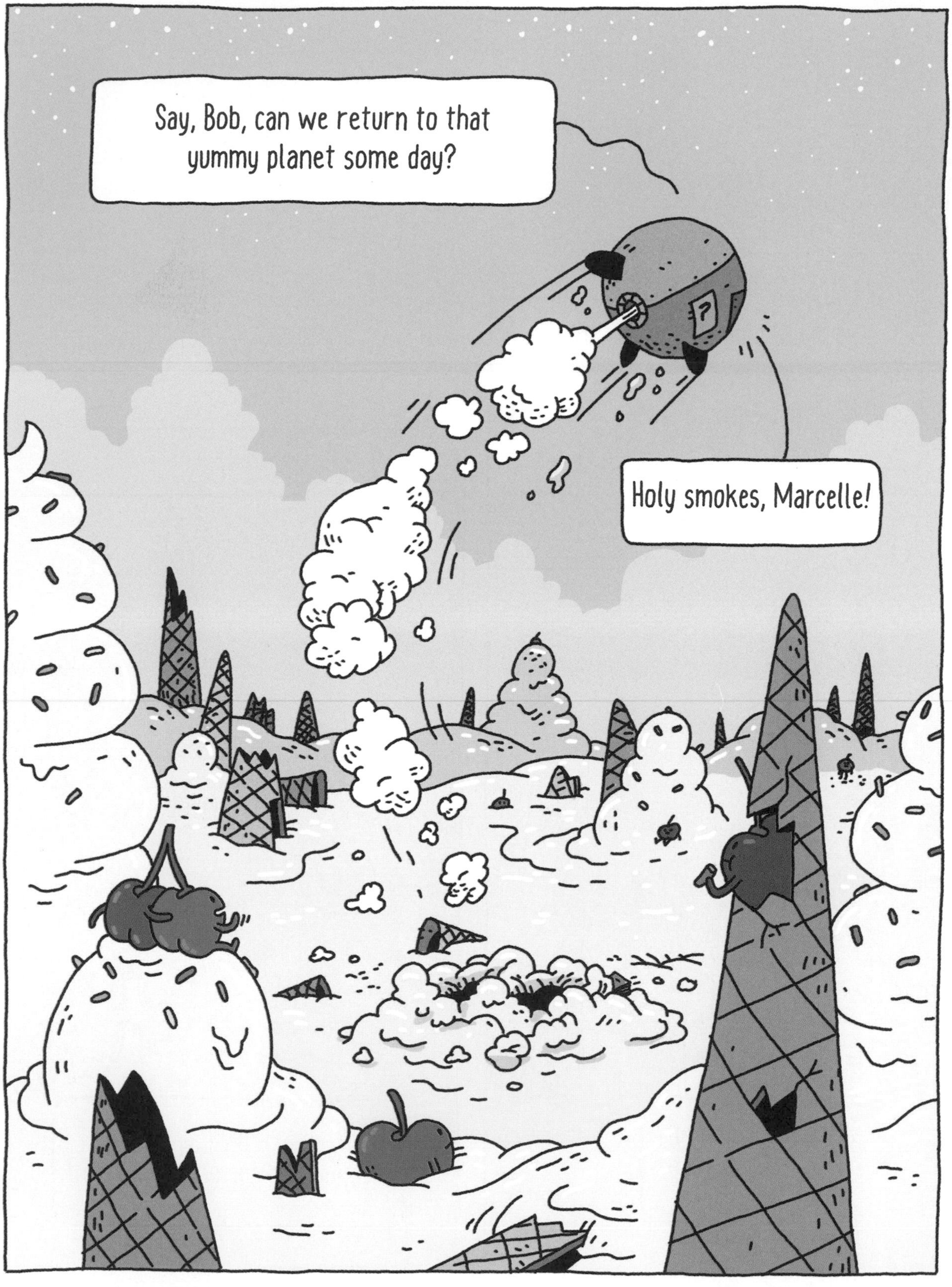
Say, Bob, can we return to that yummy planet some day?
Holy smokes, Marcelle!

STOP
#6

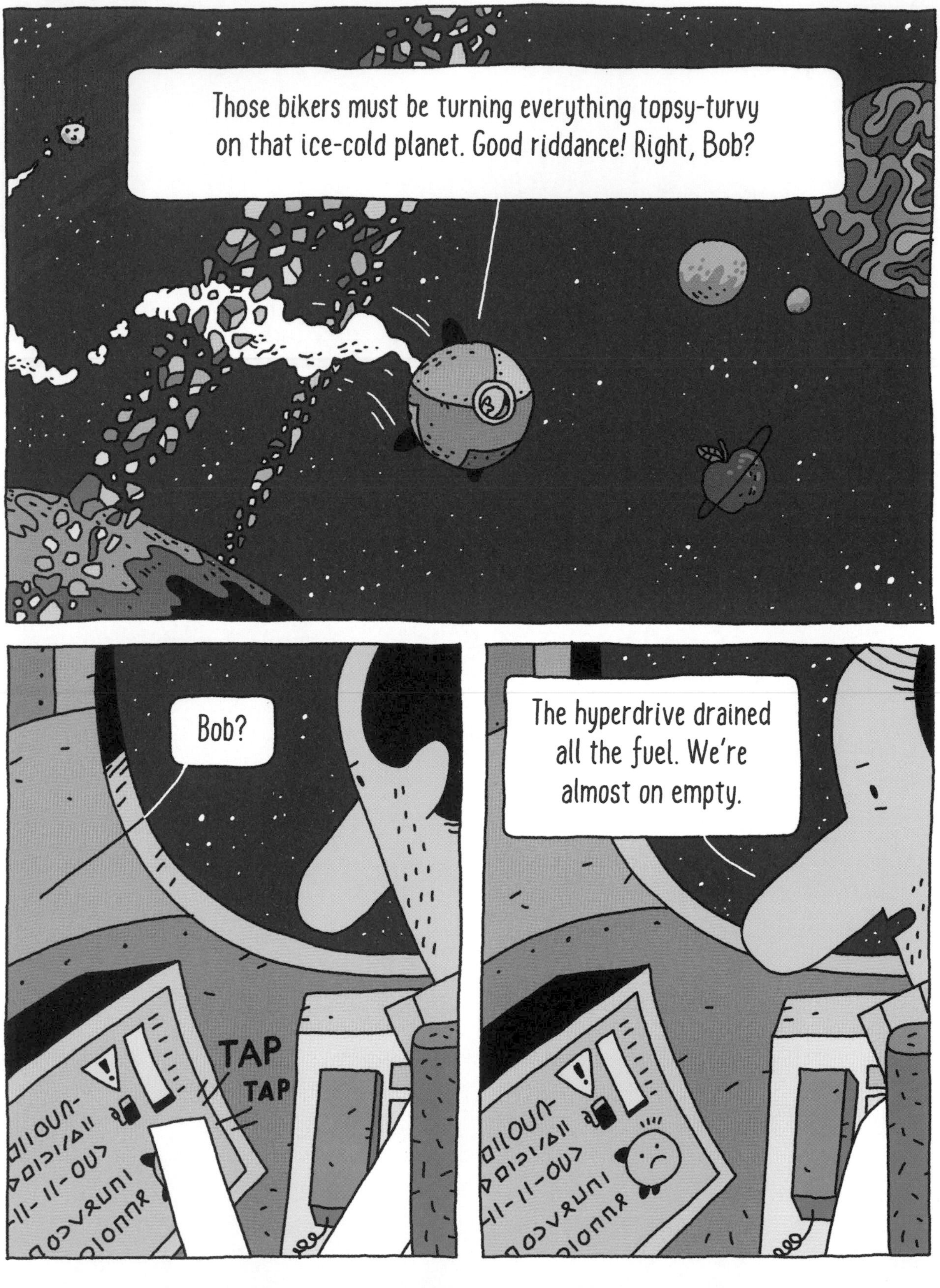
Those bikers must be turning everything topsy-turvy on that ice-cold planet. Good riddance! Right, Bob?
Bob?
TAP
TAP
The hyperdrive drained all the fuel. We're almost on empty.

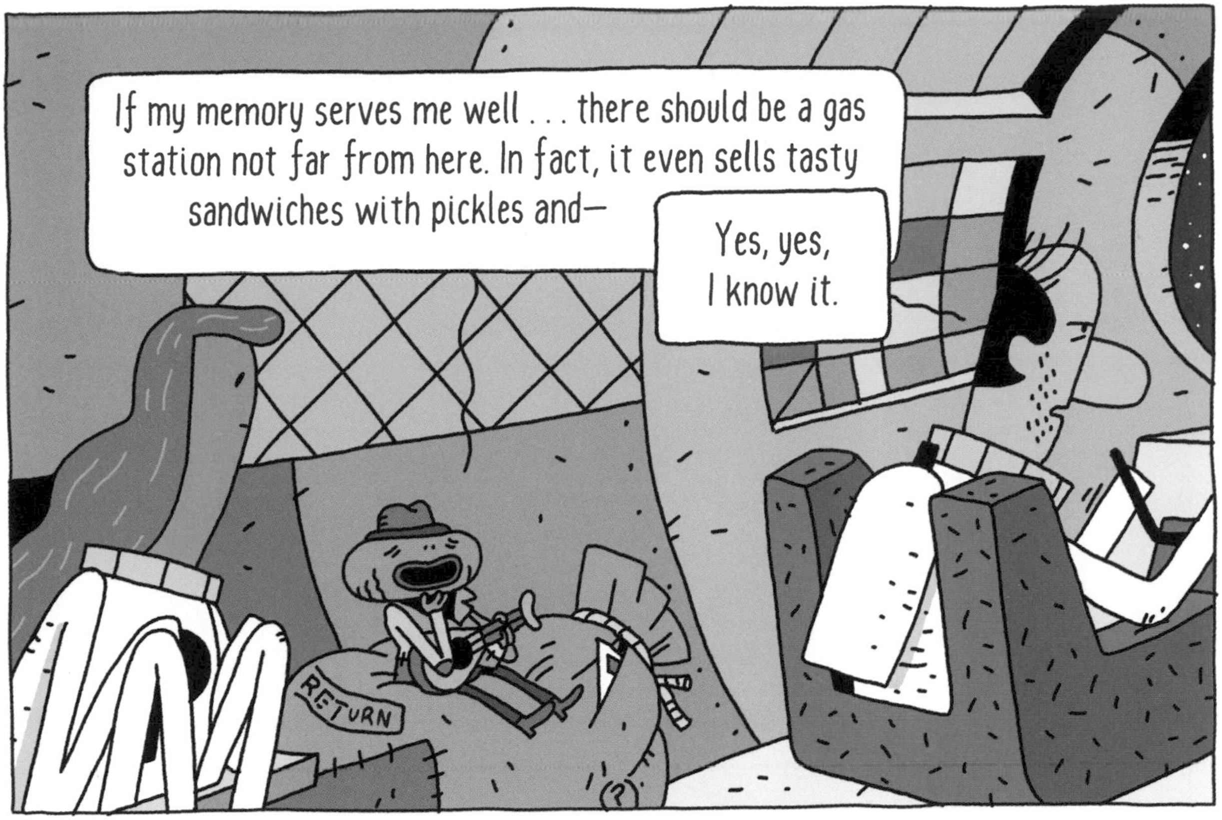
If my memory serves me well . . . there should be a gas station not far from here. In fact, it even sells tasty sandwiches with pickles and—
Yes, yes, I know it.
RETURN

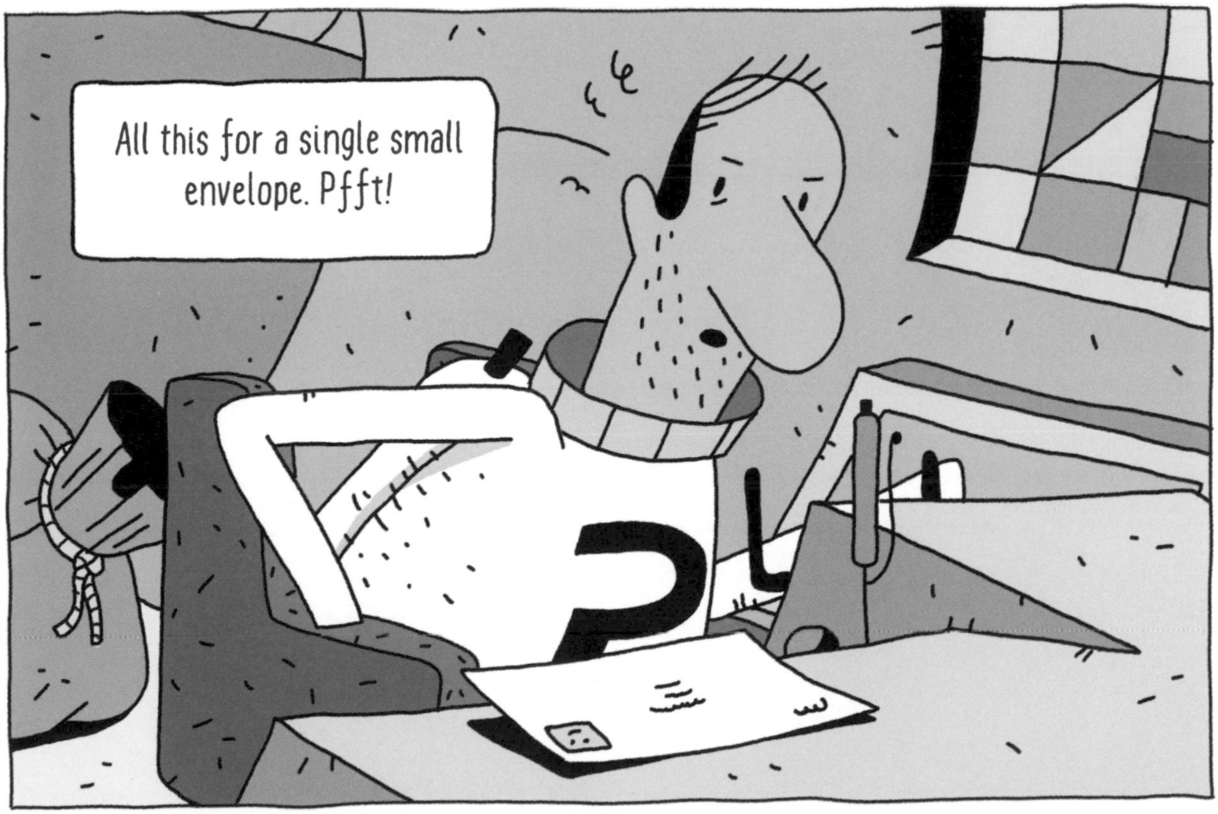
All this for a single small envelope. Pfft!

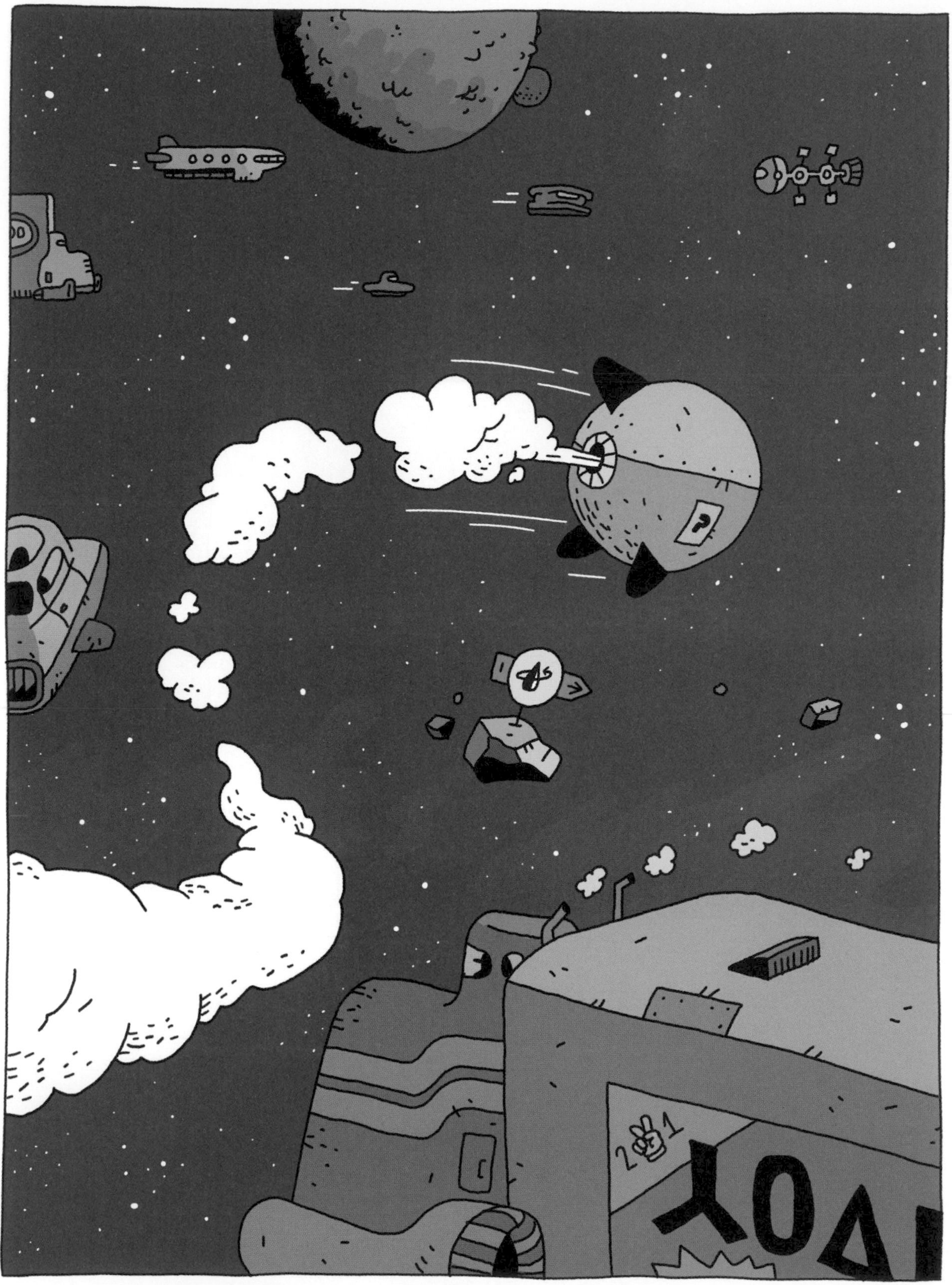

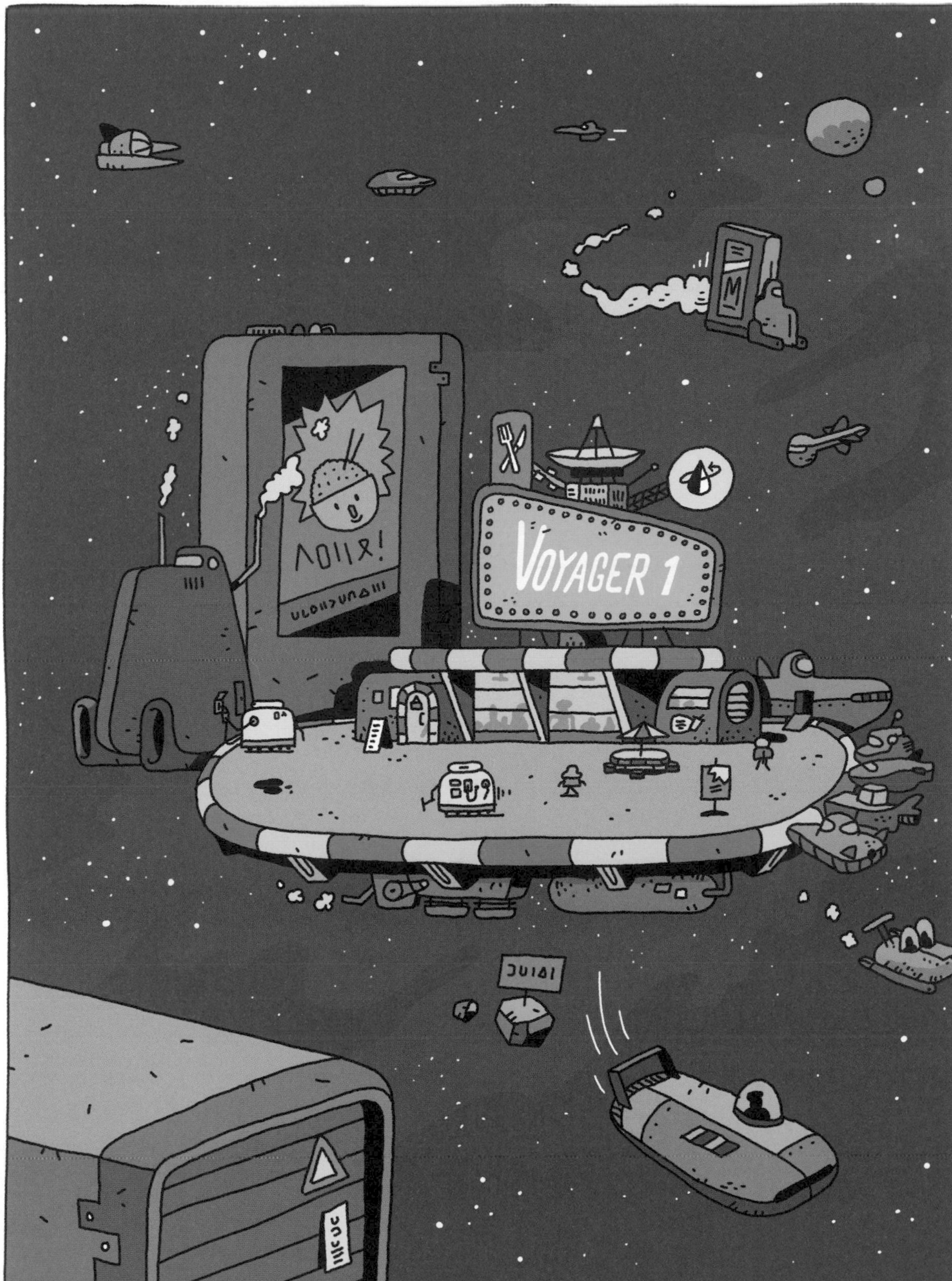
VOYAGER 1

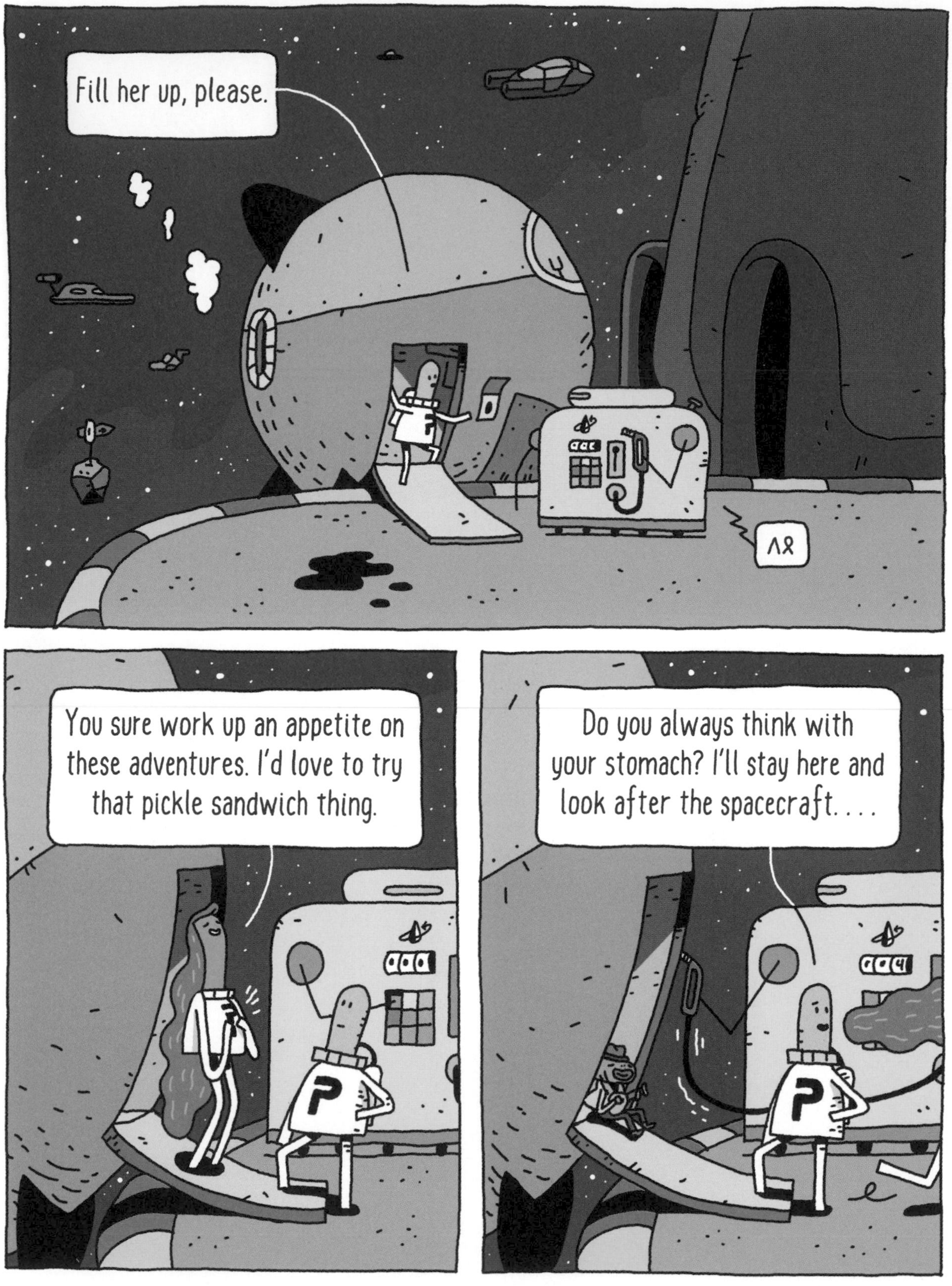
Fill her up, please.
You sure work up an appetite on these adventures. I'd love to try that pickle sandwich thing.
Do you always think with your stomach? I'll stay here and look after the spacecraft. . . .

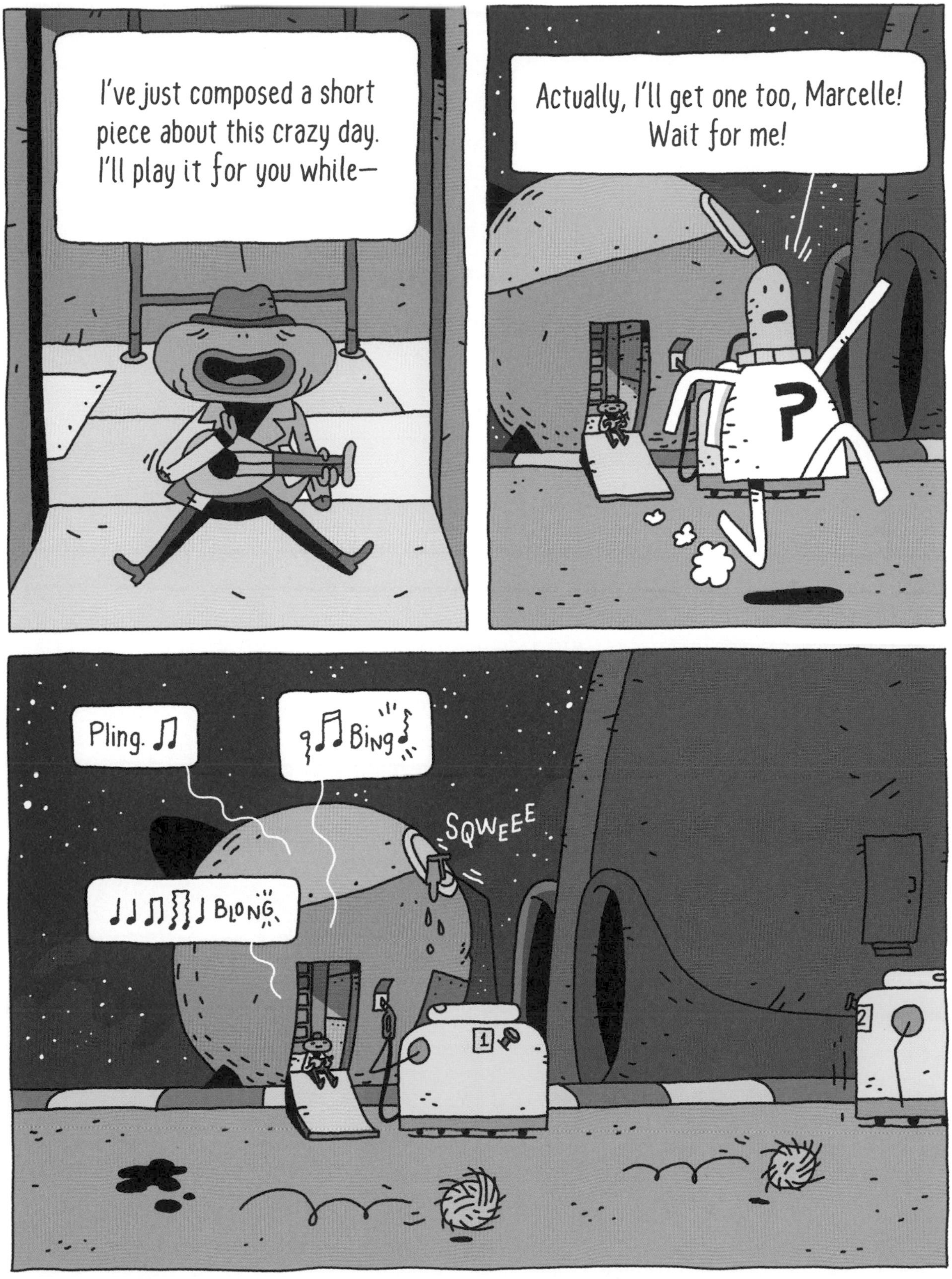
I've just composed a short piece about this crazy day. I'll play it for you while—
Actually, I'll get one too, Marcelle! Wait for me!
Pling.
Bing
Blong
SQWEEE
1
2

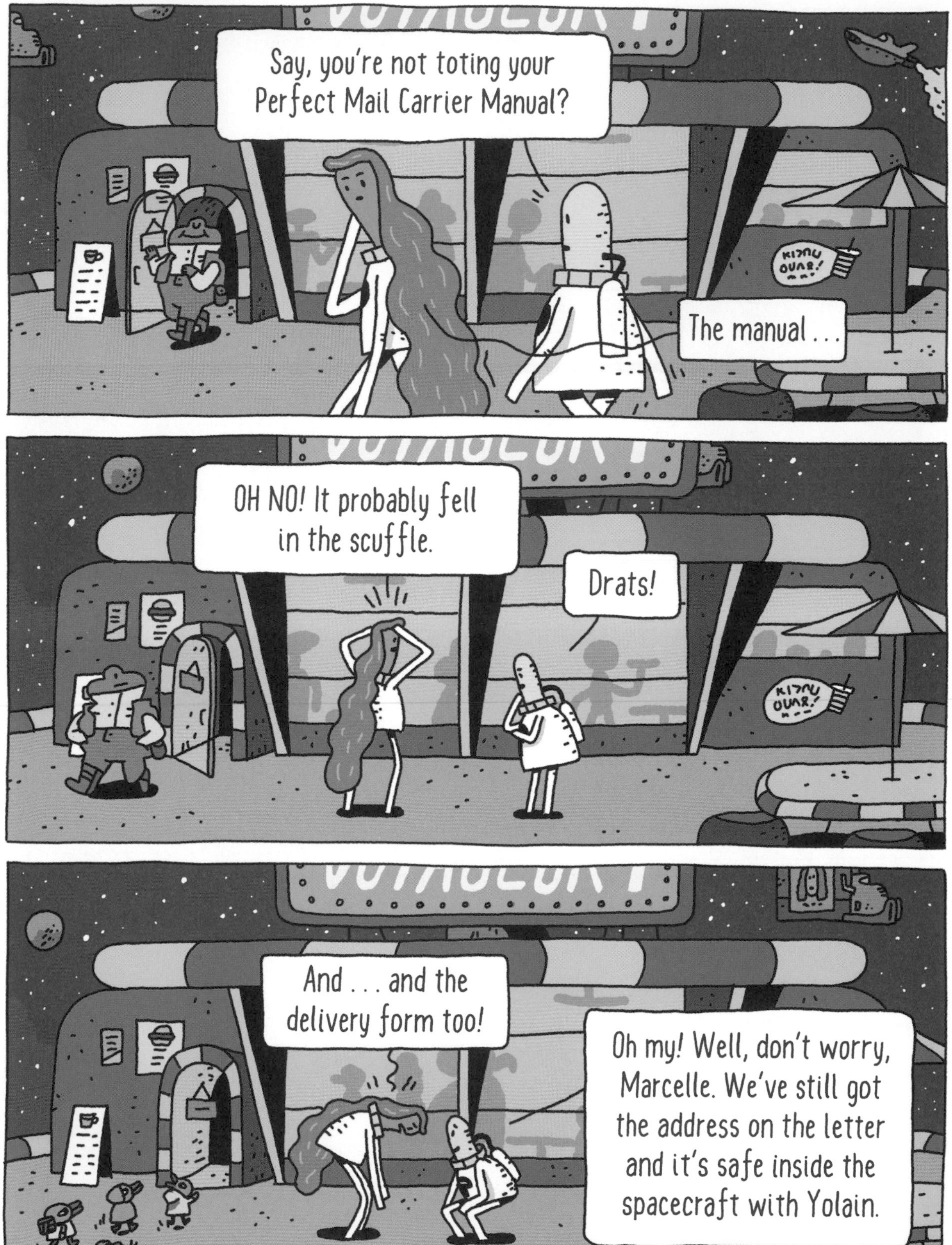
Say, you're not toting your Perfect Mail Carrier Manual?
The manual . . .
OH NO! It probably fell in the scuffle.
Drats!
And . . . and the delivery form too!
Oh my! Well, don't worry, Marcelle. We've still got the address on the letter and it's safe inside the spacecraft with Yolain.

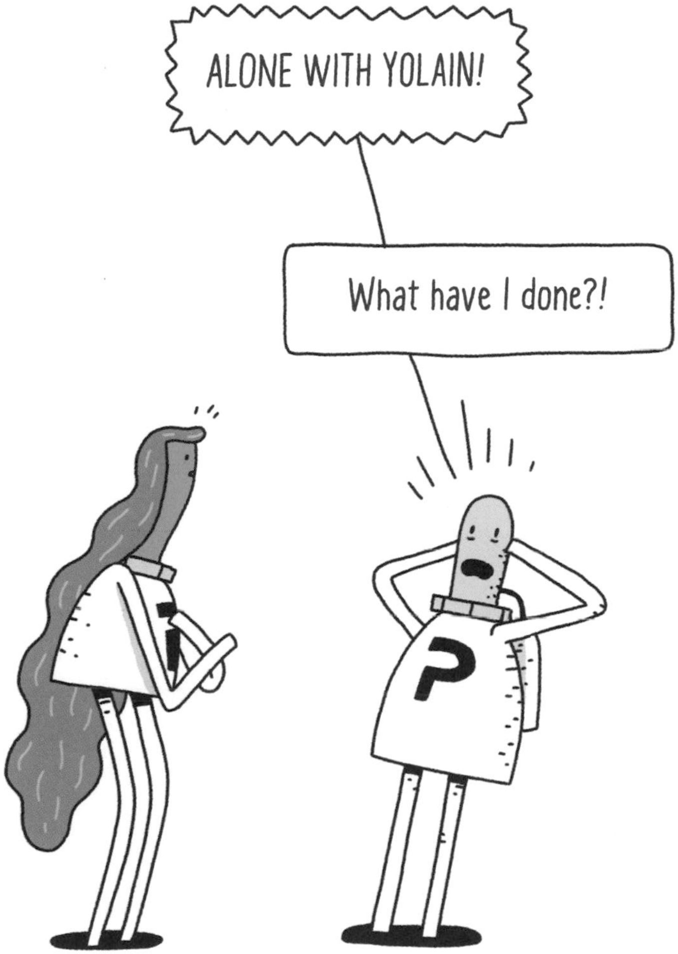
ALONE WITH YOLAIN!
What have I done?!

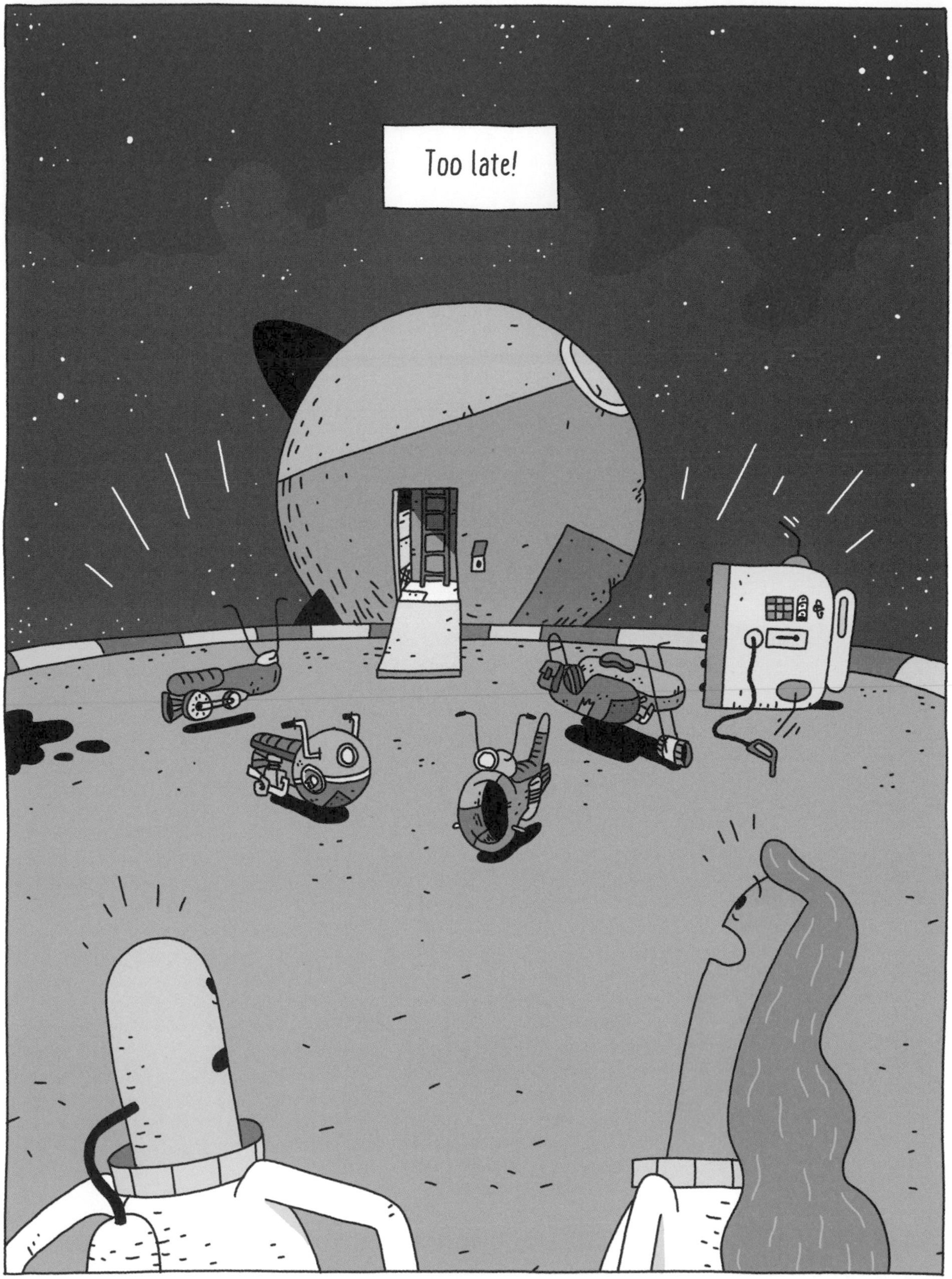
Too late!

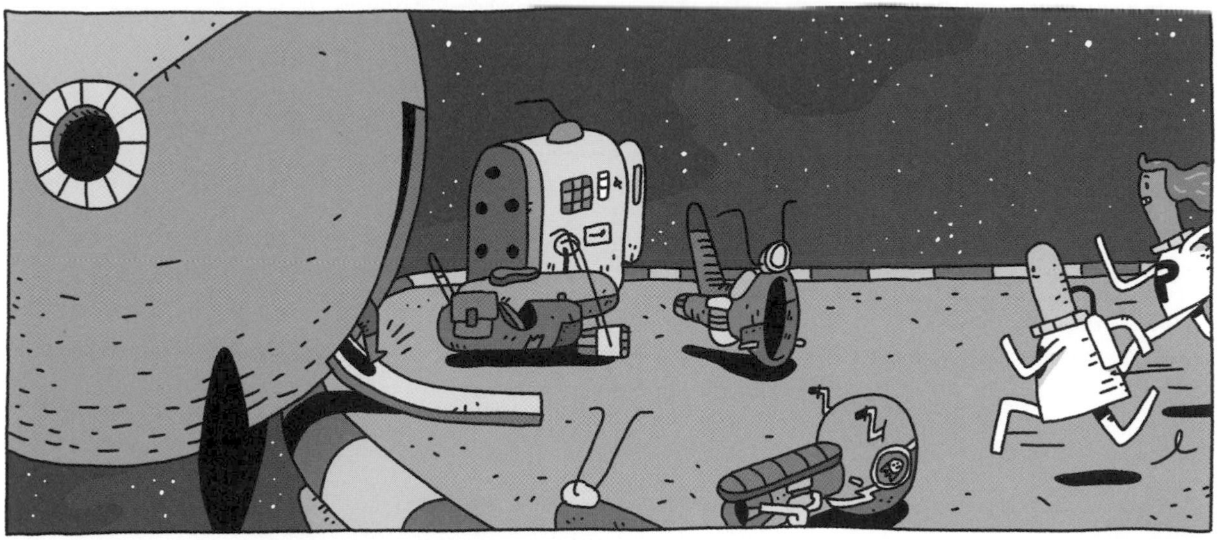

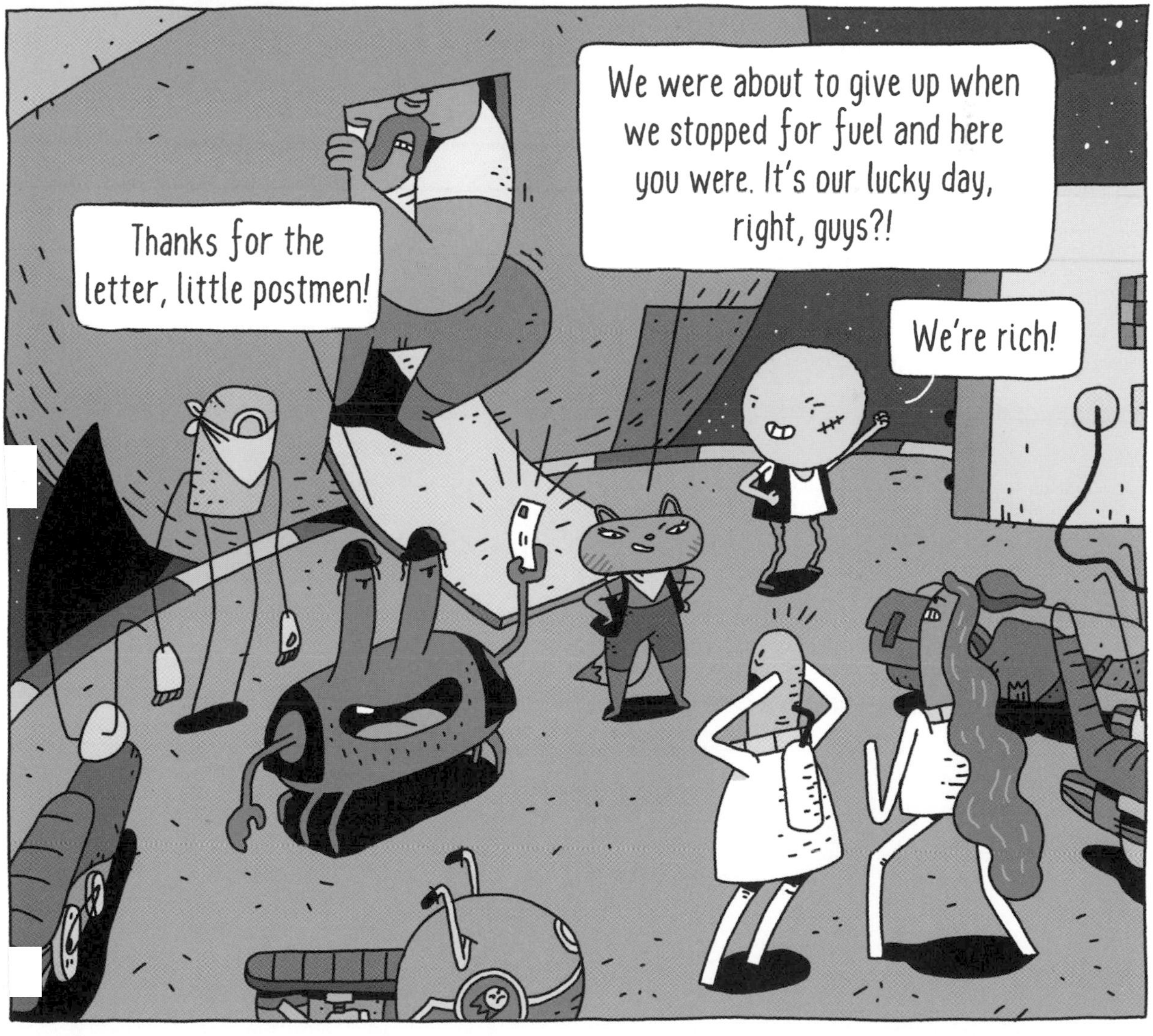
Thanks for the letter, little postmen!
We were about to give up when we stopped for fuel and here you were. It's our lucky day, right, guys?!
We're rich!

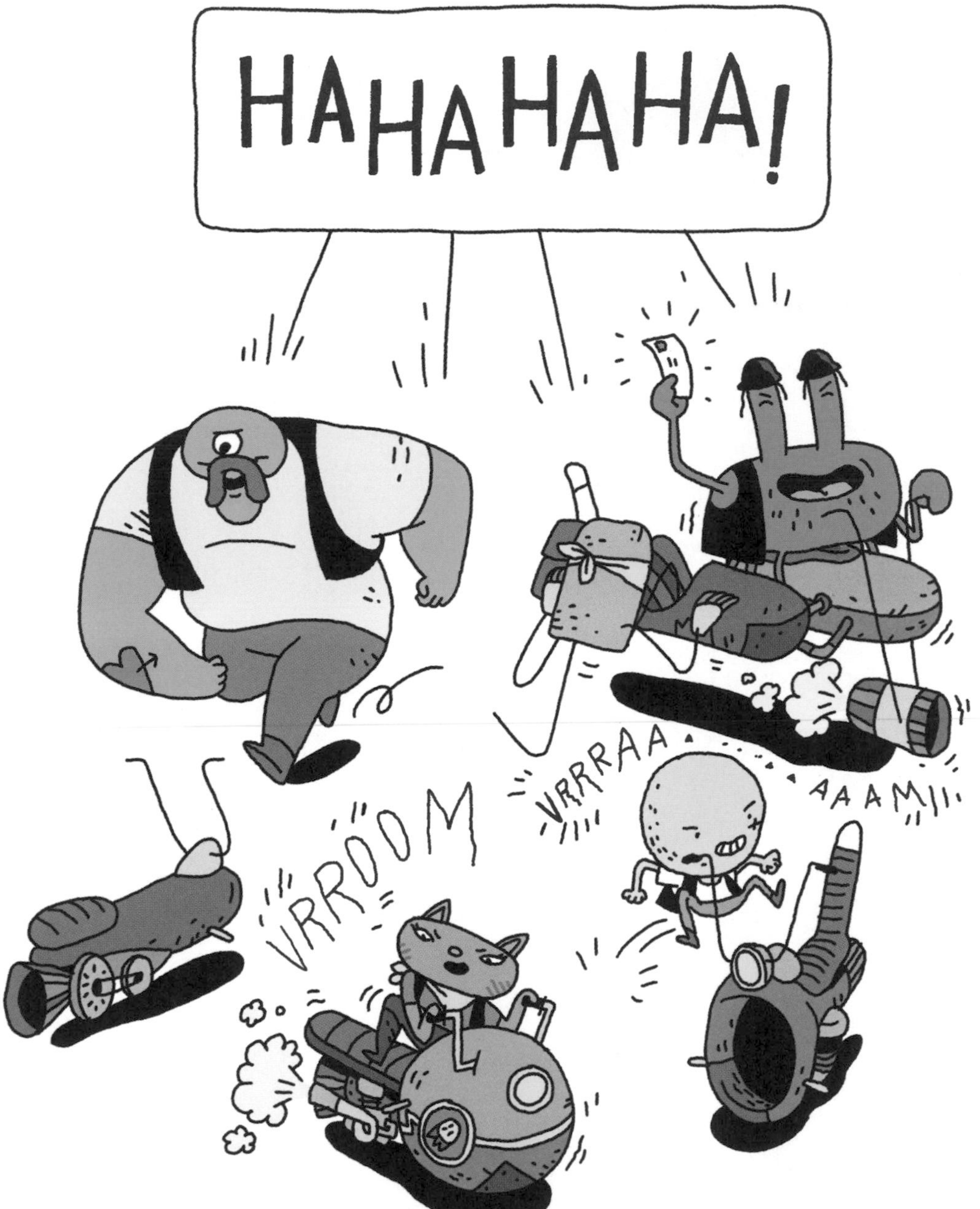
HAHAHAHAHA!
VRRRAA AAAM
VRROOM

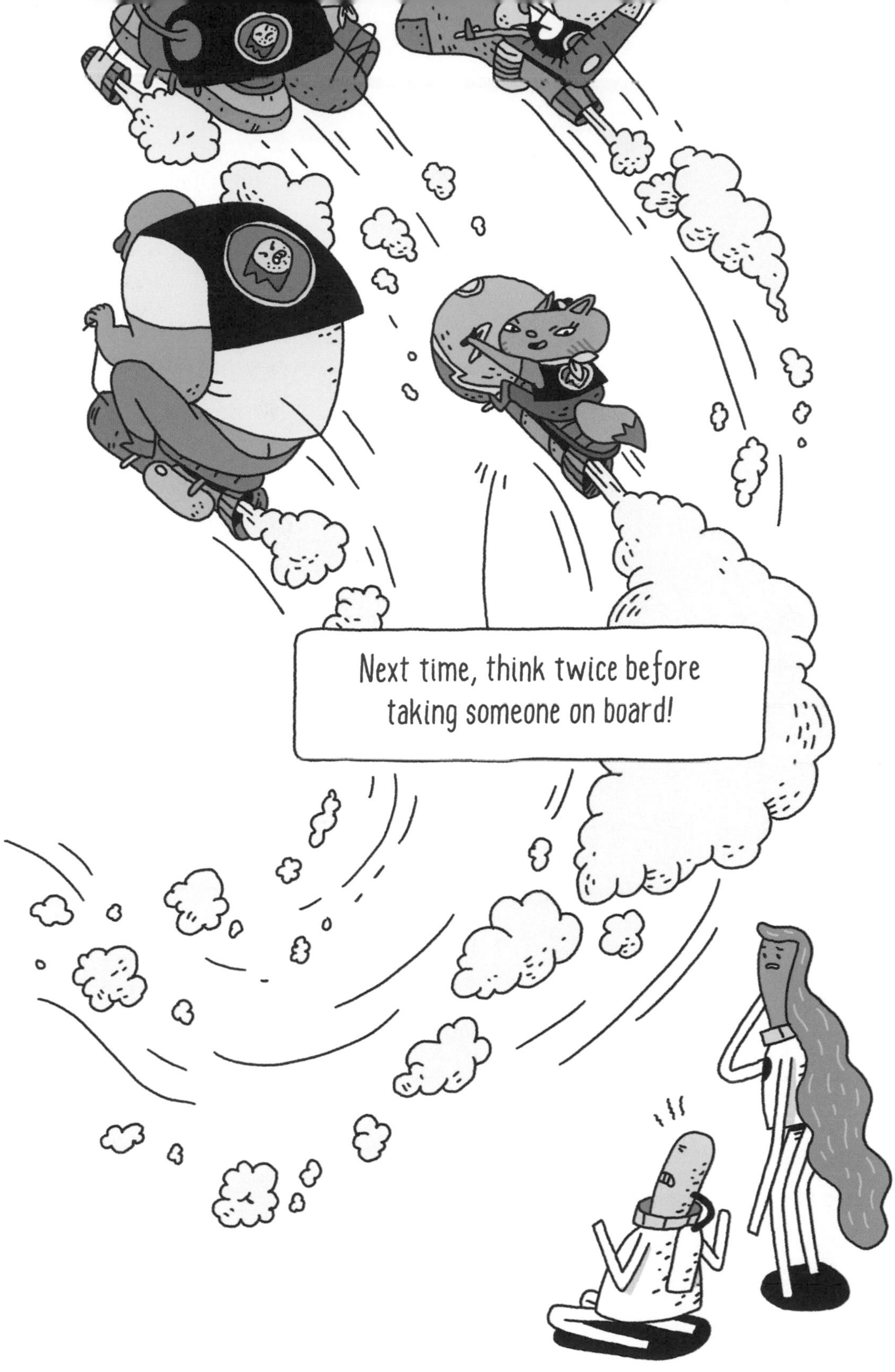
Next time, think twice before taking someone on board!

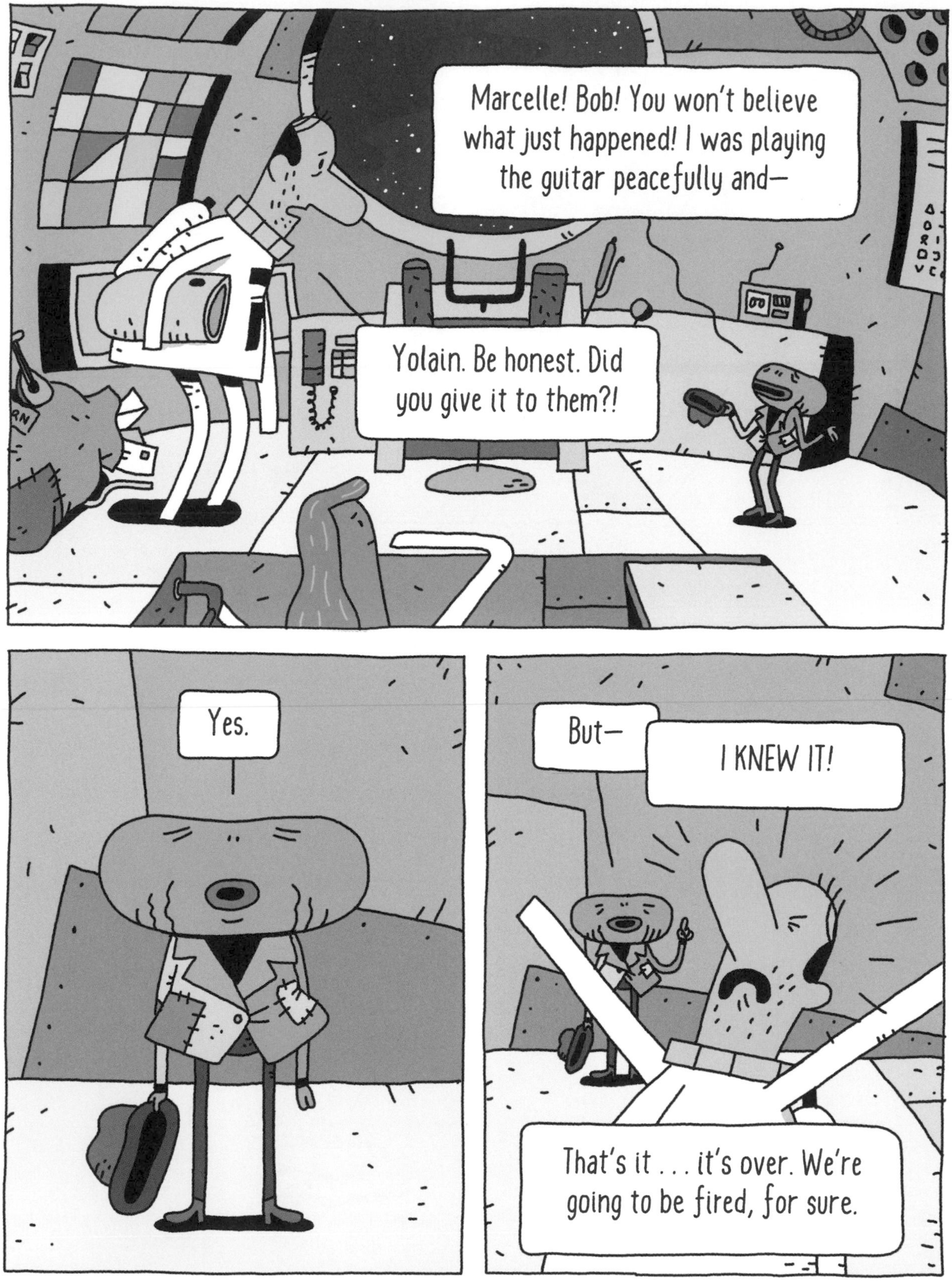
Marcelle! Bob! You won't believe what just happened! I was playing the guitar peacefully and—
Yolain. Be honest. Did you give it to them?!
Yes.
But—
I KNEW IT!
That's it . . . it's over. We're going to be fired, for sure.

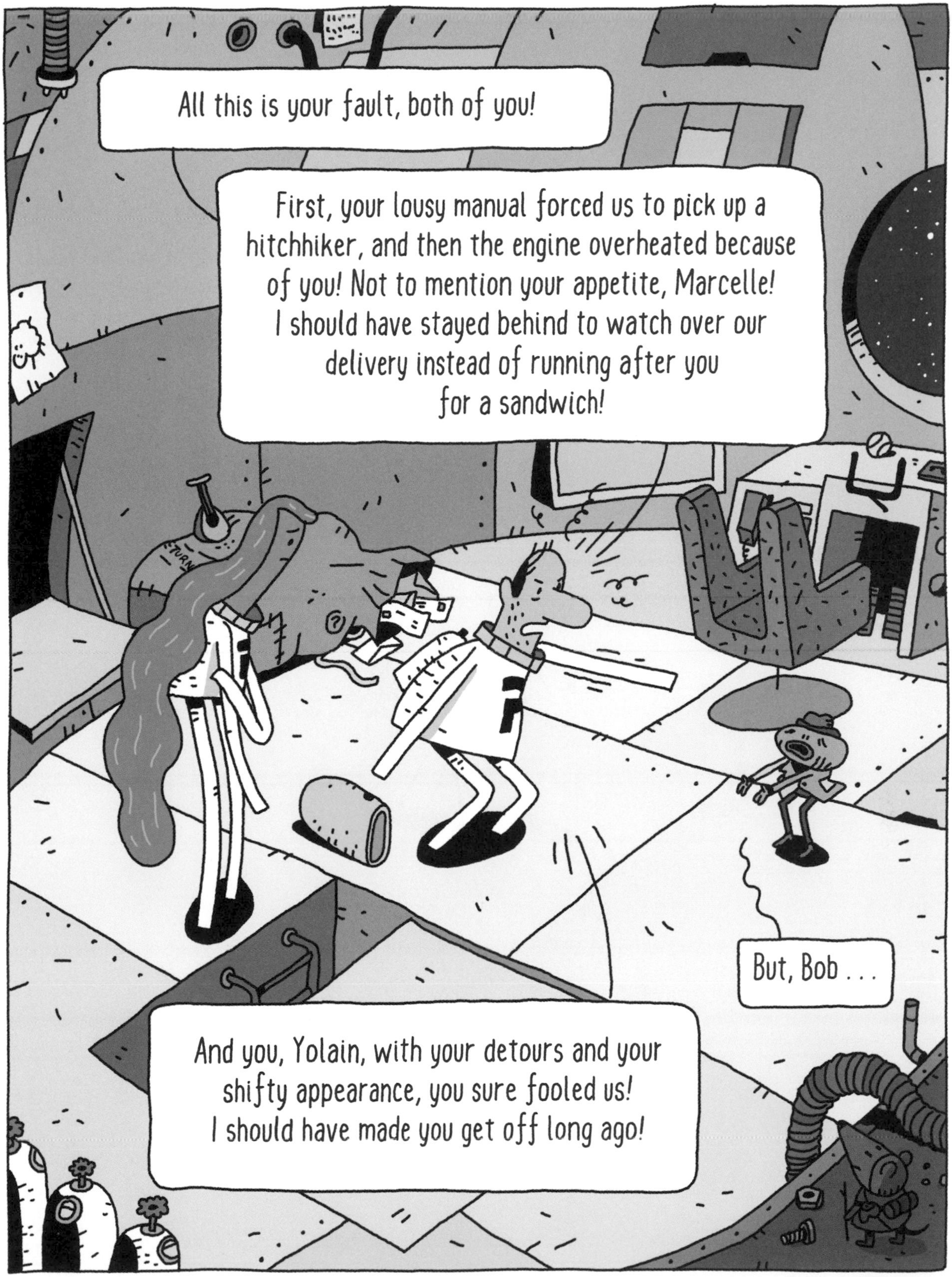
All this is your fault, both of you!
First, your lousy manual forced us to pick up a hitchhiker, and then the engine overheated because of you! Not to mention your appetite, Marcelle! I should have stayed behind to watch over our delivery instead of running after you for a sandwich!
But, Bob . . .
And you, Yolain, with your detours and your shifty appearance, you sure fooled us! I should have made you get off long ago!

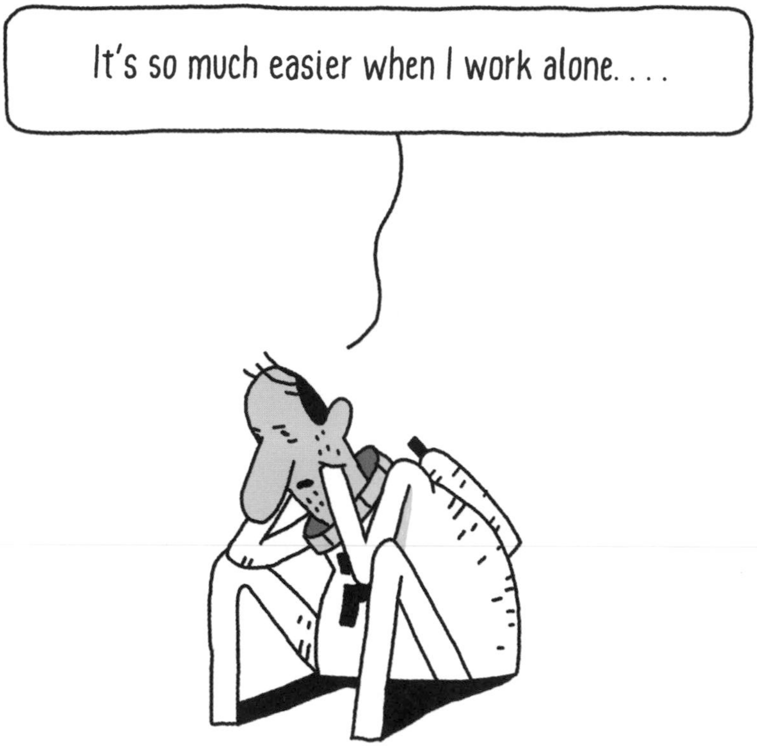
It's so much easier when I work alone. . . .

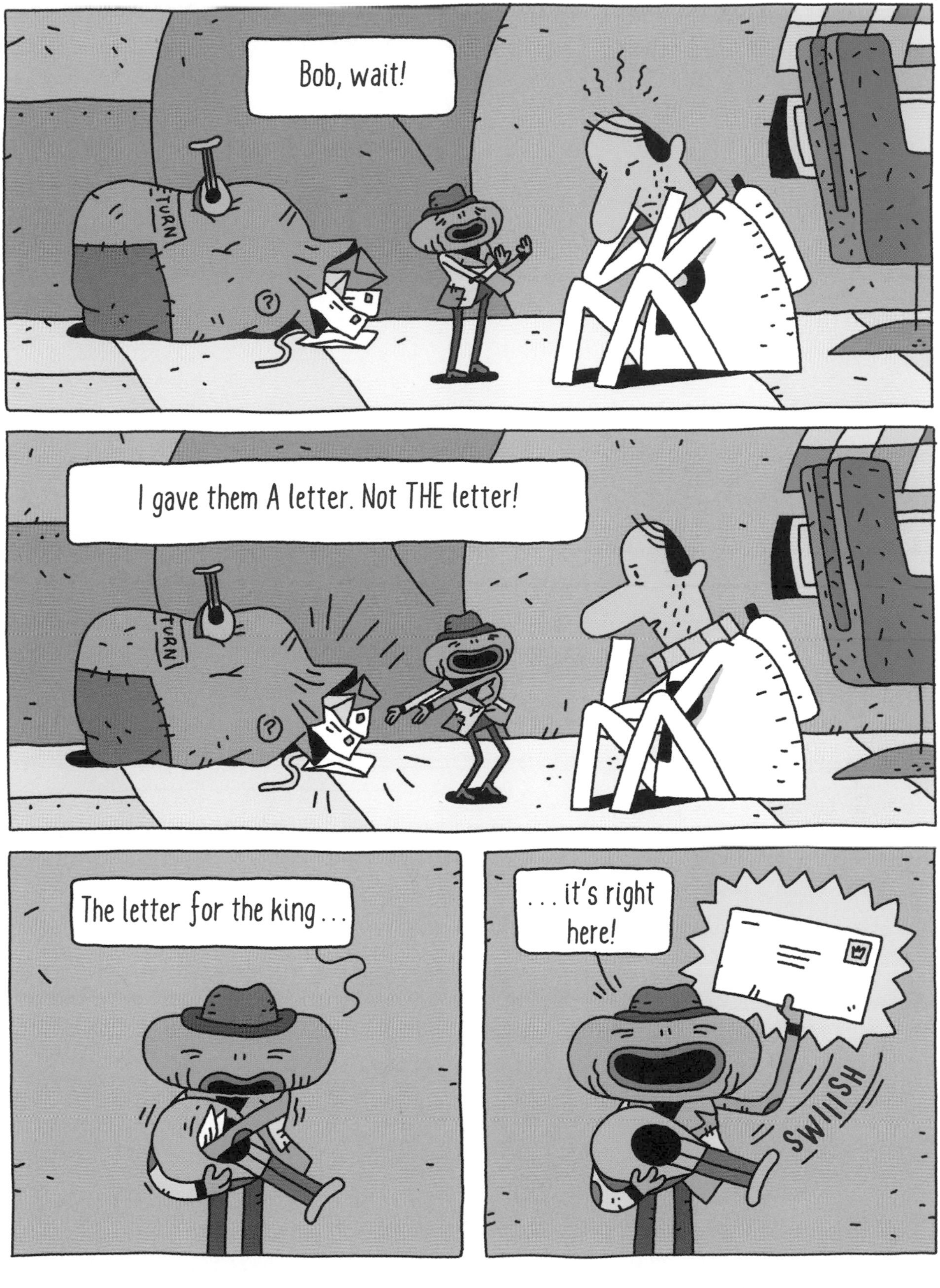
Bob, wait!
TURN
I gave them A letter. Not THE letter!
TURN
The letter for the king . . .
. . . it's right here!
SWIIISH

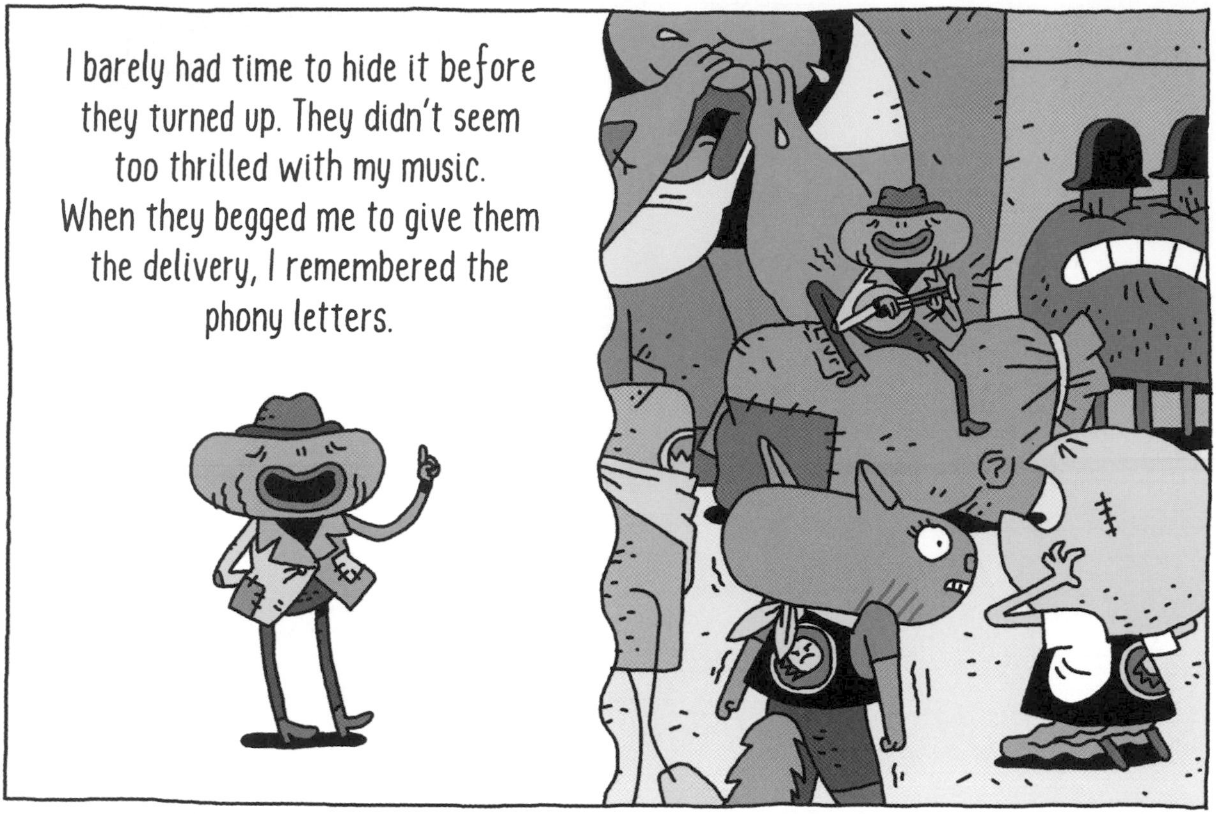
I barely had time to hide it before they turned up. They didn't seem too thrilled with my music. When they begged me to give them the delivery, I remembered the phony letters.

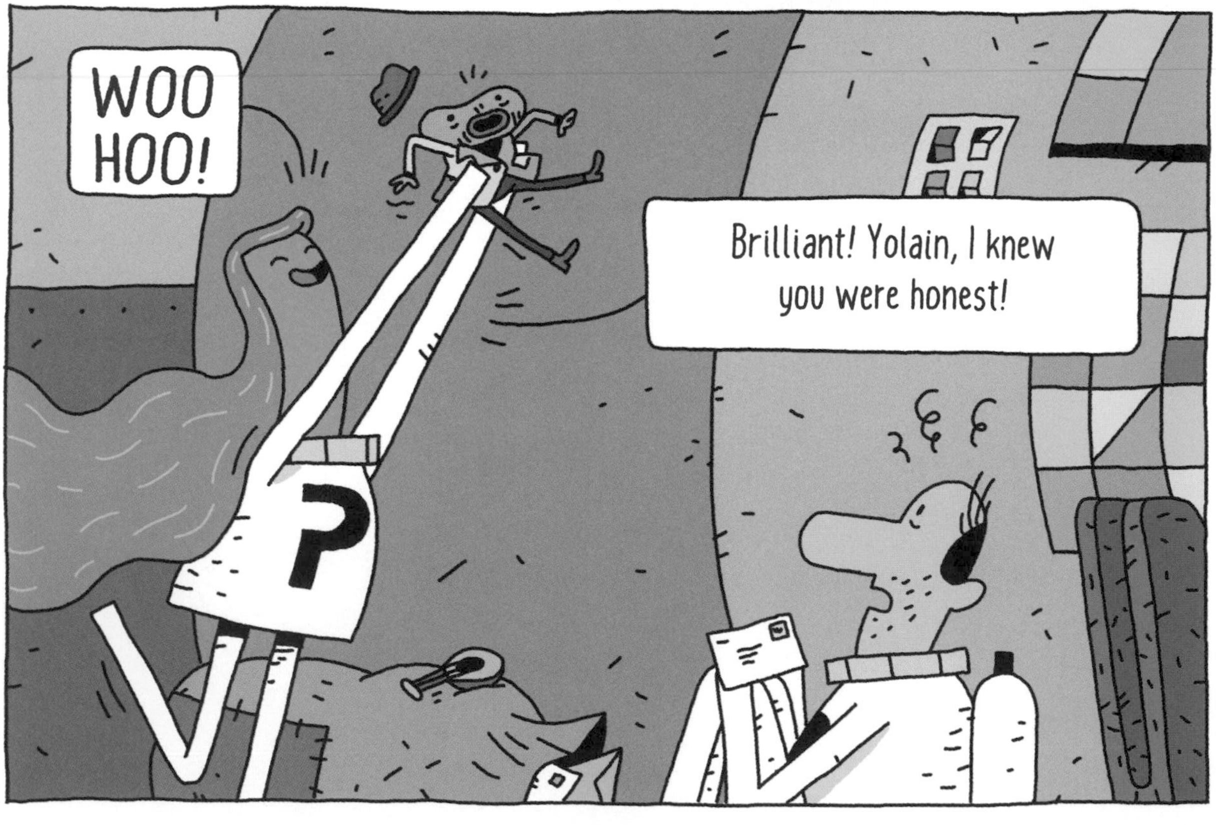
WOO HOO!
Brilliant! Yolain, I knew you were honest!

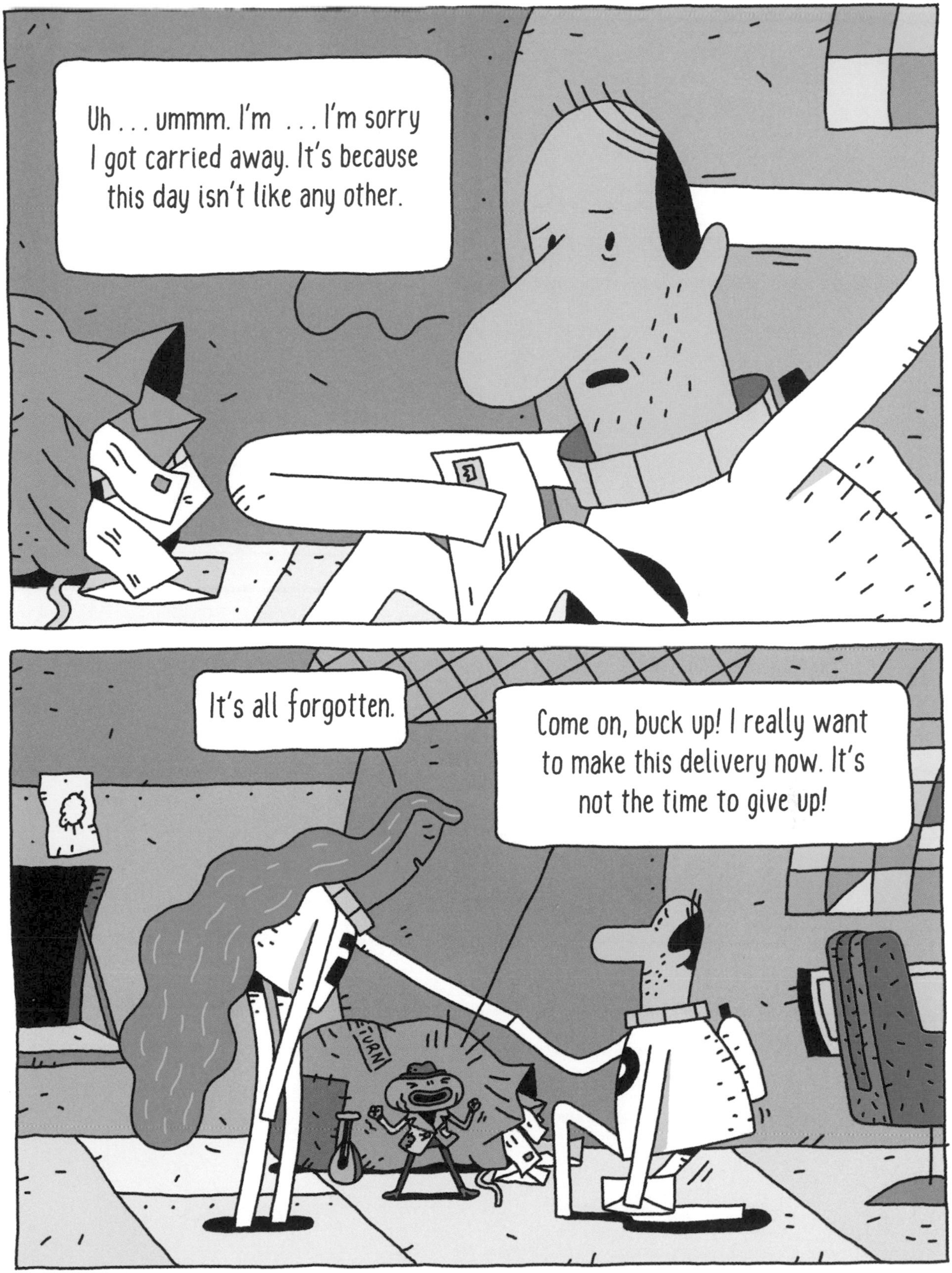
Uh . . . ummm. I'm . . . I'm sorry I got carried away. It's because this day isn't like any other.
It's all forgotten.
Come on, buck up! I really want to make this delivery now. It's not the time to give up!

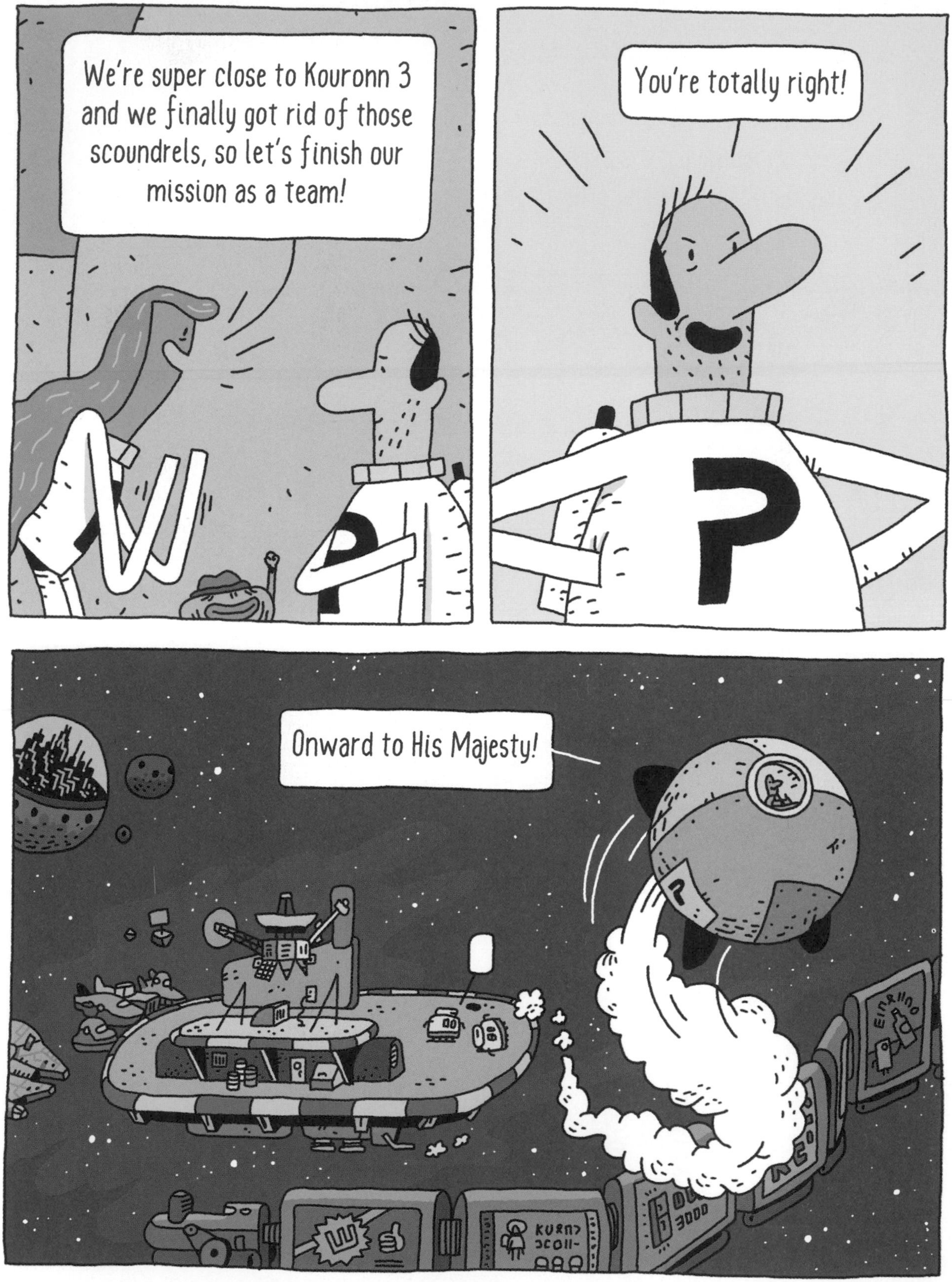
We're super close to Kouronn 3 and we finally got rid of those scoundrels, so let's finish our mission as a team!
You're totally right!
Onward to His Majesty!

STOP #7

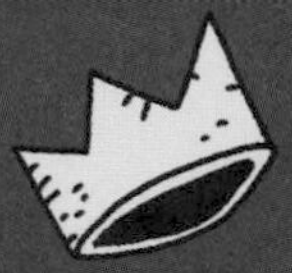

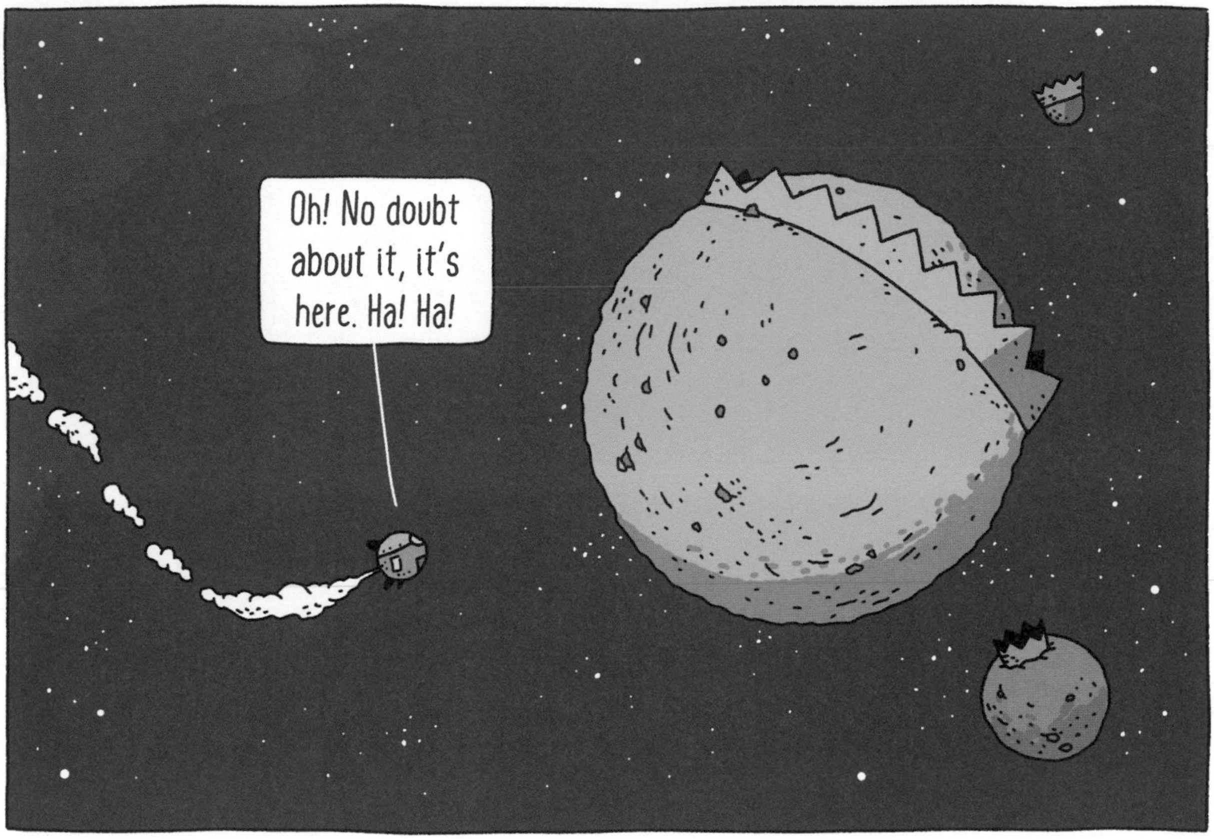
Oh! No doubt about it, it's here. Ha! Ha!

At last, Kouronn 3.

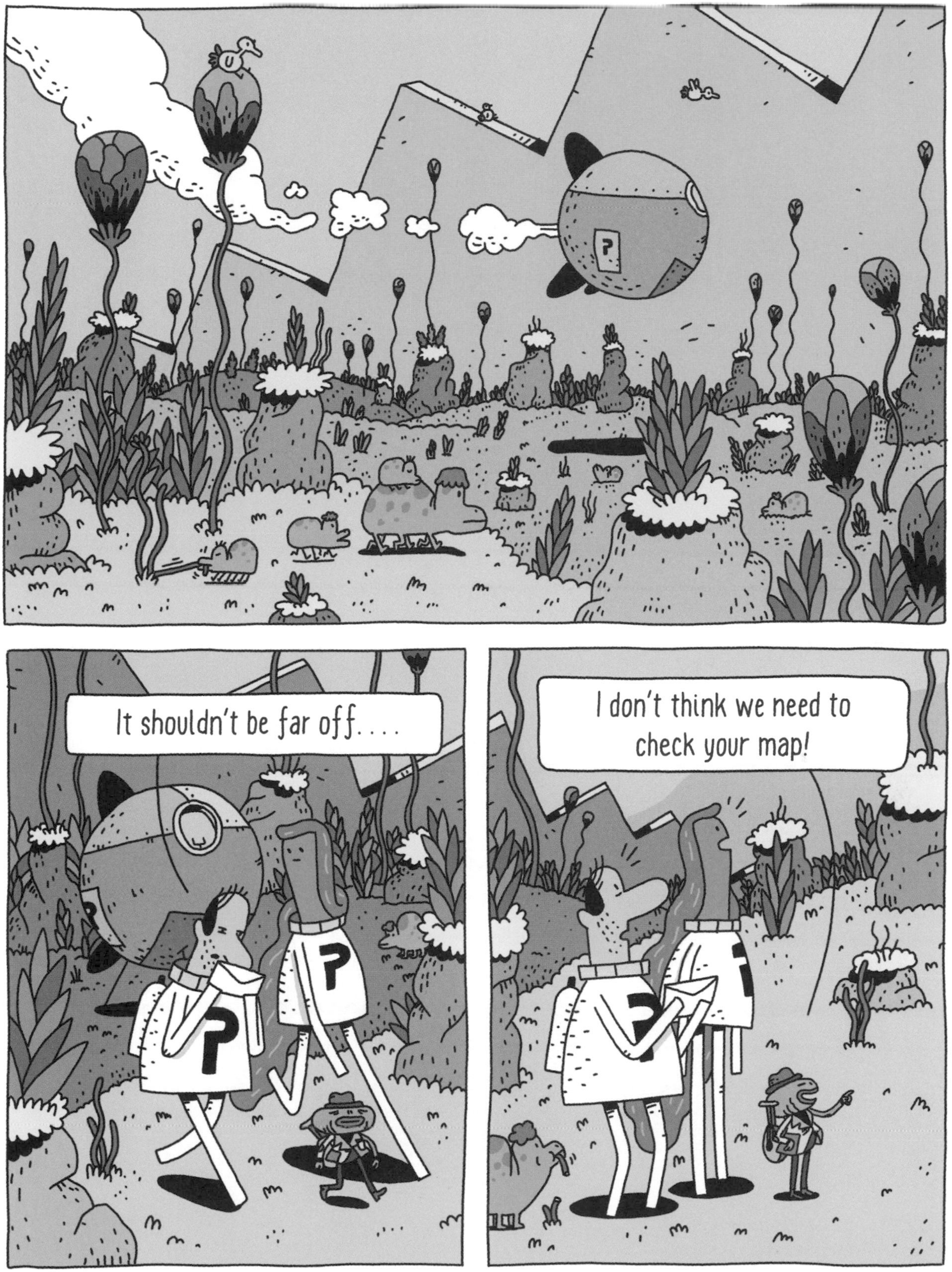
It shouldn't be far off....
I don't think we need to check your map!

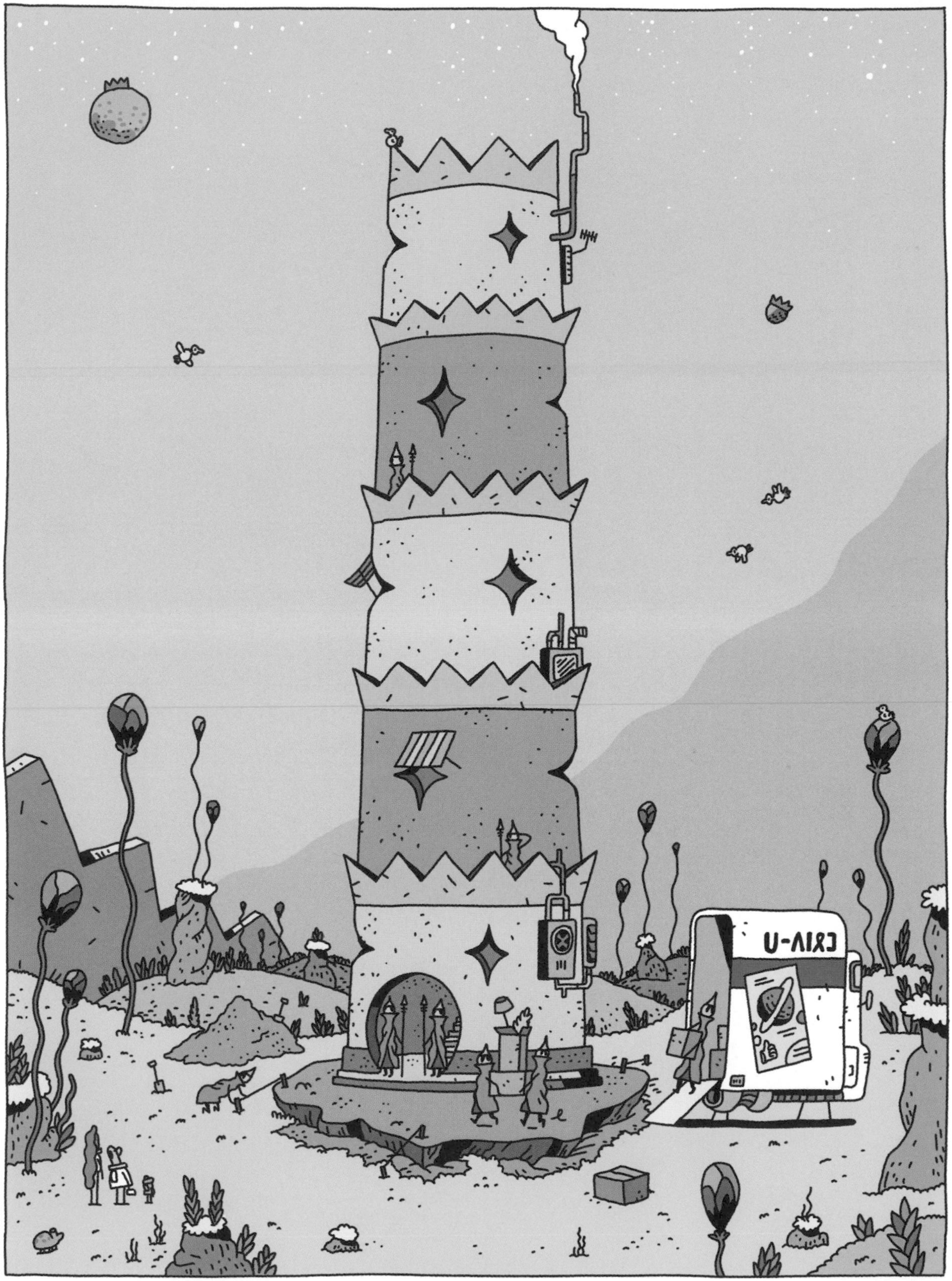

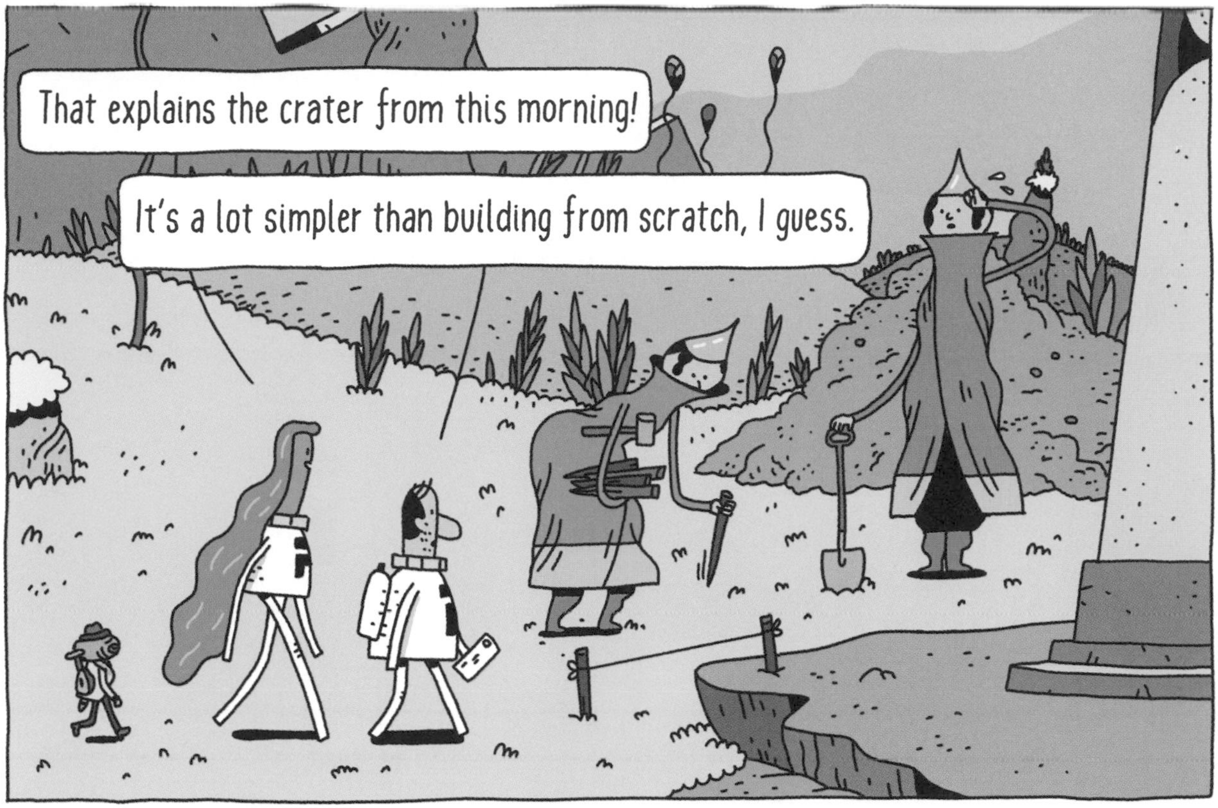
That explains the crater from this morning!
It's a lot simpler than building from scratch, I guess.

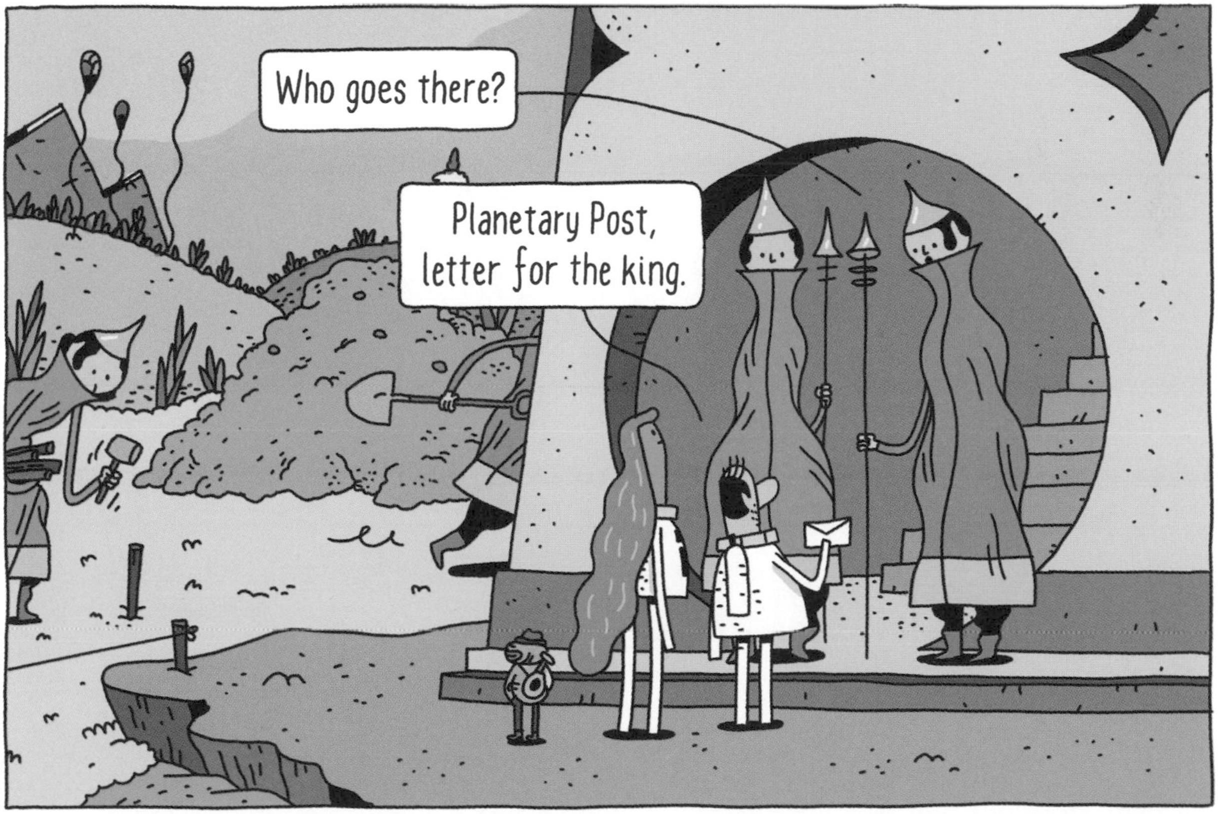
Who goes there?
Planetary Post,
letter for the king.

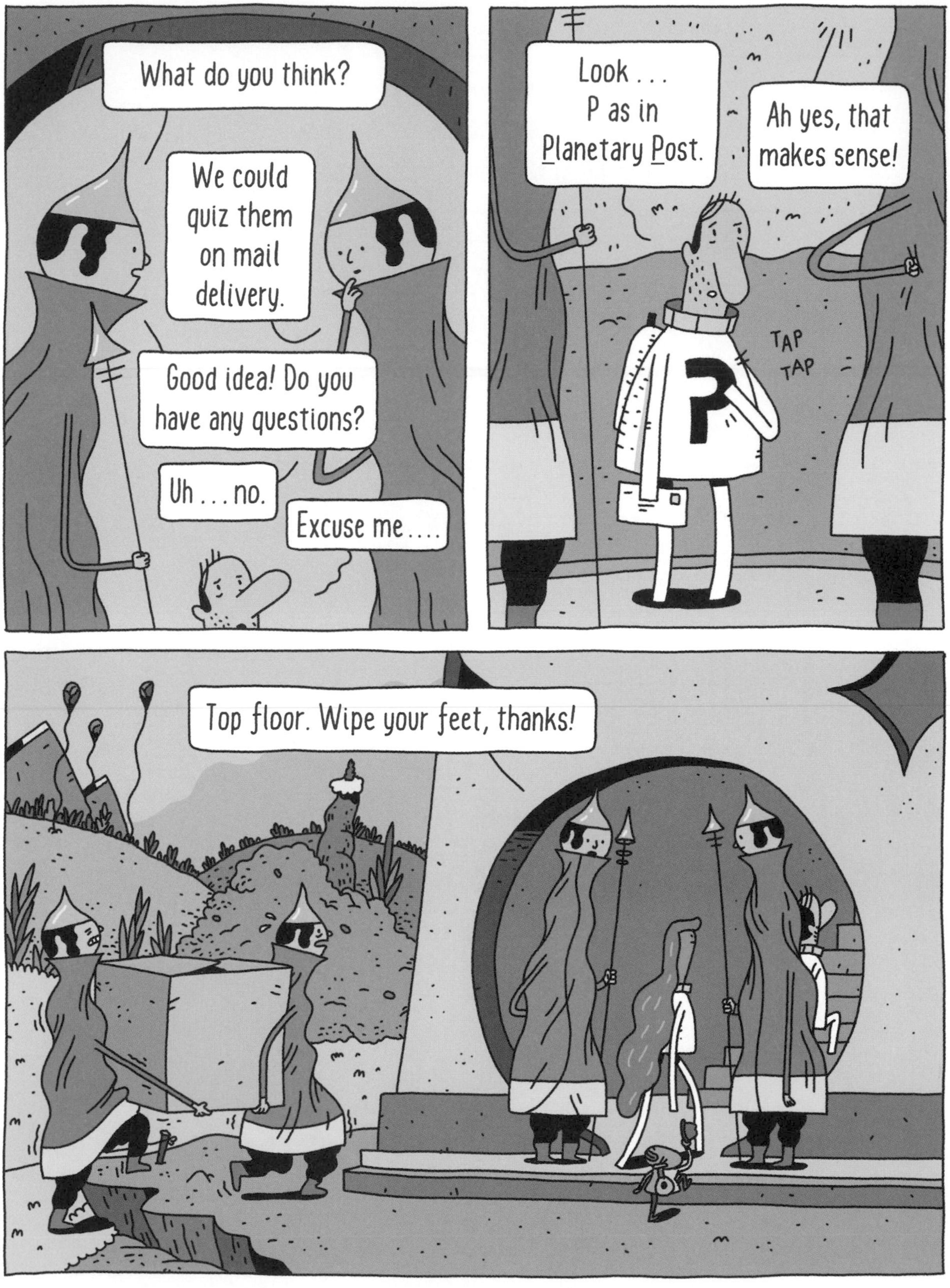
What do you think?
We could quiz them on mail delivery.
Good idea! Do you have any questions?
Uh . . . no.
Excuse me . . . .
Look . . . P as in Planetary Post.
Ah yes, that makes sense!
TAP TAP
Top floor. Wipe your feet, thanks!

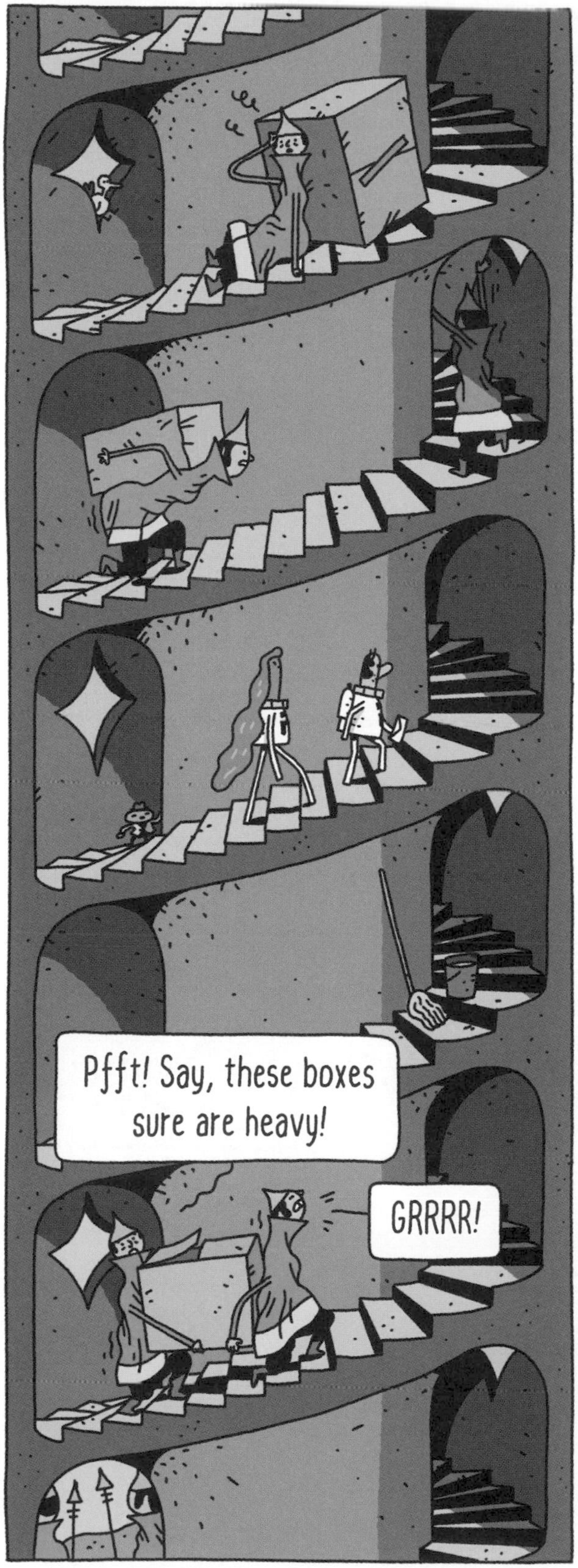
Pfft! Say, these boxes sure are heavy!
GRRRR!

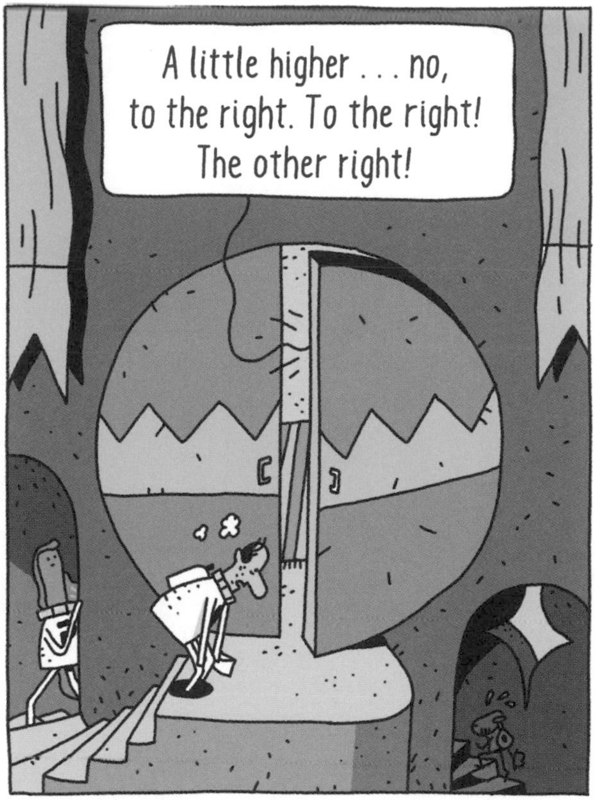
A little higher . . . no, to the right. To the right! The other right!

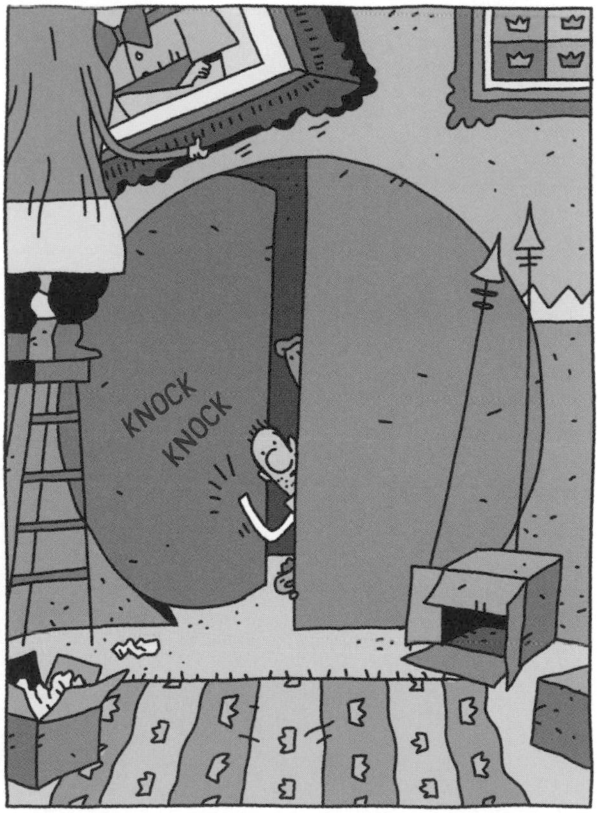
KNOCK
KNOCK

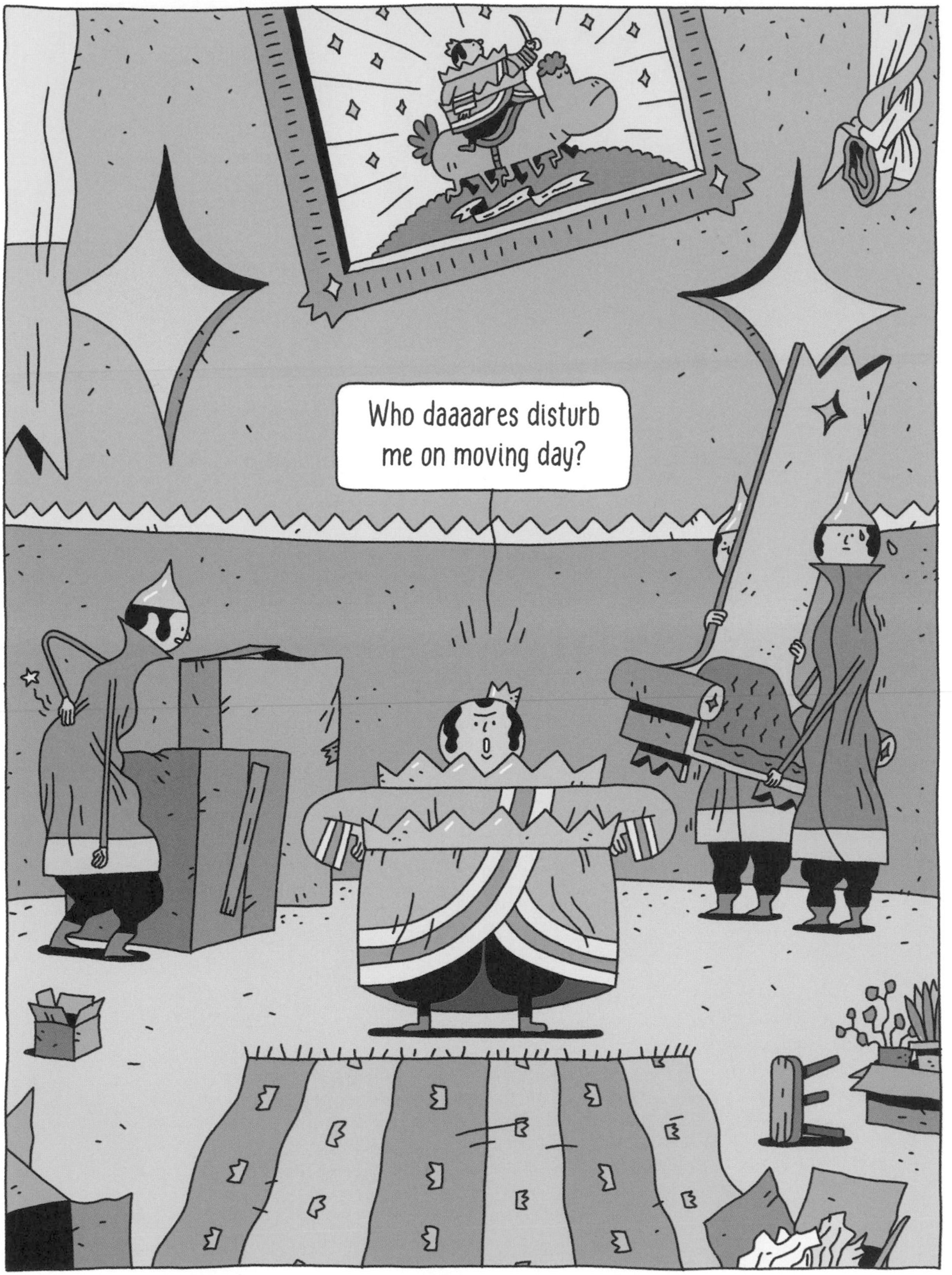
Who daaaares disturb me on moving day?

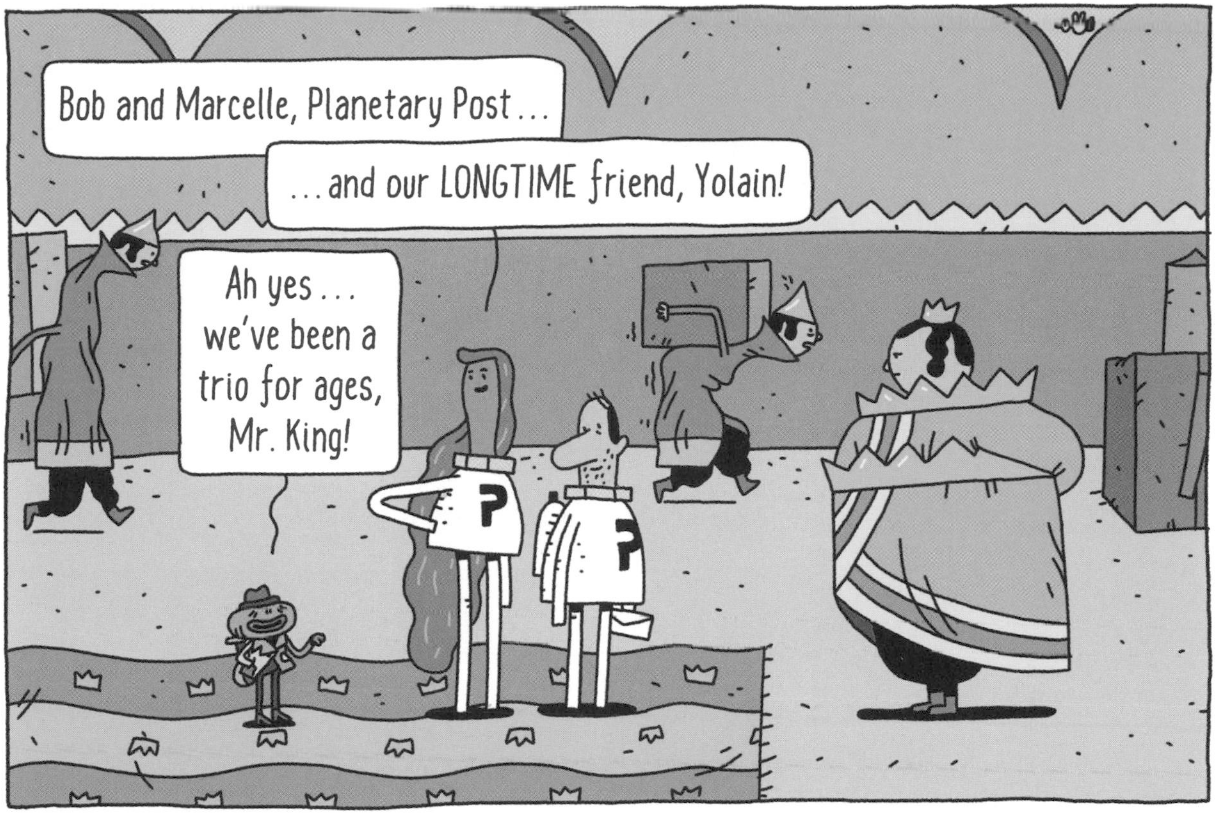
Bob and Marcelle, Planetary Post...
...and our LONGTIME friend, Yolain!
Ah yes... we've been a trio for ages, Mr. King!

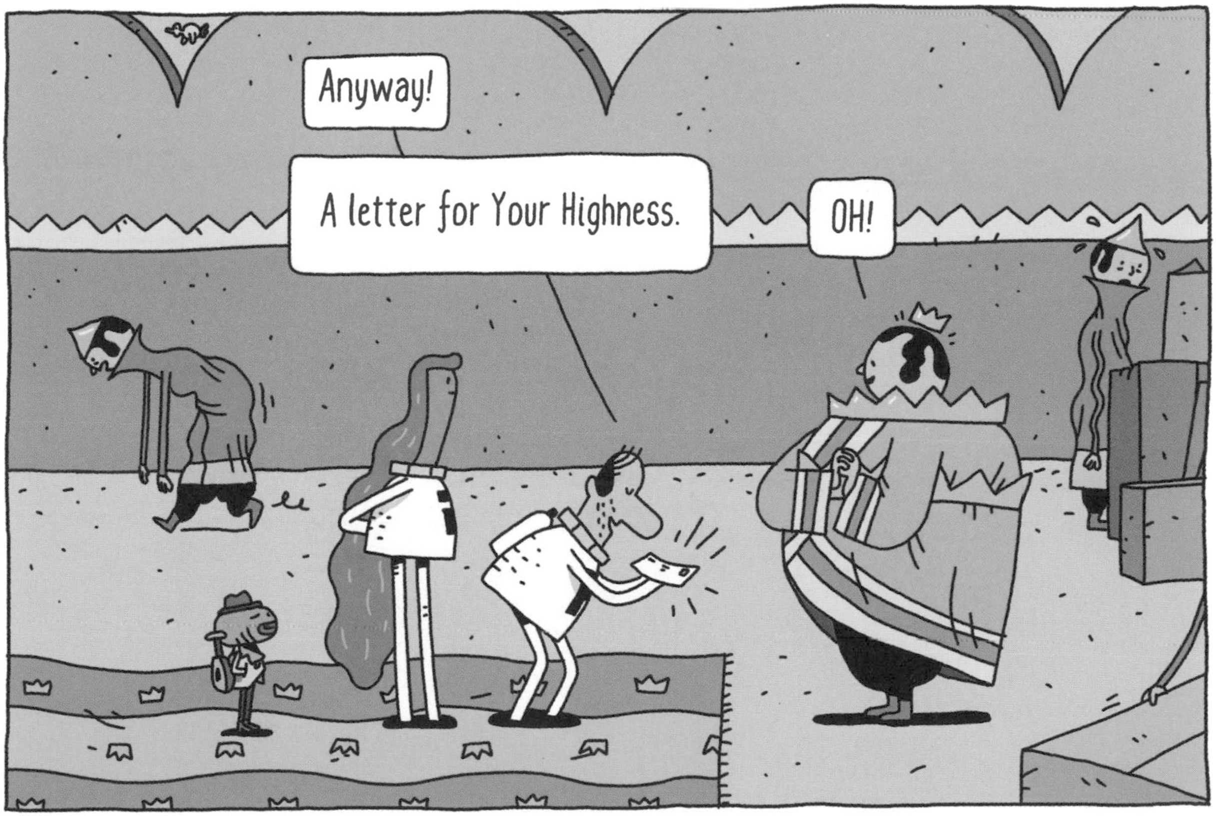
Anyway!
A letter for Your Highness.
OH!

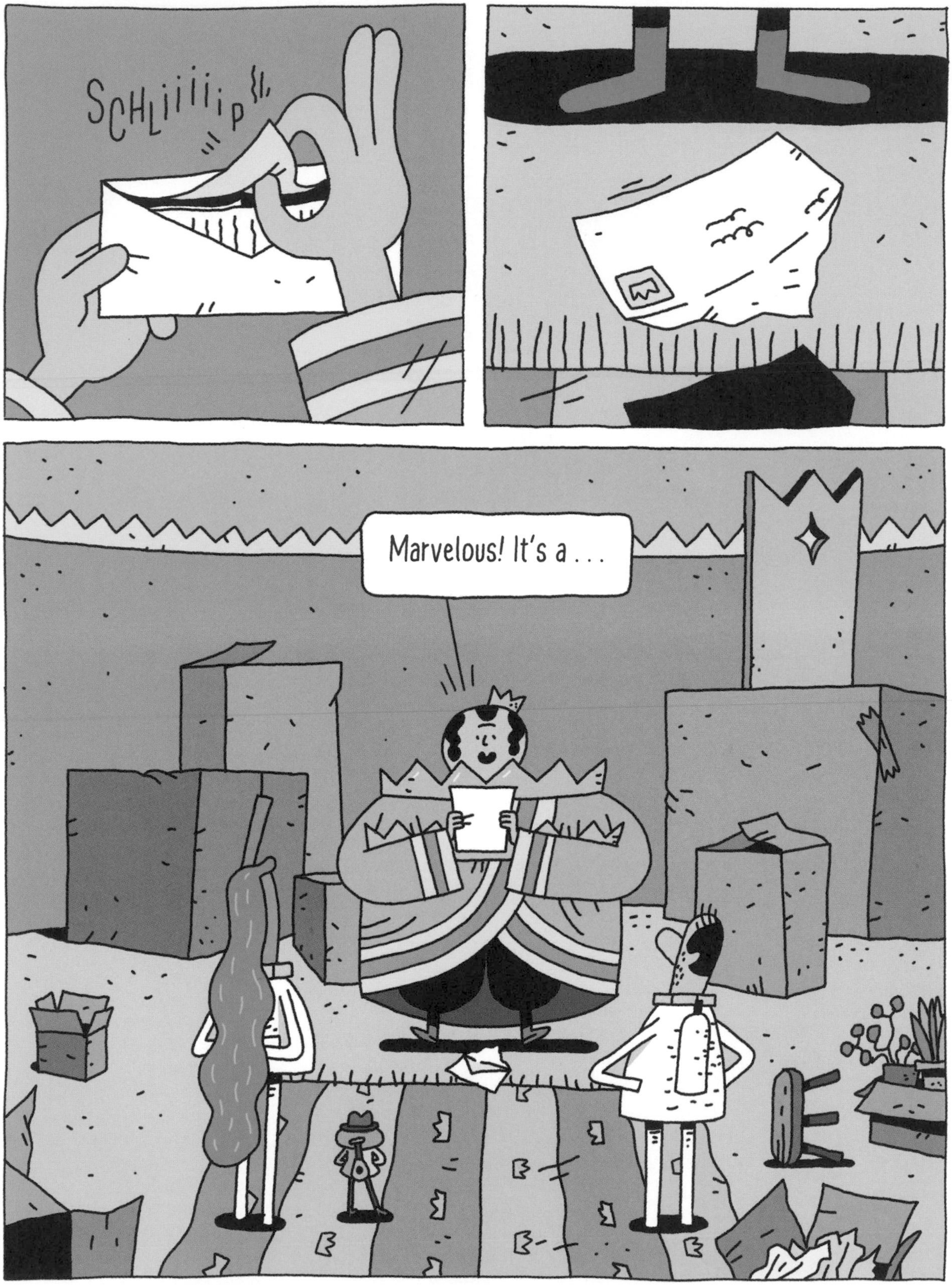
SCHLiiiiiP
Marvelous! It's a . . .

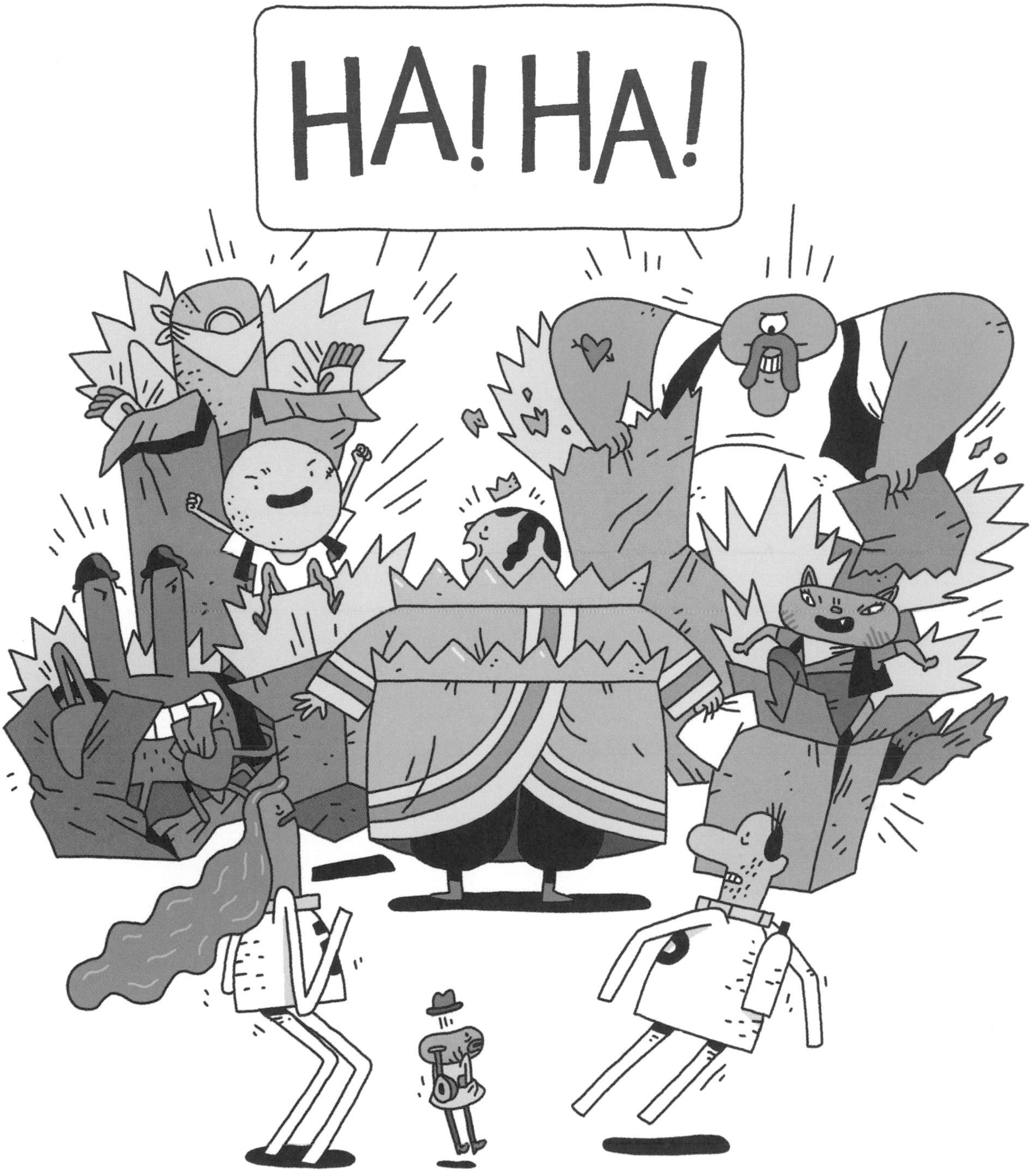
HA! HA!

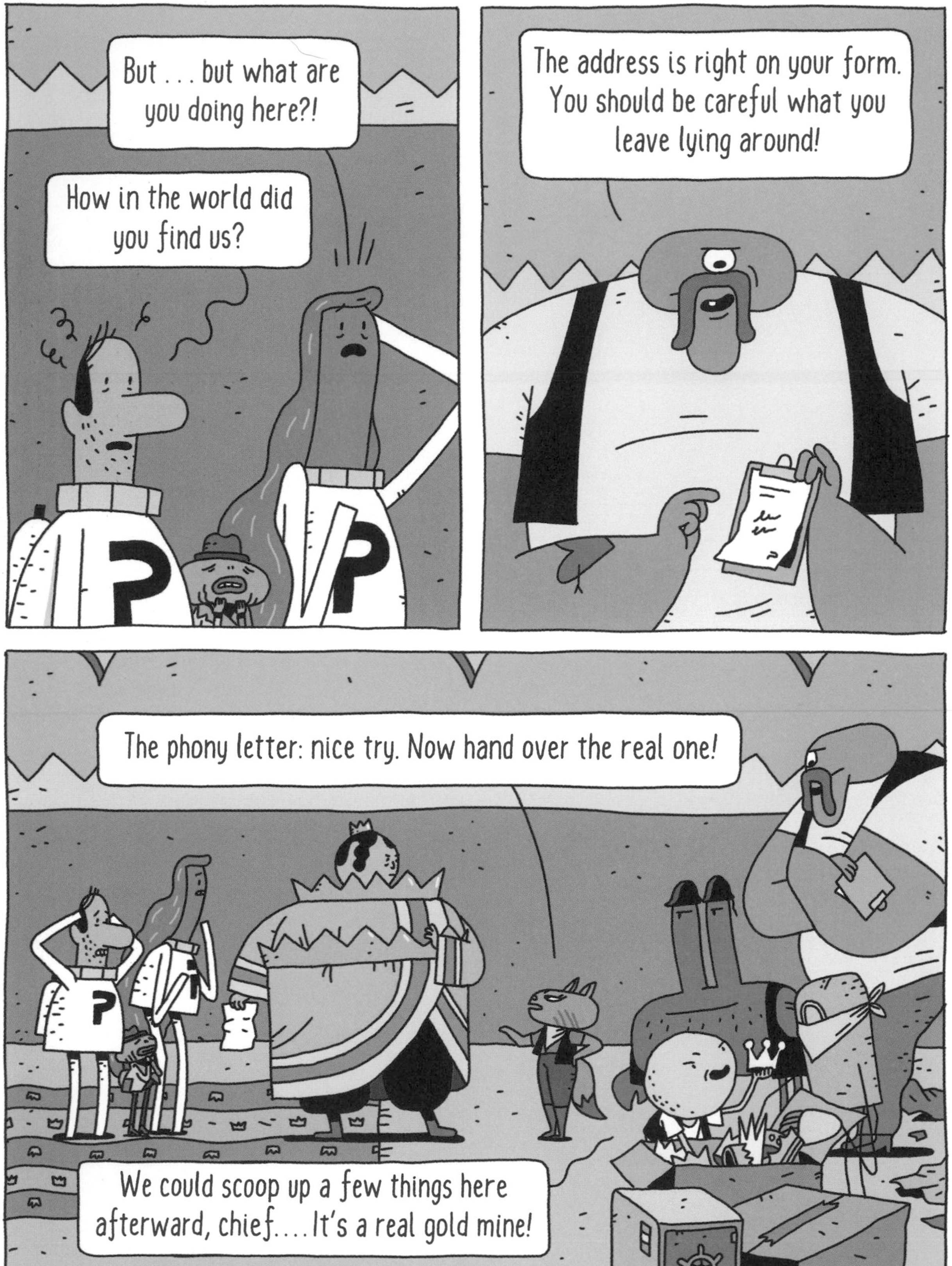
But . . . but what are you doing here?!
How in the world did you find us?
The address is right on your form. You should be careful what you leave lying around!
The phony letter: nice try. Now hand over the real one!
We could scoop up a few things here afterward, chief. . . . It's a real gold mine!

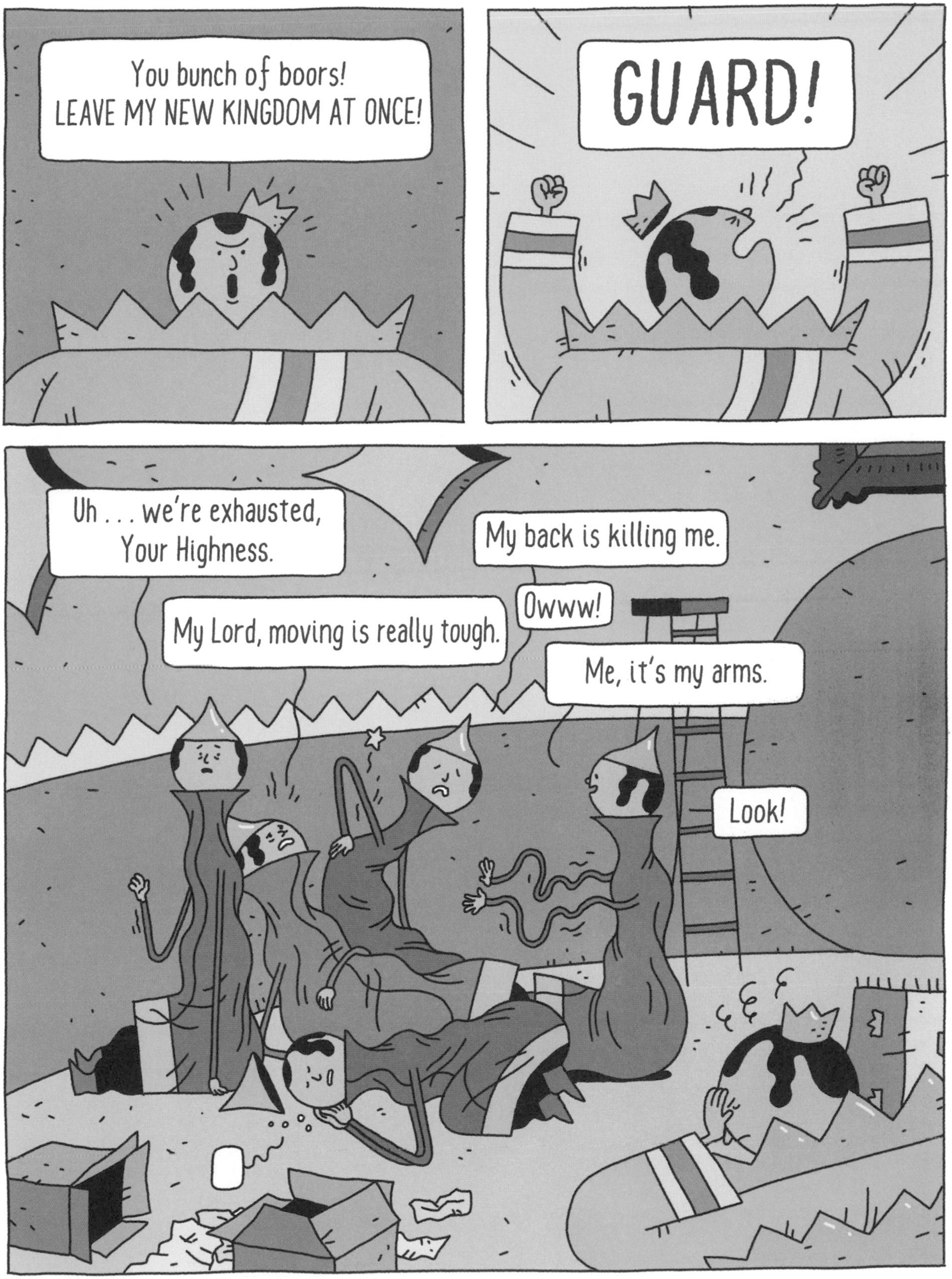
You bunch of boors!
LEAVE MY NEW KINGDOM AT ONCE!
GUARD!
Uh . . . we're exhausted, Your Highness.
My back is killing me.
My Lord, moving is really tough.
Owww!
Me, it's my arms.
Look!

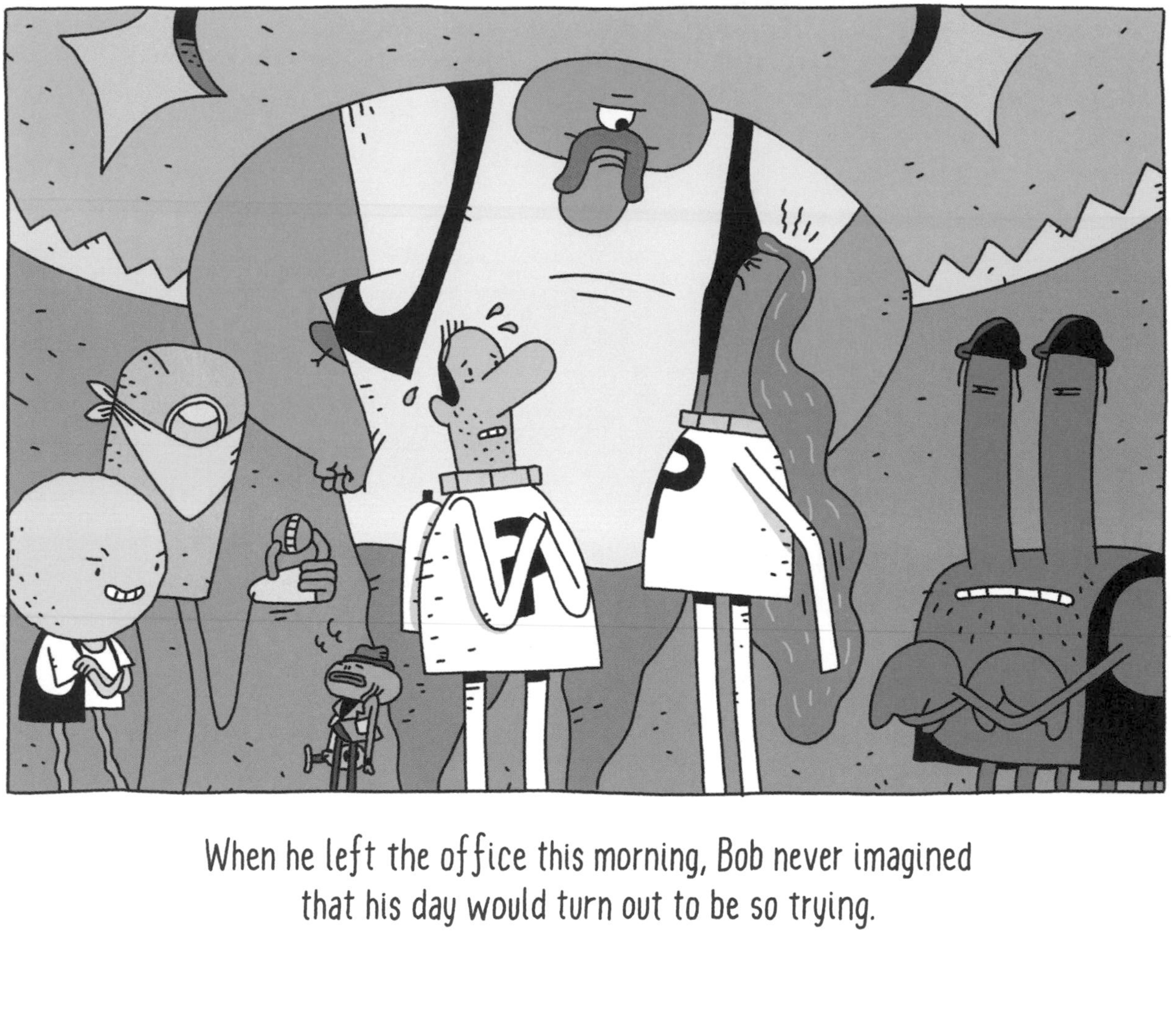

When he left the office this morning, Bob never imagined that his day would turn out to be so trying.

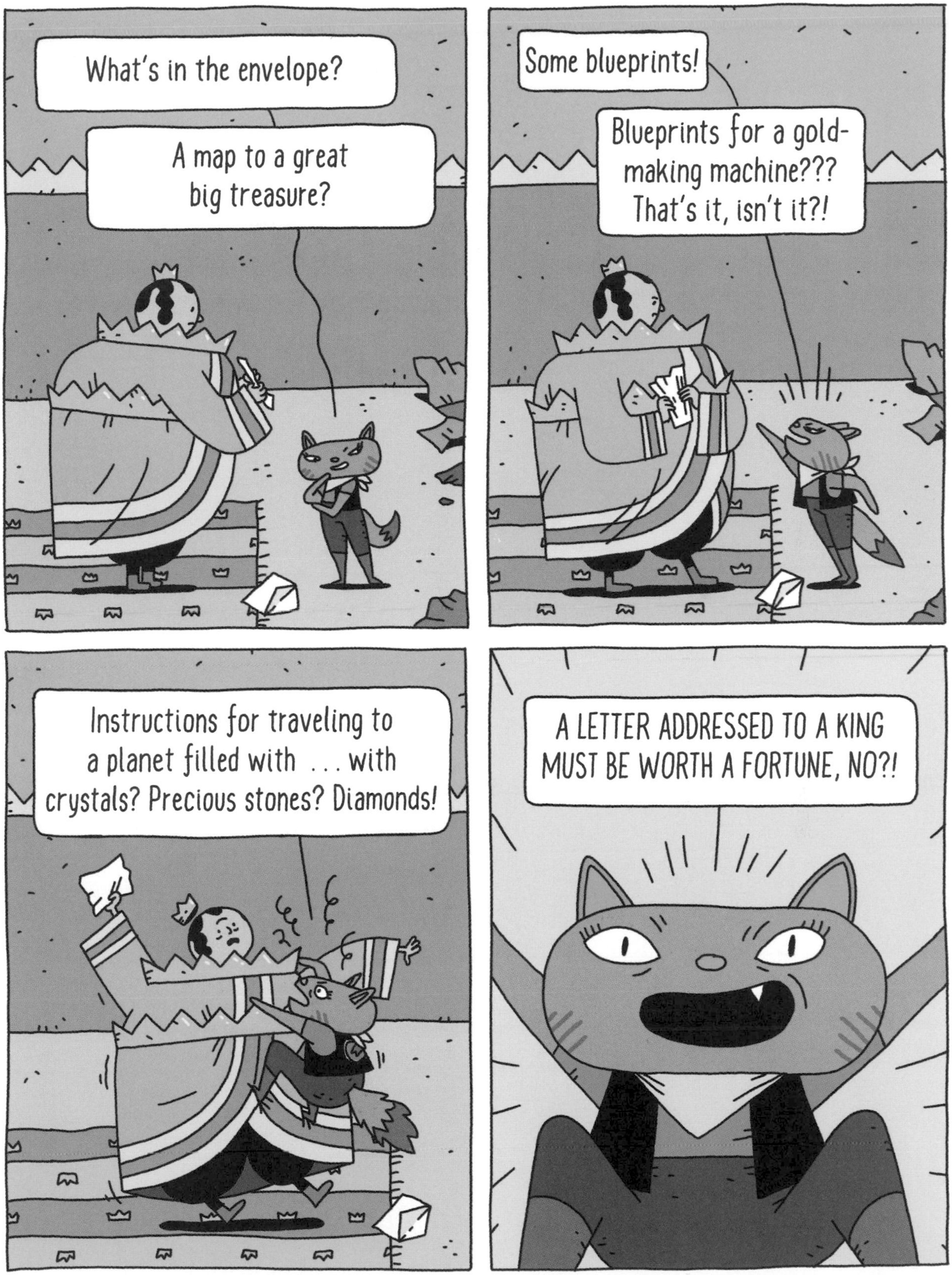
What's in the envelope?
A map to a great big treasure?
Some blueprints!
Blueprints for a gold-making machine??? That's it, isn't it?!
Instructions for traveling to a planet filled with . . . with crystals? Precious stones? Diamonds!
A LETTER ADDRESSED TO A KING MUST BE WORTH A FORTUNE, NO?!

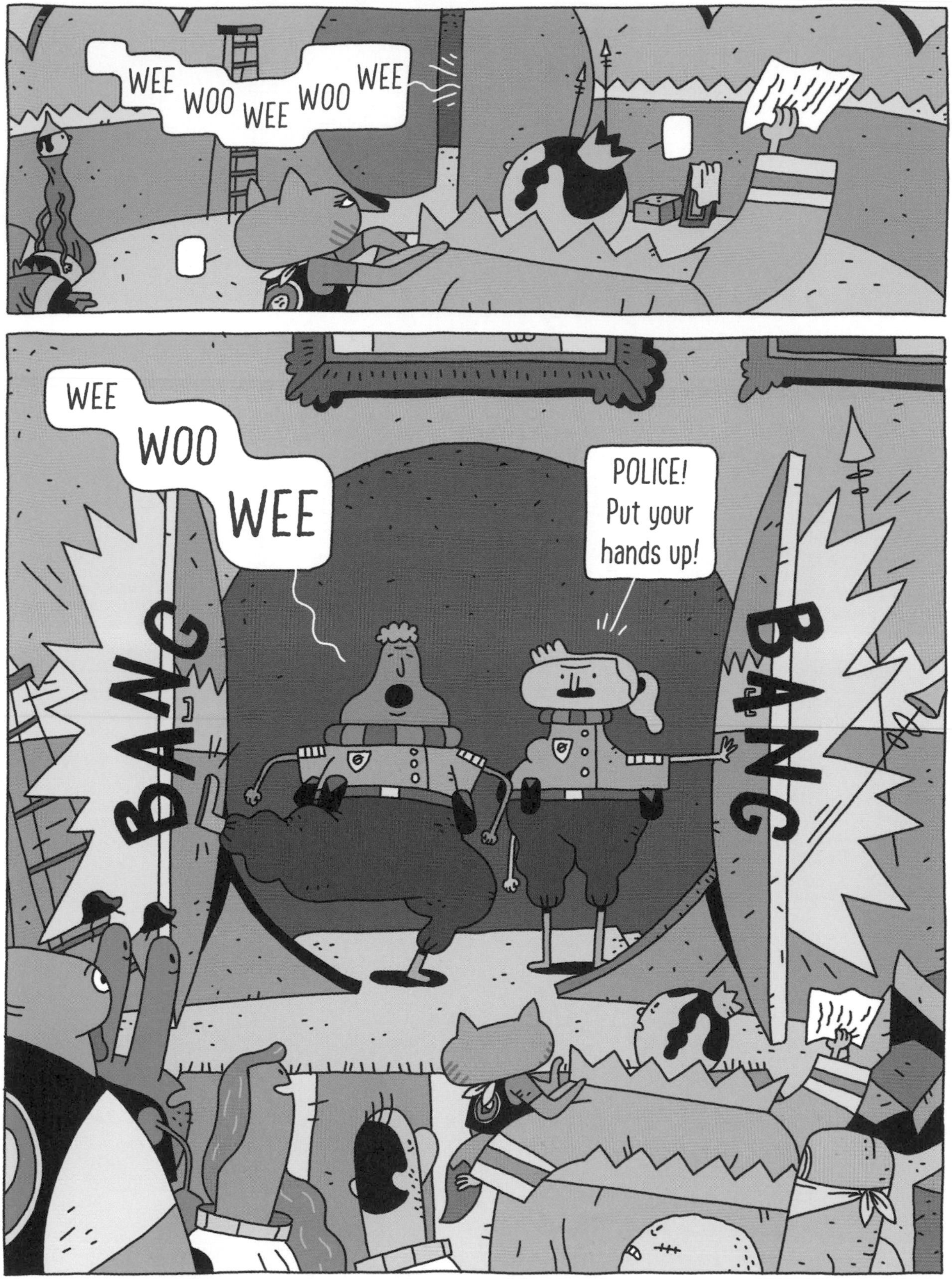
WEE WOO WEE WOO WEE
WEE WOO WEE
POLICE! Put your hands up!
BANG
BANG

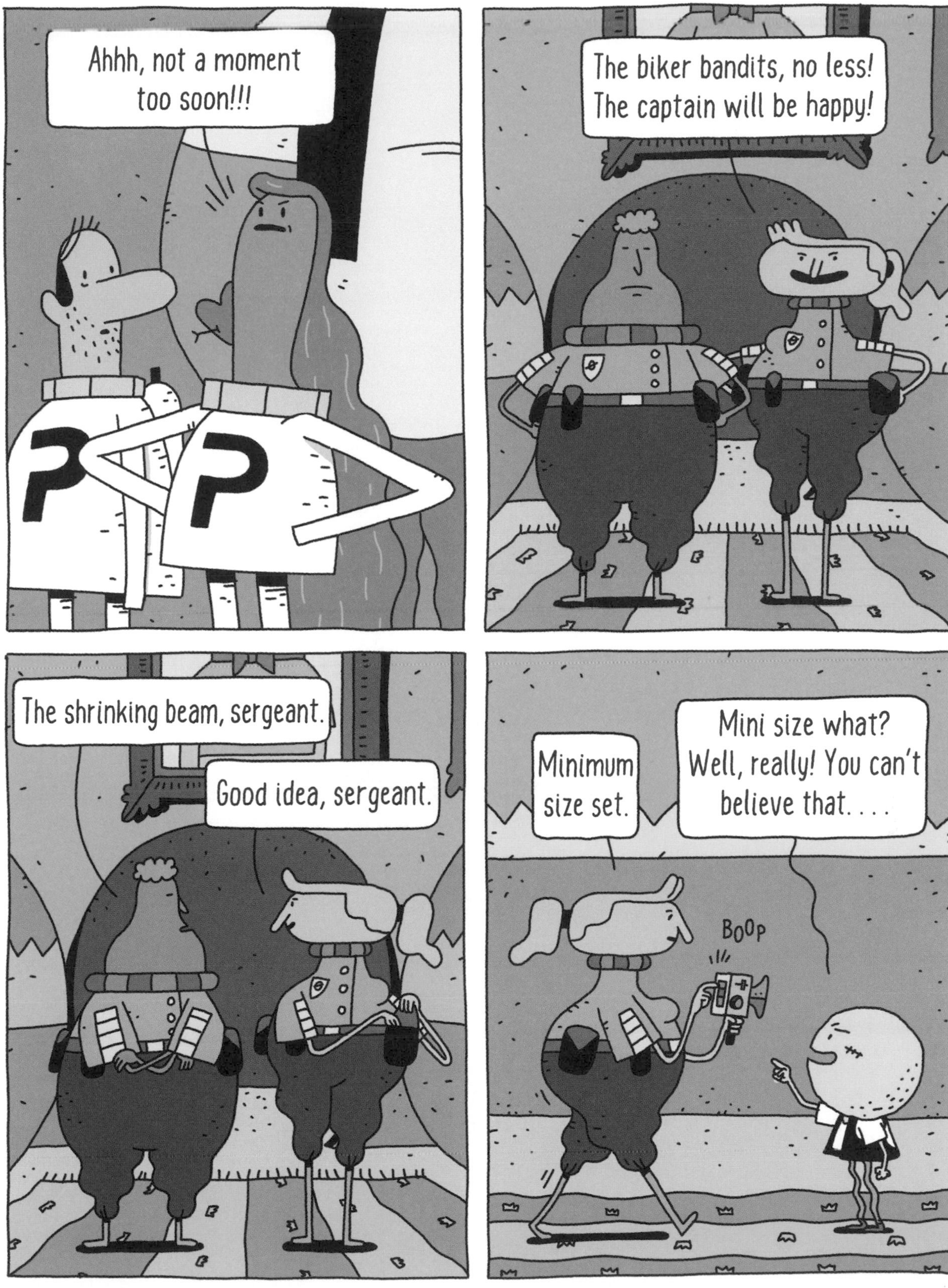
Ahhh, not a moment too soon!!!
The biker bandits, no less! The captain will be happy!
The shrinking beam, sergeant.
Good idea, sergeant.
Minimum size set.
Mini size what? Well, really! You can't believe that. . . .
BOOP

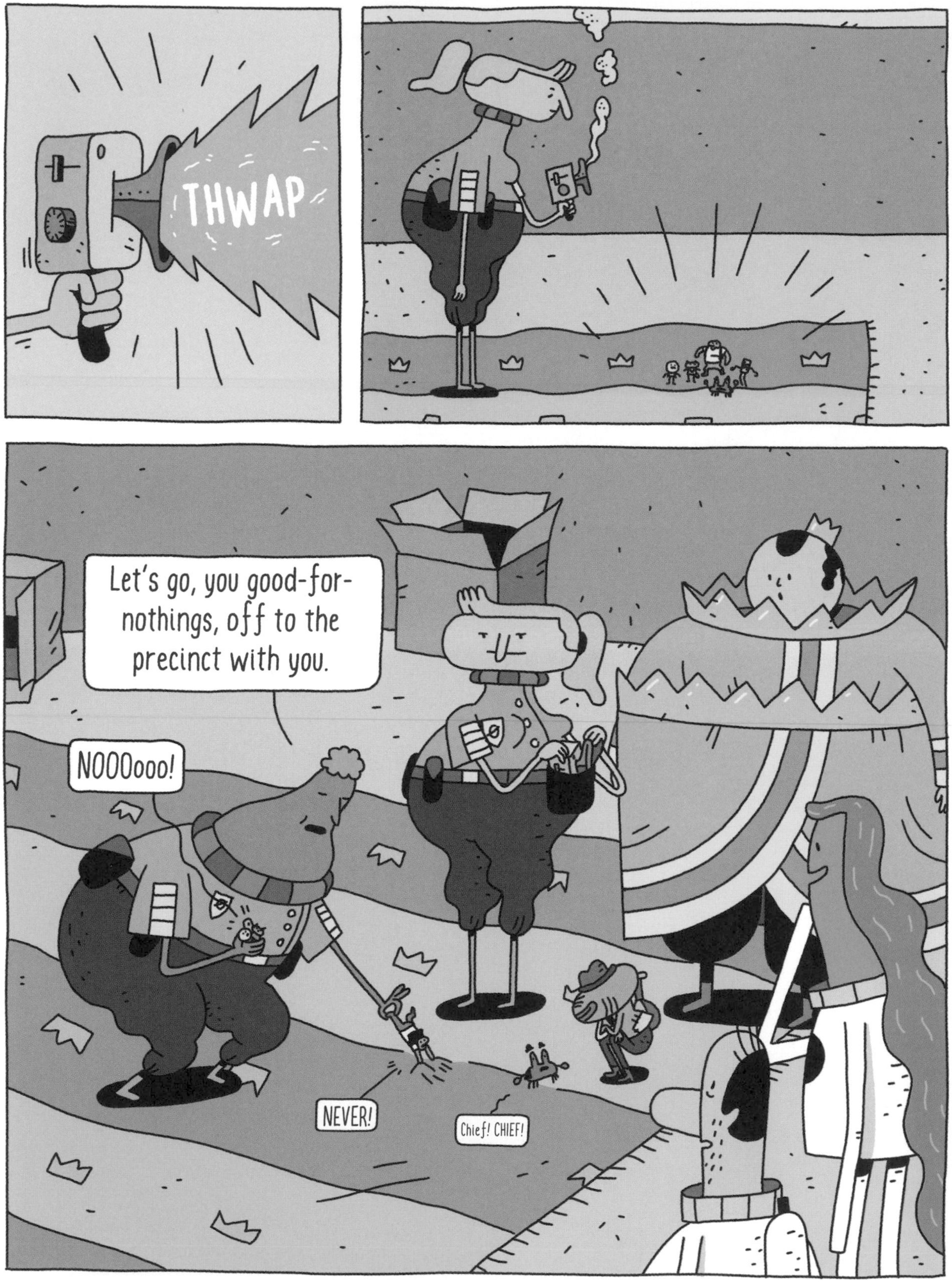
THWAP
Let's go, you good-for-nothings, off to the precinct with you.
NOOOooo!
NEVER!
Chief! CHIEF!

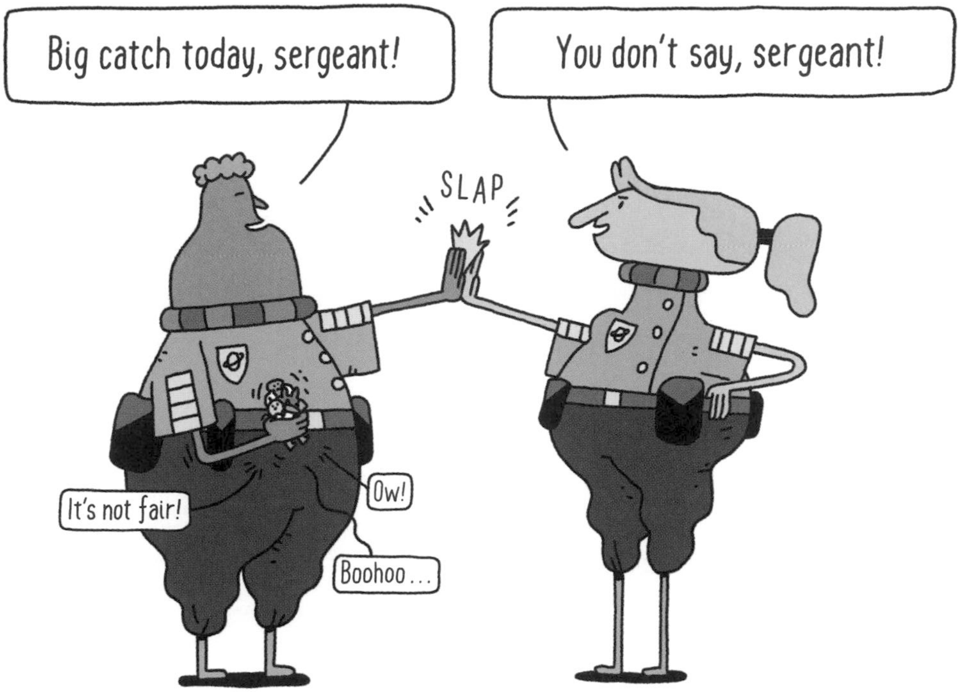
Big catch today, sergeant!
You don't say, sergeant!
SLAP
It's not fair!
Ow!
Boohoo...

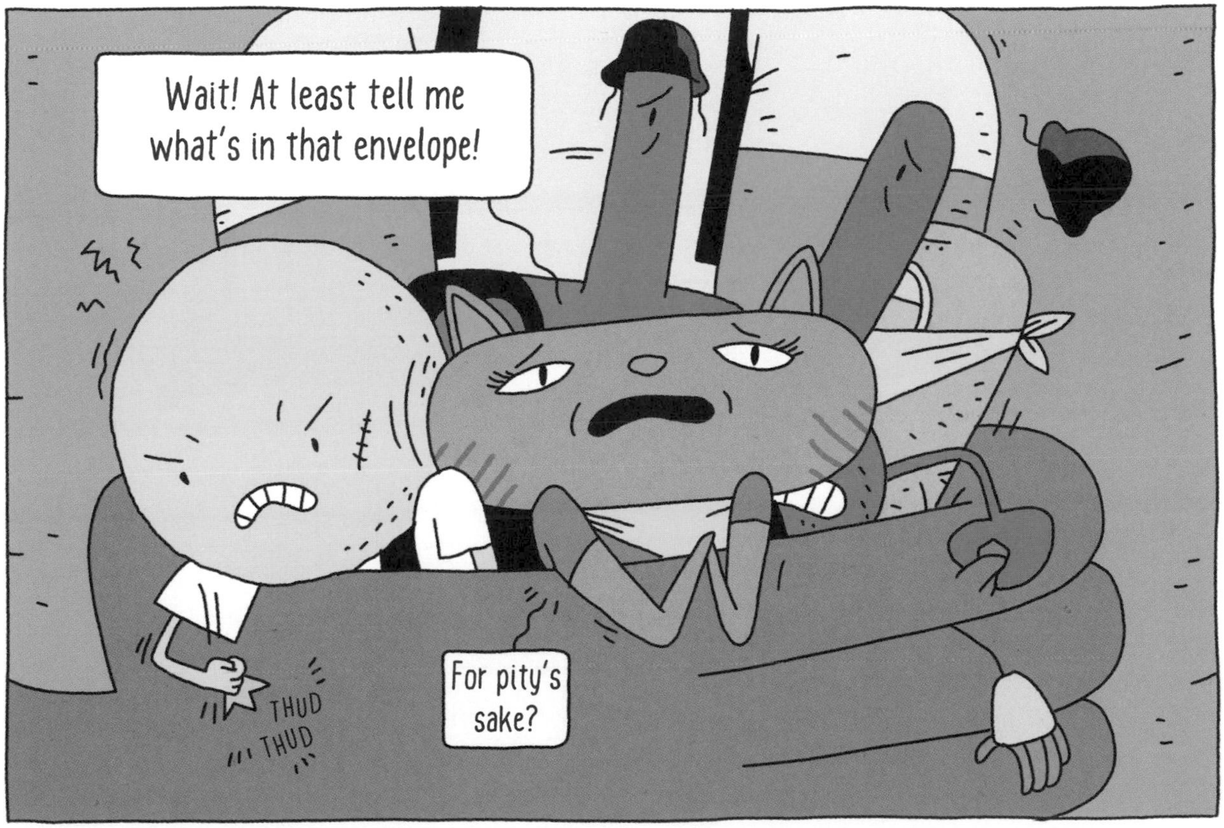
Wait! At least tell me what's in that envelope!
For pity's sake?
THUD
THUD

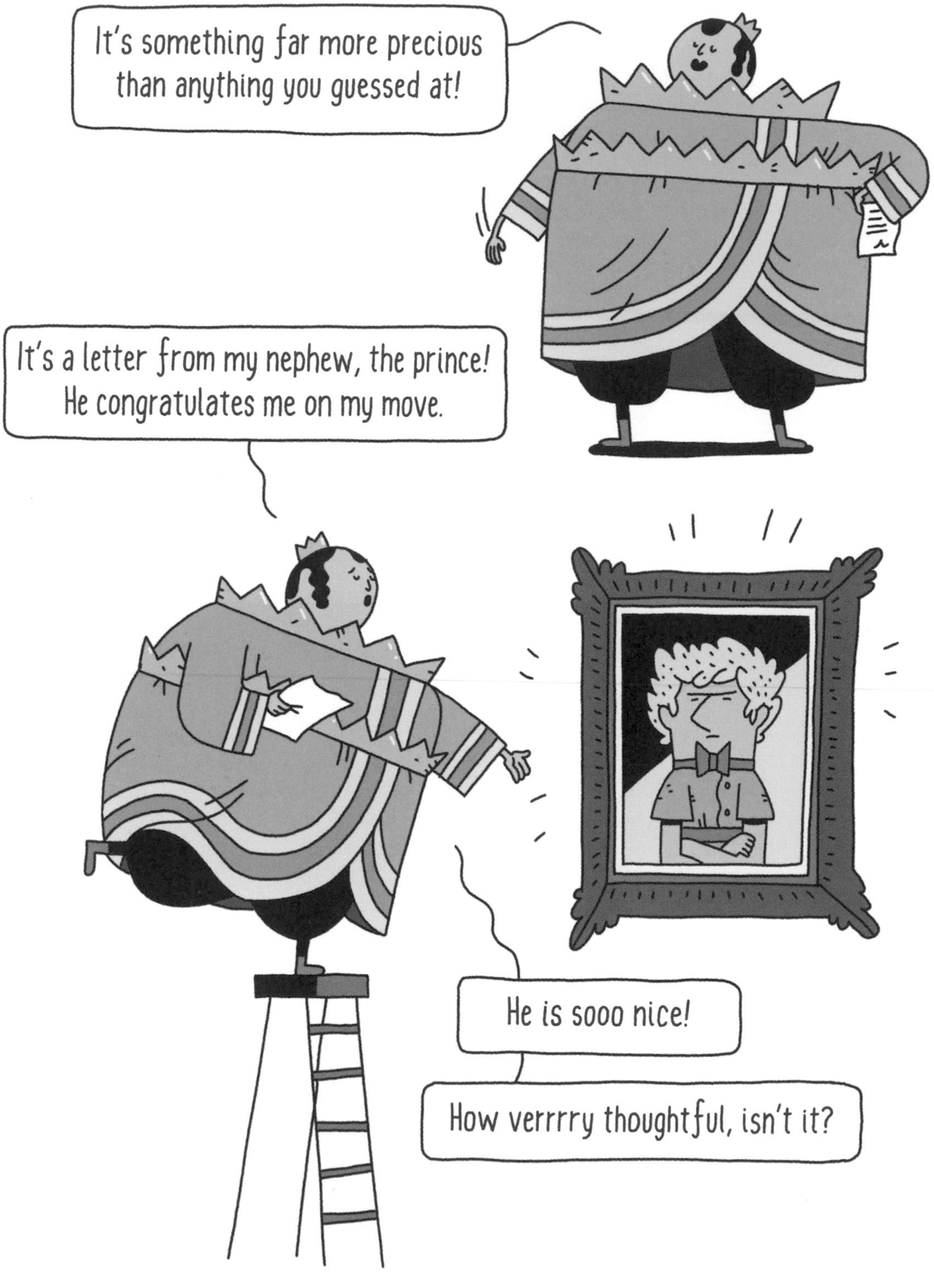
It's something far more precious than anything you guessed at!
It's a letter from my nephew, the prince! He congratulates me on my move.
He is sooo nice!
How verrrry thoughtful, isn't it?

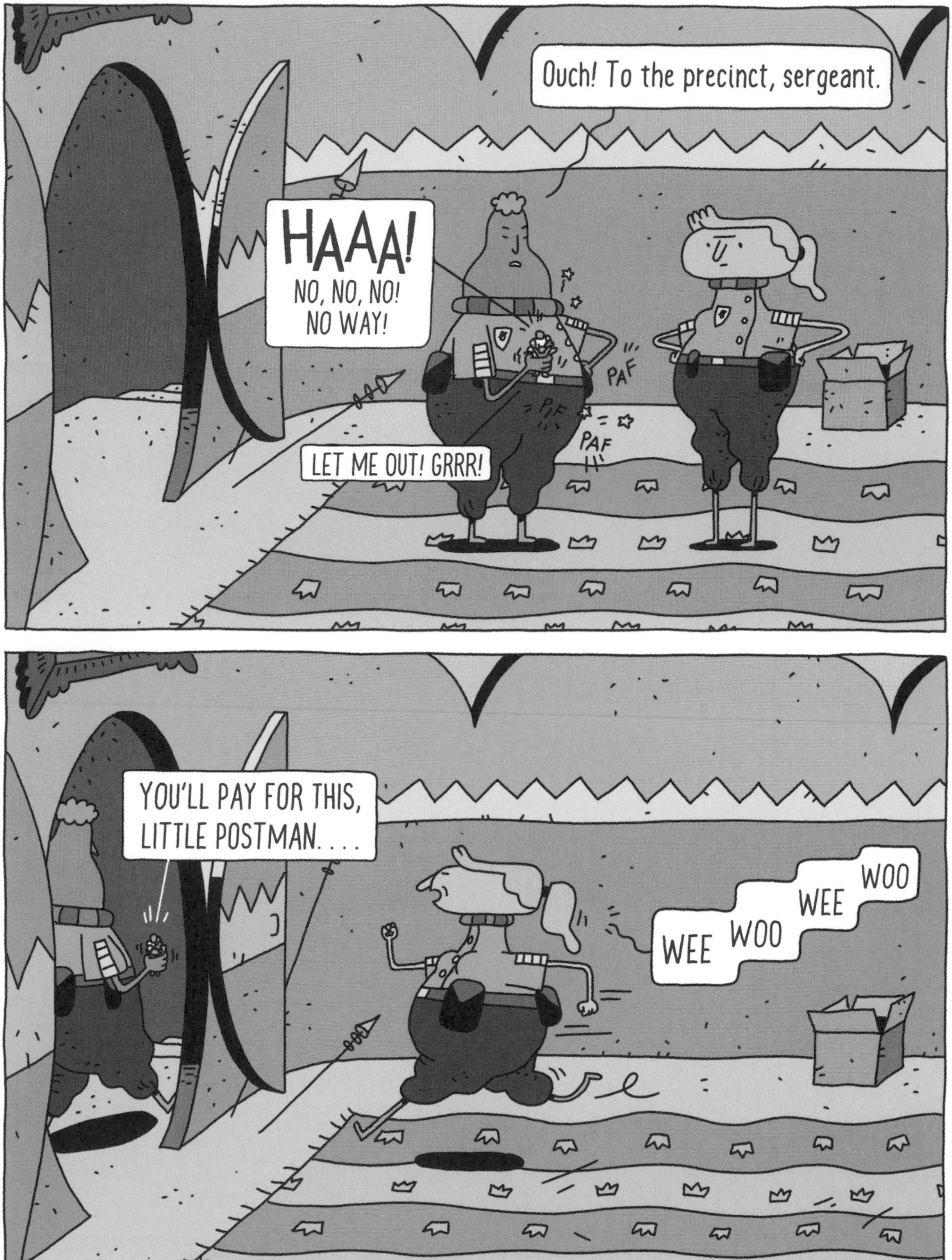
Ouch! To the precinct, sergeant.
HAAA! NO, NO, NO! NO WAY!
PAF
PIF
PAF
LET ME OUT! GRRR!
YOU'LL PAY FOR THIS, LITTLE POSTMAN. . . .
WEE WOO WEE WOO

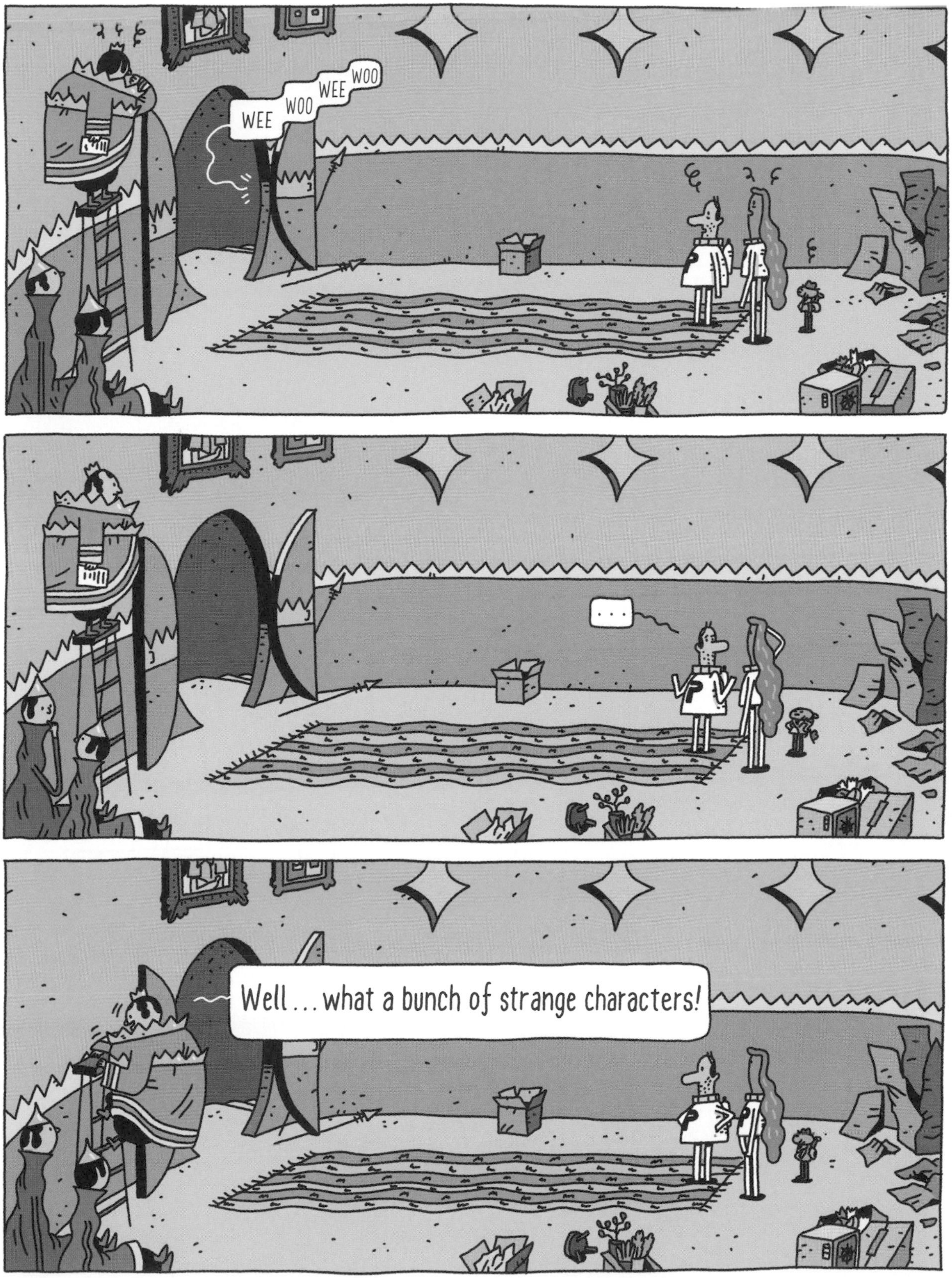
WEE WOO WEE WOO
...
Well ... what a bunch of strange characters!

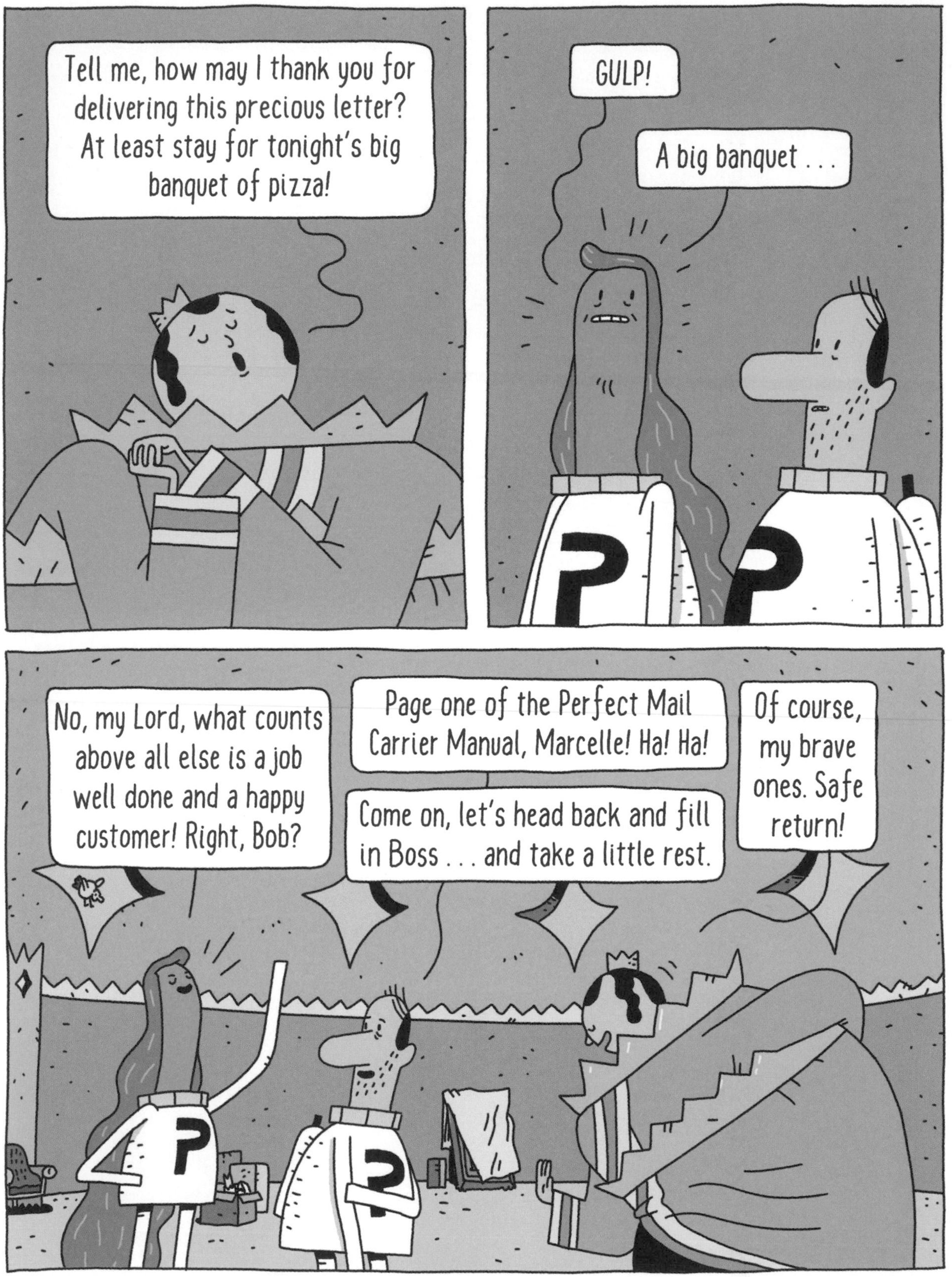
Tell me, how may I thank you for delivering this precious letter? At least stay for tonight's big banquet of pizza!
GULP!
A big banquet . . .
No, my Lord, what counts above all else is a job well done and a happy customer! Right, Bob?
Page one of the Perfect Mail Carrier Manual, Marcelle! Ha! Ha!
Come on, let's head back and fill in Boss . . . and take a little rest.
Of course, my brave ones. Safe return!

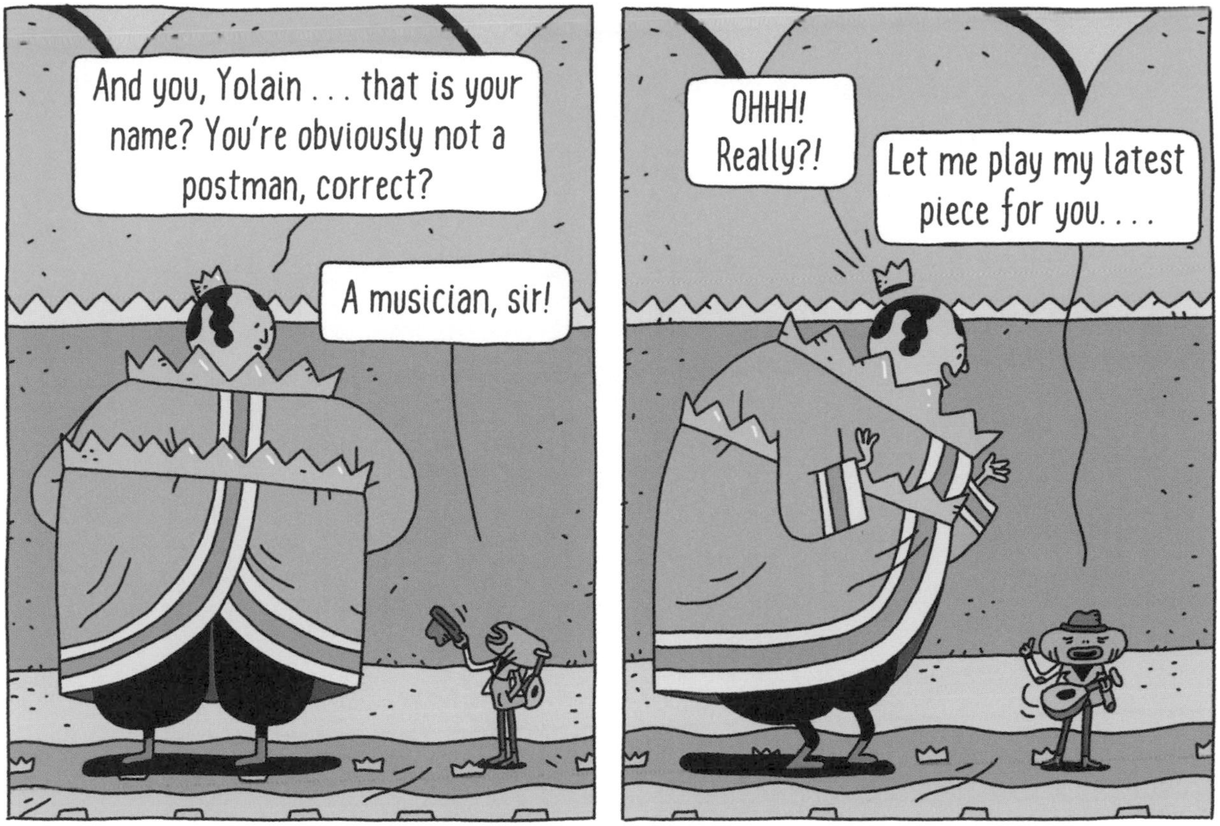
And you, Yolain . . . that is your name? You're obviously not a postman, correct?
A musician, sir!
OHHH! Really?!
Let me play my latest piece for you. . . .

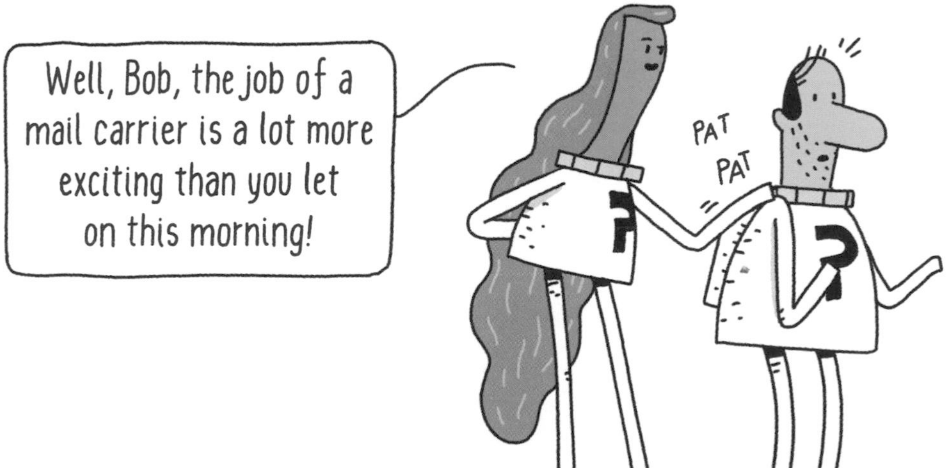
Well, Bob, the job of a mail carrier is a lot more exciting than you let on this morning!
PAT
PAT

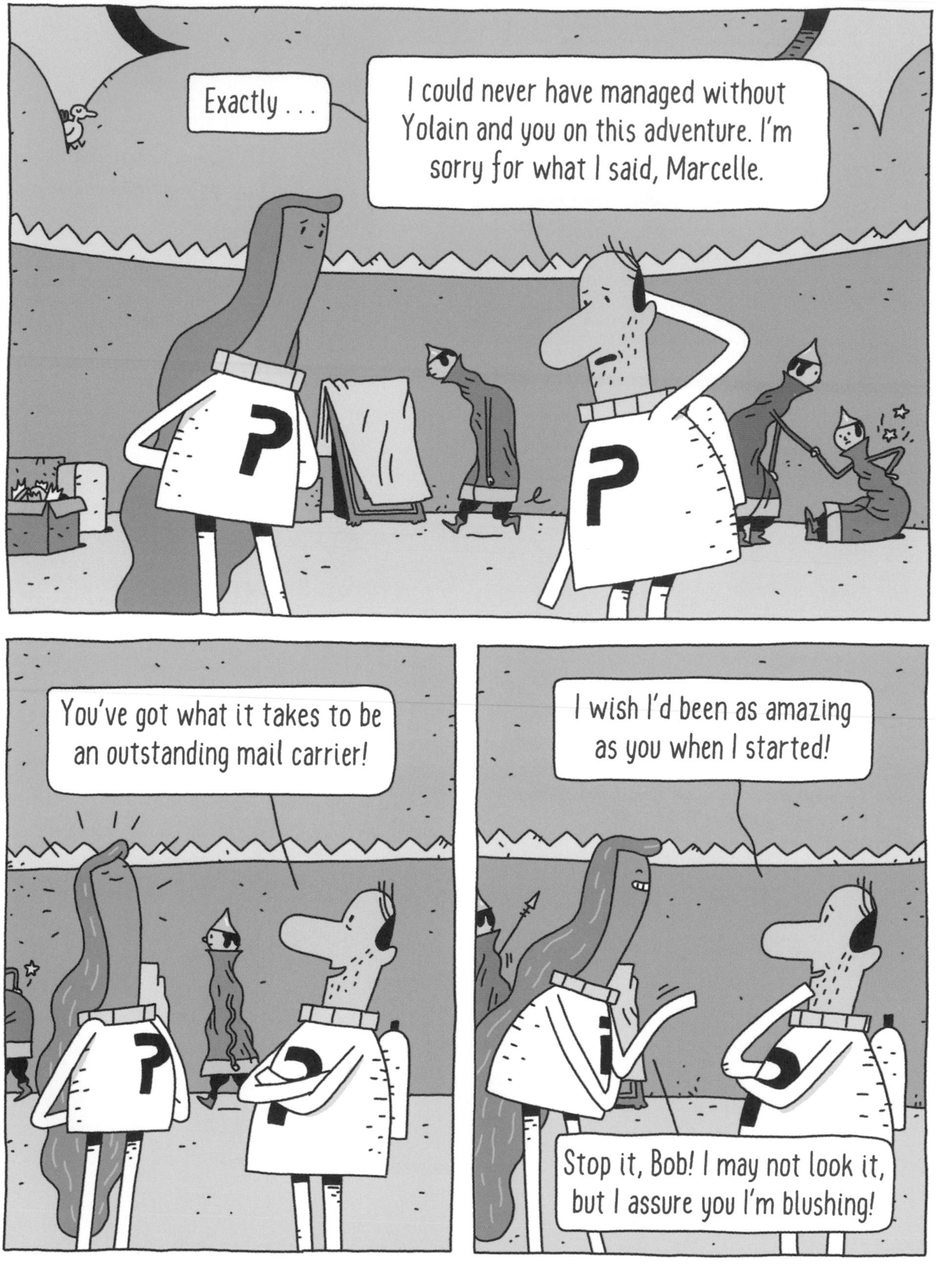
Exactly . . .
I could never have managed without Yolain and you on this adventure. I'm sorry for what I said, Marcelle.
You've got what it takes to be an outstanding mail carrier!
I wish I'd been as amazing as you when I started!
Stop it, Bob! I may not look it, but I assure you I'm blushing!

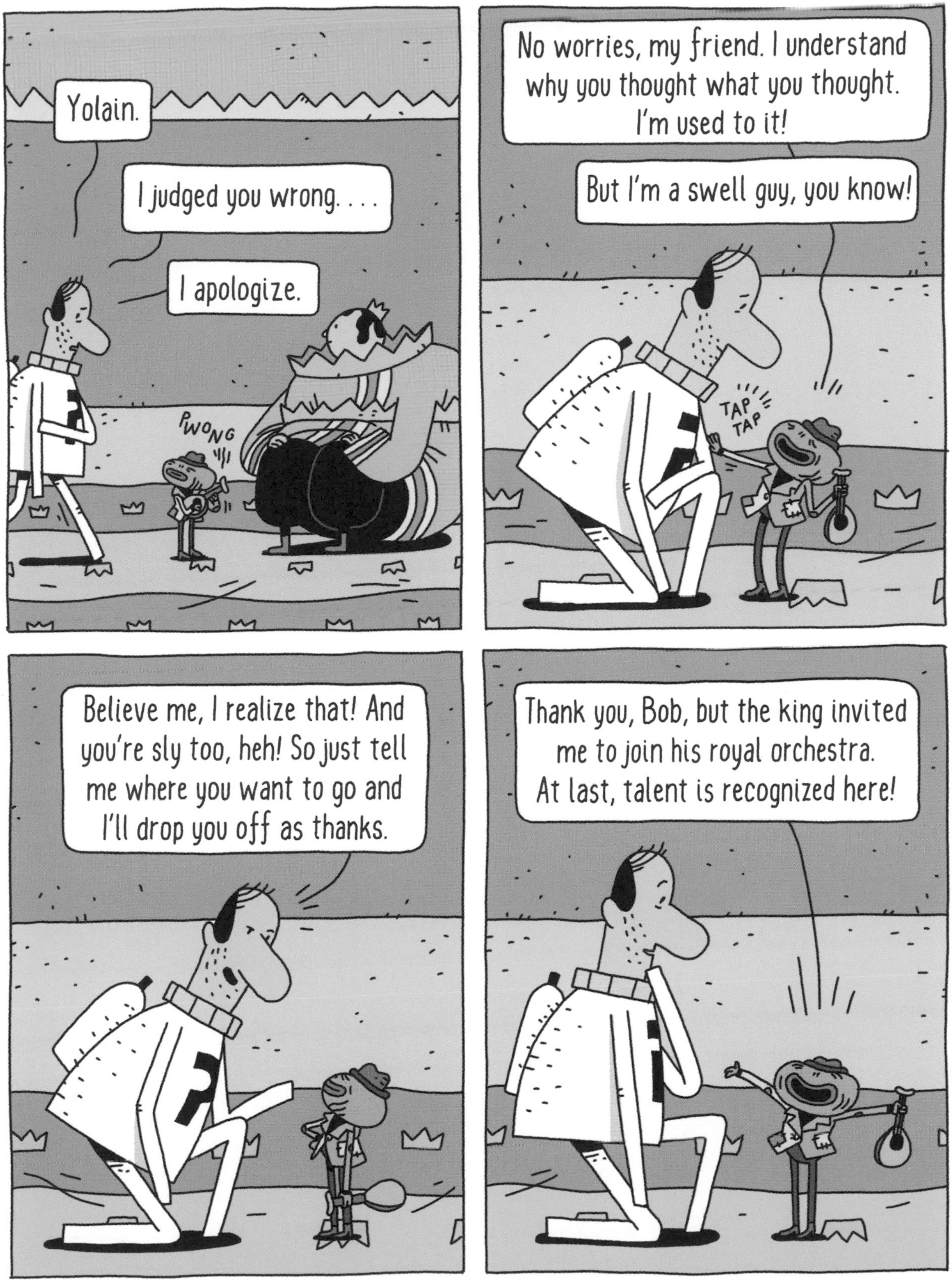
Yolain.
I judged you wrong. . . .
I apologize.
PWONG
No worries, my friend. I understand why you thought what you thought. I'm used to it!
But I'm a swell guy, you know!
TAP TAP
Believe me, I realize that! And you're sly too, heh! So just tell me where you want to go and I'll drop you off as thanks.
Thank you, Bob, but the king invited me to join his royal orchestra. At last, talent is recognized here!

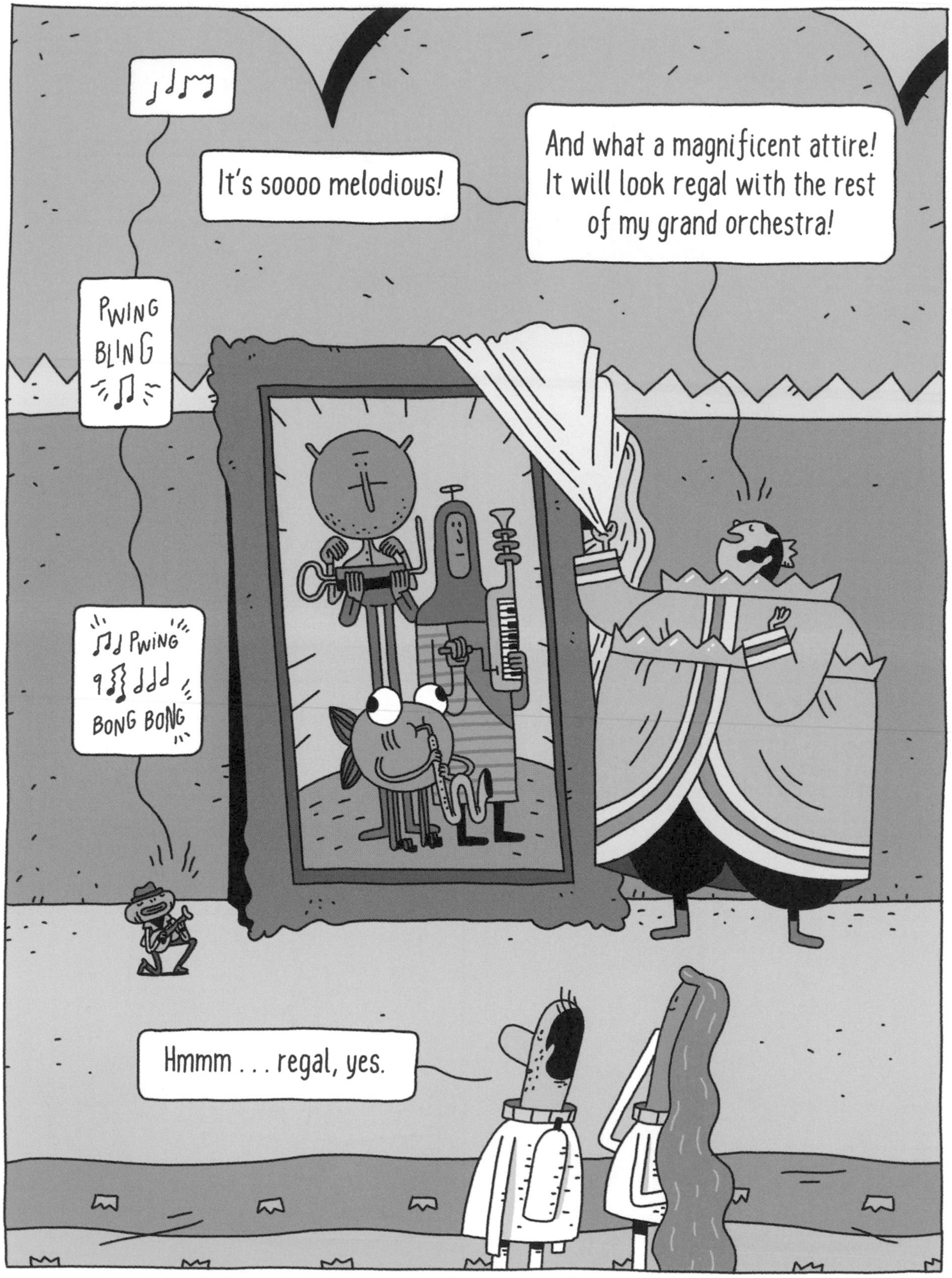
PWING
BLING
It's soooo melodious!
And what a magnificent attire! It will look regal with the rest of my grand orchestra!
PWING
BONG BONG
Hmmm . . . regal, yes.

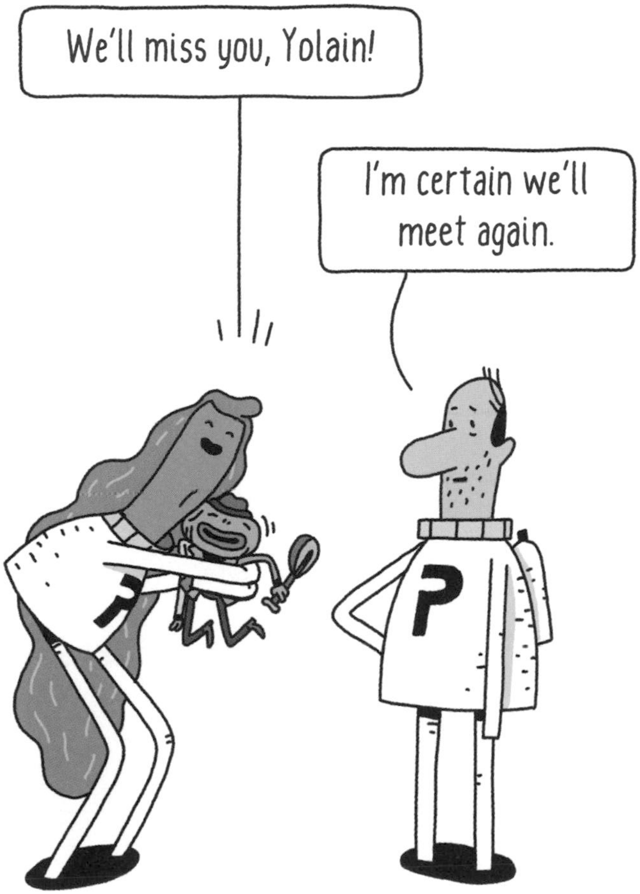
We'll miss you, Yolain!
I'm certain we'll meet again.

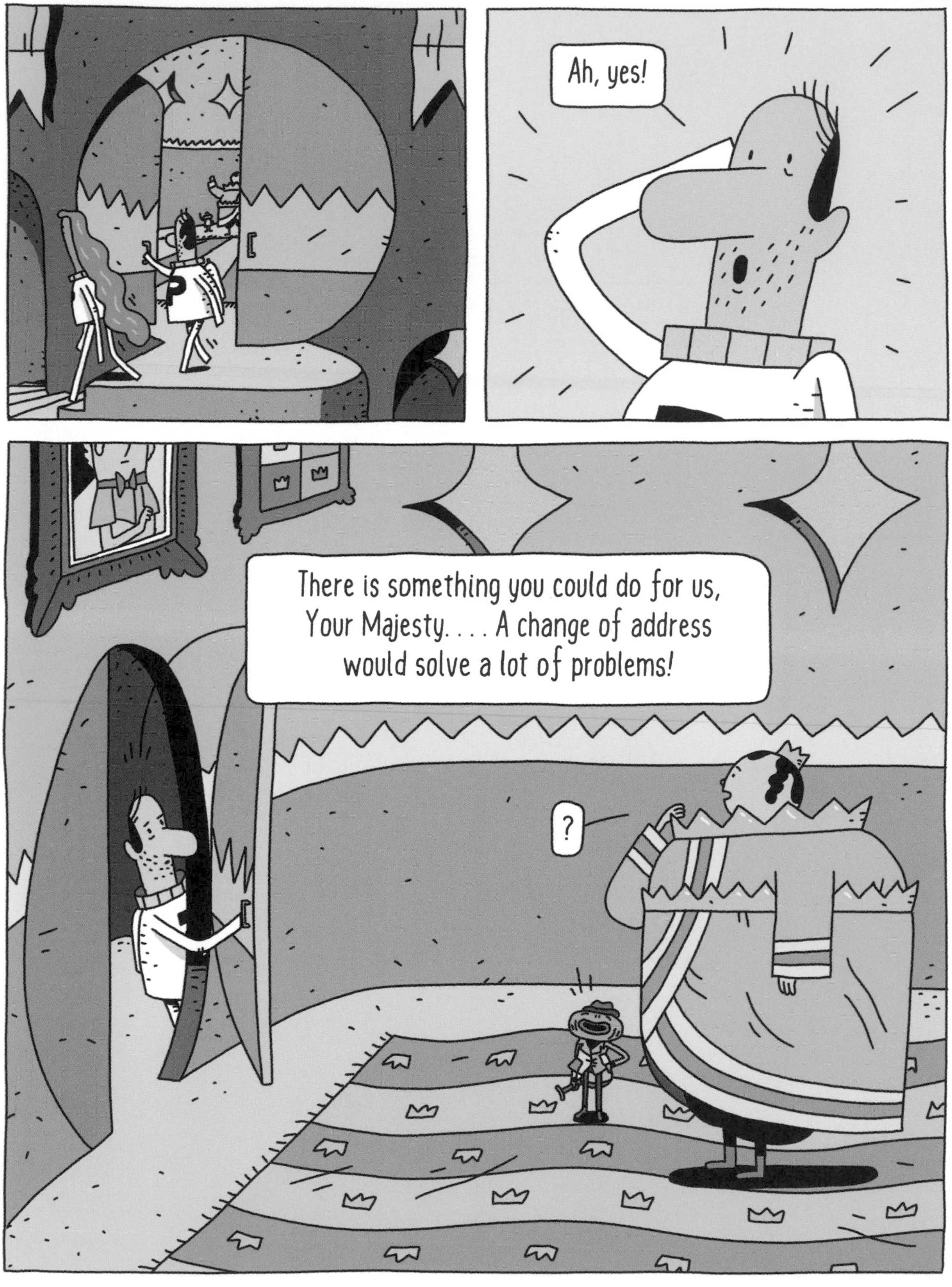
Ah, yes!
There is something you could do for us, Your Majesty. . . . A change of address would solve a lot of problems!
?

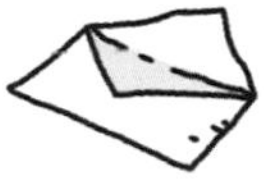

THE END

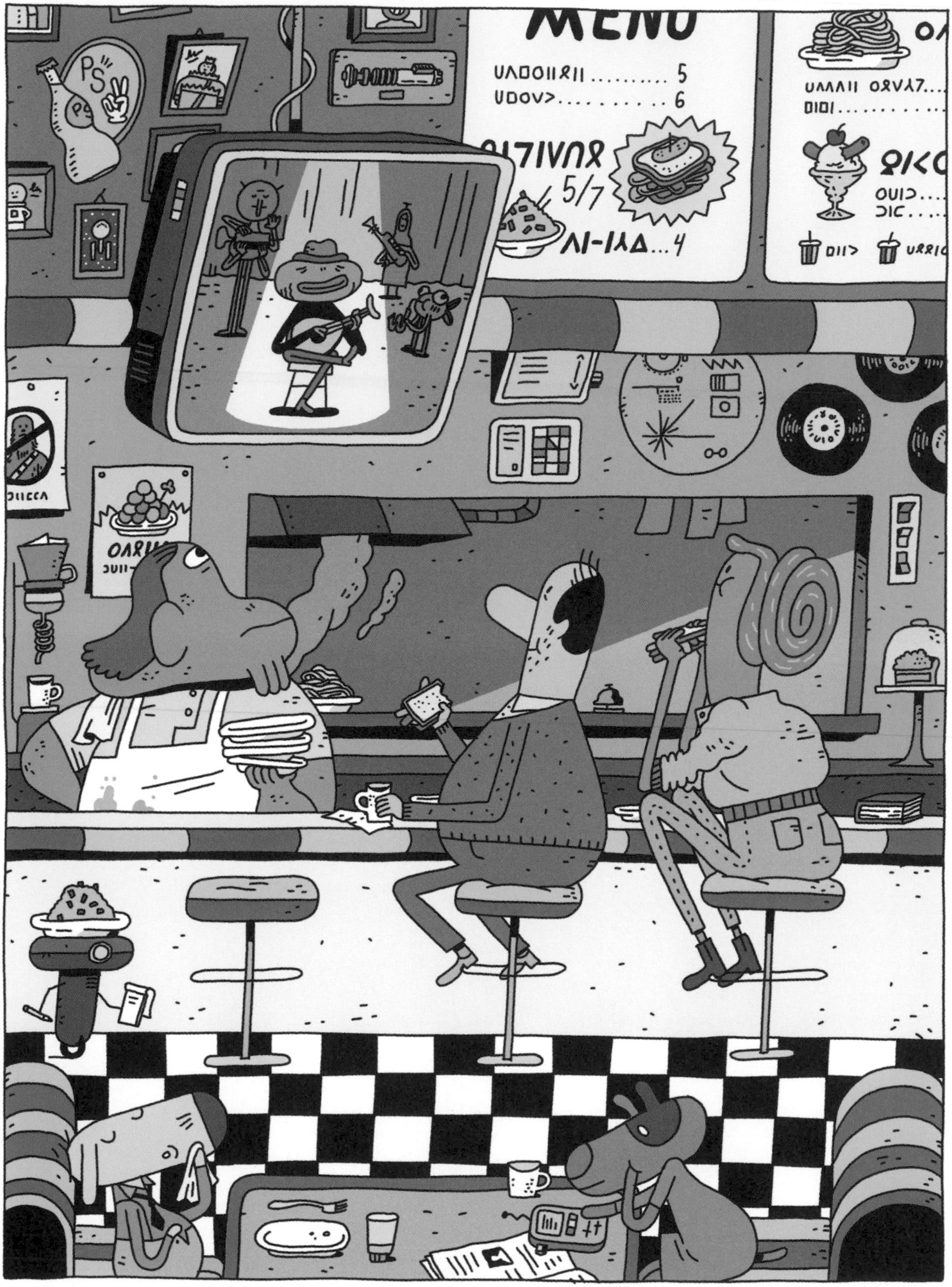
MENU

My thanks to the Canadian Council of Arts for their support.

Much gratitude to my circle of cherished friends for
allowing me to lean on you, for your advice, and the
time you took to listen; this book exists thanks to you.
Special thanks to Renaud, Rémi, Geneviève and Pascaline.
Thanks also to my editor for the adventure.

Thank you, Audrey.

ABOUT THE AUTHOR

Having failed the Planetary Post entrance exam,
Guillaume Perreault decided to illustrate and write stories
for young and old. *The Postman from Space #1* received
a Pépite des Lecteurs France Télévisions Award in 2016.

First published in French by Les Éditions de la Pastèque, Montreal as Le facteur de l'espace 2: Les Pilleurs à moteurs
Copyright © Guillaume Perreault and La Pastèque 2019
Published in agreement with Koja Agency
English translation by Françoise Bui
English translation copyright © 2021 by Holiday House Publishing, Inc.

All Rights Reserved
HOLIDAY HOUSE is registered in the U.S. Patent and Trademark Office.
Printed and bound in January 2021 at Toppan Leefung, DongGuan, China.
www.holidayhouse.com
First Edition
1 3 5 7 9 10 8 6 4 2

6|21
Library of Congress Cataloging-in-Publication Data
Names: Perreault, Guillaume, 1985– author, illustrator. | Bui, Françoise, translator.
Title: The biker bandits / Guillaume Perreault ; translated by Françoise Bui.
Other titles: Pilleurs à moteur. English
Description: New York : Holiday House, [2021] | Series: Postman from space; #2
Originally published in French: Montreal : Éditions de la Pastèque, 2019 under the title, Les pilleurs à moteur.
Audience: Ages 10-Up | Audience: Grades 7–9 | Summary: Bob is uneasy about training new mail carrier Marcelle,
although it should be an easy day, but soon they are making detours, picking up a hitchhiker,
and facing bandits on battered spacial motorbikes.
Identifiers: LCCN 2020036267 | ISBN 9780823445202 (hardcover)
ISBN 9780823449637 (paperback)
Subjects: LCSH: Graphic novels. | CYAC: Graphic novels. | Letter carriers—Fiction.
Robbers and outlaws—Fiction. | Adventure and adventurers—Fiction. | Humorous stories. | Science fiction.
Classification: LCC PZ7.7.P416 Bik 2021 | DDC 741.5/971—dc23
LC record available at https://lccn.loc.gov/2020036267

ISBN: 978-0-8234-4520-2 (hardcover)
ISBN: 978-0-8234-4963-7 (paperback)

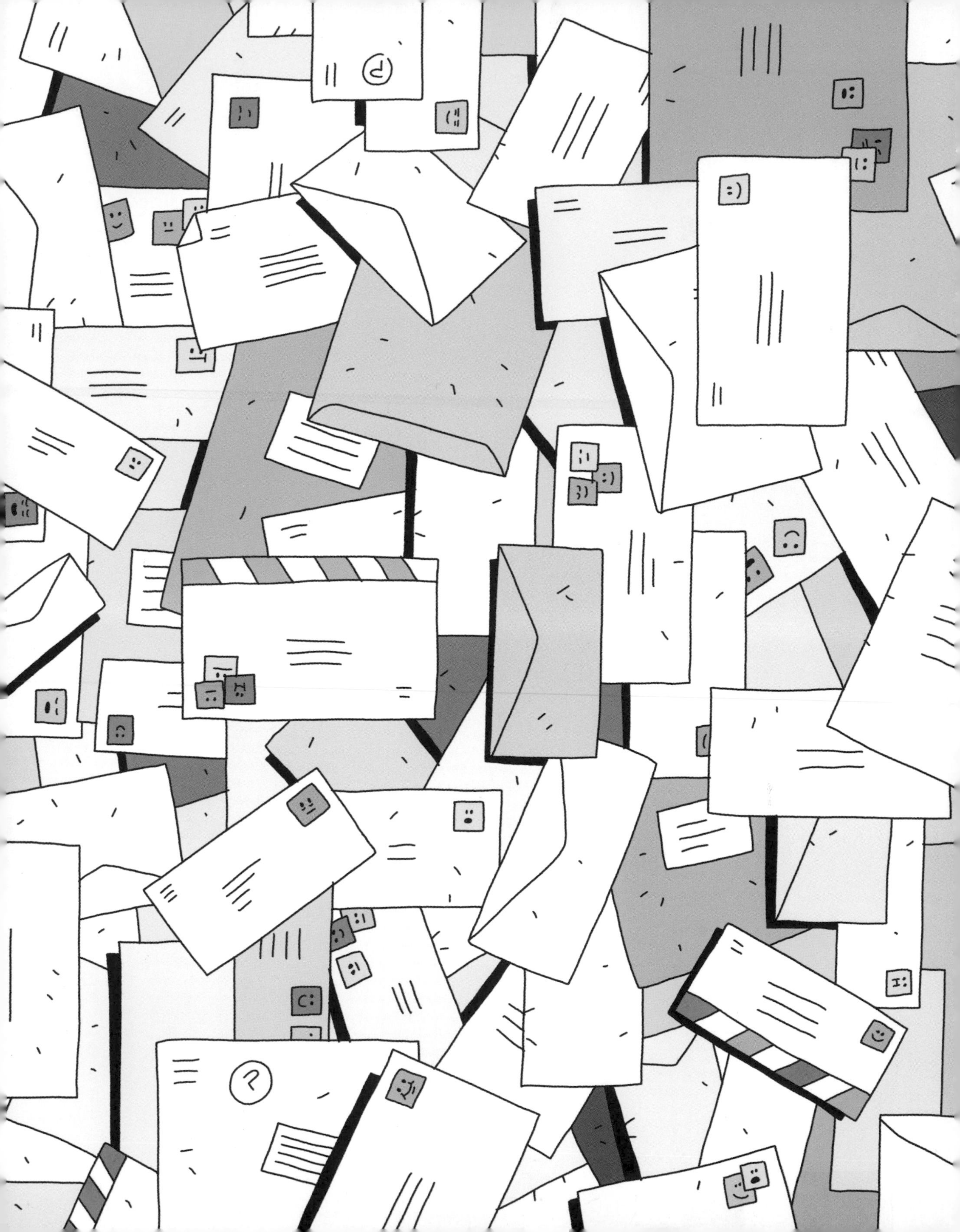